THE POSSESSED

Also by Witold Gombrowicz

Bacacay

Ferdydurke

Trans-Atlantyk

Pornografia

Cosmos

Diaries, 1953–1969

Witold Gombrowicz

THE POSSESSED

Translated from the Polish
by Antonia Lloyd-Jones
With an Introduction
by Adam Thirlwell

Black Cat
New York

Originally published in 2023 in Great Britain by Fitzcarraldo Editions.

Published simultaneously in Canada
Printed in the United States of America

First Grove Atlantic paperback edition: March 2024

Library of Congress Cataloging-in-Publication data is available for this title.

ISBN 978-0-8021-6252-6
eISBN 978-0-8021-6253-3

Black Cat
an imprint of Grove Atlantic
154 West 14th Street
New York, NY 10011

Distributed by Publishers Group West

groveatlantic.com

24 25 26 27   10 9 8 7 6 5 4 3 2 1

INTRODUCTION
BY ADAM THIRLWELL

I.

No one was better than Gombrowicz at talking about Gombrowicz. It's possible that his masterpiece is his *Diary*, which he begun writing in the Parisian émigré magazine *Kultura* in 1953, and continued until he died in July 1969. 'I must become my own commentator, even better, my own theatrical director. I have to create Gombrowicz the thinker, Gombrowicz the genius, Gombrowicz the cultural demonologist, and many other necessary Gombrowiczes.' In another brilliant work of self-commentary, *Testament*, a book-length interview with Dominique de Roux published in 1968, where Gombrowicz considers his entire oeuvre, he comes up with a constant barrage of self-definitions and aphorisms: 'I consider myself a relentless realist. One of the central aims of my writing is to forge a path through the Unreal to Reality.' Or: 'I could define myself as a little Polish nobleman who has discovered his *raison d'être* in what I'd call a distance from Form (and therefore also from culture).' But also: 'Sincerity? As a writer, that's what I fear above all. In literature, sincerity leads nowhere.'

The persona was all violence and haughtiness, but at the same time this violence was a product of a total marginalization. He had grown up in Poland in the early twentieth century. In 1933 he published his first book, a collection of stories called *Memoirs from the Time of Immaturity* (later republished in an expanded version with the new title *Bacacay*) and entered the world of Warsaw publication: of little magazines and their domestic disputes. Four years later he published a novel, *Ferdydurke*, and then a year later a play called *Yvonne, Princess of Bourgogne*. A year after that, in the summer of 1939, he had his so-called potboiler, *The Possessed*, published in serial form in a popular daily paper, using a pseudonym: Z. Niewieski.

Now, we will come back to *The Possessed*. But what then happened to Gombrowicz was a catastrophe but also a fairy tale of world history. On 29 July 1939 he took the inaugural transatlantic liner from Gdynia in Poland to Buenos Aires in Argentina, a diplomatic voyage to which he was invited by Jerzy Giedroyc, who worked at the Ministry of Industry. (After the war, Giedroyc, in his Parisian version of exile, went on to found *Kultura*.) Gombrowicz arrived in Buenos Aires on 21 August. Two days later, Germany and the Soviet Union signed the non-aggression pact, and just over a week later Hitler invaded Poland. As scheduled, the liner turned to go back to Europe. Gombrowicz took his suitcases on board and then, just before departure, in a moment of self-preservation, took them back to shore – where he remained, in Argentina, until 1963. The literary life had suddenly become a life of anonymity and poverty.

I cherish this image of Gombrowicz anonymous very much – working a terrible nine-to-five career in the Banco Polaco, a European writer lost in Argentina, while the Nazis annihilated central Europe, including his friends from literary bohemia, like Bruno Schulz. With some Latin American writers Gombrowicz worked on a Spanish translation of *Ferdydurke* – a translation that became legendary partly because of the difficulty of its production: between Latin Americans who spoke no Polish, and a Polish writer who spoke only rudimentary Spanish. It appeared in 1947, and was infinitely ignored in Latin America. Gombrowicz's next novel, *Trans-Atlantyk*, was published in *Kultura*, and therefore only read by its 3,000 subscribers. This was why in 1952 Gombrowicz began to write a *Diary* for *Kultura*. In it, he would create a personality equal to his lost ambition. It was his only method left to impose himself on the world.

II.

What I mean is that, between the Gombrowicz who finally died in the south of France in 1969, a celebrated European novelist, and the Gombrowicz who wrote *The Possessed* aged thirty-four, in the full typewriter wildness of central Europe, there is this thirty-year gap in which he offered up his early writing to the full clarity of his dominating intelligence. *The Possessed*, however, is almost an absence in this analysis. Serial publication of *The Possessed* hadn't been completed when war broke out, and on 3 September 1939 its publication ceased. And it was only just before Gombrowicz died, when he compiled a list of key dates and works for Dominique de Roux, that he acknowledged that *The Possessed* was one of his works at all. *The Possessed* therefore has the allure of a disowned work, a tacit work – a pulp novel that was written under a pseudonym, written only (so the story goes) for money: as if this novel couldn't fit into the vast work of self-commentary and explication Gombrowicz had set himself.

Just this once, I think, Gombrowicz was wrong in his auto-analysis. *The Possessed* is a true planet from Gombrowicz's galaxy. Out of its high-speed plot emerge many themes of his later self-portrait. It's true that it poses as some kind of gothic novel, or the parody of a gothic novel. It has a mad prince in a remote and ruined castle, and a haunted room, and a possible treasure. But it also has a strange layer of ultra-modernity: the dance halls and tennis courts of 1930s Warsaw. And anyway, Gombrowicz was always a writer of the fantastical: his art, he pointed out, was based on pure non-sense, on the absurd. To detach *The Possessed* from the equally parodic stories he wrote in the 1930s, or from the wild opening of *Ferdydurke* (where a writer who very much resembles Gombrowicz is abducted by a teacher called Pinko and taken back to school), *just because its genre is a fantasy genre*, is possible only through a feat of impossible engineering. In *Testament* he looked back on these early works: 'The formal apparatus I had set in motion was all my own creation. And this apparatus led me by surprise into regions I would never have risked myself if I hadn't been so high on the absurd, on playfulness, on mystification, on parody.'

The Possessed has one surface plot, which it gradually abandons. This plot concerns the machinations of the mad prince's secretary to inherit or steal the prince's art collection – a collection which has so far been unaccountably undervalued – so that he can then marry Maja Ochołowska: a beautiful, bourgeois girl who is also a tennis star. Gradually that story is overtaken by a darker narrative, which contains two different forms of haunting. The first form is the ghost of the prince's unacknowledged son, whose presence is figured in the uncanny movements of a towel at a kitchen window in the castle:

It was very gently quivering, probably because of a current of fresh air coming from the window. But this motion was strange. The towel wasn't moving freely in the draught, but quivering, and it was *taut*. And that made it look as if an invisible hand were holding onto it from below. This motion could not have been the result of air currents – it was a *different* motion.

The second form is the developing intimacy between Maja, the tennis star, and her new coach, Marian Leszczuk (whose name, until the end of chapter 2, is in fact Walczak – a change apparently determined by a wish to avoid accusations of libel by a 'real tennis coach named Mr Walczak', but really, of course, for Gombrowicz to show off the patisserie lightness of his philosophical style). From the moment they meet, Maja and Marian feel a strange frisson of similarity and resemblance, both physical and psychological, that encroaches on them until soon every conversation and interaction feels uncanny.

And at last here we are, inside Gombrowicz's studio. *The Possessed* is a fugue on the theme of resemblance. It imagines resemblance as possession by another, and therefore as a state that's both intoxicating and also to be resisted. There are likenesses everywhere in this novel, all centring on the trio of Maja and Marian and the prince's apparently dead and unacknowledged son, Franek. Among them, there are many forms of possession, because there are many ways people can be inhabited by other people: like lust or greed or grief. Everyone is vulnerable to being petrified into a form that belongs to someone else, misshapen by other people's neuroses and psychoses, or the inherited forms of invisible traditions.

This was the terrible wisdom Gombrowicz discovered in his early works, including *Ferdydurke*, his novelistic masterpiece – a wisdom partly prompted by the horror of a city's domestic literary criticism. That city happened to be Warsaw. It could have been anywhere. He had entered the world of publication and found himself deformed, into a subject of conversation and journalism. And so he had been forced into a defining philosophy, a sort of existentialism based on shame and humiliation: 'Accept and understand that you are not yourself, no one is ever themselves, with anyone, in any situation; to be human means to be artificial.' And then, as he told the revelation thirty years later to Dominique de Roux:

> I wasn't the only one to be a chameleon, everyone was a chameleon. It was the new human condition, you had to understand this very fast.
>
> I became 'the poet of Form'.
>
> I amputated myself from myself.
>
> I discovered the reality of the human race in this unreality to which it is condemned.
>
> And *Ferdydurke*, instead of helping me, became a grotesque poem describing – as Schulz wrote – the torments of human beings on a Procrustean bed, that of Form.

The other grotesque poem from this era is *The Possessed*.

III.

Yvonne, or the Princess of Burgundy, the play Gombrowicz wrote in the same period – and which was never performed until the years of his post-war European success – was about a prince who meets a woman who disgusts him in every way. Nevertheless, he is so determined to refuse the apparently universal and implacable laws of desire and disgust that he resolves to marry her. The plot then functions the same way Pasolini's *Teorema* would function – but an anti-*Teorema*, a *Teorema* of the abject. Introduced to the court, Yvonne's absolute lack of charm or beauty acts as a drastic catalyst on the prince's courtiers, so that each reveals their own vices and weaknesses – until finally, horrified at the revelations prompted by her mute presence, they all band together to kill her.

In *The Possessed*, too, people find themselves desiring people who apparently disgust them, just as everyone in the novel finds themselves hypnotized by the uncannily repulsive movement of a towel. Disgust is one of Gombrowicz's discoveries. It's also one of his wonderful lessons for the history of the novel. He was a grand stylist whose perception of the artificial and the unreal was so absolute that it included high style itself. In Buenos Aires he gave a talk called 'Against Poets', which he reprinted in his *Diary*. It was written, he announced, against 'the cult of Poetry and Poets', but as he continued it becomes obvious that what it's really written against is our continued miasma of unreality. In poets, he writes,

> not only their piety irritates us, that complete surrender to Poetry, but also their ostrich politics in relation to reality: for they defend themselves against reality, they don't want to see or acknowledge it, they intentionally work themselves into a stupor which is not strength but weakness.

Beautifully venomous, true, but earlier on in the talk he had secreted another acidic truth with possibly even larger implications: 'that all style, every distinct attitude forms itself through elimination and is, basically, an impoverishment.'

Famously, Gombrowicz kept another diary as well as his *Diary* – a text called *Kronos*, which functioned as a kind of shadow diary, an everyday record of money and sex and ambition, written almost in note form: the misshapen double of the *Diary* written for publication. That text only emerged in full in 2013 when it was first published in Polish. In the same way, *The Possessed*, which after publication in an incomplete form in 1973 only emerged in full in 1990 when the final three chapters were rediscovered (and which is now for the first time translated directly from Polish into English with beautiful brio by Antonia Lloyd-Jones) is a kind of shadow novel. Like the prince's abandoned son, it was almost entirely unacknowledged by its creator. And while it contains irrepressible moments of high literature – if you need an example, the moment at its finale where three bewildered characters are transformed into 'three speechless question marks' – it also features gleefully untalented scenes of exposition, with plot information crudely transported to the reader in impossible train conversations and purloined letters. Two major scenes of demonological investigation are detailed descriptions, shot by shot, *of a tennis match*, like some kind of magazine story for public schoolboys.

But the shamefulness, the pulp and the shlock, is also the mark of its genuine avant-garde originality. A novelist who's too precious about the creation of a style is not a true novelist because they are not a true person. They are just another ghost of unreality. *The Possessed*, this novel of mutants and doubles, is mutant Gombrowicz, double Gombrowicz. It's a modernist text remade with extra gore. It's so shameful that it belongs to the only true destination of literature, which is the future.

Adam Thirlwell, London, May 2023

REFERENCES

Diary by Witold Gombrowicz, tr. Lillian Vallee, (Yale, 2012)

Testament: Entretiens avec Dominique Roux, Witold Gombrowicz, (Folio, 1996). Citations here in Adam Thirlwell's translations.

THE POSSESSED

I.

'CAN'T YOU SEE there's a sign here that says "Do not lean out"? Do official orders mean nothing to you?'

This remark was addressed to the young man leaning out of the window by a faded, elderly man in pince-nez. It happened on a train, somewhere beyond Lublin. The young man drew his head inside and turned around.

'Do you know what the next stop is?' he asked.

'If I inquire of you whether you are aware that leaning out of the window while the train is in motion is not allowed, perhaps it would be appropriate to answer the question in the first place, and only then pose one of your own,' said the stickler for form with the face of a fish, bristly hair, and a gold watch chain hanging in the region of his belly. The young man instantly replied in a free and frivolous tone: 'Oh, sorry.'

This freedom and frivolity increased the fish-faced gentleman's irritation. Councillor Szymczyk was inordinately fond of lecturing and drilling others, but he couldn't tolerate his remarks not being taken seriously enough. He cast his victim a look of disgust.

This was a dark blond of about twenty, with an extremely neat physique. Although the summer was coming to an end and the evenings could be cool, he was only wearing a blue, sleeveless string top, grey trousers and tennis shoes on his bare feet.

Who might this be? thought the councillor. *He's got two rackets, so perhaps he's the son of a resident of these parts? But his hands are rough, with poorly kept nails, as from physical work. Anyway, his hair is not well groomed and his voice is rather common. A proletarian, then? No, a proletarian wouldn't have ears and eyes like his. But then the mouth and chin are almost working class . . . and altogether there's something suspicious about him . . . a sort of hybrid.*

The other passengers must have shared his opinion, because they too were glancing furtively at the young man, who stood leaning against the wall. Finally Councillor Szymczyk became so curious that he decided for the time being to drop further polemic on the topic of failing to attend seriously to instructions and advice given him by qualified people. He proceeded to establish the stranger's personal details, which in any case came to him easily, as even when on holiday he always considered himself an official, accustomed to filling in the blanks on forms.

'What is your employment?' he asked.

'I'm a tennis coach.'

'Age?'

'Twenty.'

'Twenty? Twenty what? Twenty years old? Please answer properly!' he said, with impatience and irritation.

'Twenty years old.'

'And where are you going?' asked the councillor suspiciously. He liked this character less and less. He always felt a certain suspicion towards persons who answered questions too hastily and compliantly; many years of office experience had taught him that as a rule such individuals either already had, or intended to have, something on their conscience . . .

'I'm going to a place near here,' the boy replied, 'to an estate where I've been hired as a coach.'

'Ah,' exclaimed the councillor, 'then perhaps you are going to Połyka, to the Ochołowskis? Eh? Of course! I guessed at once, since Miss Ochołowska is by all accounts an accomplished tennis player, sir. Are you there for long?'

'Nooo . . . Or rather I don't know how it will turn out. I'm to repair the rackets, refresh the court and practise with the young lady, as apparently she has no one to play against.'

'I'm going there too,' the councillor felt it appropriate to reveal, then stretched out a hand and said abstractedly: 'Szymczyk.'

To which the coach replied with a bow and said: 'Walczak.'

At this point they were approached by a hearty old man who had been listening closely to their conversation from the start. 'What, are you gentlemen going to Połyka?' he exclaimed. 'This is splendid, for I am going there too. Allow me to introduce myself,' he said, addressing the councillor. 'I am Skoliński, Czesław, professor, or, to be precise, art historian. Skoliński! You must be going to the boarding house, eh? I can assure you that you've struck gold – the manor at Połyka is paradise, sir, not a boarding house! Sometimes I really am pleased that the landed gentry is going bust and must establish boarding houses at their manors, for nowhere does one get as good a rest as in the countryside. I've been staying there for a fortnight now, I've been up to Warsaw for a while, but now I'm on my way back again. It's a superb place, gentlemen! À propos, Miss Maja Ochołowska, your future partner,' he boomed at the young coach, 'is also travelling on this train. Skoliński, if you please, professor, or, to be precise, art historian. I'd introduce you to her, gentlemen, but I do not wish to be indiscreet, because she is travelling with her fiancé . . . That's to say, her fiancé is travelling with Prince Holszański – you know, the prince from Mysłocz, which is next door to Połyka – so her fiancé, Mr Cholawicki, is travelling in one compartment with the prince, whose secretary he is, while she, poor lass, is in the next compartment down. The prince is a little . . . like that . . .' – he put a finger to his forehead – 'and his secretary cannot abandon him. But in any case, we'd better not disturb the young couple.'

The train sped on, swaying steadily, through the mournful land, flat and dark-green against the setting sun. More and more often the woods crept up on either side, more and more often the train sheared through a small pine copse. The two gentlemen immersed themselves in conversation, while Marian Walczak, coach for the Zespół club in Lublin, whistled a tune as he gazed at the passing landscape. He was bored. Altogether he was often bored. Sometimes such colossal boredom came over him that he found it simply unbearable. He set off on a walk down the train.

The first-class carriage he was now passing through was almost entirely empty, but one of the compartments aroused his interest.

That must be the prince, he thought, and pretending to comb his hair in the wall mirror, he peeked inside.

The sight was truly singular. Some huge, extremely old-fashioned-looking suitcases filled the racks; an open dressing case that must have seen the days of Napoleon rested grandly on a cheap, gaudy manufactured rug. An ivory encrusted walking stick was set beside an extremely shabby umbrella, and all around lay lots of parcels, bags of victuals and little boxes, all together reminiscent of the era of the stagecoach.

Amid this scattered confusion of luxury and rubbishy objects a small, slight, scrawny old man was dozing with his head against an embroidered pillow; his clothes were incredibly old, with a large patch on his right knee, but his face, for all its pitiful senility, had something so imperious and refined about it that at first sight no one could fail to understand that the smart gentleman in the perfectly cut suit sitting opposite could at most be a secretary and underling of this majestic personage. The secretary was holding an open book, though he wasn't reading, but gazing out of the window, lost in thought.

Suddenly the distinguished old man sneezed and opened his eyes – upon which he caught sight of Walczak staring at him – and at once his small, faded blue eyes began to goggle and gape as if he'd seen a ghost. His face went red, and he started trying to say something, moving his lips before shrilly crying: 'Franio! Franio!'

He stretched out his hands, but his companion turned from the window and with one good pull lowered the door blind.

Though not entirely sure what had happened, Walczak realized he'd better move along, and peeped into the next compartment. Here he discovered a sight no less curious – in some respects similar to the one that had vanished from view a moment ago, but in other ways the polar opposite. To wit, there in the compartment sat a young woman, fast asleep.

Aha, he thought, *this must be Miss Ochołowska.*

He couldn't see her face because she was hiding it with her arm, but the way she was sleeping surprised him – her smartly dressed, fine and slender body was tossed into a corner with her feet on the opposite seat, her legs bent high at the knees, her body leaning to one side, and her head almost lower than her feet – if someone had tried to find the most uncomfortable position to sleep in they couldn't have arranged themselves in a more eccentric manner, or even a more brutal one. One simply wanted to shake her by the arm and shout: 'How on earth can you sleep like that?!'

'But she's also sleeping without any care for herself,' he muttered. 'As if she had no self-respect. As if it were all the same to her if her head were lower than her feet, or vice versa . . . And yet she's so elegant . . .'

The train soared on, rumbling monotonously, everything shook and jiggled up and down, including the sleeping girl. He was so absorbed in watching her that he quite forgot where he was and where he was going. Actually he didn't find her especially attractive – he preferred older women, more ample, but there was something about her that captivated his attention. Until finally he realized.

She's sleeping in exactly the same way as I do! he thought in amazement.

Indeed, whenever he'd happened to wake in the middle of the night, he'd been in a similar position – his way of sleeping was exactly the same, and his pals had often teased him about it. Well, it was all right him sleeping like that, it was quite understandable – but for this stylish young lady to sleep in this manner, with no self-respect . . . *She's sleeping like someone at a police station, on a bench*, he thought. *I wonder if this really is Miss Ochołowska?*

Her coat was hanging on a hook by the door. There was a white envelope sticking out of the pocket. He hesitated, but his curiosity got the better of his scruples – he pulled out the letter, and with occasional glances at the sleeping girl, he began to read it. Yes, it was her. Addressed to Maja Ochołowska, the letter went like this:

My darling Maja,
If you'd like to stay on in Warsaw for a few more days, you can boldly go ahead, as I'm managing extremely well here, and the guests – regrettably – are few in number. It's dreadful that we're obliged to host strangers at our lovely old house. But what can

one do? If only it pays off! But there's something else I want to write to you about. It's your engagement to Henryk.

My dearest child, you know how deeply I desire your happiness. I leave you full freedom to make your own decisions, as I know you won't obey me anyway, but I'm finding your secretiveness awfully tiring. It's funny to be writing you this in a letter when we'll be together in a couple of days from now, but to be quite frank I don't know how to talk to you.

How painful it is for a mother to be unable to communicate with her own daughter on the most important and most personal matters. And yet relations between us are in such a state that I'd sooner discuss some of these things with a complete stranger than with you.

My darling girl, don't be angry with me for writing to you like this. I know you love me, and you know I'd give up my life for you, but we have no common language. So I'm taking advantage of the physical distance between us to try to tell you what's on my mind by letter. Please take it on board, and then we won't talk about it, all right?

For some time I've been so frightened for you that it's poisoning every spare moment I have.

I'm frightened of your beauty, of your youth, I'd rather you were less self-confident . . . How can I put it? I sense in you determination, ambition, and an unquenched desire for happiness. I think you're extremely hungry for the outside world, and you find our monotonous rural existence so deeply unsatisfying that you'd do anything to gain access to a rich, city life.

Do you really think Henryk can secure that for you? Are you genuinely attached to him, or are you just wanting to break away

*from here with his assistance? Perhaps you've already reckoned
on dropping him in a few years' time?*

*In any case, even if you do feel affection for him, isn't it based
on the fact that by nature you share the same unsatisfied craving
for pleasure? Sometimes it looks to me as if he doesn't respect
you, nor you him – that it's just calculation, the life partnership
of two completely wild animals. Oh God, what am I writing! But
let it stand as it is. If I'm wrong, if it's just a lack of understanding of you young people on my part, as an old woman, brought
up in different times and living according to different ideals, then
please don't hold it against me.*

*But you can understand how agonizing this sort of conjec-
ture must be. With each day the modern world becomes more
terrifying and more of a mystery to me. You two have no dignity
and you don't respect yourselves or others – that's the worst thing
of all.*

*You may spend all of the money you withdrew in Warsaw,
as I've unexpectedly received 1300 zlotys by virtue of settling
accounts with Lipkowski. I'm so unaccustomed to large amounts
of cash that I'm truly scared of keeping such a sum in the house!
For the time being I've put it in the left drawer in your closet.
Please ignore the expense and buy yourself anything you need for
your wardrobe, because the money for that can always be found,
it simply must! How ghastly of me to be working at encouraging
and sustaining the need for luxury in you, but I'm too fond of you
not to! That is my greatest weakness! I hope you've upped your
game during your short stay in Warsaw. Don't be angry with me,
darling, think about what I've written, and when we're together,
pretend you never received this letter at all. Do you love me?*

Mother

Walczak thrust the letter back into her coat pocket.

Yes, this was Miss Ochołowska, the talented tennis player, whose game he was to 'up' starting tomorrow – his future partner. Aha, so she wanted to marry money – sure, who wouldn't? – every girl like her wants to marry a rich man and enjoy life. *Just like me!* he thought, and laughed.

The train began to slow down. He returned to his carriage, where Councillor Szymczyk and Professor Skoliński were already fetching down their suitcases and putting on their coats. The carriages shuddered and stopped.

'Get off the train!' cried the professor. 'Just a two-minute halt!'

II.

'Are there any horses from Połyka?'

Emerging onto the porch in front of the station, Councillor Szymczyk cast this question ahead of him. A porter followed, lugging two cases and a bag of bedding.

Not receiving an answer, the councillor asked again louder, but the handful of gawping boys responded with stony indifference.

If Szymczyk had addressed one of them directly, he'd have had the information at once, but as he cast the question straight ahead of him, they just looked at him as if watching a spectacle.

'There's a fine shout for you!' cried the youngest, picking his nose.

This annoyed the councillor, and he went red. But instantly he became cold and calm, because someone had jostled him from behind.

'Excuse me,' said the councillor, looking around. 'Would you please watch out! You're jostling me with your bag.'

'What? I am? You? With my bag? A thousand pardons,' said the professor, for it was he who had accidentally driven his bag into Szymczyk's back. 'Oh, what's this I see? Miss Maja! Gentlemen, allow me to make the introductions. Mr . . . er, what was it . . . Szymon . . .'

'Treasury Councillor Szymczyk,' Councillor Szymczyk introduced himself and added: 'I sent a telegram to herald my arrival.'

'A thousand pardons. Szymczyk. And this is Mr Myńczyk . . . The tennis coach . . .'

'Excellent!' said Miss Ochołowska, offering her hand. 'We'll all fit, because there's the britzka as well for your things.'

The carriage drove up, and she and the professor sat down on the back seat, while the councillor and Walczak took their places on the bench. They drove along a muddy road amid sparse forest; here and there a vista opened onto a wide, flat, mournful region.

The sun had set by now, and the silence pervaded their ears. No one spoke. Not once did the woods retreat from the horizon, but now the road led through meadows sparsely covered in stunted trees.

'What a country!' uttered the councillor at last.

'Yes, round here it's a wilderness, poverty and sorrow,' said the young lady, laughing, and to Walczak somehow this laughter seemed familiar – he looked at her closely. She spoke very softly, whether out of coquetry or for other reasons he couldn't tell, but it gave her a tinge of mystery. Yet he recognized that laughter from somewhere. Which of his acquaintances laughed like that? Suddenly and for no clear reason his heart began to beat very fast.

What the devil is it? he thought.

As darkness fell, the veil of approaching night started to cover the boughs of the trees. A great moon was rising over the meadows. Dogs were barking in a distant village. Walczak couldn't ward off a strange sense of anxiety; as he tried to penetrate the increasing shadows, all of a sudden he thought he was dreaming . . . A large and ancient coach of a kind not used for at least a hundred years by now, drawn by four horses, rumbled right past them at immense speed with a rasp and clang of metal and disappeared in clouds of dust.

'What was that?' cried the councillor.

The professor leaned out and gazed in curiosity after the mammoth vanishing into the distance.

'That was the prince from Mysłocz,' he said.

'Yes,' said Maja. 'He's on his way home from Warsaw too, poor thing. You don't know the greatest attraction of these parts,' she said, addressing Szymczyk. 'Mysłocz is a few kilometres from Połyka. We're driving across Mysłocz land now.'

'But why on earth does he use such a strange means of locomotion? Like something from the days of Queen Bona!' said Szymczyk. 'It's both uncomfortable and noisy.'

'Why? Because he has bats in his belfry!' said the professor. 'That's why, my dear councillor! Since time immemorial the poor old prince has been an oddball, to put it mildly. I'm amazed he was in Warsaw – he never puts his nose out of his great big castle. Mr Cholawicki must have had a good deal of bother with him,' he said, turning to Miss Ochołowska.

'Quite so,' she replied. 'Henryk only just managed to persuade him to make the trip, but business required it. In Warsaw he wouldn't let Henryk leave his side.'

'Look, look, sir!' cried the professor to the councillor. 'From here you can see the castle, but I don't know if it's not too dark.'

But by now the moon was beaming over the boundless plains, dotted here and there with the fantastic silhouettes of trees. In the pale glow, a white stretch of water appeared – it was the Muchawiec rolling slowly and idly across the flatlands, creating giant pools, almost unable to move from the spot.

The vast sheet of water that appeared to the councillor's view could have been called a lake if not for the reeds, rushes and osiers rising above it in the most unlikely spots. It looked more like a flood than a lake, or a large number of individual ponds. In places, the earth and water were so mixed together that it was hard to tell which element prevailed.

The surprise in this hopeless, wetland scenery was a hill that soared above the water, inexplicably rising out of nowhere. And even more astonishing was the vast edifice built on top of it.

Being short-sighted, Szymczyk could not distinguish the details, but he was aware of a great mass of stone, from which an enormous tower shot up, possibly six storeys high, ragged and ruined at the top. Solitary, noble and feudal, it dominated the landscape. Mist was gradually enveloping the foot of the castle.

'What an immense pile!' exclaimed the councillor.

'Bah!' replied the professor. 'One hundred and seventy ruined bedrooms, living rooms, ballrooms, halls, atria and whatever else you care to mention! But for an art historian it is of no significance. No style, you see! Ruin, neglect, a typical lordly mansion in a state of total collapse. Poland, as you know,' he went on didactically, 'is not rich in architectural monuments. In former times there were some splendid castles, but they were almost all destroyed during the Swedish wars, and the rest have been consumed by their owners' negligence and barbarism. How many of these monuments were simply demolished for the stone . . . Now they say Łańcut is the finest palace in Poland. But Łańcut is an infant, a callow youth without a past! True, it has splendour, orangeries, marble stables and God knows what, but it has no patina. At least Mysłocz is some six hundred years old!'

'Six hundred?' wondered the councillor. 'In these parts?'

'Why, yes,' replied the professor. 'It was the ancient fort of the former princes Holszański-Dubrowicki. There has been a stronghold here since time began . . . This castle,' he added, with a note of despondency, 'had its glorious episodes in the past, but now . . . it's just a heap of stones stripped bare and that's all! The dismal seat of a madman, the tomb of a dying clan . . . For the past hundred years no one has lived here but madmen.'

They drove into forest again. It grew darker, because the moon only rarely peeped through the branches, and an infinite sorrow gripped Walczak's heart. At the same time, he was seized by such anxiety that he had to stop himself from jumping out of the carriage and fleeing into the bushes.

The despondency of this gloomy terrain also infected the professor, who fell silent; only the councillor began to hold forth on such typically Polish failings as disorder, disarray, dishevelment, the lack of proper care, the lack of organization in conservation. No one was listening to him, as they were all engrossed in the forest, in the past, and perhaps in their own, hidden anxieties.

Suddenly Miss Ochołowska turned to Marian.

'We're going to play!' she said.

'Sure!' he replied, and laughed.

Did he imagine it, or had she looked at him carefully? Yes, he caught her inquiring gaze, peering furtively at his face. It occurred to him that perhaps she had noticed his underhand doings with the letter – but no, it was impossible, she'd been asleep.

So why was she looking at him like that?

He shook off his reverie, and just then the professor announced: 'Oho, we've arrived.'

Sure enough, they had driven into a large clearing, then through a gateway and there were dogs leaping around them.

Połyka was a large, old manor house with a distinctive high roof and a small porch. Marian stood to one side, waiting for the introductory formalities and greetings to be over.

'Ah,' said Mrs Ochołowska at last, to whom Maja had whispered a few words. 'How wonderful that you're here. My daughter has been dreaming of you for ages. Marysia, show the gentleman upstairs and then take some supper up to his room.'

She offered him her hand in a friendly manner and disappeared with the remaining guests. Preceded by the maid holding a candle, Walczak climbed a narrow, creaking staircase. His room was a small cubbyhole in the attic. The maid was extremely neat and sensible, though young.

'Here's a bowl and water,' she said, 'I'll bring a towel at once. If you need anything, please ring, but I think that's everything.'

'Do you have a lot of guests here?' he asked, sitting on the bed.

'Hm . . . no. Apart from the ones who arrived today there's a doctor's wife from Lwów and one other lady. It's only the start of the season.'

She said goodnight and left. He went up to the window and tried to open it, but couldn't, so he merely opened the vent. The old trees in the park were gently rustling, while just beyond them stood the forest, deaf and silent. Once again he had a sense of anxiety. He felt as if he shouldn't have come here, and that even now, even if on foot it would be better for him to run back. But where was he to go back to? The course of his life so far had been entirely random.

Quite by chance, at the age of ten he'd become a ball boy at a tennis club in Lublin. His father, a locksmith by profession, was pleased with his son's 'position', especially as the boy often brought more money home in tips than he earned all day doing hard work. The boys at the club did in fact receive regular remuneration of a few groszy per hour, but often one or another of the richer players would give the lad an extra fifty groszy or even a whole zloty. And eventually Marian had learned to keep this incidental revenue for himself.

Noticing the reduction in income, and with no opportunity to control it, his father began to beat him, which made the boy even more determined to keep the money. He hated his father and refused to give him a single groszy, even at risk of being battered to death. With every year that passed their relationship worsened as the son matured. He learned not to come home for the night but would stay with friends, only showing up a couple of days later, but afterwards there was always a beating.

Meanwhile at the club there were smooth courts strewn with red clay, sunshine, ladies and gentlemen dressed in white, jokes, shouts and merriment. Ah! Marian felt at home here; he learned how to wrangle money out of people with saucy wit and brazen cheek, while at the same time borrowing a racket from the players in the breaks between one set and another to try out some classic strokes. Mieczkowski, the ageing coach and manager of the club rolled into one, noticed the boy's remarkable talents and decided to train him as a coach. He gave him the permanent loan of a battered old racket.

By the age of sixteen, Walczak knew how to serve the balls correctly to beginners and spent hours coaching schoolboys and schoolgirls. He also learned how to string a racket and – to an even higher degree – how to string along the guests, persuading them they had unusual talent.

At this point another happy accident occurred: his father went off to the provinces to take up a job, and the boy moved in with Mieczkowski for good. On top of that he earned extra money at the club restaurant, or rather canteen, which Mieczkowski had been gradually and imperceptibly transforming into a 'restaurant' that was also designed for guests from the street.

But Walczak had started loafing around on the court and in the restaurant. He was bored with coaching duffers, he wanted to play – he started paying more attention to his own playing than his opponent's, and would 'finish' the ball with a killer smash instead of passing it gently to his opponent's racket, on top of which he became difficult, wayward, disobedient, moody, dissatisfied and rebellious. He was bored. He couldn't have said why. He went to the cinema, read cheap thrillers, and sighed for a different life. He felt he was wasting every hour he spent here, that instead of sitting around at Mieczkowski's he could do something – go somewhere, start on something, come up with a plan to get into something better at last.

At night he was sometimes overcome by such awful despair that he wanted to put an end to himself forever. He was going to ruin. He felt he was going to ruin, an utterly lost cause. He liked to read *The Sporting Review*, knew the names of all the greatest players by heart and imagined their travels abroad, their matches, the successes and the ovations . . . Why the devil did he have to sit in a provincial town, at a second-rate club instead of travelling and winning, like those fellows? Bah, they had talent – they were real players. While he could beat all the local no-hopers when he wanted, he had never yet seen good playing at first sight.

He was so bored with it all that when an engineer he knew had asked if he could go to Połyka for a couple of weeks he'd agreed at once, and begged Mieczkowski to let him. He'd read about Miss Ochołowska in *The Sporting Review* as one of the most promising female players of the younger generation.

'I'm going!' he begged Mieczkowski. 'She must be stuck in the countryside, and there are no players out there – she's no one to play against. I'll practise with her and restring the rackets, and I'll pay for my keep like that. You'll manage without me for two stupid weeks, Mr Mieczkowski! I'll only escape for a few seconds!'

And he had got away . . . But now as he gazed out of the window at the motionless rural linden trees, he was starting to regret escaping. Maybe this old manor, maybe the gloom wafting from these godforsaken parts was the cause of his disquiet and strange sense of sorrow. He thought about everything he'd encountered on the journey – the prince's mysterious exclamation, the letter he'd read, Miss Ochołowska's manner of sleeping, her laughter, her glance, the money that was hidden away in a closet somewhere in this house – and couldn't imagine which bit of it could have got him so worked up.

He stretched blissfully until his bones cracked in their joints. Aaaaah! and he laughed softly, frivolously, at the thought of all the unexpected events that still lay ahead of him in life.

At the very same moment, in her room Miss Ochołowska, half undressed, was stretching in an identical way, with exactly the same smile on her lips as she thought about some of the plans and projects she had for the near future. A light breeze arose and the linden trees started to rustle outside.

Next morning, dressed in white, Walczak and Miss Maja strolled across the lawn towards the tennis courts, from where they could already hear the voices of the kids who'd been summoned to pick up the balls. It was a splendid day, with no wind, just some feathery white cloudlets scudding across the pale blue sky.

Each of them had two rackets tucked under an arm.

Walczak, who was extremely well versed in the inside story of the sport, knew that although Miss Ochołowska had yet to take part in the major tournaments, she had carried off some unofficial victories against leading players, and that was among the men. The experts often noted her exceptionally versatile style, promising the highest hopes and the greatest successes abroad for her.

As for Walczak, there was really no one at the club who could dream of winning a set against him, but nor was there anyone to represent the higher class of player. So he decided to limit himself to nothing but serving her the ball and helping her to practise her individual strokes. In any case, Miss Ochołowska probably wasn't expecting any special thrills. She walked along in silence, apparently thinking about something else – sullen and inattentive, with her eyes fixed on the ground. When she stopped at the courts – which were excellent, as Walczak could immediately judge – she didn't say a word but just rapidly withdrew beyond the baseline.

'Forehand!' she called.

He served the ball and it went into the net. The second one was out. The third was finally in, but Miss Maja had to run up to catch it on her racket. The next few landed chaotically, too near or too far away.

'But you haven't a clue!' she finally shouted.

'Everyone does as best he can,' he replied without thinking.

She stopped. 'What a pity you can't do better,' she said, shrugging. He sent her a new series of balls, which she returned with fine, well-practised swings.

He swore to himself that he wouldn't return any of her balls – the disrespect she had shown him had deeply wounded his ambition.

Now Miss Ochołowska began to practise her backhand, especially on the high balls, which she returned with a deep twist at the waist, retracting her racket with both hands almost behind her back. Her strokes, hitting the baseline, were so superb that Walczak couldn't resist after all, and when one of the balls presented itself to his racket, he hit it. The ball passed an inch over the net. His opponent bent at the knees, drew her racket right back and returned it with a lightning crosscourt shot.

He lunged for the ball almost before it had been returned, and that was the only reason why he managed to reach it at all.

He returned it.

'What??' she cried, already on the run, leaning forwards.

There followed an exchange of very sharp crosscourt shots deliv-
ered backhand – the rackets began to ring out rhythmically and fast.
Miss Maja herself had no idea when she was thrown off the court
by her opponent's long, killer shots. At the same time Walczak ran
up to the net, and when she tried to get past him with a high lob, a
killer smash followed, which left her totally helpless.

'We'll play a set!' she shouted.

Walczak was surprised by his own success. He realized he had
played the ball extremely well, but perhaps – fancy that! – there was
also no great difference between them as players? He concentrated
and received her perfectly sharp, well-placed serve. The rackets rang
out again. The first point was his!

'Either she plays worse than I thought,' it occurred to him, 'or I
play better.'

And suddenly, somewhere in the very depths of his being he felt
an almost mystical connection with nature, the sort of confidence
and certainty that sometimes comes over a sportsman or a card
player. He realized that he really was in excellent form. He narrowed
his eyes and killed her service with an unerring smash, whacked
into the corner, and won himself the first game.

In the next game Miss Maja started to play more cautiously – the
balls arced far above the net with changing fortunes. Meanwhile,
lured by the sound of the game, the boarding-house guests had
appeared on benches at the side of the court.

The presence of spectators excited them even more, and imperceptibly the match turned into one of those unique, impetuous
encounters that intoxicate the players and the gallery to equal
measure. Walczak's sense of abandon, of losing himself in the
game, was accompanied by insane joy at discovering and revealing
his talent – now he was in no doubt at all, every stroke confirmed

the truth that he was better than this girl prodigy, that he was a class player, on the road to becoming a champion! And on top of that he had a sense of satisfaction that it was her he was beating as he pleased.

For some strange reason he felt tremendous ferocity towards his opponent – clenching his teeth, he struck the ball as if he were hitting her, straining his sight, he caught all her actions, foreseeing her every move with animal vigilance.

But as well as astonishment, such a keen ferocity, bordering on anger, had appeared in Miss Maja too that she herself was surprised by it.

They fought in total silence; though incapable of understanding the technical details of the game, the people sitting on the bench were excited enough by its fury to stop applauding.

In the quiet of the deciding game a hushed comment by one of the ladies watching was clearly audible: 'How similar they are!'

'Indeed,' replied the other. 'It's quite astonishing!'

At this point Miss Ochołowska did not run up to the ball. She stopped and left the court.

'Thank you,' she said. 'That's enough.'

'What?' he asked in amazement. 'Aren't we going to finish the set?'

Both were breathing heavily. She cast him a glance.

'No.'

She was pale. Walczak went pale too, and had to stop himself from swearing. What was wrong with her? He didn't reply.

The company received them with cheers.

'Why did you stop? That was incredibly thrilling!'

'You're a superb player!' called Mrs Ochołowska to Walczak. 'I'm quite a good judge . . . Where have you been hiding? Who taught you? You make some basic mistakes, but you have phenomenal talent. You're not a coach, you're a player – you could do with a coach yourself!'

'You're a phenomenal player!' cried one of the ladies, an obese blonde with bulbous eyes. 'Especially those diagonal shots . . . Exceptional!'

'Beyond compare!' said another lady, thin and bony. 'Although for my taste a little too powerful. My daughter and her friend can pass a single ball to and fro for far longer. Naturally, that's not an argument, you play gloriously, and your daughter,' she said, turning to Mrs Ochołowska, 'plays like an angel, an angel!'

'More like a devil!' replied the fat woman. 'What a temperament.'

'Now now,' said Councillor Szymczyk, 'let us not exaggerate. One should never overdo one's praises. If we knew how much praise can swell a person's head, we'd be more cautious about giving it. An atmosphere of healthy criticism is far better,' he added, wiping his pince-nez. 'And there's no need to overestimate the role of sports!'

'They played exquisitely!' said the plump doctor's wife with an ecstatic sigh. 'And they're altogether a lovely couple. How similar they are – you'd think they were brother and sister.'

'I can't see any similarity,' replied Mrs Ochołowska coldly.

'For sure, for sure, dear lady, nothing of the kind! Of course! And yet there's something in common, the same temperament, the same tenacity, ferocity – naturally it's just a superficial impression . . . Please don't take it literally, dear madam.'

Mrs Ochołowska gave a faint sigh. Councillor Szymczyk's over-critical and didactic attitude was nothing compared with the diffi-culties she had with these ladies. The thin one was sour and cold, while the fat one was sweet and hot in her endearments, but neither of them missed a single opportunity to antagonize her by making impertinent remarks.

Both were convinced that Mrs Ochołowska, as a landowner forced by material necessities to run a boarding house, felt it an indignity and regarded her guests with repugnance. As a result – although Mrs Ochołowska had never once shown any kind of repugnance, and deep down was even sincerely grateful to them for coming to stay –they had decided to adopt a defensive position just in case, and to make it clear to the lady of the manor that they were not so easily impressed!

On the whole, the lady of the manor received their sarcastic comments with complete calm, but this time the tubby doctor's wife's remark touched her to the quick. There was some truth in it! Maja really was like the coach in some way, and her mother found this similarity alarming, as it wasn't a similarity of features, but something else, something elusive . . . The mother, who was so fearful for her daughter, had a bad feeling about this similarity, though she couldn't think where the connection between Maja and this . . . well, this Mr Walczak came from.

Oh, there was no pride in her feelings – Maja's mother had none of the gentry's bad habits; she was too well-versed in the nature of the great social revolutions that were gradually but inexorably levelling all classes and castes. So if it worried her so much, and even wounded her, it wasn't because of inopportune snobbery, but for reasons of a moral kind.

It looked to her as if what connected them was a common trait of character, an affinity of natures . . . Something elusive, but definitely bad, or even ominous. Mrs Ochołowska ran a hand over her brow – but then maybe it was an illusion!

'Let's go in to lunch,' she said.

'Ah, lunch, my dear madam!' gushed the overflowing, plump and goggle-eyed doctor's wife. 'I can imagine how delicious it's going to be! They really know how to eat in the countryside – one does nothing but eat from dawn to dusk!'

'But think how many people are dying of hunger while we're eating more than we're able,' said the thin woman sourly, rising from the bench.

'The regulation of food,' said the councillor. 'The reorganization and normalization of both substances ingested and substances apportioned is from the economic point of view a state necessity that should be implemented by means of special rules. Each citizen should consume only as much as he requires in order to fulfil his duties to the state in the proper manner.'

They strolled off towards the house.

Walczak, who as soon as the game was over had crossed to the other side of the courts to calm down, could not hear what they were saying, but he could feel their gaze on him. But now he felt that someone else was watching him too. It wasn't Maja.

She was talking aside to a tall, broad-shouldered and impeccably dressed man, whom he instantly recognized as the gentleman who'd been with Prince Holszański in the train compartment.

He had plainly come to visit on horseback, as he was in riding clothes and was flicking a crop against his boots. It was this clean-shaven, well-groomed, burly man, Prince Holszański's secretary and Maja's fiancé, who was looking at him. While talking to Maja, he never took his eyes off him, with the nonchalance of a very self-confident person who doesn't give a damn about others. Walczak was familiar with this lack of concern, typical of the golden youth who sometimes frequented Mieczkowski's club and restaurant.

Why the hell is he staring at me like that? he thought angrily.

Everything inside him was quivering with rage. Playing against Maja had angered more than bewildered him. It was that the girl hadn't said a word to him after leaving the courts that angered him most. She was talking to her fiancé quite indifferently, as if she hadn't been fighting with all her strength only minutes ago.

But at lunch (this time he ate with everyone else in the dining room downstairs) Miss Ochołowska's indifference ceased to annoy him. On the contrary, it started to amuse him.

She must have been furious with him for beating her and for clearly being the superior player. It wasn't indifference, but quite the opposite – anger and humiliation at the fact that he, a common coach, had proved better than she was.

She's upset! he thought, and it made him feel utterly intoxicated, while also putting him on familiar terms with her.

Sitting at the dull end of the table, he suddenly felt that he was closer to the girl than anyone else – including the fiancé – and for some reason he was gripped by certainty that she wanted to appear to be ignoring him, while in fact she was fully tuned to what he was doing.

To make sure, he cast her a glance across the table – though not looking in his direction she instantly went as red as a peony.

She lowered her head, but just then her fiancé, Mr Cholawicki, started telling a joke and everyone burst out laughing.

Yet it was all unclear. Why had she blushed? Was it only because of losing the game?

And why had she been looking at him in the carriage?

And why had Cholawicki been watching him?

And why had all the other people furtively shifted their gaze from her to him and from him to her, as if they couldn't stop themselves?

One after another they cast a seemingly accidental glance at him, then at her, or vice versa – even Mrs Ochołowska had done it . . .

Straight after lunch, Walczak set off for the forest, striding ahead along an overgrown path through the shrubbery, flicking away the large, heavy flies that kept landing on his bare arms.

He was bursting with wild joy. He couldn't think about anything except the game against Maja, and kept reliving every moment of it, with the racket strings ringing in his head.

Could it really be true that he had talent? Why hadn't anyone told him that before? Admittedly, at the club he played carelessly and was never able to show what he could do – neither to himself nor others. But he'd always had a hunch he was better than they were – was that why he was so unhappy? That was why he felt he was going to ruin! That was why he wanted to escape into the world outside. Ah, he had to go to Warsaw at any cost, he had to let them see him, assess his potential and help him to improve – and then he'd travel the globe, like Tłoczyński! He suddenly felt hot, and stopped in his tracks for sheer joy.

And once again his fevered imagination offered him several wonderful balls that he returned from almost hopeless positions. No, he decidedly played better than she did! He was a whole class ahead! She was nothing compared to him! He resolved to speak to her that evening and ask for her help to make contact with the players in Warsaw. She probably wouldn't be jealous of his playing for long – after all, she was a woman, so they couldn't compete with each other.

And suddenly he found himself by a river, sleepily rolling through the forest. He undressed and plunged into the warm, idle current. He swam a short way – and came to land on a small sandbank bathed in strong sunshine. Intense weakness assailed him.

He fell asleep.

When he awoke, the sun was starting to set. The water in the river had turned greenish-violet with silver glints on its surface and the forest was fragrant as Walczak swam across to the bank and put on his clothes. He turned towards the house, but the thought of a career, of trips, journeys and triumphs dogged him at every step, keeping pace with him through the sparse tall-treed forest.

He was seized by a wild craving for pleasure. Finally, to give vent to his feelings he started to run, racing ahead as if running away from himself . . .

On he ran for two kilometres, until he stopped, exhausted, at the foot of a large oak tree. He pressed his face into wet moss.

Suddenly he heard a voice coming from above.

'Is someone there?'

Astonished, the boy looked up. Somewhere in the oak tree, very high up among the branches, he could see a human shape. The voice spoke again.

'Help!'

'What's wrong?' he called.

'Please help me to get down. I can't do it, I'm feeling dizzy.'

Walczak climbed the tree easily, and once he was halfway up he discovered . . . the professor, straddling a branch almost at the top, and clinging tightly to the trunk.

The sight was so ludicrous that he snorted with laughter.

'I'm coming!' he shouted.

'Quick, or I'll fall! Please save me!'

But it wasn't easy. The branches at the top were thin enough to snap under the weight of two people. The slender trunk was swaying alarmingly – and on top of that the professor latched onto Walczak with both hands, digging his fingernails into him – his body was shaking. The boy began to lower him from branch to branch, ignoring the scars left by this operation on the clothes of the poor rascal, who simply groaned: 'Aaaargh!'

He fell to the moss, where it took him a few minutes to come to his senses, and then finally he cried: 'Where are my binoculars?'

'They're here,' replied Walczak, racking his brains to think what an old man could be doing up a tree with a pair of binoculars.

'Young man,' said the professor solemnly, 'if not for you, I'd have fallen, because I cannot bear heights.'

'Then why on earth did you climb up there?' Walczak asked naïvely. 'Were you trying to get a look at the castle?' he suddenly guessed.

Following the professor's gaze, he caught sight of some boggy ground that started beyond the forest, and further on, a couple of kilometres away, a massive heap of stone walls and two corner towers, above which loomed the main body of the castle and its sloping roof. From roughly the middle of the buildings, the biggest, four-sided tower shot up, the one he had already seen on their drive from the station. Here and there the black holes of narrow windows appeared, and the severe, jagged walls exuded grand, lifeless solitude. Close up, the castle looked even more formidable and somehow more fantastical . . .

'Hm, among other things . . .' said the professor cautiously. 'Among other things I was trying to look at the castle. But where did you spring from?'

'I was in the woods and I got lost.'

The professor gave him a searching look.

'You are an outsider here,' he said, as if considering something. Walczak was amused by his stale, wrinkled little face in eternal motion.

'Young man,' said the scholar at last, 'in the first place please know that I'm a good judge of people, and I only have to look at you to know with whom I am dealing. A person's character is written in his bodily physique – as long as one knows how to read it, of course. You are a far more dangerous type than you appear to be – do you know where I'm inferring this from? Right here,' he said, touching Walczak's face – 'it's the combination of these cheekbones and the shape of the mouth, that nose with those eyes. Watch out, because if you fail to control your passions, you'll end up in the wilderness, from where, hm . . . That's not the point. I think you have a violent but upright nature. Well, so I'm ready to let you in on a secret, naturally on condition you don't squeak a word to anyone about it. I'd like to get inside the castle, and if you can make it easier for me, I shall reward you.'

'So may one not enter the castle?'

'No, one may not! That's the point, it's impossible!' he shouted furiously. 'The old prince is a madman, his father was a madman too, and so was his grandfather. For a hundred years no one has been able to get inside the castle, all the more since the . . . the secretaries are hostile towards people who . . . I tried to enter the normal way, through the gate, but it's locked and bolted, and the flunkey, that senile old fool, peeped at me through a hole and gibbered away that the prince forbade any admittance. There are only three people living in the whole of that vast pile – the prince, his secretary and that flunkey, no one else. The other servants have no entry to the inside and cluster in those nasty little hovels, over there on the left. They don't let anybody in, but I must get inside – I must, even if they set the dogs on me.'

'Why must you?' asked Walczak, observing the old man's fury with interest. The professor scowled and cast him a look of contempt.

'It's a waste of words! You wouldn't understand even if I spent a hundred years explaining! Young man, if I am not misled by my presentiments, my suspicions, the conclusions and pieces of evidence I have come upon in the course of my research, then inside this castle is a store of priceless treasure, the only one of its kind in all Poland, a mine, mark me, a mine of marvels! It is exceptional! Unique! A revelation!'

He was breathless.

'Mark me, sir, on the outside, those walls are purely defensive in nature. The castle was not built without reason, so from the outside it's an ancient fortress, austere and warlike . . . And all my life I thought that the castle at Mysłocz had nothing distinctive about it except for its great age – as you should know, the north wing is almost six hundred years old. Meanwhile, one day in a Roman library I came upon the correspondence from Poland of the seventeenth-century nuncio Almari. It turned out the nuncio had visited Poland, and among other things had stayed at Mysłocz as a guest of Prince Holszański. So, in writing about the castle Almari mentions the splendid paintings he saw there. That puzzled me, but I'd have overlooked the whole matter because, good Lord – I thought the Italian was flattering the magnate – until in the records of the Radziwiłł family, closely related to the Holszańskis, I also chanced upon a document from Mysłocz, dating from the eighteenth century, titled "Register of sums expended", and dear Lord, what entries I read! "To the artist for restoring two ancient plafonds painted by Dolabella . . . Repair and embellishment of two paintings by Jordaens . . . one depicting the Adoration, and the other Ceres." When I read that, I tell you, it almost took my breath away . . . Well, I shan't explain it to you, because you won't understand anyway. All I shall tell you is that Gabrielle d'Estrées' chairs, the famous chairs given to her by her lover, the French king Henri IV, also featured in this inventory. And armoires made by Hugues Sambin too! Mark me! And it only listed items that had been renovated. So how many other antiques are those walls hiding? What is there inside? What marvels! What masterpieces of brush and chisel.'

Having just accused Walczak of passion, now the professor himself fell prey to it. He was close to tears. Old-age passion and youthful passion looked each other in the eyes, incapable of mutual understanding, each living for himself, in his own world . . .

'Oh!' cried the professor. 'I must see it, I must touch it, I must know for sure what's in there. Because it's all going to waste, deteriorating with every passing minute . . . It has to be saved!'

'How much might one of those pictures be worth?' asked Walczak.

'What a funny question!' roared the professor. 'Things of that kind aren't valued in terms of money. But I'll tell you. One such picture could be worth as much as a million!'

'And nobody knows all those valuables are in there?'

'That is what amazes me! How on earth has such an oasis been preserved in Poland, a sanctuary nobody has discovered? But I understood when I found out that for one hundred and fifty years no civilized creature has been allowed to pass through the castle gates; the last three generations of that family were drunkards, gamblers and womanizers, people who hadn't a clue what they possessed, incapable of telling the Renaissance apart from the Gothic. And further back, which of these aristocrats had an ounce of imagination about art? The masterpieces passed from father to son, and they grew so used to them that finally they ceased to notice them. But there will always be secretaries – who not without reason refuse competent people the right to enter on the pretext that . . . the prince has categorically forbidden it!'

He lowered his voice and began to wink at Walczak, then a little later he shouted: 'Where are my binoculars?'

'It seems Mr Cholawicki is the prince's secretary,' said Walczak, letting his gaze slide over the majestic residence.

A whitish haze was just starting to rise at the foot of the castle, making the walls look higher. In the distance the sky was tinted by the last rays of the sun, and below dense darkness was coming closer.

The boy sighed, and without knowing why, was once again crushed by a sense of sadness.

'Mr Cholawicki, secretary, cousin, administrator, plenipotentiary, confidant, household member and steward!' recited the professor disdainfully. 'A typical specimen of the elegant cad! A cad in toff's clothing! A debonair brute! Ha, but perhaps there's nothing there, perhaps all my assumptions are false,' he said aghast, and goggled at the castle, which was receding, rising and melting to greet the approaching night.

Dogs began barking from the buildings on the slope of the castle hill. But the air above the floodplain was growing denser, heavier, suffused with fog, ready at any moment to gather in a white cloud.

The terrifying emptiness of the vicinity, the malarial, unhealthy climate, the loneliness and misery of the reed-clogged marshes, here and there cut through by a causeway, further intensified the atmosphere of tragedy and magical mystery of this ancient lair, the seat of a dying clan of eccentrics, slowly tumbling into ruin and death along with their castle.

Walczak felt more and more frightened, who knows whether of ghosts or the darkness, or something else entirely, something that might suddenly creep under his feet, or jump out of the gloom or a thicket. It was in his nature to swing abruptly from joy into grief, after which sorrow and fear took total possession of him. Meanwhile the professor kept his eyes glued to the darkening edifice, as if in an effort to pierce the armour of the walls.

Suddenly a light shone in one of the small, elongated windows in the corner tower. Strangely, this one single, feeble, solitary light within the entire bulk of the building further deepened the impression of emptiness – a shiver ran through the boy at the thought that for one hundred and fifty-something rooms there were only three people – the prince, his secretary and the butler, three people trailing about those dark, damp, empty chambers, amid riches crumbling to dust . . .

'There's always a light in that window,' said the professor. 'It must be the prince's room. Well, let's go, we'll be late for supper anyway. It's almost four kilometres from here to the manor. Now you understand,' he said, gesticulating and tripping over the stones, 'what I need your help for. There must be another entrance, not just through the gate; I'm inclined to believe that on the western side the walls are badly impaired, partly in ruins. But the whole problem lies in the fact that one cannot go too close without being seen from the windows. I don't want to arouse suspicions. That, young man, is why you must help me, for which you will be rewarded, whatever. You will have to go up to the castle at night under cover of the mist, and thoroughly investigate how one might get inside. Tomorrow night we shall go together, and if we succeed, I shall conduct a discreet inspection of this junk store. At least I shall know if it's worth making further efforts.'

'But what if they catch us?'

'Pshaw!' said the old man. 'Lily-livered, are you?'

The boy cast a sideways glance at the professor, who was gamely tripping along beside him.

But he didn't take the proposal too seriously. It made no sense for him to get involved in such machinations – after all, if they caught

him, he'd be thoroughly compromised, and his tennis plans would
fall through.

If he didn't refuse at once it was only because he'd taken a liking
to the professor, and besides, all these stories stirred his unruly
imagination. Bah! If not for the tennis . . .

I must have a chat with Maja this evening, he thought. *I have to
find out what she thinks of my playing.*

'We'll talk some more,' he said to the professor, once they'd finished the supper left out for them.

Some of the company were playing bridge in the little parlour,
from where they could hear the voice of the thin lady clerk who
interwove her bids with acid remarks about the unsuitability of
such amusements, when at that very moment someone incurably
sick might be dying in appalling agony, et cetera.

'Then why on earth are you playing?' snapped Councillor
Szymczyk at last.

'Oh, pardon me! Am I the only one to be deprived of all pleasures?' she said, and tartly bid a small slam.

Maja was standing by the window with her fiancé, who was
explaining something to her in a whisper – it looked as if they
were quarrelling.

At the sight of her, Walczak's impatience rose – he wanted to
talk to her now, immediately, though perhaps it would be better to
wait until tomorrow – what if the moodiness she'd shown him that
morning hadn't passed off yet?

The girl's face did not bode well; she wore an expression of scorn
and contempt.

But he had to talk to her! He absolutely had to know right now
what chance he had, and what he should do.

Suddenly Miss Ochołowska walked away from Cholawicki, inter-rupting his arguments in mid-sentence, then she bid farewell to the company and left the room at a swift pace.

Walczak caught up with her in a small lobby at the top of the stairs as she was opening the door to her room.

'Excuse me!' he called.

'What is it?' she asked in her quiet voice. 'What can I do for you?'

Her tone was spiteful and unpleasant. At once he lost all his self-confidence.

'Excuse me,' he stammered, 'I'd like to ask you something . . . I'd like to have a word . . . I have a request . . .'

'Does it have to be right now?' she asked, glancing at her watch. 'All right, then,' she said, opening the door. 'Well, say your bit,' she snapped impatiently. 'It's getting late.'

'I'd like to go to Warsaw to show my playing! Perhaps someone would be interested. You know everyone in the administration there, maybe you could give me a letter of recommendation or some-thing . . . You told me I have talent, Miss.'

He sensed he was talking like a complete idiot.

With a hand on the doorknob, Miss Maja did not take her eyes off him.

'What if you did have talent, so what?'

'What do you mean, so what?' he stuttered. 'Things would be entirely different.'

'For sure,' she said. 'Entirely different.'

'For sure . . .'

'Right now you're a miserable little coach, but you could be a famous player! And then everything would open up before you. The world . . . Fame . . . Money . . . Women . . . Travel . . . Pleasures . . .'

She said this so avidly, with such understanding and somehow in such a familiar tone that she suddenly became terribly close to Walczak. They looked each other in the eyes.

She laughed softly, nervously. He too began to laugh, pained but also excited.

How well she knew his desires!

All of a sudden she went pale, and anger appeared on her face.

'Why are you laughing?'

He was stunned.

'You're laughing too,' he stammered, not knowing how to reply.

'I am free to, but you . . . but you . . . You're carried away by your imagination. What an idea! Talent! You play hardly a touch better than average so you can knock that out of your head! I didn't feel like playing today!'

Without a second glance she ran downstairs.

He stood rooted to the spot, as if thunderstruck. He didn't believe a word she had said.

But the way she had spoken to him!

If he could, he'd have hit her, for that spite and contempt of hers! She'd treated him like . . . like scum! What could he do to her, what could he do to her so she'd remember . . . There was nothing he could do to her!

Suddenly through the half-open door of her room he caught sight of the closet, and remembered what he'd read in the letter – that there was money in there, one thousand and several hundred zlotys.

All right!

If she's going to mock me, then I'll mock her – I'll swipe that cash. I don't know how to play, but I'm capable of stealing!

He looked around. Glazed doors led from the lobby into the guest rooms – there were no lights anywhere, so nobody was there. They were all downstairs.

He went into Miss Ochołowska's room.

It gave him pleasure to enter her room without permission – it put him on a par with her . . . First of all he checked whether there was another way out. There was. A second door led into one of the guest rooms.

If anyone came, he could go through that room and back into the lobby.

He hesitated.

He had never taken a single penny off anyone before.

But he'd take it off her! He'd rob her!

That was the one thing he could do to her!

He'd do it to her!

He tiptoed up to a solid piece of furniture by the wall and opened it: there in its depths were Maja's dresses on hangers, filling more or less half the closet.

The money had to be in one of the two drawers at the bottom – but which? They were both shut.

Just then he heard voices on the stairs. He ran into the adjoining room, intending to get through into the lobby, but here he met with disaster: the door into it was locked from the other side!

Quick as a flash, he raced back into Maja's room and was just in time to hide in the closet. He hid among the dresses and closed the door tight.

Into the room came Maja and Cholawicki. Walczak could hear every word they said, and could even see them through a crack.

They were quarrelling . . .

'Perhaps you'd leave me alone,' said the girl, as quietly as ever, but sounding extremely exasperated. 'I'm tired. Let's stop this now.'

'I'm not leaving until you give me an explanation!'

'I have nothing to explain! You're ridiculous.'

'I know I'm ridiculous,' he hissed. 'It's absurd that I'm forced to have a row with you about that boy! What a thought: me, you, and the coach, Mr Walczak! What a trio! It sticks out a mile! Do you think I didn't notice you blushing at table? And on the court you behaved like a lunatic. Why did you break off the game? Do you think I can't see you watching him? And just now you had a conversation with him upstairs and came back shaking! What's the meaning of it?'

'Just you think about what you're saying. You're insulting me! It's utterly vile of you not to trust me. And to be jealous of . . .' She broke off. 'You should have more respect,' she continued.

'I? For you? Respect? Do you think I don't know why you got engaged to me? You calculated that it'd be worth being Cholawicki's wife for a couple of years because any day now Cholawicki might make a fortune – and you can't imagine living in poverty. And, at the same time, I'm stylish enough and quite handsome, with a good name – perfectly suitable as a husband for a nice little beauty who . . . has her appetites . . . and wants to shine. And I am supposed to respect you, when I know you're marrying me in a calculated way, for a fortune.'

'So maybe you think I don't know by what means you aim to come by this fortune?'

For a while he said nothing.

'So you know – in spite of which you got engaged to me?'

There was now fury in his tone.

'And you know that I know, in spite of which you got engaged to me?' she said.

They fell silent again.

'Now I know what you're like!'

'What? What am I like? If you don't respect me, why are you marrying me?'

'Shall I tell you what you're like? You are . . . you appear to be refined, but in fact you're vulgar, like someone from the demi-monde. Vulgar! You're offended because I'm jealous of that boy . . . With you one can be jealous of everyone. You know perfectly well why I'm jealous! You know that if you weren't so similar to him it'd never have crossed my mind . . .'

'I? Similar? To him?'

'Don't lie – you're well aware of it yourself! That's why you keep looking at him like that. It's as if you're moulded from the same clay – everyone has noticed it. He has your smile, your look, your gestures – it's scandalous! That . . . that Walczak! Everyone can see it! You know it better than anyone and you're furious!'

'Get out!'

'All right, I will!'

Miss Maja was left on her own. She leaned back against the wall and gazed into space . . .

Her lovely little face froze in an inscrutable expression. She sighed.

So it really was true!

So he too had discovered her wild, improbable, idiotic resemblance to Walczak.

It was incredible. In the carriage, as they'd been driving from the station she had already noticed something about him so akin to herself that it had given her a fright . . . And then on the courts, when they'd battled against each other with exactly the same ferocity . . .

And she was horrified that it was obvious to other people too. She, Maja Ochołowska, conspicuously similar to a tennis coach!

She was perfectly familiar with every little detail of her own appearance. She knew that the likeness did not arise from shared features. They had different mouths, eyes, hair, and their colouring was different too.

It was a deeper commonality, of a physical kind, in the facial expression itself, in the gaze, in the laugh, and in something deeper and more elusive too.

Although it was hard to put a finger on it, she had realized that everyone was linking them, that the boarding-house guests were constantly shifting their gaze from her to him and from him to her, seeking reasons for the similarity . . .

Ugh, it was unbearable. Maja had no prejudices, and could easily have put up with a chance coincidence in appearance . . . But to share such a resemblance with a boy who didn't concern her, who meant nothing to her, a resemblance with a tennis coach – that was ridiculous!

It made her look a fool! It exposed her to silly scenes, forced her to blush idiotically, made her dependent on him against her will!

It was absurd! – for an optical illusion to be able to impose itself on people to that extent, including her!

She stood before the mirror. The blood rose to her cheeks again. The thing that agonized her most was that she was so embarrassed. She, who never went red, was now betraying herself with blushes.

'If there weren't a similarity, surely he wouldn't dare to tell me I'm vulgar!' she whispered.

Cholawicki had hit her weak spot. She knew that her type of beauty was very refined, she had petite hands and feet, she was in love with her own elegance and perhaps that was the main reason why she had to marry Cholawicki – he alone could dress her suitably.

She could never get enough of the dexterity and refinement of her own movements. But now it all turned out to be similar – and to whom?!

That Walczak was ridiculing her. He was compromising her! He was making her beauty laughable and trivial. She looked in the mirror with horror.

Suddenly she knitted her brow. She could hear her fiancé's footsteps on the stairs. He was coming back!

She ran to the door to lock it shut. She didn't want to see him at any price – she found him despicable!

But as soon as she remembered that there'd been no key in the lock for ages, she stepped back abruptly.

And then she went through exactly the same experience as Walczak half an hour earlier. She looked around in panic, seeking refuge, took a few steps towards the neighbouring room, backtracked at the last minute, abruptly opened the closet door, and before Walczak could do a thing, Maja was inside the closet right beside him and had slammed the door shut.

Simultaneously, after knocking a few times to no effect, Cholawicki entered the room.

'Maja!' he called.

The answer was silence.

Convinced she had just gone out for a moment and would be straight back, he sat down on a chair and impatiently began to drum his fingers on the table. He absolutely had to talk to her before going back to the castle, he must make up with the girl, who seemed increasingly attractive to him the more trouble she caused.

He decided to wait.

It took Maja a minute or so to take in the incredible, unlikely impression that . . . she was not alone in the closet. It was pitch dark in there.

She was standing so close to Walczak that the back of her hand was touching his. Impulsively she reached out and touched somebody's fingers.

Who on earth was it?!

She leaned the other way, shrinking as much as possible. She wondered if she was going crazy. They both froze still and held their breath.

Walczak was convinced that any moment now she'd start screaming, then Cholawicki would rush to the closet and a scandal would erupt throughout the house.

But Miss Ochołowska was so afraid of ridicule that it sobered her up. Now her greatest worry was that this mysterious fellow would start screaming and would leap out of the closet – for fear of her. Who could it be?

A thief?

Or maybe there was no one there. Perhaps she was imagining it?

She was afraid to touch him a second time. But she could feel his warmth, and she could virtually hear his heart beating violently right beside her. In any case her own heart was beating so fast it felt as if it would blow up the closet. Once again she began to think feverishly – who could it be? Total darkness reigned.

Then she remembered the money in the drawer. Ah, yes! So it was a thief!

Cholawicki had picked up a magazine from the side table and was leafing through it. Then, seeing Maja's absence was prolonged, after several glances at his watch he decided to write her a letter. He

took a fountain pen from his pocket and wrote nervously, taking
deep drags on a cigarette.

Dear Maja,

*I choose to ignore your last words. I'm putting them down to
irritation prompted by my own remarks. What's more, I admit
that I too was carried away. Perhaps my suspicions were errone-
ous and unjust. If so, I apologize. Lately I've been very anxious.*

*I see that you entirely fail to appreciate the difficulties of my
present situation, he continued. If you had more sympathy for
me, you wouldn't wear down my resistance with such preposter-
ous scenes. ('In fact it was I who made a scene to her,' it occurred
to him, 'but never mind.') You should understand in your own
interest that now, when the situation – you know which one – is
coming close to resolution and will require my full attention, I
cannot be troubled by differences with you, because that could
have an effect on business! I'm sure it's a mistake on my part to
attach undue significance to your caprices, but since I have this
weakness, you should respect it! I can assure you that I am working for your future too.*

*Naturally, not for a moment do I believe you could drop me.
You are too reliant on me and we are too well suited to each
other. Your attitude to me is entirely egotistical, but you need
me and I need you – and in fact I'd rather our relationship were
based on mutual need rather than affection. That is a solid basis.
But that's not the point. Despite knowing that you regret your
conduct, I'm afraid I may be forced to think about it too much
tomorrow and for the next few days.*

*You know I cannot go far from the castle now. The prince
is becoming increasingly difficult as his strength declines, and*

the trip to Warsaw has worn him out entirely. I must attend to him constantly. I will not be able to come to Połyka any time soon. The fact is that I refuse – and it's my right! – I refuse to be upset by this misunderstanding between us. I have other troubles to deal with. So please come and see me at the castle tomorrow <u>without fail</u> (these two words were underlined). *Obviously not through the main gate, but via the underground passage. I shall be expecting you at nine on the dot. It's rather unpleasant . . .*

He stopped, wondering whether he'd better not subject the girl to walking down that dark tunnel. Too bad! He leaned over the paper again.

Meanwhile, frozen to the spot inside the dark closet, Maja was growing more and more certain that it was Walczak.

They were standing side by side, so close that she had to huddle, contracting her muscles as hard as she could to avoid coming into contact with the alien, stranger's body.

And at the same time her mind was racing non-stop, feverishly – was it him, or not, was it Leszczuk* or not . . . If it was, then what? Then what? Surely it was monstrous! What was to be done?

Meanwhile Cholawicki went on writing.

---

*   As there has turned out to be a real tennis coach named Mr Walczak, with the author's permission we are changing this name to Leszczuk. What a strange coincidence!
[Translator's note: the book was originally serialized in a journal, hence this unexpected footnote from the editors. In fact, little did they know, but they'd been called with this complaint by a satirist named Jurkowski, a friend of Gombrowicz, who was annoyed by the writer's continuing miserliness despite the fact that he was being paid well for the serialization of this work. In another account, the joke was played by letter, and Gombrowicz took part in it.]

It's rather unpleasant, but at least nobody can see you in either direction, and there won't be any gossip.

Please be sure to come, because if I have risked writing you this letter and you don't come, I shall think you really have taken offence and have broken with me, and then I'd likely be even more annoyed. If you aren't going to come, write to me – but that's no good either, because the prince will instantly find out and be alarmed. You see what hell I have with this man, so don't be surprised that sometimes my nerves can't cope. I'll be waiting!
H.

He stood up and reached for an envelope. At the same time Maja snuggled up to Leszczuk, though she wasn't sure if it was him, she snuggled up gently, but recklessly, with total abandon.

It took so little for her to snuggle up – she only had to let her muscles go a tad. And what happiness she felt when a rough hand seized hers in the darkness.

She returned his grip with insane, secret joy.

Cholawicki sealed the letter, addressed it and sat down again, drumming his fingers against the table. Where could she be? Should he go on waiting? He sat out another five minutes and then left.

Once his footsteps had died away, Maja leaped out of the closet and without looking back ran out of the room; Leszczuk ran off too, as fast as his legs could carry him, and shut himself in his attic room.

III.

ON HIS WAY down to breakfast next morning he had no idea what lay ahead of him. Would they order him out of the house immediately? Or worse than that? He was prepared for anything.

However, these expectations did not come true. Mrs Ochołowska greeted him with a friendly nod, and after breakfast Maja appeared with the rackets.

'We'll play!' she said.

'How impetuous your daughter is!' cried the plump doctor's wife enthusiastically to Mrs Ochołowska. 'There's nothing like youth, ducky!'

'Not everyone can be young,' replied the thin lady clerk drily.

The company took their places on a bench to watch the game. After a dozen preliminary strokes Maja suggested a set – but even Councillor Szymczyk soon realized there was nothing worth watching, and the overflowing doctor's wife exclaimed: 'Just look how they're playing today! Dismally, dear lady! And your daughter looks unwell – maybe she's sick?'

'They both look unwell,' said the lady clerk unexpectedly.

Mrs Ochołowska got up, and they all strolled off into the formal garden. Leszczuk and Maja went on playing.

He was returning the ball ever more badly and ever more impatiently. His mind was racing. Was Cholawicki still here? He wasn't – evidently he'd left for the castle. *And why did I want to steal? Why did I want to steal? What on earth happened to me?*

Why did I want to steal? What came over me? They'd have known at once that it was me!

But one excellent certainty predominated: *she hadn't said a word to anyone.* She'd kept it all to herself! What's more, she had suggested they play tennis, as if nothing had happened.

He'd noticed her tiredness, the pallor of a restless night, the distraction in her playing, and he longed for the moment when he'd find himself on his own with her. His impatience rising by the minute, he missed a few of the easiest balls.

Six times Maja served out or into the net, and finally she left the court.

He caught her up at the point where the trees shielded them from the boys picking up the balls as well as from the house.

'Just a moment!' he called.

She turned round.

'Are . . . are we going to play this afternoon?'

'No.'

'Don't you have time?' he asked the silliest question in the world. He didn't know how to talk to her, how to refer to the incident in the closet. She cast him a look of surprise.

'No.'

Her indifference was so total that he was close to thinking he'd dreamed the events of the night before. He caught her by the hand. But at that she shouted: 'What are you doing?! Have you gone mad?'

And with all her might she struck him with her racket. Luckily he managed to step back and took the blow on his left arm. Miss Ochołowska walked away.

What on earth was that? So she thinks nothing happened between us . . . Ha! so that's her take on it. He rubbed his stricken arm and plunged into the garden.

Never before had he been so unhappy. All the mixed emotions he had felt for her during the night boiled down to hatred and fury. He went up to a tree and started snapping its twigs, one after another.

Meanwhile in her bedroom Maja had put the rackets on the bed and was sitting staring blankly at the wall.

'The insolence,' she whispered. 'What on earth does he imagine, that . . . thief?'

Thief!

She had no doubt he'd been trying to steal the money from the closet. Trying to commit a common theft and run off with the money. Yes, he was a common little crook!

Maja was amazed to find that the sudden discovery of Leszczuk's true nature, that his display of churlish, crude, coarse behaviour could shake her so very badly. He became so detestable to her that she'd have to force herself to play against him.

Everything inside her cringed at the thought of him. Perhaps it was actually the similarity between them that caused his miserable, boorish dishonesty to affect her so directly – making her feel it as if personally!

When they had first met he hadn't seemed to her either dishonest or crude and calculating. She had thought him a simple but decent boy. But now . . .

'What on earth does he imagine? That what? That I . . .'

That something like this would occur, that the moment of weakness to which goodness knows how and when she had yielded yesterday, would turn his head, would make him unruly, impudent and familiar – of this she was sure.

She knew this because . . . well, because in his place she'd have become unruly too. But she never supposed he would dare so insolently to . . .

He got what he deserved, she thought with pleasure. *Now he'll know.*

The worst thing was that today they were *both* pale and clearly hadn't slept – once again they resembled each other, even more, this time as the result of an identical experience.

Had those women noticed their mutual pallor? Had they connected his tiredness with hers?

I must say he has to leave, she thought. *I must make it clear to Mama that he has behaved improperly towards me, and then Mama will find a way to get rid of him tactfully and discreetly, before the end of the day. Yes, a single word from me and he'll be gone today. That's essential! Mama won't ask me any questions.*

But she knew she wouldn't utter that single word. No! It was simply impossible to understand how on earth she could have forgotten herself so badly yesterday.

At the memory of that moment, she was seized by such anger with herself that she bit her lip until it bled and clenched her fists. And where had it occurred? In the closet! In the closet with that Leszczuk! No, that was the height of absurdity!

And on top of that it had lasted a long time . . . maybe ten minutes! until Cholawicki left. Ugh, ten minutes! That was even worse than if they'd kissed . . . because a kiss would have been a caprice, a more or less scandalous whim . . . but they had stood there, hand in hand, intoxicated, frenzied . . . That was serious . . . it was just like love . . .

Love with Leszczuk!

And to cap it all he had overheard the scene her fiancé had made! He'd found out about their similarity – if he hadn't already noticed it himself.

So he had to stay a few more days. He had to stay so that she could undo everything she'd done with him. Make it clear to him and everyone else and to herself that she couldn't care less.

'He'll atone for it!'

She washed her face in cold water and went downstairs, now tenacious and indifferent. When she stopped by the dining-room window someone gently took her by the arm. She turned and met the worried, uncertain look of her mother.

'Maja,' said Mrs Ochołowska, dropping her gaze, 'it seems to me that you don't have much use for the tennis coach, and I'd like to put Marysia in his room.'

'I'd rather keep him for a few more days,' she replied.

Mrs Ochołowska sighed. How constantly, endlessly she feared for her daughter, so pretty and so difficult . . . Sometimes she even wanted her to marry Cholawicki, so great was her horror of the girl's self-reliance, secrecy and obstinacy.

But without daring to ask any questions she went back to her household occupations, which took up almost all her time. From afar she saw that Maja was slowly and thoughtfully reading a piece of paper – oh dear, why was there such a gulf between them that made it impossible to have a chat, to help or give advice?

Meanwhile Maja was reading Cholawicki's letter for the third time. Go or not go? In normal circumstances she'd have just shrugged . . . But this time there was something telling her to take notice of her fiancé.

She wanted to make peace with him, re-establish the relationship, gain his support. After all, Cholawicki was stylish, he was from her world – Maja felt a violent need to be reconciled with this man who looked right, from the same environment as she was.

At the same time she was bursting with desire to take action. She had to do something, her character was such that when moved and shaken she had to let off steam by taking immediate action. So she decided to go, and once dusk had fallen, after supper she slipped out of the house in a gaberdine overcoat and with an electric torch in her pocket.

At any rate, she need have no fear of the dogs – they knew her – and she could even come back very late at night without attracting attention, because she had an arrangement with Marysia, the housemaid, with whom she had a friendship, whereby whenever she knocked, Marysia would let her in through the window.

Maja ventured into the woods, among the pine trees, completely black after nightfall. Whistling, rapidly and nervously she moved on amid the nocturnal secrets of the forest and was soon in an excellent mood.

The night and the forest excited her, gave her pleasure, and at the same time calmed her down by blunting the torment of ambition and wounded pride.

But when she emerged from the woods at the edge of the great swamps below the castle, a slight shiver ran through her. The hopelessness of the surrounding area was acute.

Clouds of mist floated above the floodplain, over the reed-choked marshes and the clumps of bushes. There was no end to this confusion of the elements of earth, water and mist, in which one's vision drowned and lost its way, unable to find a resting place.

The mist reached almost to the foot of the stone walls, solitary and superior as ever. The barking of dogs in the distance sounded dreadful, like the voice of suffering.

Maja wasn't afraid of anything she might encounter in life, but she was afraid of death. And to her mind the empty, uninhabited castle amid the waters and marshland was death – it was a dying creature, doomed to extinction, sent mad by its own greatness, collapsing under the burden of the centuries, it was antiquity breathing its last.

And not without alarm she spotted the solitary light in a window of the corner tower. Nevertheless, she moved onwards.

Now she was walking along a causeway, and at once the characteristic dampness of mist enfolded her. Here one had to be careful. It wasn't hard to go the wrong way and find death on the treacherous, boggy ground that in places changed imperceptibly into a quagmire.

After forty-five minutes of arduous trudging, she finally reached the slope of the castle mount. In fact it could only be called a mount compared with the totally flat plain from which it rose. It was actually a hill no more than fifty metres high. But the good thing was that the fine mud clinging to her feet had come to an end.

Close up, the castle loomed through the mist even more uncannily – there was something unreal about the fantastical, mediaeval edifice with its oriels, battlements, arrow slits and shingle-roofed towers. Here and there within the stone walls were ordinary little windows with glass panes, and some unstylish, ugly details also further accentuated the mouldering building's antiquity.

Maja began to move with greater caution. The higher the ground, the sparser the mist, and in the moonlight it wasn't hard to spot her silhouette.

Luckily a clump of bushes appeared just in front of her – here was the entrance to the underground tunnel, the other end of which was connected to one of the castle cellars.

One time, Cholawicki had escorted her along this passage, more for a joke than with serious intentions. The tunnel's original exit was much further on, in the forest, but that stretch of it had been impenetrable for as long as anyone could remember. One of the later owners of the castle had joined the tunnel with the outside world at this spot, perfectly camouflaged by bushes and almost inaccessible.

I wonder what for? thought Maja. *Maybe a woman came to see him this way?*

She forced her way through the undergrowth until she came upon some narrow stairs going down. She switched on the torch – she was in a dark dungeon, dripping with damp – startling the rats, she headed off as fast as she could. Then came more stairs, this time leading upwards, and here was the vaulted cellar. Cholawicki came running to meet her.

'Thank you,' he whispered.

She had to catch her breath. In spite of all, that passage was exhilarating. He led her up a winding staircase.

They passed a couple of ground-floor chambers, utterly ruined and bare, then climbed another set of stairs, so narrow that a single person could only just squeeze through.

Then there was an enormous atrium, cold and empty – and they entered a small room lit by an oil lamp. A fire was dying down in the hearth. Two wardrobes, a small table, a few chairs, a bed in the corner – these were the spartan furnishings. But at any rate it was an inhabited room – and as Maja stopped in the middle she felt a sense of relief.

'Are you drinking?' she said, seeing a few bottles on the table.

He went up to the door and set it slightly ajar.

'We must keep quiet,' he said in a hushed tone. 'Do you realize where you are? This room stands roughly in the middle of the south wing. There are six large halls between it and the prince's room, which is located in 'Dorotka', that's to say the south-west tower. I'm leaving the door ajar on purpose, as one can never be sure he won't come out of his room. In that case you'd have to go downstairs. Grzegorz, the butler, lives on the other side of the castle.'

'I admire your nerve!' said the girl, gripped by the terrifying silence.

'And you're surprised I drink!' he erupted. 'If I didn't drink I'd go mad like the old man! You have no idea what it's like to spend day and night in this blasted place, at the mercy of all the whims of a madman. But it won't be for much longer!'

He uttered these final words with such joy that Maja turned her face away from the fire.

'Could it be that bad already?' she asked.

'Yes!' he replied. 'The state of his nerves is clearly worsening, and that's proof of a physical decline. Last night when I got back from Połyka he made a dreadful fuss, weeping and moaning that I was abandoning him . . . I won't be able to leave the castle for even an hour now, I must sit here – but it's not for long now – and then we'll sail onto smooth waters.'

He drew her towards him.

'I knew you'd come! Not for a moment did I suppose that you could seriously fall out with me. You are attached to me! You must be, since we understand each other – we're both sober, clever and courageous. We're a fine couple! When we set about something, it's bound to succeed. I am the one you need! Let's not be upset by trifles.'

She gently pulled free of his embrace.

'Are you sure you won't run into disappointment?' she said. 'I'm talking about the prince. After all, he's not sound of mind.'

'The will has been made. No heirs or relatives. And there's no question of him changing anything.'

Just then Cholawicki pricked up his ears.

'I thought I heard him calling. You cannot imagine how tiresome he has become since the journey to Warsaw. It undermined him greatly – he has aged by ten years. Yes, the will has already been made and no one has formal grounds to invalidate it. Anyway, who would want to put themselves at the risk of legal proceedings – the properties are mortgaged – I'm the only one who knows there's still something to be got out of the estate. They all think it's totally bankrupt. What's wrong? You're not angry, are you?'

He took hold of her hand, but she drew back abruptly.

'What's this?' he said, frowning.

'Nothing.'

'Don't you love me?'

'No.'

'So why are you here?'

'For business reasons!'

He burst out laughing. That pleased him. He liked that tone of hers, sharp, ruthless – she got him with that. Not for a moment did he doubt her love – he was too sure of his own merits. But he liked the fact that she never went to pieces or melted into sentimentality.

Meanwhile, aware of his total self-confidence, Maja got all the more pleasure from saying the worst possible things to him. In any case, she infinitely preferred this coldness, sobriety and sincerity with her fiancé to that ghastly, shameful going to pieces in the closet!

He took her by the hand again, and this time she didn't pull free. But suddenly the memory of Leszczuk came over her with such force that she went pale and closed her eyes, gripping the table tightly with her other hand.

'You're in love!' he whispered, pulling her close. 'You're in love!'

'Leave me alone!' she cried.

Just then they heard a feeble cry: 'Henryk! Henryk!'

Coming from somewhere within the suite of empty chambers, the old man's quavering voice horrified her.

'It's the prince!' he hissed. 'I must go. Wait here!'

He hurried out of the room. Maja was left on her own. She sat down and stared a while into the dying embers in the fireplace, her face pink in its glow.

Only once Cholawicki had gone did she understand that an extended stay in this place really was bound to exhaust the strongest nerves. Neither the forest at night nor the underground tunnel had stirred such anxiety in her as this giant accretion of uninhabited chambers.

Aroused to the utmost, her senses caught every rustle coming from the furthest recesses of the building, living its own, separate life . . . Something over there was crumbling . . . something occasionally creaked . . . then a large rat appeared in the doorway and instantly vanished.

Ugh! she thought. *What am I doing here?*

She began to feel afraid, not just of the castle but of her fiancé too. Until now she hadn't given much special thought to his existence here. She knew he was the prince's secretary and the only person whom the old crank would tolerate, apart from Grzegorz, the butler. She knew that Cholawicki was hoping to inherit some fifteen manor farms from him, which constituted the residue of the Mysłocz estate, and that these properties were less ruined than was generally believed. All this was bearable. She regarded her fiancé as a hard and ruthless person, but by and large a decent one.

He could fake an affection for the prince in order to seize his property, but she doubted he was capable of anything . . . of any deeds of the kind suggested by the gloomy, demonic atmosphere of the castle.

Indeed – anyone who spent a long time in here was bound to be haunted by thoughts of crime and evil, cruel, murderous acts. And in order to go on living here at all one had to have an extremely thick skin, as well as extreme passion.

Maja realized that she had never appreciated Cholawicki's strength before.

A faint shiver ran through her. She peeped through the gap in the door into the next chamber – apart from a feeble gleam coming from the windows there was total darkness inside, rats rustling in the corners and a profound sense of desolation. She listened hard to the castle, to the wide scale of mysterious whispers and murmurs. Bats circled outside the windows.

These stone walls must be a metre and a half thick, she thought.

Suddenly a light flashed in the distance. She quickly retreated.

It was Cholawicki on his way back from the prince, and shortly after he appeared, holding a torch.

'Well?' she asked.

'It's nothing! He dozes pretty much around the clock. Every couple of hours he wakes up, and then he calls me, to make sure I haven't abandoned him.'

'So do you have to go to him at night too?'

'Naturally! But not for long now,' he said, pouring himself a glass. 'Would you like some?'

'Go on,' she said.

He picked up the bottle, but froze with the glass in his hand. He went pale.

'What are you . . .'

'Shhh . . . There's someone in the castle.'

'Where?'

'Quiet! I have an ear for it by now. There's definitely someone here – an outsider.'

His hand began to shake, causing liquid to spill from the glass. She listened hard, but she couldn't detect anything in particular.

'You're imagining it,' she whispered, but he was staring at her vacantly.

'There's definitely . . . there's definitely someone here . . .'

Suddenly they both shuddered. In the silence they heard the prince shouting with insane clarity – five or six exclamations imbued with madness, shrill and piercing: 'Franio! Franio! Franio! Franio! Franio!'

'What's that?!' shouted Cholawicki. He grabbed a Browning and the torch.

Maja ran after him – she wouldn't be left alone here for anything! They raced through the empty rooms. He reached the prince's bedroom and disappeared behind the door.

She could hear his soothing voice and the old man's prolonged, wheezy, helpless weeping, which immediately changed into coughing. She took cover in the window frame so no one could surprise her from behind. And once again she heard him moaning: 'Franio! Franio!'

Cholawicki came back, but just signalled to her to wait, and ran into the depths of the castle. It was quite a time before he reappeared, his face betraying serious alarm.

'Somebody was here. He saw them! That's why he shouted. That somebody must have gone into his bedroom, woken him, and when the old man started to shout he ran away. It must have been a young man. The prince has this mania – he daydreams about this Franio character! He can't bear young men, because they remind him of his Franio. Anyway, here's the proof that somebody was there. Look, I found a penknife.'

He put a small folding penknife with lots of blades on the table.

She recognized it at once. Yesterday after lunch Leszczuk had peeled an apple with the very same penknife.

'Aha!'

At once she averted her gaze, only realizing after the fact that she was doing it on purpose to avoid telling Cholawicki whose penknife it was. No, that was going too far!

'I know whose it is,' she said, in spite of herself, enraged. 'That's Leszczuk's penknife.'

His hackles rose.

'What are you saying?! Are you sure it's his property?'

'At least he has one that's identical.'

'In that case it's even worse than I thought.'

She smiled.

'Aren't you exaggerating?' she asked with derision.

She was prepared for a new fit of jealousy and even wanted to provoke it – but to her great amazement Cholawicki simply muttered: 'You don't understand a thing. Come with me.'

He led her through the same rooms they had just been in, but before reaching the prince's bedroom he turned right, into a side gallery. It was long, and above all high – in the dim torchlight she could see traces of a faded painting on the ceiling. Tripping over holes in the stone floor they went through a small cloister, from where they turned left, and then he unlocked a heavy oak door.

Maja was wrapped in a cloud of stale air as Cholawicki pressed the button on his torch.

'Look,' he said.

It felt as if this large, vaulted hall, supported by a single central column, was packed full of furniture, so strongly did it contrast with the abandonment Maja had seen until now. There was a wide frieze running the length of the ceiling, effaced in places, depicting martial scenes. The walls were covered in tapestries, and two large Persian rugs gone grey with dust carpeted the floor.

Against the walls stood heavy Renaissance wardrobes and carved chests, also coated in dust as if untouched by human hand for the past hundred years. A few small, old-school paintings completed the whole, which did not in fact create the impression of any luxury, but instead evoked the acute despondency of a jumble of abandoned objects.

'What's the point?' she asked, looking at the carved family crests above the fireplace.

'The point,' he replied, 'is that if I've been flogging myself to death here for the past two years, it's only for these blasted bits of junk! I haven't told you about this before, because why would I? The Mysłocz properties really are in ruins. The devil himself won't squeeze anything out of them. But either I'm very much mistaken, or else these objects represent millions – millions, I tell you!'

'This stuff is supposed to be worth millions?' she said, pouting. 'Can you be sure?'

'That's just it, I'm not sure!' he erupted. 'I'm clueless about these things, and you'd have to be a seasoned expert to judge just the approximate value of one of these pictures, for example. They're definitely genuine antiques, the furniture has been here for about two hundred years, but whether it's worth tens of thousands or several million, I couldn't say.'

'Several million?'

'Yes! Or so one might assume from certain pieces of evidence. A legend to that effect is told about the castle. One time, Grzegorz, the butler, who goes back to the days of the current prince's father, told me something of the kind. He said that before he went mad, the old prince wanted to take a few paintings abroad to get rid of his debts. I also found a mention of it in letters the last prince left behind – a fairly vague mention, but it was there. And then my old man has a strange attitude to these objects too – a sly one, I'd say, as if he were hiding their value from me. That's the typical spite of a madman. I tell you, I have serious grounds for believing that all the Mysłocz manor farms rolled together wouldn't be worth enough to buy this room. And there are eight rooms like this one.'

'Why don't you bring in an expert?' asked Maja, stupefied.

'I'm no fool! Bring in a dealer to blab about it all, and the very next day the entire Polish press would announce that treasures had been found at Mysłocz Castle. Creditors would come running, distant family, in short everyone who's now leaving me in peace. Bah! I'm playing too risky a game to let myself in for that sort of a sensation. I've often thought of taking one of the paintings to Warsaw to be valued. But if I happened to pick out a painting that's too good, the work of a famous master, there'd definitely be a stir and I couldn't be sure of anyone's discretion. But I don't know my way around these paintings at all.No, I can't put myself at the mercy, or the lack of mercy of dealers and specialists, I know all too well that they'll go to any lengths if they get the scent of treasure, and what treasure! I'd rather be cautious. I'd rather hold off evaluating these things until I'm their master and owner!'

His voice was shaking. She understood what violence he must have been doing to himself by communing with these objects on a daily basis, while all this time cautiously holding back from clarifying these doubts . He touched one of the canvases with his fingertips.

'No, no, this has to be valuable,' he whispered, 'it has to be! How much? What do you think? Maybe this particular picture is worth two, three hundred thousand? And what about this rug?'

It occurred to her that if he suddenly found out they were worthless copies he'd be sure to go mad. With horror she noticed his pallor.

She was starting to grow more and more afraid of her fiancé. How different he looked at Połyka compared with here, at the castle. She was shocked by what he was saying. This whole business looked completely different from how she had thought of it too. It wasn't to do with the manor farms, but the furniture.

'Why have you never told me about this?' she asked.

'I didn't want to let you in on it. The fewer people know, the better! If I'm telling you now, it's because you're the only one I can rely on, and now I can tell I won't be able to manage on my own. Do you realize what that boy's nocturnal visit means for me?!' he erupted. 'Especially with that professor staying at your place!'

'The professor?'

'Exactly! He's an expert, an art historian. Do you suppose he came to your house just like that, for a quiet *villeggiatura*? No, he's probably caught the scent. He has already approached me to say he'd like to look around the castle.'

He closed the door carefully. She glanced out of the window and stopped: in the moonlight, surrounded by a cobweb of half-ruined cloisters, the castle courtyard was like a dream. She was starting to believe in the treasures.

But Cholawicki tugged at her sharply.

'Let's go!' he hissed.

They went back to his room.

'You have to help me! Remember, this isn't just my affair. It concerns our future!'

'What's your point?'

'You have to find out if Skoliński has guessed something. Was it definitely Leszczuk? If it was, then what was his purpose for coming, and above all, was he acting at Skoliński's instigation? That's the most important thing! Do as you wish, as long as you find out. That boy will tell you.'

'Why should he tell me?'

'It'll be easier for you to communicate with him than for me,' he muttered, and the look he cast her filled in the real meaning of his words. Ah, yes, she was like him, wasn't she?!

'Aren't you jealous any more?' she asked scornfully.

'That's all nonsense!' he erupted. 'Stop goading me! I'm not in the mood. No one but you can do it. You have to extract everything you can from him . . .'

'I refuse!'

'What? What? You refuse? Why? You refuse to do this tiny thing for me?! I have to do everything myself. Why do you refuse?'

'I don't want to!'

She turned away so he couldn't see her face. She found the thought of being obliged to get close to Leszczuk and draw confidences out of him extremely repugnant. Enter into some sort of collusion with him?

'Don't demand it of me,' she said quietly.

'Why not?'

'Surely you understand that after what you said to me yesterday I don't want to talk to him, especially about these matters and in such a way!'

'Have you gone crazy? You care what someone like Leszczuk thinks. For you he should be a total zero, thin air! If he really did mean nothing to you, you wouldn't be ashamed, not even if the whole world told you that you resemble him! What do you care?'

'All right. I'll talk to him.'

'But do it cunningly!'

'I'll try to do it – cunningly.'

'And carefully, without giving him any ideas.'

'I'll try to do it carefully . . .'

'Come here tomorrow at the same time. Once we know some-thing specific, we'll consider what to do next.'

'I'm not sure I can find anything out by tomorrow.'

'Come anyway! It's dreadful being stuck here like in prison.'

IV

LESZCZUK had concluded it would be best not to tell the professor that he'd been in the castle the day before. Even now he felt shivers down his spine at the memory of the old prince's mad shouts, and of his own panic-stricken escape through the labyrinth of stairs and chambers.

It was sheer luck that, when suddenly roused from his nap, the prince had evidently mistaken him for someone else, seeing he had shouted the name 'Franio'. The young man was hoping to get himself out of the affair in one piece, on the condition he didn't breathe a word to anyone.

In fact he'd had no intention of going there at all. But the day before, when he'd gone into the woods after the quarrel with Maja, and at some point had ended up close to the castle, he'd remembered what the professor had said – that on the western side the walls were badly impaired.

'I'll go there!' he'd thought. He had to do something, find some occupation – it was like being drunk, it didn't matter what – anything to divert his thoughts from what had happened with Maja.

Twice he was forced to undress and swim across some horrible, slimy water. Indeed, at close quarters the smooth stone wall of the castle turned out to be full of cracks and fissures; here and there some of the stones had fallen out entirely, creating large holes at roughly first-floor height. After a few unsuccessful attempts he managed to climb up to one of them, by hanging onto holes in the crumbling brickwork.

He was inside the castle. He looked round in every direction and said to himself: 'As I'm here, I'll take a look . . .'

Cautiously he'd entered the courtyard, and then the building, the holes left by broken window panes gaping in the darkness. A desolate void. No treasure anywhere. Large chambers, damp, bare, and shabby. Not a living soul anywhere. Rats.

He walked along, more and more at his ease, until finally he turned the handle of a door, and the following occurred: facing him in the candlelight he saw an old man on a bed, who on catching sight of him raised a shout. He slammed the door shut and raced off like mad, back towards the exit. Luckily he didn't lose his way. In a couple of minutes he was beyond the stone walls, and in two hours he was at Połyka.

That was all.

Why on earth did I blunder my way into this? he thought, as he walked down a garden path, chewing on a blade of grass. *What a damnable coincidence! First the closet, and now the castle! In the short time I've been here, I've come within an inch of being caught twice . . . Yet I've never stolen a single groszy from anyone in my life before! What's going on? It'd be best for me to pack up and leave and be done with it.*

He felt a deep-seated animosity towards Maja. In fact he'd rather she'd screamed and shouted at that moment in the closet, behaved normally. Things would at least have been clear. But as it was?

He had no idea if he was still an honest person, or had ceased to be one. And that bothered him. But at the same time he was profoundly shocked by Maja. That was not how a decent young woman should behave. It was all because of her!

He couldn't fully understand it, but he knew that it was all because of her.

He looked round.

Maja was standing right next to him with a playful smile on her lips.

'I'd like to return something to you,' she said.

She showed him the penknife.

'Where did you find it?' he asked in amazement.

'In the castle.'

He stiffened.

'In that case it's not mine!'

She smiled.

'Don't try to pretend,' she said in her soft tone. "I know you were there . . . I saw you. I was there yesterday too. Don't be afraid, I won't tell anyone.'

'You won't?'

'Noooo . . .'

She flashed her eyes at him, and suddenly he could tell that she definitely wouldn't tell anyone. As if they'd had an understanding for years. She moved nearer to him.

'Why did you go there?' she asked at close range, leaning one hand against a tree. With another faint smile, she raised her head and looked up at the crown of the tree, then at him again. It was all very friendly, as if she were nudging him with an elbow.

When he hesitated to answer, barely moving her lips, she very softly, but insistently repeated: 'I won't tell anyone. Was it for . . . what you went into my closet for?'

Should he say he'd only wanted to take the money out of spite, to be revenged on her? No – she wouldn't believe him anyway. Besides, there was something in her tone of voice – something avid, insatiable – that made him feel he didn't need to excuse himself. So instead of giving a plain reply he burst out laughing, and she instantly reciprocated with the same provocative snigger he'd heard once before – that time in the lobby, when she'd asked if he wanted to have a career.

'To you it is . . .' he said, not sure what he wanted to express.

Involuntarily, laughing, they watched each other with curiosity – were they really so alike? And the likeness gave both of them great joy, it brought them closer, made them familiar and connected.

'So how did you know there was money in the closet?' asked Miss Ochołowska, just as if she weren't the owner of the closet and the money, but an accomplice in theft.

'When you were asleep on the train I removed the letter from your overcoat pocket and read it.'

'Ah, you read my mother's letter. That's right, she wrote about the money! So why did you remove the letter?'

'Out of curiosity!'

They laughed aloud again. They understood each other so superbly. But then she asked casually: 'And how did it occur to you that there was something worth taking in the castle? Who told you? Professor Skoliński?'

'How did you know?'

She squinted.

'I'm interested in the matter. After all, my fiancé lives in the castle and he's the prince's secretary. I am *in-te-res-ted* in it. But . . . Do you want to be completely frank with me?'

'All right.'

'Shake on it?'

'Yes.'

They shook hands.

'So Skoliński sent you to the castle?'

'Yes, he did. He told me there might be great treasure in there, he said he'd read about it somewhere, in some old documents. He sent me to see if there really is anything. And I thought to myself, I'll go and see, just in case. But you've promised not to tell anyone.'

He gave her a brief account of his adventure.

'Well? And?'

'Er . . . I only saw a few rooms, but they were empty. Bare walls. Maybe there's something in some of the others. So is there treasure at the castle or not?' he asked with curiosity, but she didn't answer him.

'Did you talk to Skoliński when you got back?'

'Not yet, but I'm going to.'

'Please don't say anything to him . . . for now,' she said. 'Please hold off until tomorrow. I'll give it some more thought. You're not going to say anything?'

'I can keep quiet.'

'Well, let's go and play! It's dry now.'

Off she ran at full pelt. They were racing each other, but not far from the house Maja slowed down.

'Cool it,' she whispered. They fetched rackets and balls.

The first strokes immediately convinced them that this time the game would be superb! They both played with the greatest delight, forgetting the entire world, with joy. Maja was amazed to be miraculously returning balls she couldn't have dreamed of hitting before, while with every stroke he was discovering new worlds within himself. No one was watching them. And the likeness in playing style, the kinship of temperaments meant that they understood each other in a flash, they were well-matched in the fight and drew the maximum skill, agility and effort out of each other.

Maja was losing. She was losing more and more as he grew ever bolder, developing, arousing his potential – but she continued to defend herself tenaciously, blow for blow.

At one point, as they were changing ends he wantonly asked her: 'Well, then?'

In a breathy whisper, almost inaudibly she replied: 'Superb!'

But near the end of the set she suddenly threw down her racket and fled into the house. Left behind on the court, he couldn't understand how all this had happened between them. How was it that he'd told her everything at once? How come they'd suddenly started talking to each other as if they'd been acquainted for years? How come their game had worked out like that? And why had she run off, what had bitten her this time? He was clueless. He felt completely foolish, while at the same time his heart was flooded with a mixture of joy and anxiety.

After lunch, when the professor accosted him to ask about the castle, he replied any old how, saying that yes, he had tried to find a way through the day before, but hadn't been able to get to the castle, because there was water or mud everywhere.

'I'll try again this evening, but I'm not going inside. If you want to explore it, do it on your own! I don't want to get involved.'

'All right,' said the professor. 'I'll manage without your help.'

But Leszczuk was already thinking about something else. He tried to find Maja, but she didn't show up, and at lunch she hadn't cast him a single glance.

That evening she slipped out to visit her fiancé. With her hands in her overcoat pockets and her head down, she advanced swiftly along the causeway between the sleepy, overgrown waters. The moon was rising.

Henryk should be satisfied, she thought as she walked nervously along the slippery path. *I've found it all out even faster and more easily than I'd imagined. I gained his trust and now he won't do anything without me! Yes, Henryk will be satisfied,* she repeated, as the water splashed beneath her feet, *he'll be satisfied!*

But as for herself, she was not satisfied. She was very far from satisfaction. When she recalled that conversation of theirs, her own smiles, the ease with which they had instantly come to an agreement and then the race for the rackets, the blood rushed to her cheeks, she quickened her pace, like someone trying to escape, she clenched her teeth and fists, as if at the memory of a painful blunder, while trying in vain to persuade herself it was all just a deliberate game, stooping to the level of the boy. How ridiculous she thought herself! And how similar to him! Ever more similar to him!

No – it could drive you mad!

Cholawicki was waiting for her in the cellar and took her to his room. She briefly told him everything she had heard from Leszczuk.

'I wasn't mistaken,' he whispered in horror. 'So the professor does know something! From the start I suspected something of the kind. What is to be done?'

'If I don't want him to, Leszczuk won't tell him he was here at all. He promised me!'

'Ah, I see you understood each other.'

'We understood each other,' she replied.

'No, that's nonsense!' he said, pacing the room and rubbing his hands together. 'Who can vouch for me that he won't tell? Besides, do you think that nosy aesthete will stop sniffing around? You don't know them! He'll have to be pacified for good.'

'What do you want to do?' she asked.

He laughed.

'I simply intend to persuade him there's nothing to be done here, there's no treasure and that's that. After all, he's not entirely sure. Ah! I've got it! Here's what we're going to do.'

He drank a glass of vodka and listened for a while. Every few minutes he stopped talking, listening hard to the sounds of the castle – in case the prince had woken up – had he started on his walk around the rooms? But it was all right.

'Every item that one might suspect of greater value will have to be hidden away. In the first place the pictures and tapestries. Ultimately the wardrobe or some other piece of furniture could be better or worse, but it's not a work of art on a grand scale. He won't be tempted by that. Once he's convinced there's nothing else here, he'll leave us in peace. We'll have to get him to come here and see.'

'How?'

'That's not so difficult. Shhh . . .'

Someone was walking about; there was a noise of slippers shuffling along, and soon after an old man's dry cough resounded at the end of the suite of rooms. Then Maja heard a subdued, feeble call: 'Henryk, Henryk . . .'

Cholawicki cursed and went off.

She was left on her own. Oh, how unbearable it was to be alone in the castle – while her fiancé was with her and while they were having a matter-of-fact conversation she could still cope with it – though risky, everything seemed more or less sober and normal. Maja wasn't frightened by tangible risk or the problems to be overcome.

But whenever she was left on her own, when the silence, despondency and desolation of the castle accrued from all directions, assailing her from every nook and cranny, at once the whole tangle of events she'd fallen into seemed horrid and ominous, sinful and dreadful, and the girl was pervaded by an acute sense of being on a slippery slope that would gradually and imperceptibly lead her to monstrous things.

She feared the castle – she feared her fiancé – but most of all she feared herself, and the dangers lying in wait for her deep down in her own nature, too bold, too restless and far too thirsty for happiness. The ancient, gloomy stone walls, engrossed in the past, seemed to be whispering woe to anyone who too frivolously pursued the ephemera of happiness.

But she did want to be happy! She had to be happy! Everything she did, she did in order to be happy and fully delight in her own youth and beauty.

How far all this is drawing me in! she thought in terror, as she stood in the middle of the room, immobile.

She preferred to keep still – she felt as if any move would be noticed and remembered by these silent, all-seeing walls.

How far all this is drawing me in! I'm already Henryk's accomplice! And what about the other one – Leszczuk? How will it all end? Maybe I should talk to Mama? – the thought dawned on her, but she instantly rejected it. Seek help from her mother? No, she'd manage on her own.

Meanwhile Cholawicki knocked on the prince's bedroom door, and without waiting for an answer he quite unceremoniously entered with his hands in his pockets and a sullen, disgruntled look on his face.

It was a peculiar room: fairly small, with a low, vaulted ceiling, and round – since it was the inside of a tower – with three windows set into such thick stone walls that the window recesses were two metres deep. The walls were clad to halfway up with shabby oak panelling that had a barely visible pattern.

There was an enormous four-poster bed right in the middle, as well as two armchairs, a washbasin – and lots of odds and ends, an infinite number of small bottles, boxes, items of clothing, toiletries, empty jam jars, little plates, knick-knacks and other bizarre objects strewn about the entire room.

For years the prince had refused to let anything be removed – he hadn't the strength to tidy up for himself, and had a neurotic fear of something being taken away that might come in handy. As Grzegorz, the old butler, was also quite decrepit, fantastic filth prevailed throughout the room. The bedclothes were virtually grey because the prince had been dithering for a few months over whether or not to hand them in for laundering. He hated any kind of change.

The small, skinny old man with the bird-like, aristocratic face was sitting on the bed. He cast Cholawicki a look of terror.

'You called me, Prince?' asked the secretary sternly.

'Far from it, far from it, Henryk – you're hearing things. Why on earth would I call you when I know you don't like it?!'

'What's the matter?'

'It's nothing, it's really nothing.'

'I'm asking you what's the matter. Please tell me, because I know that as soon as I leave this room you'll call again. Better tell me right away.'

'But Henryk . . . Very well, very well then, I'll tell you!' he cried in a shrill tone as Cholawicki turned towards the door. 'You see, Henryk, I'd like to tidy up, there's an awful lot of rubbish in here. I've just started with this little bottle – but I don't know, perhaps it'll come in handy?'

'Then don't throw it away.'

'But maybe it'd be better thrown away? What use could be made of it?'

'Then do throw it away.'

He burst into tears.

'What a life I have with you! Never, from nowhere, nothing at all – no help, no understanding, no consolation, no solace, no forgetting!'

'If you're going to be a bore, I shall move out of the castle!' said Cholawicki, looking with unconcealed hatred at the prince who had changed his life into hell. He wasn't cut out to be a nurse! He couldn't bear these conversations with an idiot – he found them extremely tiresome.

'Please don't abandon me!' cried the prince with wild dread. 'I won't stay here on my own for any treasure! In the castle? Alone? Never in my life! This is an evil castle,' he added more quietly and as if with much thought.

'Why do you say that?' asked Cholawicki.

He was always hoping the prince would let something slip about the treasure; sometimes he suspected the old magnate was more rational than he appeared to be, and was just playing the fool on purpose, out of some senile delusion or maybe out of malice.

'Why is this castle evil?'

'On the whole it's good. Of course. But there's one evil place in it.'

'Which place is that?'

'There is one . . . One chamber.'

On this point the prince was implacable. He was never willing to reveal which chamber was the evil one and why. Cholawicki suspected there was a secret involved, and had often endeavoured to extract more detailed information from him, even following the old man as he wandered about the castle, but he'd never managed to figure anything out.

That place must have been associated with a truly terrible memory for the prince, because whenever he spoke of it he closed his eyes, which was evidence of extreme terror. This time too the old man closed his eyes, and for quite a time his pale lips gasped for breath.

Finally he said perfunctorily: 'Pretty much the whole place is haunted.'

Cholawicki shuddered. This was the maniac's other favourite hobby-horse. He was always hinting that the castle was haunted, and he said it spitefully, with some cunning and cussedness.

Sometimes Cholawicki thought the old man was playing on the nervous anxiety he was unable to conceal – his nerves really were shot to bits and he lived in constant fear of something . . . he had no idea what . . . that lurked in the deserted chambers. So perhaps it was craftiness and perversity on the part of the prince, the malice of a madman, the childish idea of the haunted castle. But it was plain to see that the prince really was afraid of something – he dreamed up all sorts of things and had strange hallucinations, but he looked like someone utterly terrified, for good and all, hounded by constant fear.

Even his laughter was unduly shrill – and he was always looking about, his eyes were constantly at work, plunging into dark corners.

In fact Cholawicki was aware that he made a similar impression himself. It must have been the elusive but intense atmosphere of the castle that affected both of them this way.

Another thing that always came to mind as he observed the prince, his eternal anxiety, his terrified cunning and the dread lurking in his eyes, was that there must be something horrible weighing heavily on the old eccentric's past. His madness probably had a special cause, and wasn't purely the result of physical degeneration.

What on earth could have happened to him? Why did he shout 'Franio'? What did he mean by 'Franio'? All he knew about the prince's past was that in his youth he'd had a riotous time enjoying himself in all the capitals of Europe. Then he had married, but his wife had died in childbirth.

At that point he had settled at the castle and led an entirely solitary existence. The nature of the Holszańskis had come to the fore in him. A couple of years ago, when Cholawicki first saw him, he already looked exactly the same as he did now, and was just as prone to anxiety attacks.

Why was there so much terror in his demeanour? Grzegorz was unable to explain these matters to Cholawicki, who in any case found the prince's mental eclipse to his advantage. Thanks to it, on catching sight of Leszczuk in the night the prince had taken him for 'Franio' – plainly, he thought every young man was this 'Franio' of whom he was never willing to speak.

'Why don't you take some drops?' he said. 'Your nerves are bad again.'

He poured him a double dose of a strong sleeping draught and went back to Maja. He was sure that after taking the drops the prince wouldn't wake up all night, which would enable him to move the paintings without attracting his attention. For quite a time he talked to Maja, and then, once she had left, he headed for the ground floor and called in an undertone: 'Grzegorz!'

'What is it?' answered the old butler from inside the small cubbyhole he occupied near the main staircase.

'Come with me, Grzegorz. There's work to do.'

'Give us a moment, I'll put my clothes on. I ask you! At night . . .'

'Hurry up!'

'Give us a moment . . . Bah, ordering folks around!'

The butler loathed Cholawicki, but he saw in him the future master, so he preferred not to fall out with him. Generally he conducted a policy of strict neutrality. He didn't tell the prince his suspicions about the secretary's scheming, nor did he share any information with Cholawicki.

'I don't know,' he replied whenever the secretary tried to sound him out. 'I don't spy on the masters, so I don't know nothing!'

Cholawicki would have most readily done without his help but he didn't want Grzegorz to assume there were some machinations going on behind his back.

'You're going to help me,' he said. 'Some of the paintings will have to be taken down and moved to another spot.'

'But what for? They've hung here for all this time, let 'em stay put.'

'Don't argue with me, Grzegorz! I've spoken and that's final! And don't say anything to the prince. I need to show the paintings to a certain gentleman. They're badly damaged, they need to be restored.'

'Much good restoration'll do those daubs!'

Nevertheless, he set about taking down the pictures pointed out by Cholawicki. With some effort, they took down almost all the canvases – apart from a few so ugly that there couldn't possibly be any illusions about their value. They rolled up some of the tapestries and rugs.

'Where's it all to be stored?' asked Grzegorz in a voice hoarse from dust.

Cholawicki wondered. The idea was not to lug the things far, but hide them somewhere nearby and secure. He remembered a corner chamber, known as 'the old kitchen'.

This room was to one side of the main halls; no one ever looked into it, and on top of that it recommended itself with a heavy oak door reinforced with iron fittings and locked with a key.

'Come on,' he said. 'We'll take it to the old kitchen.'

'To the old kitchen? But why to the old kitchen?'

'Why not? What's the matter with you?'

'It's . . . dirty in there.'

'It's dirty everywhere. Come on, then. Do you have the key?'

He picked up a lamp and walked down a narrow passage, with the old man behind him. But once they were standing at the door, the butler spoke up again.

'Perhaps it'd be better in the Arian Room?'

'Open the door!' cried Cholawicki, who was starting to suspect something. But the butler held out the keys to him.

'Open it yourself.'

'What's the meaning of all this?'

'Nothing . . .'

Cholawicki turned the enormous key in the lock.

'You'd better not open it, sir,' whispered Grzegorz feverishly.

'Why not?'

'It's . . . haunted in there.'

Aha – the thought flashed through Cholawicki's mind – *Could this be the 'evil' chamber?*

He opened the door. Before him was a fairly large whitewashed room, which must genuinely have served as a kitchen in the past, because it still had a stove with a chimney and a grill.

The air in here wasn't bad, thanks to a couple of missing window panes. He was surprised to see an ordinary iron bed against the wall covered with a blanket, and beyond it a washbasin and a wardrobe . . . it looked as if someone had been living in here relatively recently. There were some old newspapers lying about on the floor.

He was about to go inside when Grzegorz grabbed him by the hand.

'Sir,' he warned, 'don't start trouble . . . better leave it be. This is an evil place.'

'Is there a ghost in here?' he asked with curiosity. 'Have you seen it?'

'Lord protect me! But in my memory two folks have come to a sorry end out of fear in here. It'll be fifteen years since Mr Rudziański, the apprentice, said he wasn't afraid of ghosts and spent the night in here on purpose – next morning I found him under the stairs, he was just sitting there, rocking to and fro, with his hair sticking straight up like a brush. He never uttered another word – he'd gone completely mad. I'll stay the night, he said, I'll see for myself. Well, he stayed the night, and he saw for himself . . . and now he's in the nuthouse, holding his hands to his face all the time, so they say he's got sores on it now. And as for the other one, Wicuś, the cook's son – he went totally daft too, and died straight after of that daftness!'

'What silly nonsense. Perhaps they were seeing things?'

'Like as they were and they weren't. You'd better come out of there. Besides, there are signs here plain to anyone. Anyone can tell at once there's an evil force in here. Anyone can see it.'

'What do you mean?'

'I'm not going to say.'

Cholawicki raised the lamp, but he couldn't see anything unusual. The white walls looked quite nice and bright compared with the other rooms. And yet there was something abnormal . . . On closer inspection one had the feeling there was something going on in this room that went against the laws of nature, but God knows what it was.

Finally Grzegorz nudged him and without speaking, reluctantly pointed a finger at a towel, grey with dust, hanging on an old iron peg. It was very gently quivering, probably because of a current of fresh air coming from the window.

But this motion was strange. The towel wasn't moving freely in the draught, but quivering, and it was *taut*. And that made it look as if an invisible hand were holding onto it from below. This motion could not have been the result of air currents – it was a *different* motion.

'What exactly is that?' he muttered, scrutinizing the phenomenon.

The sight of the taut, quivering towel had an off-putting effect – there was something horrible about it. Overcoming his disgust, he tried to go closer, but Grzegorz seized him by the arm.

'Leave it!'

'Nonsense! There must be a reason for it.'

'You can be sure there's a reason!' muttered the silver-haired butler, roughly crossing himself.

'What reason?'

'There is one.'

He realized he wasn't going to learn a thing. No force on earth could wring any more detailed information out of Grzegorz. Anyway, although he didn't believe in ghosts, he had a nasty feeling too. He burst out laughing.

'All right, calm down, Grzegorz. There's never been a castle that didn't have its ghost. We can always store the things somewhere else, though here would be best, because there aren't any rats.'

'You can be sure there ain't no rats. No rat would show up here,' he replied superstitiously, closing the door. 'They're wiser than people.'

'Does the prince look in here on occasion?'

'Never ever.'

They moved the things into one of the adjoining vestibules. But it took Cholawicki a long time to rid himself of a horrible feeling – not exactly dread and not exactly disgust – that made the silence and emptiness of the castle even nastier than before.

V.

Professor Skoliński was following a path through the forest, as if on a walk, but in reality to take another look at the inaccessible yet highly desirable castle walls.

As he ambled along, he pondered ways to get inside, and occasionally spat on the woodland mosses with disgust. To think that he, a professor, an intellectual, should be obliged to play such a role in his old age! Fie! Fie! It could all end in a fiasco! He felt quite unfit to be a burglar.

And yet he was sure he had right on his side. Could one really allow riches beyond measure and outstanding works of the human spirit to be lamentably wasted at the mercy or lack of mercy of a demented aristocrat?

In our country everything goes to waste! he thought bitterly. *After all, these treasures would increase the national wealth. Doesn't the state take out loans against the gold reserve at critical moments? So the fate that befalls these objects is not irrelevant to the common good. Quite apart from their spiritual value. Limiting oneself to the purely financial aspect.*

But in our country everything goes to waste. It's true that in this regard things are improving from day to day, but still . . . People are going to waste just as much as pictures. That Leszczuk, for example! The boy's all but bouncing with vitality, but he's disorganized, disorderly, you could say he's immoral, amoral. He could just as easily

*do something positive as something evil . . . Whatever's appropriate,
however the circumstances unfold.*

*And what about Maja? Exactly the same. Wild vivacity, an unreg-
ulated river that breaks its banks and floods the fields, instead of
driving mills. Like the Vistula . . . And those two ladies, one thin, the
other fat. One bitter, the other sweet, but both equally narrow-minded
and limited. And Councillor Szymczyk? Well, I never! On the one
hand impetuosity, and on the other bureaucracy, conformity, artificial
perfection, petty administrative fuss. And the paintings in the castle
are going to waste . . .*

'Fie, fie! Good morning, young lady! Where did you spring from?'

This last exclamation was addressed to Maja, whom he had spotted emerging from a thicket opposite. She seemed hesitant, yet at
the same time serious.

'It's excellent that I've run into you, Professor,' she said. 'I need
to have a word with you.'

'With me?'

'Yes, you. It's to do with . . . a certain building that interests you.'

The professor had no intention of denying it.

'Aha,' he said, eyeing her closely, 'did Mr Cholawicki tell you I'd
like to tour the castle?'

'I heard it from someone else as well.'

Briefly she told him about her visit to the castle yesterday and
about Holszański's shouts.

'Henryk didn't guess a thing and put it down to the prince's
momentary hallucinations, but I found Leszczuk's penknife and
guessed it was him. I didn't tell Henryk about it, but today I talked
to Leszczuk. He came clean, and . . . apparently it was you who
encouraged him?'

The professor bit his lip. So Leszczuk had spilled the beans. That might have been expected.

'If you please,' he said with dignity, 'I have nothing to be ashamed of, nor do I have anything to hide. I do indeed wish to get inside the castle, but I am driven solely by pure intentions. If only your fiancé hadn't put obstacles in my way I wouldn't need to resort to such stratagems.'

'That,' she said, 'is exactly what I want to talk to you about. Henryk refuses to show anyone those things.'

'Ah, so you know about that too? But this means there are some things after all.'

'There are. There are several furnished rooms . . . But I cannot judge their value . . . And if you'd like to see it in secret without Henryk knowing, I could take you there. I know a passage. There's no risk, no one will see.'

He was watching her with increasing amazement. How could it be? She herself wanted to show him the castle – and behind her fiancé's back? What on earth did it mean?

The professor felt an instinctive mistrust towards young ladies of Maja's kind, who shocked him with their independent way of life, untimely maturity and unrestrained freedom. Could she be trying to take him in? If Cholawicki wanted to hide the things, then why did she want to show them?

Maja was standing by a tree, chewing a blade of grass.

'You see,' she said casually, almost childishly, 'I'll tell you. Henryk has his sights set on a legacy from the prince, and that's the reason why I got engaged to him. I need money!' She spat out her final words impatiently. 'Lots of it! Unless he has vast wealth, I shan't marry him, because I can't bear him!'

He goggled at her in ever more astonishment. What? Why was

she telling such confidences to a stranger? Yet she spoke with a tone of sincerity.

'I can't bear him! He annoys me. I'm completely indifferent to him! I'd marry him, but I must have a guarantee that his fortune will be substantial. I've heard the legend that there are riches at the castle, but I can't get any specific details out of him. I'm afraid the items may have no great value, so he's deliberately not telling me the truth out of fear that I'll drop him. He loves me,' she added with some pride, incidentally. 'But I shan't be conned! I'll take you inside and you can see – you're an expert?'

The professor found the girl's naïve cynicism rather incredible. There was something improbable about it all.

'Child, what on earth are you saying?! You don't love him?'

'No. And he's a dubious character! I don't love anyone at all,' she blurted.

'No one?'

'No! Not my mother, nor him, nor anyone . . . Nooo, only myself!'

She said this 'nooo' in a way that instantly reminded the professor of Leszczuk. For quite a while he too had been struck and bothered by the unusual, elusive affinity between them. But this time it was even more noticeable than ever . . . to a point where to his amazement the old professor felt himself blushing like a peony.

She too had instantly gone red; through clenched teeth she quietly said: 'Nooo . . . I don't love anyone, I'm just similar! I'm similar to . . . to someone!'

She was plainly making the greatest effort to stop herself from crying, but the tears began to flow down her cheeks of their own accord and her mouth turned down. She stood straight, without covering her face, at the mercy of shame.

He took her by the hand.

'There, there, my dear child . . .'

'You too know whom I resemble . . . He's a thief! He tried to rob my closet! But I am just the same! We are identical! Are you surprised to hear me say that openly? Why on earth should I be ashamed if I am totally and utterly the same?'

The professor listened in horror, lost for words.

By now he was in no doubt at all that everything the girl was saying was true. She hated her fiancé. She wanted to show him the things. She confided in strangers. The whole story had to be the truth because – she was just like Leszczuk. And if he had learned from her that she had robbed someone, he would have instantly believed that too, so greatly had the matter involving Leszczuk turned an otherwise decent and upright young lady into someone unpredictable and eccentric.

But how she despised him!

'There's no need for contempt!' he whispered at last and walked away. He couldn't bear to hear any more of this – he needed to do some thinking. The moment he had disappeared beyond the trees, Maja burst out laughing almost at the top of her voice. She couldn't stop herself. She found her own lament so amusing.

It worked! she thought. Now she'd be able to show him the things! *Henryk should be pleased. He believed it all.*

He thinks I'm in love with Leszczuk. Excellent! What harm can that do me?! This way I can make them believe anything I please. Except that . . . I really did weep, she thought with surprise as she wiped away the traces of her tears. *All right, the similarity does bother me. But all the better. While I was ordinary, normal Miss Ochołowska I couldn't take the liberties I can take as Miss . . . just-like-Leszczuk!*

'I'm already the object of ridicule anyway!' she whispered.

On her way back to the house she ran into the fat doctor's wife accompanied by the thin lady clerk. Both ladies fell silent at the sight of her, as if they'd just been talking about her.

Maja guessed this at once from their looks. How familiar she'd become with those controlling, furtive glances over the past few days! She went up to them with a smile.

'Have you ladies seen Leszczuk?'

'No!' cried the doctor's wife. 'What is it, ducky? Do you want to play tennis?'

'Nooo, I just fancied a chat with him.'

She said this light-heartedly, but blatantly, enjoying the effect of these words on the two ladies. She knew that the 'similarity' would colour this remark of hers with a particular meaning – sure enough, as soon as she left, the doctor's wife and the lady clerk exchanged meaningful signs.

Both were convinced (though they had no proof of it) that there must be some sort of relationship between the young lady and the coach; the lack of any actual grounds for this claim merely deepened their instinctive certainty.

What's more, the professor was of the same opinion too. Except that following his conversation with Maja he wouldn't hesitate to apply the word 'love' in this instance. Miss Ochołowska's sensational behaviour during their conversation had shocked him so badly that he had almost forgotten about the castle.

He was in no doubt that either she was already madly in love with the coach, or was heading in that direction.

Astounding! he thought. *To think that I didn't instantly realize. They're quite simply made for each other! One can see it at first glance. It's not a similarity, it's a harmony, a sort of inner harmony of types – something that pushes them towards each other in spite of*

all considerations. They've met their match. They're the perfect pair!
These things rarely happen, but when they do, there's no fighting it.
Like Romeo and Juliet. I wonder if he too is already . . . He must be!
But what a scandal! Poor Mrs Ochołowska!

There's a battle raging inside her – he went on thinking about
Maja – *between ambition and the fateful power of natural selection.*
The poor girl is terrified by the 'similarity', perhaps even more by the
fact that against her will she's surrendering to it. She despises him.
What did she say – a thief? Could he really have tried to pinch some-
thing? That humiliates her, it strips her of dignity, and an unconscious
but demeaning feeling of this kind might push her into something
dreadful – especially with her temperament!

Bah! But what am I to do? Should I take advantage of her offer
and go to the castle? Out of the question! I cannot get involved in
such an affair. Yes! But then I'll lose my only opportunity to examine
the antiques – which are in fact there, as she said, in the castle!

On reflection, the professor decided to go. Perhaps he was exaggerating the gravity of the situation. There'd still be time to consider
how and to what extent he could help Maja.

After supper she winked at him, and minutes later they met in
the woods beyond the front gate.

'Let's go,' she said.

The moon was shining. The water shimmered among the reeds.
Mist wreathed the foot of the castle.

Several times he tried to start a conversation with her, but she
replied in monosyllables, taciturn and mysterious. The situation
seemed stranger and stranger – here he was, being led along by this
mournful young lady, being guided by her to the castle, which grew
the closer they came in the nocturnal darkness. But the nearer they

were to the walls, the more the passion of a scholar took precedence over everything else inside him.

She led him along the underground tunnel. At last! They were in the castle – and the professor was walking up the narrow staircase into the rooms on the first floor. Maja led him along a route agreed with Cholawicki, through the east and north wings, on the far side of the building from the rooms occupied by him and by the prince. They walked quietly.

The professor soon grew accustomed to the darkness, all the more since there was a little moonlight falling through the windows. But these chambers were empty, wrecked, ruined . . .

Here and there, traces of a Renaissance frieze above a door, the peak of a vaulted ceiling or the remains of a crumbling fireplace showed the former grandeur of these interiors, brutally stripped bare.

Approaching a window, he spent a few minutes examining the attic above the courtyard and the proportions of the cloisters. Maja watched him with curiosity. Despite having other problems, she was infected by the connoisseur's passion.

The professor's face seemed to grow wise, alert and focused. At moments he entirely forgot the necessary precautions, then, suddenly shocked, he looked back behind him again. Some of the architectural details of the chambers, though seemingly insignificant, drew his attention, but on the whole he did not display any great delight.

Only once they reached the chambers in the oldest part of the castle, which were small and cramped, with terribly thick, high-vaulted walls, did he smack his lips a couple of times in admiration.

She unlocked a door into a suite of eight Renaissance-and-Baroque rooms where items of furniture had been preserved, and lit an oil lamp that stood on a small round table.

'Here are the things,' she said.

A rat began scratching in a corner.

The professor sighed deeply – he was breathless with emotion. He cast his gaze around the entire room, as if wanting to drink in its contents at a single gulp. It didn't make much of an impression. It must have been formed out of two smaller rooms, because a badly blackened plafond divided it into two parts supported in the middle by a column of rather poor workmanship.

He went up to the small table on which the lamp was standing.

'This is Boulle,' he muttered, inspecting the inlay.

'What does Boulle mean?'

'He was a French eighteenth-century master. And this seat? This is what's known as a Savonarola chair, fifteenth century, one of the world's first armchairs. You should know that in those days even ordinary chairs were almost unheard of. People sat on chests of a kind, like this one – splendid, this is Francis the First, or on benches set into the wall, to which tables were brought up. You see, that chest is as early as Gothic. How on earth did these items stray all the way here?'

He touched the sculptures and hissed as if he'd burned his fingers. The chest had been gnawed through by rats from underneath.

He strolled the length of the antique Flemish and Italian secre-taires and Danzig wardrobes standing against the wall. He cast an eye at the plafond.

'That's nothing!' he decreed disdainfully. 'A poor Baroque mural. Where are the paintings?'

'In the next few rooms.'

Maja picked up the lamp, while he helped himself with an electric torch. They went through into the next room, an enormous one with six windows.

'Can't the light be seen in the windows?'

'No, these windows can't be seen at all from the inhabited part of the castle. In any case I've covered the lamp with paper on the side facing the windows.'

He went up to the canvases left behind by Cholawicki as entirely worthless. Indeed, they were hideous pieces of kitsch, painted so ham-fistedly that Maja was surprised how carefully he studied each painting. Increasing disappointment appeared on his face.

'Well, there's nothing here. Let's move on.'

He looked around the walls. Maja was afraid he would notice the faint marks left by the paintings Cholawicki had taken down, but the professor wasn't observant enough. Suddenly he went up to an old, almost entirely blackened canvas that was pretty large – a biblical scene, where only the faces were visible – and stared at it intently, as if bewitched. When he held the lamp close to one side of the painting, misshapen features, naïvely painted hands and the stiff folds of costumes came into view.

She smiled.

'But that's a caricature!'

Now the professor was examining the underside of the painting, and gently running his fingers over its surface. He produced a magnifying glass and inspected the uneven paint.

'Well, I never,' he muttered.

'What is it?' she asked.

'First-rate art. Either I am very much mistaken, or . . . Hmm, just a moment . . .'

'What do you mean?' she asked in astonishment. 'This is a good painting?'

'How can I put it? In all Poland there is not a single painting that would be half as good as this one.'

'But that's impossible!'

She was amazed. It was unfortunate that Henryk had left that painting! But who could have imagined – such an abomination!

But the professor had started feverishly examining some little portraits that he had overlooked before, and picked out of them one small painting in an ordinary gilded frame.

'And to me this smacks of Titian!'

'What?!'

'There really are treasures here!'

'Please would you wait here? I'll be right back.'

Maja ran off to Cholawicki.

'It's all for nothing!' she cried from the threshold.

'What's wrong?'

'It turns out the worst paintings that you left behind are actually splendid works of art! He found a Titian there and something else too!'

'Impossible!'

Cholawicki was shaken to the core. On the one hand, all his hopes had been confirmed – there were treasures at the castle! But on the other, the professor's discovery brought a risk of disastrous complications.

'What shall we do now?'

'That man will have to be neutralized somehow. Now he really has become dangerous.'

He thought a while.

'Or perhaps . . .' he muttered while looking carefully around the room.

'What?!' asked Maja, curious. But he began to laugh as if amused by his own thoughts.

'Nothing special. We just have to come to an agreement with him. There's no sense in hiding the truth from him. We must keep him at the castle. If he knows everything already, let him at least catalogue and value the pictures. And I'll gain time; I'll find a way to handle him.'

The professor was inordinately surprised to see Maja coming back with Cholawicki. But the secretary got straight down to business.

'You know by now that there are treasures at the castle, Professor?'

'I know . . .'

The scholar continued to glower from behind his spectacles.

'And you imagine I'm concerned about keeping this matter a secret?'

'I imagine so.'

Cholawicki laughed.

'No! You're wrong! There's nothing so improper about my intentions,' he said with irony. 'It's simply that the prince has bequeathed his movable as well as his immovable property to me, and I would like to avoid unnecessary difficulties and lawsuits in the event of his distant relatives finding out that the legacy is greater than is generally supposed. As you can see, my conduct is entirely in order and I am acting in accordance with the prince's wishes. This is basic caution to avoid unnecessary bother. And so – you might even be of help to me, since, as it turns out, I wouldn't be able to deal with these antiques on my own. An expert is needed here to catalogue and value them, and as a matter of fact I am pleased that Maja has brought you here. I'd like to make you an offer.'

'What exactly?'

'If you promise to be discreet about the whole matter, I could invite you to the castle for several days to take a look at the things.

But I have two conditions. First, discretion. Second, you would have to come and stay here. You see, the prince is in an awful state of nerves and he cannot bear strangers in the castle. If you were coming and going, he might catch sight of you, and it could also be noticed at the boarding house. But you could tell the folks at Połyka that you're going to Warsaw, and meanwhile we'll give you a room here somewhere out of the way – the castle is so spacious that it won't be hard to keep things quiet until you've finished the work. You could pitch up here tomorrow evening, say. In any case,' he added, 'I'll show you some other paintings too.'

The professor hesitated. This offer was unexpected. But at the same time – to spend several days at the castle in secret from the prince and at the mercy of this fellow . . . To be sure, Cholawicki's explanations sounded too reassuring; it was natural that he didn't want to expose himself to unnecessary problems with the family, but somehow the professor did not trust him. And the emptiness, the string of rooms, the silence of the castle . . .

In any case the professor knew they were trying to deceive him. Both the 'Titian' and the other painting he had discovered were in fact the ham-handed creations of some anonymous painter of kitsch from a hundred years ago. He had instantly spotted the marks on the walls, realized that some of the paintings had been removed, and had taken advantage of Maja's and Cholawicki's ignorance to frustrate their ploy. And now the secretary's promise to show him some 'other paintings' filled him with the brightest hopes.

That tipped the balance.

'I'll stay,' he said.

VI.

'THERE'S SOMETHING going on in here!'

'What could be going on? There's something going on with your nerves, that's all!'

'There's something going on in here! I tell you, Henryk, there's something going on!'

'Where?'

'Here. At the castle, I don't know where, but there's something going on. The balance has been disturbed. Something – somewhere – someone, I have no idea who, but I'm sure of it – maybe on the ground floor – or in the old castle. I don't know, but there's something!'

For an hour Cholawicki had been trying to pacify old Prince Holszański, who was thrashing about in bed out of groundless fear. Attuned for many years to the unvarying symphony of the castle, his ears must have discerned some elusive change, seeing he had never made quite such a fuss to the secretary before.

'All right, but have you heard some suspicious noises? What is the foundation for your conjecture?'

'I haven't heard anything, but there must be something – there's something new in the castle – something has been added on!'

'Onto what?'

'Oh, Henryk, you don't understand a thing! Oh God, oh God, oh God!'

He covered his face with his hands, but Cholawicki noticed that with one eye he was looking at him through his fingers. Undoubtedly his suspicion had increased – in any case, the secretary was aware that in some mysterious way the prince combined absolute trust in him with absolute suspicion.

He persuaded the troubled prince to take a double dose of bromide, and then headed off to 'the museum', as he ironically called the rooms that contained antiques.

After making sure that Grzegorz was in his room downstairs, he opened the heavy door of the old kitchen and went inside. For some time he stood right by the door and looked closely at the towel as it quivered and vibrated in the torchlight, moving monotonously, but at the same time convulsively. Then he swept a shaft of light about the entire room. He was trying to overcome the unusual revulsion this place inspired in him, when suddenly he was shocked by the idea that here he stood, focusing hard on God knows what.

It'll end with me going mad too, he thought.

He walked through several adjoining rooms to the one that Grzegorz had prepared for the professor. There was a bed in here, made up for the night, a small bedside table, a washbasin, a lamp and a water jug.

Cholawicki picked up the lamp and carried it into the old kitchen. He put it on a little table. Once again he briefly stopped and listened.

Then he went back and fetched the bedding.

He had to get a firm grip on himself to remove the mouldy old blanket from the iron bed that stood in there and then cover the mattress with the bedclothes. Disturbing anything at all in this room seemed a dangerous and reckless act.

But he got the bed ready and transferred the rest of the things. He left the lamp dimmed.

Once again he stared at the quivering towel and left the room. He'd been working in here with his fingertips, so to speak. He gently closed the door.

On his way back to his own room he stopped at one of the windows overlooking the courtyard and fell into thought. There were moments when he wanted to laugh like a schoolboy, and others when he was assailed by a muted sense of terror, far greater than if he'd been planning an ordinary attack on the professor with a revolver. What he was doing seemed to him dreadfully silly and dreadfully awful all at once.

In fact it was childishness and idiocy to imagine that the 'ghosts' in the chamber would cause the professor to lose his wits, or eliminate him in some other way. But Cholawicki hadn't the courage to dispose of the interloper himself.

In helpless fury, feeling incapable of dealing with the professor, he had come up with this childish idea – or at least he had decided to accommodate him for the night in the old kitchen. Maybe something really would happen to the professor; at the very least (if he didn't go mad like those other fellows) he'd get a fright and lose his desire to meddle in the castle's affairs.

Whatever, the experiment could do no harm. The way the towel moved really was uncanny . . . But if nothing happened to the professor, once he had him at the castle, he could always consider using some other means, conciliatory or compulsory.

He went downstairs and waited for the professor and Maja at the tunnel entrance. They arrived late, because it hadn't been at all easy to stage his departure for Warsaw. The professor had had to go by carriage to the station, and from there he'd taken a hired droshky back to the vicinity of the castle – there he had met up with Maja, who had helped him to carry a small suitcase containing his things.

'Quietly,' whispered Cholawicki, leading them through the rooms. 'The prince is worse again. Oh, here's the room for the professor.'

'Thank you. A very nice little room.'

'Unfortunately I won't be able to keep you company. I must see to the prince. Why don't you get down to examining the things at once, but do it quietly and be careful with the light. I have prepared something to eat. Anyway, you'll have to cope on your own.'

'I could spend a year here on bread and water,' said Skoliński ardently, as he opened the door into 'the museum'.

Cholawicki said goodbye to Maja and went off to the prince. The prince was asleep.

From then until late at night he circulated between the prince's bedroom and the rooms where the professor was covertly working.

Eager for the most precise information about the likely size of the inheritance, he spurred him on, demanding exact figures, though the professor explained that works of art have a relative value depending on the market and the buyer. He brought him the hidden paintings, which the scholar subjected to scrupulous examination with the help of the means at his disposal.

At the sight of these paintings Skoliński inwardly rubbed his hands together with satisfaction and in admiration of his own cunning.

What he was seeing now surpassed his boldest expectations. He had already identified two works by Jordaens beyond any doubt, of astonishing power and freshness of colours, and one small landscape by Masaccio – how on earth had these works drifted all the way here? Had one of the Holszański-Dubrowickis been an art lover, or was it the result of an extraordinary accident? How long had these paintings been at the castle?

But after a while he was overcome by fatigue, tired by the surfeit of artworks surrounding him. He was highly familiar with this sense of overload, which had often beset him in museums, and he knew he shouldn't defy it.

His eyes were tired, and he was starting to have a mild headache. He decided he should have a nap. He locked the room and went off to the one that had been prepared for him. He sat down on the bed and ran a hand down his forehead and eyes.

He yawned.

He was so tired that not even the acute silence of the castle could get through to him.

He went over to the table and turned up the lamp, then sat down on the bed again and started to undo his shoelaces.

Suddenly he stopped what he was doing. There was something going on in the room. He didn't know what, but he was sure there was something going on in here. It was a strange feeling. He looked around.

And saw nothing. Just white walls, a stone floor, a kitchen stove with a large hood – and yet there was something . . . The something wasn't a threat from the outside, but from the inside – the something was in the room. Suddenly the professor's throat was gripped by a vague but acute sensation of atrocity, as if a detestable animal were lurking close by.

But the kitchen was almost entirely empty, except for a heap of old papers in the corner. Nonetheless he had the distinct impression there was something going on, and that this something was working away non-stop.

He picked up one of the newspapers that had been left on the floor. It was a back issue of the *Warsaw Courier* dated 1923. There were two other papers with the same date.

He was kneeling on the floor, examining the newspapers, when all at once he was seized by the fear that something might be lurking behind him. He went straight back to the bed, but his terror grew to such an extent that now nothing could possibly induce him to move from this position.

He was afraid of every movement. Sweat broke out on his forehead.

These symptoms of fear shocked him even more because they had no rational foundation. What he feared most of all was being afraid.

'Why do I feel afraid?' he thought blankly.

His eyes scoured the entire room, examining every single object. The papers in the corner puzzled him – a pile of old account books and some other scraps; it was the only spot in the kitchen that he couldn't see properly, and so it attracted him. Perhaps the something was hiding under those papers – he didn't dare approach, but visually scanned it all the more thoroughly.

Protruding from under the stiff, bookkeeping covers he spotted the corner of a notebook – an ordinary school exercise book with squared paper, filled with writing in pencil. The professor was long-sighted, so he had no problem making out a few words, to wit: . . . *so far nothing has hap* . . .

The rest was shielded by the books. Except in the line below he could decipher: *12.45. Still nothing* . . .

Instantly he felt sure that this was relevant to his situation. In a few decisive paces he went up to the corner, pulled out the exercise book and immediately returned to the bed.

At the top of the exercise book, written in large letters was the word: *Minutes.*

And further on:

The minutes of my sojourn in the old kitchen at Mysłocz Castle on the 14th of December 1923, by Kazimierz Rudziański.

I, Kazimierz Rudziański, apprentice at Promcza manor farm on the Mysłocz estate, on learning that the old kitchen is said to be 'haunted', which I do not believe, have resolved to investigate and to explain the question of supposed ghosts.

I am recording my impressions for two reasons: first, as a lasting reminder, and second, to have something to occupy me, because I cannot sleep, the ghosts have not appeared, and I have finished reading the newspapers. It is twenty past twelve, and thus the hour for ghosts has already come, but so far nothing has happened.

Rudziański's 'Minutes' went on in the same, slightly humorous tone for a few pages. The professor feverishly read his way into the text, hungry to know if this person from fifteen years ago had experienced the same groundless anxiety. Here it was! After some lengthy reasoning to justify his theory that 'supernatural phenomena do not exist at all', came the following passage:

Besides, I would be lying if I claimed not to be surrendering entirely to the atmosphere. Indeed, I am still waiting for something, and although I am trying hard to concentrate fully on writing, at the back of my brain I am continuously geared towards the supposed ghosts. As well as the lamp I have lit two candles, each in a different spot, so nobody will be able to deprive me of light in one go.

As well as that I have a revolver to hand. If anyone were stupid enough to play some sort of joke, I'll shoot. But how could anyone play a joke? I have locked the door and barricaded it with the table, and no one can get through the window because it's too narrow and too high up.

At this point the text ended. The rest of the exercise book had been torn out.

'So this room is haunted?' muttered the professor.

He scrutinized the pile of old books again, and shortly after extracted some scraps of paper inscribed with the same handwriting. But they were torn into such small pieces that he could hardly decipher a single phrase. Who had ripped them up, and why? On one of these scraps Skoliński made out a word that instantly focused his attention.

It was the word 'towel'. '. . .*towel mov . . .*' – he couldn't find the continuation.

What was the connection between this towel and the minutes? He looked around the room and immediately noticed a dirty, grey-and-yellow, fringed towel, hanging on a peg in the corner. He wanted to go up to it, but at once he felt he had better not.

Was it an illusion, or was the towel moving? He laid the papers on his knees and for quite a while he tracked its steady spasm, like the spasm of an earthworm. So here was the activity he had sensed at once on entering the chamber. The something was in fact this towel. An abhorrent spectacle – it looked as if the towel were trying to vomit but couldn't. And at the same time its motion was almost imperceptible. If not for the scraps of paper he mightn't have noticed it.

A shiver ran through the professor. If not for the actual, wholehearted fear he felt, he'd have assumed he was falling victim to suggestion. But the feelings he was having instantly required him to take the situation extremely seriously.

Should he leave? Yes, he'd have to. But he hesitated. Seized by reluctance to make any distinct movement, he sat quietly, trying to occupy as little space as possible – and thought. The lamp cast a rather dim light on the room. The pieces of furniture stood mute and still. A sort of paralysis gripped the professor. Had he imagined it, or was the towel moving more and more violently? By now its motion couldn't be doubted.

And it was an evil motion – beyond any doubt evil.

The professor was a man of deep faith, but he wasn't inclined to detect signs of the evil spirit in everything he saw. He had taken part in a number of spiritualist séances and had seen some astonishing manifestations without ascribing any supernatural meaning to them at all. And yet whatever was gradually and imperceptibly coming into being in this chamber was essentially different from the spiritualist séances.

At the séances one felt aware of an unearthly but purely mechanical power. Weird things happened there, but they were neither good nor evil . . . But here the professor could sense a tangible, frenzied malice, lurking somewhere against the walls.

There was malice and monstrosity in the air, a distinct and ruthless threat. Should it really be ascribed to some forces of the de . . .

Skoliński noticed to his amazement that . . . he was afraid to think that word. In these circumstances it was so horrible that he couldn't . . . That really shocked him! Could he have lost control of himself to such an extent that he'd suddenly become as credulous and superstitious as a peasant?

'Of the devil,' he whispered, in order to get a grip. 'Of the devil'.

And several times more, as if in an effort to get the better of his rising terror he repeated: 'The devil, the devil, devilish, of the devil'.

But then he was seized by a sense of horror one hundred times greater than before. He imagined himself sitting here on the bed, his lips trembling as he kept repeating that word, which sounded like a provocation. Hadn't it been whispered into his ear? Wasn't it this that the entire order of things in this chamber was aiming for? And at the same time he was even more frightened by his own terror – afraid he was losing his grip and letting himself be carried away by incomprehensible panic.

'Easy now,' he whispered, 'easy.'

Once again he looked around the room cautiously, and as if in a bit of a stupor.

Everything was still peaceful and quiet – nothing had changed – only the towel was working away in the corner, contracting, quivering and tensing. Now its motion was patently visible and couldn't possibly be explained away by any normal cause. It looked as if it had revealed itself and stopped being ashamed. There was shamelessness about it. And at the same time this horrible, bulging cloth was oddly reminiscent of the way the medium moved during a spiritualist séance, and also a woman during childbirth – as if it were trying to cast something out of itself, to give birth to something. But that wasn't the worst thing of all.

Something was starting to happen to the light.

In fact the lamp was burning normally, but the professor suddenly felt absolutely sure that someone was endeavouring to extinguish it. Someone? Who? He could sense someone – somebody's presence. It had to be auto-suggestion, but he could have sworn there was someone else in the room with him, and he could even point out exactly where that someone was at that moment.

Maybe he should throw the towel away? Grab hold of it and throw it away?

No, better not.

So should he get out of here? Stand up and get out.

Yes, but he'd better not.

He went on sitting on the bed, as quiet as a mouse. It was harder and harder for him to move. It felt as if any solid movement would draw attention to him. And only his fingers moved, feverishly sifting tiny little bits of Rudziański's minutes. Oh, he'd give anything to know how it had ended for that fellow, who'd sat on this bed fifteen years ago in exactly the same way – and waited.

But not much was clear from these bits of paper.

twenty to two . . .
animal . . .
paralyzed . . .
blew . . .
ence ye
I fear
black, black-and-blue and thr
I am moving, alo

Skoliński's imagination was working away like mad. He was trying to reconstruct his own fate out of all these scraps. What did 'I am moving' mean? Animal? A black animal? Or maybe these words weren't connected at all? Get out! Escape! Jesus Christ! And only at this point was he assailed by such extreme shock that he grew numb. He felt that by now he was too frightened to run away.

All he could do was sit here – and wait. He was like a small bird hypnotized by a snake – he couldn't escape.

The two or three minutes he now experienced were probably the toughest in his whole life. Overcome by dreadful impotence, his throat tightened, he felt a chill, his shoulders hunched and his muscles tensed almost to a state of paralysis – and with all this came the awareness that with no hope of rescue he was at the mercy of fate, and what was going to happen was bound to happen.

With a final effort he tore free of the bed and bolted out of the chamber. As he ran, he could sense something lurching out of a corner and trying to make a grab at him from the side, slantwise, but he didn't look round. He slammed the door shut.

As soon as he found himself outside the gloomy room, though stretched to their limits his nerves carried him onwards. He started to run through the dark atrium and some rooms – as far as he could – until finally he sat down on the floor against a wall, totally exhausted.

Now the entire castle seemed to him to be in the possession of unclean forces, and horror loomed out of the darkness. About three quarters of an hour went by before he just about managed to get a grip on himself.

He was extremely tired. With his head in his hands, half lying on the cold flagstones, he was considering how to make his immediate escape from the castle, when suddenly he heard some soft footsteps in the adjoining gallery. He peeped through the door. At the far end of the gallery, where a small winding staircase led into the atrium, he spotted the hunched figure of Cholawicki. In trousers and a shirt, barefoot, the secretary walked to and fro a few times, then stopped, leaning an elbow against the wall.

It looked as if he were eavesdropping. Aha. Now the professor understood why Cholawicki had kept him at the castle and had put him in that particular chamber for the night.

Skoliński felt like laughing. Taking advantage of the moment when the secretary disappeared into the depths of the vestibule he made off at top speed in the opposite direction. It was incredibly hard for him to find his way through the labyrinth of winding castle passages. He longed to find a safe retreat for the rest of the night and a piece of furniture to rest on. He'd have to wait for dawn before he could get out of the castle without waking anyone or causing a fuss.

He ventured down a dark, narrow corridor. He passed an alcove – and at once was seized by the certainty that someone was following him.

He stopped in his tracks. No, it couldn't be Cholawicki. So who was it? The professor held his breath and waited . . .

The other person waited too.

The professor moved forwards – and so did he. Skoliński increased his speed – and so did he. His breathing was distinctly audible. When the professor abruptly turned into a side room, he turned too.

But there was something absurd, insane or drunken about it all. The unknown figure's movements were hesitant, uncoordinated, abrupt and tottering all at once – like those of a small child.

Was it a human being? Again the professor felt a sense of horror and revulsion rising to his throat, when suddenly the figure caught him up, and a small, sticky hand grabbed his arm.

But at the same time it was shaken by an old man's fit of dry coughing.

This cough was not unfamiliar to the professor. He'd heard it before, on the train. He guessed it was the prince.

Meanwhile the prince, with a tight grip on his arm, was furiously trying to suppress his coughing and nestling his head into the professor's jacket. Finally he regained the ability to speak.

'Who are you?!' he inquired insistently, holding the professor tight. 'Who are you?!'

He was shaking. In the weak glow from the window his face was visible, and the professor saw that here before him was an utter madman. The prince was staring at him in alarm, as hard as he could, and menacingly wagging a finger in front of his nose.

'Don't be afraid, Prince,' he said gently. 'Please calm down!'

'Who sent you?'

'Nobody sent me.'

'Don't lie. Admit that you've been sent . . . Well, give the sign, give the sign! It was he who sent you. Give the sign!'

'What sign?'

'I'll do anything! I'll carry out his every wish,' he whispered ardently, 'just give the sign so I'll know you've come from him! I've waited so many years!'

'I don't know any sign!'

'That's not true! Last night I saw him. He appeared to me. I know he has taken pity on me at last. Give the sign and tell me he has forgiven me, that this is the end, that he's setting me free, and won't torment me any more . . .'

'Please calm down,' said the professor, trying to speak in a genial and convincing way. 'You must calm down. I am a completely ordinary person. Mr Cholawicki invited me for the evening. I have outstayed my welcome, but I'm going now. I'm just about to leave.'

'Cholawicki invited you? Aha, the secretary?! So you're out to get me? Admit it, you want to do me in, eh? You're after my life, aren't you? The secretary invited you, and you say you're not here to do me in?'

He kept convulsively pushing the professor away or pulling him towards himself, digging his clutching fingers into his wrists.

'But please, Prince, calm down, I hardly know Mr Cholawicki.'

"He's an out-and-out scoundrel,' said the madman suddenly in an entirely different tone, unexpectedly pulling the professor towards him with an almost paternal gesture. 'If you don't know him, then watch out!'

'Why should he be eager for your death?' asked the professor nonchalantly.

'What?! That's a fine one! It's quite simple! Because I refuse to die. He's bored here and he's in a hurry . . . he's in a hurry to . . . well, it's all the same . . .' – the prince winked playfully – 'but somehow I am unable to die! Indeed, it is rather boring here, it's sad, gloomy, dark, and even terrifying, so no wonder a young man who's smart, pleasant and handsome . . . But I cannot leave the castle.'

'Why not?'

'I cannot. Not before time. There's something here . . . I must be here for it. There's a certain matter going on . . . a certain matter . . . there, over there,' – he pointed in the direction of the old kitchen – 'and I must be here . . . to the bitter end . . . to my last breath . . . until I am released . . . But admit it, you know this better than I do. Why are you pretending? Admit that he sent you! Give the sign! Why are you tormenting me?' he shouted in despair. 'Can't he understand that if he forces me to keep waiting here Henryk will kill me because he's getting bored?! Has he absolutely no pity for me? Tell him that – tell him that from me!'

He pushed him away, and with a pitiful wail he disappeared into the gloom of the building.

A pale dawn was breaking, driving out the deposits of darkness still hiding in the nooks and corners. The professor went back to the old kitchen without running into Cholawicki on the way. In the daylight the room looked nice and bright. His nocturnal experiences seemed quite unreal. He put out the lamp, pulled the mattress off the bed, moved it to a chamber some way off, and without undressing, totally exhausted, he almost instantly fell asleep.

He was so tired that he ignored the complications that would result if the secretary discovered his temporary resting place. Luckily he didn't sleep for long. A couple of hours later he woke up. He glanced at his watch. It was eight o'clock.

He hurried back to the old kitchen, and once he had overcome his disgust, he lay down on the bed and waited for Cholawicki to arrive. He wanted to make him believe he hadn't budged an inch all night.

VII.

CHOLAWICKI spent the night making constant trips to the door of the old kitchen and waiting for the dreadful thing that was supposed to happen behind it. He kept swinging from extreme disbelief to bizarre, unfounded certainty that something was bound to happen.

But halfway through the night, when nothing had happened in the haunted chamber, he was completely filled with doubt; furious at having let himself be tempted by such childish ideas, he undressed and went to sleep, having first drunk a few shots of vodka.

At around nine, old Grzegorz woke him.

'What is it, Grzegorz?' asked Cholawicki. 'Is the professor up already?'

'He's still sleeping . . . in the old kitchen.'

The butler cast Cholawicki a strange look.

'Nonsense! Surely you don't believe in that rot? I moved him into that room for the night because it's a much nicer one and there aren't any rats.'

'I'm not interfering.'

The secretary dressed and went to see the professor. 'Hm . . . what's happened in there?' he muttered as he knocked at the door with acute curiosity.

'Come in,' came the professor's voice.

The professor was sitting on the bed; his clothing was crumpled, his hair tousled and his face utterly drained. At the sight of Cholawicki he blinked and ran a hand down his face.

'How did you sleep?' the secretary asked the conventional question.

'Is it morning already?'

'What do you mean? It's almost half past nine.'

'Ah, half past nine. But I haven't slept. At all. Oh, so it's morning already.'

'Are you unwell?'

Cholawicki examined Skoliński's completely altered appearance with interest. One could say that the old scholar's lively, quite jovial face had disappeared without trace, and had been replaced by a weary, apathetic mask thoroughly devoid of expression.

'You'll be served breakfast shortly.'

'Oh, breakfast? I might not eat. Whatever, it's all the same.'

Finally Cholawicki couldn't hold back.

'Did something . . . happen to you in the night, Professor?' he asked. 'What's wrong?'

'No . . . Nothing happened to me. It's . . . But it's all the same.'

'What on earth is up?'

'Nothing,' said the professor, curtly brushing him off.

'Are you going to look at the paintings now?'

'Oh, the paintings? I'd forgotten. Maybe I will. But it's all the same . . . Maybe this evening.'

This was puzzling. The professor had stopped being interested in the paintings. So something must have happened. He hadn't actually gone mad, or died – but he seemed to be a complete wreck, apathetic and stupefied by some sort of dreadful experience.

From the corner of his eye Cholawicki glanced at the towel. It was moving, very faintly, but in constant agitation. A similar agitation occupied Cholawicki's soul.

He must have seen something after all, he thought.

He didn't want to ask too many questions. Anyway, it was clear that the professor wouldn't tell him. He'd keep it secret.

'If you didn't sleep well in here, maybe we can give you another room?' he asked, in order to sound him out. But Skoliński replied apathetically: 'No . . . I'll stay here.'

Cholawicki agonized in vain over the solution to this riddle. If something really had terrified the professor in the night, he should have been eager to accept the offer to change rooms. But maybe out of curiosity he wanted to test his impressions some more. After all, those other fellows had also spent the night in here out of curiosity. Or maybe he was already so befuddled and drained that it really was all the same to him.

In any case, his idea hadn't turned out to be entirely idiotic. Who knows whether after a couple of nights the professor might not suffer the same fate as those two – who'd gone mad.

He went back to his room feeling incredibly perturbed. He was no longer in any doubt that the old kitchen was haunted. He called in on the prince to make sure the old boy hadn't noticed anything.

He found him in an excellent mood, drinking his morning coffee.

'Ah, Henryk . . . How are you, Henryk? Today I must set about the tidying! Now or never, I must make an assault on this mountain of rubbish! But – what do you think, where should I start?'

There was so much mischief in his tone of voice that once again Cholawicki couldn't help suspecting that the prince was only pretending to be mad. After a short exchange he left, convinced that so far at least the professor's presence at the castle had escaped the prince's notice.

Meanwhile, once Cholawicki had gone, the professor's appearance changed entirely; having dropped his expression of apathy and stupefaction he was whistling through his teeth with satisfaction. It had worked. His pretence had achieved the desired effect. Cholawicki was confused.

The professor was afraid that if he saw him looking well and in one piece Cholawicki would expel him from the castle. That was why he had done his best to convince the secretary that the haunted chamber's poison was working – though more slowly than one might have expected – and the evil powers had already caused a certain degree of mental breakdown. With the help of this innocent claptrap he was counting on managing to remain in the castle for a few more days. Not just on account of the antiques.

Skoliński suspected – no, he was sure – that the prince really was in serious danger from Cholawicki, and that the poor old lunatic was urgently in need of help. And what on earth was the mystery that tormented him? What had happened in this chamber? It all demanded an explanation and possibly active intervention. And then Maja was dependent on Cholawicki too – she was his fiancée, she was going to tie herself up with this sinister character for the rest of her life.

The secretary hadn't even guessed what a fierce enemy he had gained in the good-natured art historian, who in normal circumstances wouldn't have harmed a fly. Suddenly the professor's face took on an expression of bafflement again, his eyes went dim and his lips twisted in a nasty scowl. Someone was approaching. To be sure, there in the doorway of the chamber he saw Grzegorz.

The butler stopped warily on the threshold.

'Breakfast is served,' he reported, stubbornly fixing his gaze on his own feet, decked in some antediluvian slippers.

'Where?' whispered the professor wanly.

'Down there. I've served it in the hall.'

As the professor ate, Grzegorz stood behind his chair, watching him in awe like someone who has come back from another world. *What the devil – he spent the night in there and nothing happened to him! But wait! Not so fast! It's plain to see that something's wrong – his movements are ponderous, he's hardly touching the food, he's wiping his brow – he must have seen something, the devil has already put the screws on him in there . . .*

He crossed himself roughly, but curiosity got the better of him.

'How did you sleep in there, Your Honour?' he asked politely. Not receiving an answer, he cleared his throat, and a little later asked again: 'Did the secretary tell you about that chamber, Your Honour?'

Skoliński discerned deeply hidden suspicion and dislike in his tone of voice. Could it be that the old butler felt antipathy towards the secretary? In that case this ancient retainer and probably friend of the prince would be suitable as an ally.

The professor cast him a vacant look and whispered as if to himself: 'No, he didn't say a word.'

'Well, I never!' stammered Grzegorz and wiped his face with a large neckerchief. 'Don't stay in there!' he burst out. 'Your Honour, it's evil in there! And the secretary ain't well-intentioned, that he ain't!'

'If you only knew what I went through last night,' said the professor, 'your hair would turn white on the spot!'

This rhetorical remark was rather unfortunate because Grzegorz's hair was as white as snow. But Skoliński's toneless voice had an effect on the butler.

'Well, then?' he whispered. 'Did you see? What did you see?'

Curiosity and terror were battling inside him. He crossed himself again and again, while at the same time his eyes bulged with curiosity.

'What I saw,' said Skoliński solemnly, 'I shall never tell anyone to my dying day.'

'Thank goodness it didn't end in nothing worse,' muttered Grzegorz. 'But I'll tell you something. It was the secretary who arranged it. I'd prepared a different room, but late at night the secretary shifted the bedding to that accursed kitchen. Please be on your guard, sir, I don't want to have it on my conscience. The secretary must have something against you if he put you in there. But don't tell the prince or him that I told you so, or I'll be out on my ear.'

It was plain to see that Grzegorz was struggling between two fears – on the one hand he was terrified of Cholawicki, on the other he was even more terrified of the ghosts. Skoliński decided to put his cards on the table.

'Grzegorz,' he said, 'pay attention to what I'm about to tell you. I shan't reveal what I saw in the night, because . . . because it's a secret. But I'm already aware that the secretary has evil designs on the prince. We must save the prince from him. That scoundrel should be thrown out of here, expelled from the castle!'

'I'm not interfering in nothing.'

'But I'm advising you to interfere, Grzegorz, or it might end badly for you too. You don't understand that if someone's plotting evil in the vicinity of that terrible place, it's as if they were lighting a fire around a powder keg.'

'And what? There really is evil in there?'

The professor had noticed that spending a night in the haunted chamber had given him almost total power over the butler's soul.

'Don't be too curious, Grzegorz. I'll just say this: right now, that one single chamber is haunted, but the "evil" can easily spread about the entire castle.'

'In the name of the Father, the Son and the Holy Spirit . . .'

Until now the old butler hadn't been afraid the ghosts would look in at his little room on the ground floor too. In his eyes Skoliński was now the ambassador of the world beyond, entrusted with a momentous and difficult mission.

'Oh yes, indeed,' he fervently affirmed, 'I'm not the type to help. For sure, for sure! Evil must be fought with fire and sword! Oh, the dev . . . those ghosts have been at rest for all these years, and now it's starting again.'

'Exactly. He's an evil man and he has joined forces with those evil powers, he's stirring and inciting them. If with the help of God, he can't be prevented from doing it, he'll stir up those evil spirits even more and you'll see what happens here!'

'I shall do all I can! Everything!'

Skoliński thought a while.

'Have you been at the castle for a long time, Grzegorz?'

'Oh, it'll be about fifty years now. The late prince took me on as a boy when I were just so high.'

'Then you must know a thing or two. Can you tell me when that chamber was first haunted and why? And why is the prince mentally ill? Because the former and the latter must be connected, eh?'

White as a sheet, the butler replied gloomily: 'I will tell you. I'll tell you all, as at holy confession. I've never spoken to nobody, but now I shall, and may the hand of God hold me in its care! But not right now, because the secretary might come in. I'll take a guess at a good time to come and have a quiet chat. Now I must go – to work.'

He took the breakfast tray and disappeared behind the door. Skoliński's feelings were similar to those that had so recently shaken Cholawicki. He too was oscillating between horror and absurdity. The whole story would have been extremely funny if not for the very real fact, verifiable at every waking second, of the abnormal shrinking and quivering of the towel . . . if not for the terrifying reality of supernatural forces. And he too felt profound anxiety at the thought that here he was, recklessly playing with these forces by scaring Grzegorz with them and trying to divine their secret. But knowing that he was doing it with good intentions made it easier for him to bear the pressure – while Cholawicki, on the contrary, had no armour and no shield against the evil that he was inciting.

As he waited for Grzegorz, the professor got on with examining the antiques, ready at any moment to adopt an expression of apathy and bewilderment in case Cholawicki called by.

But his connoisseur's passion had entirely evaporated, and not even the most interesting discoveries were capable of restoring it. Finally he dozed off in a large Dutch armchair, and his snoring filled the Baroque-and-Renaissance drawing room, packed with writing stands, escritoires, wardrobes, tables with innumerable legs, rugs, tapestries and pictures.

VIII.

CHOLAWICKI looked into the drawing room several times, but on seeing that the professor was sleeping the sleep of someone totally exhausted, he withdrew discreetly. He glanced at his watch impatiently. He had arranged with Maja that she would come to the castle at five in the afternoon; meanwhile it was almost six, but the girl hadn't arrived.

What could have happened to her?

The secretary felt the sting of jealousy again, though for some time it had been dulled by the rapid course of events and had ceased to bother him. It was unbearable – to be forced to sit here, like in prison, knowing that she was gadding about at liberty – maybe with Leszczuk? He closed his eyes and saw them together – so 'similar' to each other, so close-knit in this similarity that he almost hissed. If there was ever a time when he shouldn't be leaving the castle, on account of the professor, the prince and the chamber, it was right now – but what if he rode over to Połyka for just an hour or so? Nothing could happen in such a short space of time. The prince was asleep too.

He had his horse saddled and twenty minutes later he was riding up to Połyka. He emerged from the forest into a large clearing, with the Połyka park looming beyond it. Here he slowed down and rode at a walk along the forest wall, to avoid causing a sensation by arriving on a foaming horse.

Suddenly he spotted Leszczuk, who came out of the park and walked diagonally across the meadow, heading for the forest.

Cholawicki stopped his horse, then quickly rode into the forest. He was seized by the need to take another look at that boy. To check whether the similarity really was there. To monitor his own impressions. This need proved so acute that, ignoring the branches that were whipping him in the face, he spurred on his horse and cut ahead of Leszczuk.

He stopped behind a clump of bushes, from where he watched out for the boy, who soon appeared.

Leszczuk was lost in thought. With his head down and his hands in his pockets, he was walking along whistling, and Cholawicki could plainly see that the 'similarity' was there, that every movement, every glance, though not strictly the same, had something of Maja about it, was connected with her . . . Oh, it was insufferable. The secretary drilled his eyes into his young rival until he disappeared behind the trees.

At this point he planned to turn back towards Połyka, when deep in the forest he caught sight of Maja, moving between the trees. She was walking fast and cautiously – following Leszczuk.

Cholawicki jumped off his horse and tied it to a tree. He started to sneak on foot through the undergrowth, after those two. So was that why Maja hadn't come to the castle? She had some business with Leszczuk?!

Cuckoos were cuckooing in the woods. Maja quickened her pace and circled Leszczuk at a large distance, then turned back. The secretary understood her manoeuvre. She was aiming to meet him in the forest as if by accident.

Sure enough, he was the mute, desperate witness of this encounter. Maja emerged from the forest opposite Leszczuk. They stopped. Cholawicki couldn't hear what they were saying. They talked for a couple of minutes, while Maja drew shapes in the sand with the tip of her shoe. Then they started to walk slowly towards the house together.

The secretary went after them, his heart full of despair.

The last of his doubts had dissolved. But he couldn't quite believe that Maja could really be interested in Leszczuk – in any case he was counting on the girl's ambition, even on the plain difficulty of communicating with the boy, with whom she may be able to exchange balls, but not thoughts and feelings. He didn't suppose she was capable of that. And yet he could see it with his own eyes.

They were walking along together as if they'd known each other for ages. Never had their mysterious bond been so obvious – the striking harmony in the way they moved, the painful sameness in the way they turned their heads as if the same habits governed both. He was sure she was happy with this harmony – it made him furiously jealous to see that she must be a hundred times happier with that fellow than she'd ever been with him.

But at the same time he noticed to his amazement that she was the active party here. How come? Could she really be unbridled enough to seduce him? She was urging him to do something. She was explaining something to him, as she walked casually beside him and by laughing she was stirring him up, rousing his imagination.

Cholawicki was suffering! If before this Maja had captivated him with the modernity of her behaviour, the boldness of her antics and her 'sober' take on the world, then now he was getting his just deserts!

After all, he himself had challenged every moral principle she had, and had taught her to seek happiness by taking the shortest path. He had brought this on himself – he'd let her force him into rivalry with Leszczuk! Cholawicki was incredibly sensitive to social considerations. He'd have forgiven Maja a flirtation, but he'd never forgive her for flirting with a tennis coach!

But if he could have heard their conversation, he'd have been far more astounded.

'There are some odds and ends there, for instance, miniatures,' she said guardedly, looking underfoot. 'There's a cupboard full of miniatures.'

'Miniatures are a sort of small picture, right?' asked Leszczuk.

'Yes. Anyway, there are silver and gold-plated cups too. And table silver as well. Small knives with mother-of-pearl handles. Lots of valuable odds and ends.'

She stopped.

'I'll have to tell my fiancé to hire a night watchman. The castle isn't guarded at all. The best proof is that you got all the way to the prince without anybody stopping you. But the prince can't bear to have guards. It's an impossible situation.'

Leszczuk didn't answer. What did this mean? Was she trying to persuade him to go back to the castle again? He gave her a sideways glance. She smiled in a rather strange way . . .

Their relationship was turning out to be so stormy and confusing that it was hard for him to understand anything at all. He was starting to suspect her of some ill-defined intentions.

Sometimes he thought she was making fun of him.

And sometimes that she wasn't – or even quite the opposite . . .

Despite the whole 'similarity', the conversation with her was making him feel dreadfully awkward. When he was playing tennis with her, or when they were walking beside each other in silence, everything was fine and they were in perfect harmony; but when it came to conversation, difficulties and ambiguities instantly arose.

'I often find myself itching to take something from there,' she suddenly said in an undertone and with mad impatience. 'I'd have

money. I'd take it, and that'd be that. I'd be independent. I'd have
enough for the rest of my life!'

'I'd like to lead an honest life,' he quickly replied, as if to defend
himself. She took it with a smile.

He didn't know how to explain to her that there was a misunderstanding between them, that she was wrong to take him for a
thief, and that if he had wanted to take the money from her closet
that day it wasn't for gain but to get revenge on her – no, he had no
idea how to explain.

'I'm not the kind of person you take me for,' he said.

'I know what kind of person you are!'

'How do you know that?'

'You're forgetting that . . . we are very much alike. Everyone says
so. I know what kind of person you are . . . because I know what
kind of person I am.'

He looked at her dark face and small ear. Perhaps it was true?
Maybe she was right. Could this sophisticated, upper-class young
lady really be capable of dubious intrigue? What if she could? After
all, she was similar to him. But at the same time she was behaving
strangely – no, she definitely wasn't one of those normal young
women with higher education. All right, but so what if she was like
him? He wasn't a criminal, was he? True, but then again he was
similar to her. So if she was suspicious, he was suspicious too. And
if he was suspicious, then so was she . . . Leszczuk was losing his
head entirely.

But at the same time he still suspected that either she was mocking him, or else she was trying to trick him, and sometimes he
thought she hated him more than she liked him. Now and then her
eyes flashed so proudly and with so much hate – and there was that

same wild ferocity aimed at him that he had already experienced while they were playing tennis.

Meanwhile, watching him furtively, Maja was thinking: *Yes, it wouldn't be hard to persuade him – to do anything.*

She wanted to find out what he was like at last. He wasn't being frank and open with her. He was keeping his true nature hidden from her. So, to embolden him and at the same time test him, she'd started by trying to get round him.

But in tempting and encouraging him, she was also tempting and encouraging herself. Her unruly imagination was drawn to the idea of robbing the castle, though of course she would never do it. But there was something pleasing about it . . . She took a stealthy look at his face.

Suddenly she shuddered.

Somehow, Leszczuk looked different than usual.

Something about his face had altered. At first glance she couldn't quite tell what it was that had changed. It took her a few seconds to realize that his lips were blue. Almost black. No, it wasn't an illusion. And they weren't parched, as in a fever, but revoltingly blue – she'd never seen anything like it before. As if they were painted.

'Are you ill?' she said.

'Why do you say that?'

'Have a look at yourself.'

She took out a pocket mirror. He examined himself with curiosity and abhorrence. Maja too had feelings of overwhelming disgust. It was wild. Brutal. Garish.

'That's the second time they've gone like that,' he said.

'What do you mean, the second time?'

'It happened to me yesterday morning too, while I was shaving. It must be an illness.'

'Do you feel unwell?'

'Noooo . . . I'm fine . . . I have no idea what the cause might be. I like chewing various things when I'm walking. Maybe it's because of that.'

He was embarrassed . . . A sort of unease took hold of them and they quickened their pace. Maja noticed to her relief that the blue colour was fading and Leszczuk was returning to his normal look. What on earth was it?

By now they were coming up to the park. Suddenly Councillor Szymczyk appeared in the gateway, followed by the two ladies – the doctor's wife and the lady clerk – and Mrs Ochołowska. The latter with a very unhappy look on her face, obliged as she was to listen non-stop to their more or less transparent allusions and remarks. The 'lady of the manor' would have preferred not to join in these walks, but that would certainly have been interpreted as a show of disdain and contempt. So despite having countless chores and just as many cares, Mrs Ochołowska had to go on a daily afternoon walk with the boarding-house company.

The company was hellishly bored. All these persons, removed from their everyday jobs, condemned to inactivity and gathered by chance in a single manor house, didn't know what to do with themselves. They had no idea how to amuse themselves and no opportunity to work. Hence grudges, sulks and frictions were arising.

The doctor's wife was of the opinion that the lady clerk was too thin, and she let her know this with her customary effusive sincerity.

'Ah, my dear lady, you should eat more, you're so thin, as thin as a rake.'

The lady clerk felt hurt, not so much by the statement that she was thin as by the comparison with a rake. She regarded the doctor's wife as tactless, and she made that plain to her by saying: 'I

would not wish to grow too fat, because fat people can sometimes
be too . . . heavy.'

'I spoke out of the goodness of my heart!' exclaimed the indignant
doctor's wife. 'I spoke to you in all sincerity, but you've answered
me venomously! They're right to say being too thin makes a person
resentful. I'm surprised at you!'

'And I'm not surprised at you!' replied the lady clerk, glancing
not without irony at the doctor's wife's somewhat over-exaggerated
curves. 'I'm not surprised at you in the least. It is hard to be in control of oneself when one is spilling in all directions. Isn't that so?'
she said, addressing Mrs Ochołowska.

'Do excuse me, I didn't hear what you ladies were talking about,'
replied the embarrassed proprietor, not wanting to be mixed up in
their quarrel.

'You're always floating on a mental cloud, miles away from your
guests,' said the lady clerk, very sweetly this time.

'For God's sake! Mrs Ochołowska must have had it up to here
with our company by now,' cried the doctor's wife in her usual frank
and direct tone. 'Can one really demand it? Are we relatives, or
invited guests?'

'You ladies do not know how to get on with one another,' put in
Councillor Szymczyk sternly.

This compelling statement prompted the company to fall silent.
However, both ladies resented Mrs Ochołowska for not coming to
their defence. Besides, the doctor's wife, full of rancour, was planning her revenge. She had noticed long ago that the lady clerk had
a dreadful rash on her back, which was visible through her light,
transparent blouse and she'd already wanted to tell her this several
times, 'in her own interests' – but so far had held back. Now she
decided not to restrain her spontaneous sincerity any longer.

'But in your case, dear lady, one can see the pim . . .' she began tunefully, when suddenly they caught sight of Maja and Leszczuk on the path ahead. The two women exchanged knowing looks. This had all the appearance of a scandal. Poor Mrs Ochołowska! Could she not see what was happening?

'Have you two been out for a walk again?' the lady clerk stressed clearly, and cast a glance at Mrs Ochołowska.

Maja walked up slowly, toying with a penknife. Leszczuk stopped at a certain distance.

'And are you saying again that we've been out for a walk again?' she said arrogantly through clenched teeth. There was so much lordly disdain in her tone of voice, such plain confidence that she, Maja, had no need to care about this woman's opinion, that the face of the lady clerk went pale with red blotches.

'Each chooses his company according to his own taste!' she replied.

'Quite so. And I think it would be cruel to make trouble for those who aspire . . . to better company!' Maja gave the lady clerk a look that left no room for doubt that this remark was aimed at her, and then she turned to her mother and said: 'Aren't you feeling the chill, Mama?'

'Maja dear,' whispered Mrs Ochołowska, 'go to the house and wait for me upstairs. I'll be right there.'

There was so much gravity and pain in her voice that the girl was disconcerted.

'All right,' she replied flatly.

After she had gone the lady clerk addressed Mrs Ochołowska.

'I would like to have my bill this evening. I am leaving tomorrow,' she said.

'Very well. You will receive your bill today after supper.'

Mrs Ochołowska bid the ladies farewell with a nod and headed towards the house. She tried not to think about what those two raving busybodies might be saying now, what oceans of bile, invective, and squalid suspicions they were pouring on her and on Maja. Whatever, it all paled in comparison with the urgency of talking to Maja – before it was too late. The tennis coach must leave as soon as possible! But should she speak to her openly, or in a roundabout way? It might be better not to suggest suspicions to her youthful imagination that could lead her seriously astray. She couldn't see any harm in free camaraderie with Leszczuk on the basis of sport.

'Why did you do that?' she asked her daughter once they were alone in her room together. 'I've lost a guest. Miss Wyciskówna has demanded her bill and is leaving tomorrow.'

'I'm very sorry. She shouldn't take liberties, the vulgar creature.'

'Maja, that supercilious attitude makes no sense at all, and these days in our circumstances it's simply absurd.'

'If she paid a heap of gold, I still wouldn't keep her. You heard her stupid allusions. I'm not going to let just anyone rebuke me like that.'

'But you'll go to the forest with just anyone.'

'So you see it the same way as Miss Wyciskówna, do you? In the first place Leszczuk isn't just anyone, he's better than I am,' she said childishly.

'How is he better than you?'

'Better because he beats me at tennis. And secondly he's an ordinary boy, almost on a par with a servant. Can you really suspect me of flirting with Leszczuk?'

Her words quivered with an undertone of resentment. Her mother was aware of her daughter's incredible ambition – she hadn't the courage to speak to her of the 'similarity'.

'Maja,' she said, warmly taking hold of her hand, 'I don't know . . . perhaps you're right . . . But people see it differently. You have the best proof: Wyciskówna . . . So if you're willing to do this for me, let's have him leave on this or another pretext. Give up this arrangement.'

'Oh, no, I won't,' said Maja slowly through her teeth.

She was very pale and turned her head away.

'It's insulting for me! I refuse to take account of such extraordinary . . . It insults me. I'm amazed you can't see that it insults me. I advise you never to treat me this way or I . . . Leszczuk is staying and that's final!'

She ran out of the room. Mrs Ochołowska threw up her hands. She was quite incapable of dealing with her daughter!

But Maja's violent and disdainful reaction did at least reassure her that there could be no question of any romantic danger. Ambition would give her better protection than the best maternal advice.

But why was the girl so full of contempt? *How is it,* she thought, *that I, brought up in different circumstances and less democratic times, have never had such an utter sense of superiority?*

Mrs Ochołowska started to prepare the bill for Miss Wyciskówna, but this task proved unnecessary, because just after Maja had gone, the lady clerk came to see her.

In an icy tone she announced that she put Maja's improper behaviour down to her young age, and that she did not wish to embarrass her by leaving on the instant. Besides, the goodwill she felt towards Mrs Ochołowska would not permit her to take this radical step, for she was sure that – by token of agitating the other boarding-house guests – her departure would prompt other persons to leave too. So she had decided to ignore Miss Maja's antics for the time being on condition, naturally, that Mrs Ochołowska would come to bear on her daughter. As for Miss Maja's walks and games, she did not intend to interfere in those matters, leaving concern for them to her mother.

Mrs Ochołowska thanked her quite coldly. She didn't show the relief she felt deep inside; the lady clerk's departure might indeed have been a disaster for the newly founded boarding house. But she did not know that she owed the happy resolution of the incident above all to the doctor's wife.

Because the doctor's wife was terrified that Miss Wyciskówna would leave before she'd had the chance to inform her, with the best will in the world, about the pim . . . that she had noticed under her blouse. As a result, she had spared no pains to talk her out of leaving prematurely.

Besides, the unpleasant episode was wiped from memory for other reasons too. Namely that just before supper two new persons had arrived at the boarding house – Maja's good friend and school-mate Krysia Leniecka and her distant cousin, law student Gustaw Żałowski – Gucio to his friends. This provided a welcome diversion when spirits were low.

The two young ladies were thrilled to see each other. Like a skilled politician, Mrs Ochołowska took advantage of the opportunity to have a bottle of good wine served at table, thanks to which the supper took on a festive character. Even the lady clerk and the doctor's wife, disregarding the very recent misunderstandings, put on formal attire; incidentally the doctor's wife found that even through this dress it was plain to see Miss Wyciskówna's pim . . . of which the unfortunate creature was wholly unaware.

But during supper a new complication arose. There was a sound of hoofbeats, and moments later Cholawicki appeared. His visit was not entirely desirable. Mrs Ochołowska was pained to notice the meaningful glances that the doctor's wife exchanged with the lady clerk, and which seemed to be saying: 'Ha, ha, he's come just in time!'

But she was more alarmed by the dangerous sparks in Maja's eyes and her excellent mood. She was enjoying herself! She seemed delighted by her friend's arrival. She was laughing almost non-stop.

After supper Cholawicki drew her to one side.

'I want to talk to you!' he whispered.

'Why aren't you stopping at the castle?'

'I have something to discuss with you!'

'All right, but not now. Later! Let's go for a walk!' she cried. 'It's such a lovely evening.'

This idea met with the approval of the young people, and Cholawicki had no option but to drop the conversation for the time being.

Maja nodded at Leszczuk.

'You're coming with us!'

'Who, me?'

He was already on his way to his room and had stopped halfway up the stairs. He didn't want to go with them and he was afraid of Maja, but he didn't know how to excuse himself.

'I'd like to go to bed,' he said.

'You can get some sleep later. Anyway, you'll be useful – if only to carry the coats. Actually it's too warm to wear them now, but we should take them because it might be cooler in the forest. Krysia and Gucio, pass your coats to Mr Leszczuk, he'll carry them.'

'But there's no need,' protested Żałowski politely, seeing that Leszczuk had already taken Maja's jacket. 'At any rate I'll carry mine and Krysia's.'

'Mr Leszczuk can carry all of them!' she cried petulantly and stamped her foot. Leszczuk went red. Cholawicki went pale.

'You're depriving us of the honour and pleasure of carrying our own finery,' said Żałowski, laughing, in an attempt to erase the nasty impression. They headed down a path that glowed silver in the moonlight. The dogs began to fawn upon Maja.

Cholawicki went first, trying to get a grip on himself and regain his sang froid. Some way behind him came the two young ladies and the student, and last of all Leszczuk. But Żałowski, who was well brought up, slowed his pace to talk to Leszczuk. Miss Leniecka turned to Maja.

'What on earth are you doing with the tennis coach, Maja? He might be upset.'

'Oh, he'll be fine! He's not soft-skinned, I tell you.'

'Sorry? What?'

'Well, if you can say thick-skinned, you can say soft-skinned. No, actually, you say thin-skinned, don't you?'

'Maja, there's something wrong with you,' said her friend. 'What's happened to you? You've changed.'

'How should I know?'

The air was heady, the forest, the park and the glades were filling their lungs. The trees cut into the bright, starry sky like dark stains. The great sweetness of the evening pervaded the landscape.

'Do you love him?' asked Maja, with a slight backwards nod. Leniecka pressed up to her.

'At long last!'

'What do you mean, at long last?'

'At long last I've fallen in love. Oh, Maja, Maja, Maja!'

'What about him?'

'He has too.'

She sighed deeply.

'As soon as he finishes his studies we'll get married. His parents are friends of my parents. It'll be like extending the family. You know what, I still can't believe it's true, because it's too . . . too . . . but what's wrong? Are you crying? You're crying?'

'Don't be silly!'

'Your tear fell on my elbow.'

'It wasn't a tear, just dew . . . from a tree.'

Why couldn't she love like that – steadily, calmly, happily? Why, instead of having such a nice, decent young man of whom there was no need to be ashamed, with whom one could be sure of one's fate, did she have these two men who were tormenting her, ruining her? With whom she was ruining herself?

'Don't waste time on me. An evening like this one isn't a daily event. Gucio,' she called, 'come over here! Krysia's upset with you for not linking arms with her.'

She moved away from them and walked slightly to one side, on her own – in between Cholawicki who was walking ahead of her, and Leszczuk who was walking behind her – entirely on her own. How had it happened, and whose fault was it that for all her eighteen years, for all her beauty, she couldn't enjoy this night, but had to struggle and suffer, while that girl, though not as pretty, was in the full bloom of love? Was pure accident to blame? Her upbringing? The innate dangerous tendencies in her nature? She slowed down to let the happy couple go ahead of her.

Gucio briefly let go of Krysia to catch a firefly and, holding it in his closed hands, he leaned over it. Maja caught the look full of tenderness that the girl cast at her lover before hurrying over to him in the shadow of the trees.

Would I be able to gaze as tenderly, sweetly and loyally? thought Maja with envy. But at whom was she to gaze like that? At Cholawicki, walking ahead of her, or at Leszczuk, walking behind her? What would happen if she tried to look at Leszczuk that way? Well, just

as an experiment, it was dark, no one was going to see . . . just for
fun . . . to find out whether it could be done at all, whether it was
possible to look at him like that . . .

She slowed down even more, and once she was right at the back
she cast a glance that seemed strange to her, too tender for her, at
the boy's outline. And instantly lost herself in that glance, immersed
herself in it entirely, she sank and drowned in her own gaze. A wave
of heat flooded her heart, which began to beat . . . until she had to
press it with a hand.

She quickened her pace and suddenly she was right beside
Leszczuk. The night lent her an air of lightness. Slender in her summer dress, she materialized at his side so nimbly and imperceptibly
that he shuddered. She didn't utter a word, but simply walked a few
steps along with him; he saw her large black eyes turned towards
him, full of regret and affection. But that same instant disgust and
revulsion appeared in her eyes.

Leszczuk's lips were as black as pitch! No – not black. That was
just an effect of the night. They were blue!

How horrible! It was some dreadful, repulsive illness. Where
could he have caught it? It was – wild!

She stepped back. She quickened her pace. She fled – to her fiancé.

Cholawicki only noticed her presence when she slipped her hand
under his arm. He couldn't resist the bliss that filled him at her
mere approach.

All the fury he had been feeling evaporated, to be instantly
replaced by happiness – especially when he felt her pressing against
his arm, firmly, tightly, ardently.

At once suspicion prompted him to suppose that it was a deliberate manoeuvre on her part to get him to lower his guard where
Leszczuk was concerned. But he was too happy. He had suffered

too much in the past few hours – when he'd followed them, and then wandered about near the manor. He took hold of her hand, hugged her close and refused to know any of the facts – or to ask any questions. Maja gently rested her head against his shoulder and they walked along like that for quite a time.

She was testing. Testing to see if it was at all *possible* to walk along like that with her fiancé. Could she manage it? She was doing what she could to warm her heart towards him, to force an emotion on herself with the aid of external factors. He was from her world. He didn't steal. He wasn't wild and uncouth. He didn't have any disgusting illnesses. But her heart remained cold, while there, behind them, remained the one she'd been looking at moments earlier, the compromising one . . .

She moved away from her fiancé just as suddenly as she had arrived by his side; before Cholawicki knew it, she wasn't there anymore. She walked in solitude again, slightly to one side of the path, and having let everyone pass, she followed them, disconsolately bringing up the rear.

Warm and fragrant, the night was heavy with the balsam of herbs and shrubs, and cast a dark-blue veil over both happiness and unhappiness. The ecstatic faces of the happy betrothed couple as well as the pale, anguished face of Cholawicki – and the desperate, rather child-like face of Maja – and also the doubtful face of Leszczuk.

Krysia approached and gently put an arm around her. For some time they walked together without talking. In the past they'd been very close, if that was possible, considering Maja's secretive, haughty nature.

'Who is this Leszczuk?' asked Miss Leniecka quietly.

Maja went pale. Why was she asking this? Had she already noticed their similarity too?

'A tennis coach.'

'That I know. But beyond that?'

'Beyond that I know as much about him as you do. What can one know about a boy of that kind? Where he was brought up? What he has done? With whom he keeps company? He's a boor – a wild nature, uncouth, oh, look, just like that!'

She pointed to a large clump of weeds, lushly burgeoning near the water.

'How can you know what's lurking in there? There could just as well be flowers as frogs!'

Her voice was cold and hard.

'You're exaggerating,' said Leniecka, casting her a keen glance. 'Maja, you're maligning him for no reason!'

'You think that . . . that . . . Why would I be exaggerating?'

'You just are!'

'Why? Tell me what you're thinking!'

Just then Żałowski called out: 'A squirrel!'

The little animal skittered from under his feet and quickly climbed a pine tree. Halfway up the squirrel stopped and, clinging to the trunk, looked at the people from over its huge tawny tail, then scrambled even higher. It was clearly visible in the moonlight.

They surrounded the tree.

'It can't escape,' said Żałowski.

Indeed, the squirrel had chosen the wrong tree. It was too far from any other for a jump to be possible. Cholawicki took out his Browning and cocked it.

'Don't shoot!' shouted Miss Leniecka.

But the shot had already been fired. The squirrel leaped from branch to branch. The secretary fired a second time. What bliss to be able to let off steam at least in this way!

'Why on earth are you murdering it?' asked the student in disgust. Maja said nothing.

'I must hit it!' snapped Cholawicki. 'Third time lucky.'

But when he failed to hit it a third time, he raised his gun again. He was angry, his hand was shaking, he couldn't accept the fact that he kept missing. The lust to kill had him in its grip.

'I'll catch it alive,' cried Leszczuk, and before Cholawicki could shoot he was already up the tree. He climbed with great speed.

The secretary was going to fire again, but Maja grabbed him by the sleeve.

'That's enough!' she cried.

'Have no fears,' he muttered.

Meanwhile Leszczuk was getting close to the target. He couldn't bear the persecution of animals and had only climbed the tree to make it impossible to shoot. But having announced that he'd catch the squirrel, now he had to. It had fled to the very top of the tree and was cowering among the branches.

As he continued to climb, the narrow trunk began to sway alarmingly under his weight.

'You'd better come down!' called Leniecka.

Leszczuk climbed even higher, while the crown of the tree bent so much that his back was virtually parallel with the ground. Suddenly the squirrel began to struggle like crazy. In panic-stricken terror it hopped across the thinnest little branches until finally, seeing that it couldn't escape, it leaped from the tree straight to the ground. He caught it in mid-air – but just at that moment the treetop snapped with a crack, followed by a scream from those watching below.

Luckily it broke quite slowly. Without dropping the squirrel, Leszczuk managed to seize hold of a bough that the treetop had hooked on while falling, then he slid down the branches and finally jumped to the ground.

'Are you all right?' cried Leniecka.

'I almost strangled it!' he replied. The squirrel was trembling in his hands.

'What a sweetie!' they said, carefully touching its fur.

'I'll let it go.'

'No, don't do that, let's keep it a while!'

Leniecka, who hadn't been to the countryside for a long time while busy with her studies, couldn't get over the thrill of this fresh, sweet-scented inhabitant of the forest.

'Let's take it home and then let it go. Let's see what it does indoors.'

'I'd rather let it go now,' said Leszczuk, who could feel the squirrel's heart beating like mad in his hands.

Leniecka cast Maja a playful glance, and once they had started walking on to see the castle at the edge of the forest, she said: 'He must be a thoroughly decent chap!'

Maja didn't answer.

'Look how he's petting it. Anyone who's so fond of animals can't be bad.'

'Is that what you think? Animals aren't that afraid of good people!'

'The castle!' they heard the student exclaim. They stopped at the edge of the forest, and there before them the silhouette of towering stone walls appeared, subtle and majestic. The air was unusually pure, which made the castle seem much closer than it actually was. Cholawicki clenched his fingers. What was going on in there? Why was he wasting his time here? Oh, it was madness to be unable to break free of this girl! Meanwhile, on the pretext of wanting to stroke the squirrel, Maja went up to Leszczuk again.

His lips were less black now – but they still weren't the right colour. Anyway, it was hard to tell at night. She touched the squirrel. In his hands the little animal was stiff with fear, motionless. Maja thought it seemed overly afraid. But as she stroked its fluffy coat she suddenly felt something strange. The squirrel was undulating. Undulating? No, that wasn't the right word – more like throbbing. As if it were moving internally, or puffing up. As if he were steadily crushing it with his hands. Though Maja took no special notice of this, once again she was left with the impression of something wild and repulsive.

Could he kill the squirrel? the question occurred to her. *If his lips were like that . . .*

Leszczuk would have been more than happy to leave, to drop the squirrel and get away. Everything in him was straining towards her, towards her exquisite face in the moonlight, her hair almost black in the night, her petite hands. And at the same time everything in him was running away from her. What did she want from him now?

'Would you kill that squirrel?'

'But why?'

'What if I asked you to?'

'But why?'

'Just because. I made a bet with my friend that if I asked, you'd kill it . . .'

She looked him in the eyes and he heard her laughter – provocative, impatient, insatiable, cruel. Just for a moment she laughed and flashed her teeth at him.

'Well?' she whispered, as if they'd already agreed on it, as if it went without saying. He laughed, as she had, and without a second thought he hurled the squirrel with all his might against a tree. It squealed painfully and rolled into a ball.

Everyone leaped towards it. Maja stood still, panting.

'But that's pure barbarity!' cried Leniecka. 'What had it done to you?'

'It bit me,' said Leszczuk hesitantly.

The squirrel's eyes misted over. It was dying.

They were all looking at it. Only Maja couldn't tear her eyes off Leszczuk.

'How crude!' said Cholawicki curtly, nudging the corpse.

Maja began to sob. And before anyone had time to take it in, she'd raced off into the forest. At once Leszczuk, who'd been standing there disconsolately until now, leaped after her and disappeared in the darkness.

Cholawicki set off in pursuit of them, but tripped on a protruding root and fell. He instantly jumped up and without losing time ran in great bounds.

'Stop! Stop!' he shouted.

After a long race Leszczuk caught up with Maja and grabbed her by the arms. He pushed her against a tree, making her recoil among the branches. He caught hold of her again and hurled her to the ground.

Down on one knee, she stared at him with her eyes wide open, and he stared back at her, as if seeing her for the first time. He raised her head.

'So you're . . . like that . . . like that?'

She was sure he was going to kill her, just like the squirrel. She was expecting cruelty. She knew she'd feel it at first hand. His fingers were tightening around her neck and his eyes had narrowed.

'It's you who's *like that*!' she whispered, as if not believing her own eyes.

He hit her hard. Maja lunged. He held her firmly. She bit him. Then, losing control entirely, he pushed her and they rolled onto the ground. They started to hit each other at random, reeling over the moss. They were seized by savagery!

It was as if each wanted to destroy the other, to kill, murder, annihilate – the terrible ferocity towards each other that had assailed them while playing tennis had been let loose.

He was shocked by her fury. But this fury merely increased his own. And although Maja was in no doubt that her final hour was nigh, she wasn't thinking about that – all she knew was that his hands were pulling her hair, scratching, hitting, destroying whatever they could – determined to slaughter her with the dreadful, dark and unseeing strength of a murderer.

Both of them were murderers! Each was only alive to murder the other. They hated each other infinitely!

He was the first to be horrified by her, or by himself too – and fled.

She lay breathless, powerless – her lip was cut and the blood was trickling onto her fingers. All her bones ached. Her mind was a blank. Apart from one single thought: *like this? like this?*

Ah, so this is what he's like – and I am like this too – and it's like this? . . . like this? . . .

Cholawicki was calling from somewhere deep in the forest: 'Maja! Maja!'

She jumped to her feet, and holding her torn blouse in place, took a roundabout route back to the manor. Luckily she managed to reach her bedroom without being noticed. She wasn't crying.

She was just distraught, humiliated, shocked to the core. She looked in the mirror. Her red, bleeding lips stood out in her pale, bruised face. She had a black eye. Her clothes were torn to shreds. The skin on her knees was grazed.

She remembered how once on the way home from the theatre with her mother they'd seen a crowd in the street – a policeman had detained two streetwalkers who'd had a fight. They looked just as she did, and just like her they weren't crying at all, but panting – unable to catch their breath – and staring into space vacantly, helplessly.

She sneaked into the bathroom and turned on the tap. She was plastered in earth.

And was it really possible – that fury? That incredible ferocity? That utter brutalization? They'd bitten each other, torn out each other's hair, and yanked with such furious hatred and with such lust for destruction – not even dogs bite each other like that!

Ah, so that's what I'm like? I'm like that inside . . .

And he is like that too . . .

Someone knocked at the door.

'Maja?'

It was Cholawicki. She raced to the door and turned the key. She locked herself in. Did he know what had happened?

'I want to have a chat with you.'

Silence.

'Maja, we must talk. I have to go back to the castle. I want a word with you.'

He sounded very serious. She didn't answer. She heard him walking away. She went back into her bedroom, locked the door, put out the light, got into bed and long into the night she lay on her back, with her hands under her head, staring into the darkness, incapable of a single organized thought. Nothing but shreds. And appalling grief, crushing sorrow, as if for something irretrievably lost, for a sort of refinement that used to be in her – but had been murdered, pulverized by loutish crudeness, bestial fury, hideous brutality.

And that squirrel too, the squirrel they'd jointly smashed against the tree – that small, dying animal at the foot of the tree!

She bore Leszczuk no grudges. She wasn't rebelling against him anymore. She was just surprised to find that he was like that, and she was like that – both of them were like that and such was their true nature.

Someone was opening the door.

Maja couldn't tell if she was asleep and had been woken by a rustling noise, or if she was just so preoccupied that she had lost her sense of time. Dawn was breaking. Someone had stuck a knife into the gap in the door and was trying to force the lock. At once she was sure it was Leszczuk, but she didn't move an inch. She had no right to deny him anything, because she was the same as he was! Just the same!

As if in the grip of a bad dream, she calmly watched, without blinking, as the door gave way and he slipped into her room, then quietly closed the door behind him, listening out in case someone had woken in the vicinity. His profile, focused and alert, was clearly visible in the half-light.

He went up to the closet. He took the key from the upper lock and opened the drawer containing the money.

He took no notice of Maja at all. He didn't even glance in her direction. Evidently he too was aware that there could be no resistance from that quarter because . . . they were like each other, they were just the same.

He took out the banknotes and left, and like an accomplice, Maja stood up and closed the drawer again; she even picked up a one-hundred-zloty note that he had dropped on the floor.

IX.

MEANWHILE SOMETHING had indeed been happening in the castle, which in the rising darkness stood among the flood waters, a mighty, thousand-year-old outcrop, a proud, ominous stack of walls, petrified in eternal reverie – a ruin of bygone splendour, a memento of past glory – and now a sad and tragic place where desires, terror and madness led a fateful dance?

Taking advantage of Cholawicki's absence, Grzegorz was acquainting Skoliński with the secrets of the past. His attention rapt, the professor was listening to the old servant, who kept looking round behind him, while spitting out scanty phrases with the greatest reluctance. Skoliński had to keep spurring him on and pressing him with questions.

'I don't know much,' said the butler warily, 'but what I know, I'll tell you, like at holy confession.

'I was brought up at the castle from when I was a very small boy. In the late prince's day I was a scullery lad, and the present prince Aleksander grew up with me, because we were almost equal in age. In those days there weren't no devilry yet.

'The devilry only came later on – much later . . . You want to know? To my mind the devilry's to do with the person of the footman Franek, that's to say the prince's son. But I'm not at all sure.'

'So the prince was married?' asked Skoliński.

'He was, but his wife died without an heir, and he had the son with another woman. So at least people said. But I'll tell it in order.

'About forty years ago a boy came running in to the castle with a letter for the prince. He refused to say from whom. That very night the prince rode out and didn't come back for two days after. About a fortnight later the prince called me to his study, and there was that same boy who'd come with the letter. The prince says to me: "Grzegorz, I've taken a liking to this boy. Show him to the scullery. He's an orphan with no father or mother," he says, "I will care for him."

'So he remained at the castle. He was about twelve years old then. It was idiotic. When I asked him about his parents he said his father was a stove-fitter and his mother had died recently. His name was Sikorski. But people said he must be the prince's son – though the prince didn't bother with him at all . . .

'Once he was grown up, the prince set him a wage and gave him to me as my helper. But the way I see it, by then this Sikorski fellow had realized that the prince had reasons of his own for keeping him at the castle. And people most definitely told him he was his son. In any case there was a likeness between them. With age he became more and more like the prince. The same nose. Eyes exactly the same. And when he spoke, his voice was similar too. Anyway, he was a nothing of a fellow.

'The prince could see the likeness, but he was ashamed. Just like a prince – it was awkward for him that the servant was his spitting image. The prince was a stickler, shamefaced, always very mindful, he didn't like to associate with people . . . So it was awkward for him that his sins were so plain to see in this likeness.

'What's more, when Sikorski saw that he looked exactly the same as the prince, he became very audacious. He didn't dare present his grievances, but he managed to force the prince to recognize him as his son. Many a time he came to me in the kitchen and said the prince's humiliation was coming soon. He had to recognize him!

And one day he went to see the prince, but he cursed the fellow so soundly that it could be heard downstairs. He flew into such a rage that God protect us!

'"Your head has turned!" he shouted, but to every room in the castle. "Begone! Get out of here! Out of my sight! Not a minute longer! It's a pack of barefaced lies."

'But Franek asked for forgiveness and swore he would never, ever do it again, so the prince let him stay at the castle. And somehow those ideas blew out of his head, he feared the prince, and hid it all inside. About three months went by like that.

'Until, as I remember to this day, along comes Franek to the kitchen, not the same. He smiles sort of sweetly, but spitefully, contented but evil – it was so odd that it struck me.'

Grzegorz lowered his voice and crossed himself roughly.

'That was the moment when it started!' he said solemnly. 'From then on the devil took over! So as I say, he came to the kitchen and said: "Well, now I'm going to even the scores with him!"

'"With whom?" I say, and he replies: "With the prince, my father." "Mind he doesn't throw you out on your ear," I tell him, because he's jangled my nerves with this jabber. But he just smiles and says: "He won't throw me out, though he'd like to."

'"And why wouldn't he throw you out?"

'"Because he loves me."

'"As long as he doesn't smash you in the teeth out of love!" I say, and then he says: "You can come to my room at night, Grzegorz, and see for yourself how much he loves me."

'I was curious, and that night I stood behind the door as he told me to. I look, and here comes the prince, barefoot, very quietly. He walked towards the bed where Franek was asleep, right up to the bed with a candle, I tell you, and for a long time he gazes at him, sighs, whispers something to himself and very, very gently strokes his hair with his fingertips – and there are tears trickling down his face, he strokes and sobs – sobs and strokes . . .

'Then he went away and came back again, stroked him some more with such burning, fatherly emotion . . . He loved him so much, he loved him so much – never in all my life have I seen such affection.

'And that rascal lies there pretending to be asleep, snoring a bit now and then – and when he got tired of that he moved around, as if in a dream, and the prince ran off at once.

'At this point Franek sat up in bed and spoke these words: "Well, then? Did you see? He loves me! And now I'm going to settle scores with him for good and all! For ill-using me! At night, when no one can see, he loves me, but in the daytime he's ashamed. Very well, then, I'll show my darling daddy!"

'And that was when it started. Because Franek' – at this point Grzegorz crossed himself – 'began to spoil himself to spite the prince. He spoiled himself! That's the source of the devil at the castle – and nothing else.'

'What do you mean, he spoiled himself?' asked the professor, deeply shaken by the old butler's tale, told as if his watery eyes were seeing long-gone times again.

'He made himself evil,' Grzegorz replied curtly, 'he deliberately made himself evil! Out of rancour! To show the prince what sort of fate he'd condemned him to. I've never seen such spite in anyone, in all my life. He began to drink vodka. He consorted with whores, picked fights, and damaged his own health. The worst things anyone could devise he came up with and carried out. It was all too little for him! Many a young pup will do plenty of harm to others out of stupidity, or even for amusement, but he did it out of evil – so the prince would know how evil he was. There was no infamy he wouldn't perform and then boast about it in public. "You see," he'd say, "my father didn't give me an education, he's ashamed of me, so I'm like this!"

'And what's more,' said Grzegorz, looking around in trepidation, 'he started poisoning himself. I don't know what sort of poison he found, but with every month he dwindled, his skin went yellow, he hardly ate a thing and lived in a fever.

'And all for the thrill of hearing the prince at night when he came and wept bitter tears over him!

'I was a fool, because I dared not tell the prince the reason why it was happening. I thought he would settle down, for whoever heard of a man destroying himself like that? It's just a whim, I thought, it came and it'll go, and I'd better not tell the prince.

'Until one day at supper the prince started to ask me questions – did I know what was wrong with Franek to make him look so ill? I didn't want it on my conscience anymore, so I told him the whole truth. I told him he resented the prince for hiding his paternity, and that to spite the prince he was trying to ruin his health and was even taking some medicine. Jesus Christ! First the prince went red, and then as white as this scarf.

'So I tell him there's nothing to get upset about, it's just a whim, they come and go – he's a young pup, that's all. He gave no answer, just told me to summon him at once for a conversation. "And not a word to anyone, Grzegorz!" he says.'

Grzegorz hesitated.

'And so what transpired during this conversation?' asked Skoliński.

'That I don't know.'

'Come on, you obviously eavesdropped. Better tell me frankly.'

'During the conversation,' said Grzegorz, 'the prince acknowledged him as his son, embraced and kissed him, fell to his knees before him and asked his forgiveness. "You shall be my son," he said, "I'll proclaim it to the world, I'll give you my name and access to my fortune, pardon me! I'll give you an education, I'll open my heart to you, just forgive me!"

'I found it strange to see a born prince rolling in the dust before his own footman. And as for Franek – he'd have none of it. He stuffed his hands into his pockets and just stood there watching and not moving.

'"I refuse!" he said. "You should have acknowledged me at once. But now I refuse! I don't need this belated love. I don't love you, I hate you!" he shouts. "I'll destroy myself! To hell with me for the fact that my own father was ashamed of me!"

'He raced out of the study (for in those days there was still a study at the castle, it's not here now) and dashed through the castle. So at once the prince called for me and ordered me to keep watch on him.

'"Go after him, Grzegorz, and don't take your eyes off him – he's ready to kill himself!"

'I raced after him and I was only just in time. I dash into the woodshed and he's tying a rope to a beam. The moment he saw me he stepped back and brushed me off with jokes.

'"If not today, then tomorrow," he says with a laugh, but it sounded like someone smashing ice.

'I reported this to the prince. "Christ!" was the only word he said at first. And then that he must be guarded. "Grzegorz, you're the only one I trust! We must guard him night and day until he recovers!"

'What days and nights followed at the castle – may God preserve us! The everlasting pursuit of that madman. Endlessly guarding him. Endless fear that if we stopped watching him for a moment he'd take his own life.'

Grzegorz closed his eyes and for some time said nothing.

'I shan't tell you more,' he said firmly. 'Why dig up the past? It's been and gone, may it sleep peacefully, in eternal rest.'

'You know it's not asleep at all . . . Evil never sleeps . . .' the professor warned him, pointing vaguely towards the old kitchen. 'I'd advise you to speak.'

'Your Honour! Better not wake the devil!'

'And I advise you to speak!'

The butler yielded, but he spoke so quietly that he was barely audible.

'The prince and I kept watch by turns continuously. When the prince slept, I was awake, and vice versa. One of us was always near Franek, watching to make sure he wasn't seized by any more mad ideas. And he quietened down and became so well-behaved – but it was plain to see that he was only thinking about one thing, how to kill himself, utterly destroy himself! He bided his time like that for several days.

'And then it began! Mother of God! Again and again! He tried to stab himself with a knife in the kitchen! He tried to jump off the tower through a window! He tried to smash his head against the stone wall over there by the gate! Completely mad! The prince and I kept watching out to see what he was doing, what was whirling around in that crazy mind of his. So then the prince gave orders to lock him up, and we decided to shut him in the old kitchen, because it had a heavy door, with metal fittings, and no way to jump out of the window because it was too narrow.'

At this point Grzegorz stopped again, and then suddenly asked the professor in an odd tone of voice: 'Pardon me, Your Honour, but why are your lips quivering like that?'

'My lips?' asked the professor in surprise. He raised a hand to his mouth. It felt as if his lips were chapped. But as well as that they were throbbing.

It wasn't as if they were moving. Yet when he touched them he could feel that they had swollen and seemed to be rippling.

It was horrible. Instantly the towel in the kitchen sprang to the professor's mind. The worm-like wriggling of his lips was related to the quivering of the towel. What a monstrous idea – his mouth, affected by that horrible twitching? He felt as if he had lost control of his lips, as if his mouth had changed into a revolting creature moving of its own accord – on him.

Grzegorz too was observing this effect – in silence. They exchanged glances. Finally, to avoid stirring panic, the professor explained: 'It's nothing. It sometimes happens to me. It's a nervous tic, you see. Nothing serious. Carry on with your story.'

The throbbing was gradually subsiding.

'All right,' muttered Grzegorz without conviction. 'As I say,' he continued, 'the prince decided to lock him in the old kitchen.

'I told him to go there to tidy up, but as soon as he went in, we told him that as things were he must stay there until his mania passed, and he was to hand over all the objects he might use to do himself harm.

'At that point, carried away by his madness, he lunged at us, hitting, biting, howling like a dog, kicking and foaming at the mouth – there must have been a dark force at work, because that raw lad, only eighteen years old, very nearly defeated us – fully grown men in our prime. For someone to bite and howl like that – neither man nor beast is capable of it.

'But we managed to stun him. We took away his trouser belt and even removed his shoes. We locked the door and set up sentry duty. I was on guard by day, and at night it was the prince.

'I wanted to fetch a priest or a doctor too, but the prince said: "No, there's no need. I shall talk him out of it myself, I shall persuade him. If he won't listen to me, nobody can help him. I alone! I alone can do it!"

'And from then on a new horror began.

'He crashed about in that kitchen, while the prince hovered at the door, trying to reason with him.

'Perhaps that was when something attacked the prince's brain. I tell you, Your Honour, they talked through that door for hours. The prince begged and wept, then shouted and raged, while on the other side of the door Franek kept on aggravating and exciting him, laughing, shouting and cursing with abandon. But apart from me, nobody knew about it.

'By then there were hardly any servants at the castle, just one housekeeper, or cook, Mrs Ziółkowska, but I told her Franek was seriously ill and that the prince had forbidden anyone to go to him.

'Until one day the prince came to tell me I wasn't to guard him any longer. He alone would stay on watch by the door day and night, he'd prepare himself a bed, and I was simply to bring food to the next room and leave it there for him.

'Under no pretext was I to dare come to him. He would remain alone with his son – he alone would talk his son out of it – he would get the better of his son.

'What was I to do? Now I know I acted foolishly, because I should have notified someone, asked for help – but at the time no one could have known how it would end. After all, I thought the prince had more brains than I did. He looked dreadful, all week he hadn't shaved, he hadn't washed, he'd slept in his clothes, his eyes were flickering vacantly and he spoke with a stammer, but it never occurred to me that his mind had become unhinged. After all, father and son will always reach agreement better than anyone else.

'So I left them together upstairs and only saw the prince every few days at lunchtime. He seemed calmer, he was even smiling . . . Whenever I asked about Franek, he replied that "we're on the right track".

'"We're on the right track, my friend. He's getting calmer. We'll soon make peace. He's a reckless boy, but he has a good heart. And I have wronged him severely, oh dear, severely. But we're on the right track, just keep quiet, shush – don't tell anyone."

'All well and good. Except that after some time it seemed suspicious to me. A few weeks went by, and the prince was still saying the same thing – "we're on the right track". Something prompted me to have a key made (the prince had locked the doors so I wouldn't look into those rooms) – and that night I dropped in on Franek. The prince was asleep at the time.

'I look, and the door into the old kitchen is ajar, Franek's not there at all – not a trace, not a whisker.

'I race to the prince and wake him. "Where's Franek? What has become of him?" The prince smiles and says: "He's gone away, he's gone away, my friend. I've sent him on a journey to calm down a bit. It'll do him good. Don't worry about it – and keep mum – not a word to anyone!"

'That was when I noticed that he'd lost his mind. I never discovered what went on between them. And I never found Franek's body, though I searched the castle from top to bottom.

'Ever since, the prince has been as he is now. He refuses to talk about it, and if asked he pretends he's forgotten – but it's impossible to ask, or he immediately gets worse. I've told you the whole truth about what happened.'

'And you've never told anyone else?'

'Not a living soul! I don't want to interfere! When people start gossiping, that's the worst!'

The professor found it hard to stop his imagination from running riot. What sort of atrocities must have occurred between those two – the deranged and the possessed – during the terrible days and nights they spent alone together? Is it any wonder those experiences had not been without consequences – but had left their demonic residue in the old kitchen?

But what was the connection between this dismal tale and the mysterious quivering towel? Grzegorz could not provide an answer to this question. It was an enigma that no one but the prince could now explain. Though maybe not even he knew.

'And when did you notice that the kitchen was haunted?' asked the professor.

The butler spread his hands.

'For a long time I didn't know a thing. The prince locked the door and forbade anyone to go in there – saying Franek would be back soon. But to tell the truth, something put me off that old kitchen and I didn't look in there for about a year. It took me a long time to realize that the prince was hiding something. He was afraid of something! At night when he couldn't sleep he'd walk about outside the kitchen, but he never went in. He'd go around it at a distance, but he was always hovering near it. Sometimes he said something like "there's something going on", but I thought he was raving. Only once did he say: "Grzegorz, I'll show you something, but don't tell anyone." He guided me to the kitchen, but he didn't go inside, he just stood on the threshold and showed me the towel.

'"Look what a draught there is in here. Can you see how that towel is rippling? It's rippling, isn't it?"

'He can't have been sure if his senses were deceiving him, and he wanted me to confirm it. At first I didn't notice what was up with that towel and was about to remove it from the peg, but the prince all but shouted: "Don't touch it! Don't touch it!"

'And at that moment something happened to me. I felt sick. Somehow I felt so terrible – sickened – disgusted . . . Ugh!

'The prince fled with a scream. I slammed the door and hoofed it too! For many a year I never looked into that place again. But people started to say the castle was haunted. God knows how they found out, because I've never breathed a word to anyone.

'There was an apprentice here, Mr Rudziański. One day he came to see me. "Apparently," he says, "your place is haunted. Let me stay the night and I'll see – I know about ghosts, I'm not afraid." It was some five years after those events. I didn't care anymore, I'd forgotten some of it, as a man who's working forgets everything in time. So I let him sleep in there. Next morning I look in, and he's nowhere to be seen. I look again, and he's not there. I was just thinking he'd been spirited away like the late Franek. Nothing of the kind! I found him in a corner under the stairs. He didn't recognize me, he was shielding his face with his hands, and talking nonsense. His family came to fetch him, and apparently the doctors said he had an illness that had attacked his brain. Rubbish! There was no illness, but he must have seen something he couldn't withstand.

'It was just the same a couple of years later . . . the cook's son. They found him in the forest, the poor fool. He'd completely lost his mind, though just the day before he'd been well and happy, a joy to behold. No one knew what had happened to him. It was only when I saw the crumpled sheets on the bed in the old kitchen that I realized he must have crept in there out of curiosity and paid for it with his reason. I didn't breathe a word to anyone about that either. Why let tongues wag?

'And the fact that you spent the night in there without harm to your health is a miracle! Your Honour! I have a request. I'll tell you everything. But if I fail to resist, and ask what you saw in there, please do not say! Even if I ask. I don't want to interfere. It's none of my affair!'

'And what about the secretary? How did he manage to gain the prince's trust?'

Grzegorz scowled.

'Pshaw! The prince fears him more than he likes him.'

'And why does he fear him?'

'The secretary is cunning. A couple of years ago the prince's health improved a little. He wanted to put his affairs in order, and that was when he hired Mr Cholawicki, whom he had known long before. Because he's his distant cousin or something . . . The improvement in health did not last long, but the secretary stayed for good and managed to come to terms with the prince. The whole point is that the prince won't leave the castle at any cost, but he's also afraid of being alone. The secretary noticed this, and ever since he's done whatever he wants with the prince.'

'But Grzegorz, you should be a better friend to the prince.'

'He won't let me near him,' grunted the old man, 'because he's ashamed. He doesn't like me because I can remember the past. I'm lucky he still keeps me here at all. I'm just waiting for the day I'm thrown out in my old age and that'll be that!'

'Maybe the prince has let Mr Cholawicki in on his secrets?'

'No . . . The secretary doesn't know a thing. If he knew, he wouldn't keep questioning me. He's aware of something, he has a vague idea. He has noticed that the prince has something on his conscience, that he walks about at night and is afraid of something, but that's all he knows. Only now, unfortunately for me, I've told him there's devilry in that chamber. I lost my mind out of terror. Unfortunately for me! All these years I never said a word, and now I've said that. The worst thing to say! Now it's really going to start!'

He tapped his forehead.

'Just a minute! I'll show you a photograph of Franek. I have it in a suitcase in my room. He gave it me one day when he came back from the town because it wasn't good and he didn't like it.'

Soon after he brought a small photograph, gone yellow with age. The professor looked, and shuddered with astonishment.

The photograph was the head shot of a boy of about eighteen. A nice face, not in the least gloomy, was smiling an incredibly intense smile, though tenacity showed in the mouth and the eyes. The likeness to the prince was plain to see, though the head in the photograph bore no trace of the slightly degenerate, upper-class refinement of the prince's head. Instead it was a mixture of peasant and noble features. But something else prompted Skoliński to examine the photograph closely.

The face reminded him of someone. Not just the prince. Someone else as well. The art historian's eye, used to identifying influences and likenesses in portraits, could see a certain influence here too . . . a certain likeness . . . a likeness . . .

Suddenly he realized: Franek looked a bit like Leszczuk.

No, it was an illusion. It was just their youth that made them look alike. They must have been the same age. In any case, the professor felt he was being hypnotized by similarities. Maja's similarity to Leszczuk, Franek's similarity to the prince, Franek's similarity to Leszczuk – there were too many of these likenesses.

'Grzegorz,' he said, 'do you know anything about a sign? What sort of a sign is the prince waiting for? He seems to be waiting for an emissary from this Franek fellow – as if he's going to send someone to him and forgive him – and this person is to reveal his identity with a certain sign, isn't he?'

'I've not heard of any sign.'

'It's very important. If we knew what sign it was, we could cure the prince,' said Skoliński pensively, 'and get him out of here.'

'Just once . . . But it was Mrs Ziółkowska.'

'Well? And?'

'She was the housekeeper here. Mrs Ziółkowska. One time the prince and I fell sick simultaneously – in those days there were severe winters and we caught the flu. Mrs Ziółkowska was looking after the prince, and she mentioned a sign too . . . Oh yes. She said she brought the prince some medicine during the night and . . . I can't quite remember – she may have raised her hand, because she was going to sneeze, or something like that – and seeing this, the prince began to shout: "The sign, the sign", and took her for a ghost. But she fled instantly.'

'Try to remember! If we can identify this sign, we can do anything with the prince, like with a child.'

The butler squinted, scratched his head and wiped his brow.

'I can't remember at all.'

'Do some more thinking. And this Mrs Ziółkowska, where is she now?'

'She went to live in Grodno, at least twelve years ago. But where she is now, that I don't know.'

The professor wondered what to do.

Find Mrs Ziółkowska? Yes, that was the priority. That sign gave one power over the madman's soul. With its help he'd be able to destroy Cholawicki's plans – force the prince to dismiss the secretary, and cure him, dispel the complex that was paralyzing his ailing psyche.

But for now he must take advantage of Cholawicki's extended absence. He might succeed in extracting a few more details.

'I'm going to see the prince,' he said.

'Don't, because any minute now the secretary will be back,' warned Grzegorz, nervously looking out of the window at the boundless plains, enclosed by the dark border of the forest. 'I don't know what can have caused him to stay away so long. But the prince doesn't know you and he might start shouting – or have a fit.'

But the professor was relying on the fact that the prince wouldn't have forgotten their nocturnal encounter.

What should he say to him? How was he to get through to his hermetic, deranged mind?

Cautiously, he opened the door a little way. The prince was sitting on his bed, holding a small, empty bottle. He shuddered, but when Skoliński bowed he responded with a polite nod.

'I hope I'm not disturbing you?' asked the professor, as gently as he could. His heart wept at the sight of the poor old man.

'Not in the least!' said the prince. 'I'm just getting down to some tidying. I must sort out all this rubbish. You're not disturbing me at all – if you don't mind, I shall carry on doing my work.'

It wasn't hard to spot that despite these niceties, the prince was trembling all over. He still had his perfect manners from the past – but Skoliński's sudden appearance must have terrified him to the core.

'You're going to have a hard job, because there's an awful lot of rubbish in here!' said the professor amicably.

'Yes indeed! A lot. An awful lot. Isn't Mr Cholawicki there?' he said fearfully, glancing at the professor.

The professor reassured him that Cholawicki had just gone downstairs for a moment to see Grzegorz. At once the little bottle the prince was holding fell from his hands.

'Shall I pick it up?'

'No, no, thank you.'

'What if I were to help you to tidy up?'

'Oh, no, thank you very much. I'm just working out a plan,' he began to explain feverishly, 'but I don't know where to start. Henryk – excuse me, that's to say, Mr Cholawicki – always refuses to give me advice; but I don't know, I really don't know . . . Oh, I am most terribly sorry, I'm boring you with my . . .'

He sank into gloom again, took a deep breath and sat looking ruffled, like a bird.

Skoliński realized that the old man was saying all this just to avoid bringing up the business of what had happened in the night. The prince may not even have been sure they had spoken in the night: reality and delusion must have been inseparably tangled in his madman's head.

Nevertheless, the professor took a few steps forward and said, as if talking to a child: 'In fact it's not at all hard to begin tidying. I'd advise you to start from this corner, and then gradually slide along the walls to the right.'

The prince looked at him.

'Yes indeed! Of course, from this corner! Yes, yes! But why from this corner, and not that one?'

'This corner is closest to the bed.'

He raised his hands in a gesture of astonishment.

'Quite so,' he whispered.

'By your leave, we can start at once.'

The professor leaned over the rubbish.

'Just a moment! Just a moment!' cried the terrified prince. 'We don't know what might come in handy. Better not touch it! Don't throw anything away! It's not at all easy!'

'I wouldn't throw anything away at all. In my view, any item might come in handy. You never know.'

'Exactly so . . .'

'But that's not a reason to have this heap of rubbish in your bedroom. As it is, you can't make use of anything, because it's impossible to tell what's here. I would suggest sorting the rubbish according to a system, and then putting it in the next room. Nothing will be thrown away, but at the same time there will be order.'

'You know what, that's a thought!'

The prince looked at him like a saviour. Skoliński realized he had found a way through to the madman.

He started to expound his sorting method, established five categories of objects, suggested drawing up a list, to be supplemented with an index, and introduced so many technical improvements that the prince rapidly felt liberated from the dreadful heap of refuse that was poisoning his life. He forgot about his mistrust. He jumped off the bed and they got down to work together.

But Skoliński found himself in a difficult situation. He was afraid that Cholawicki would appear at any moment, but the tidying was going to take a long time. He tried offering various excuses to leave, but every time the prince held onto him tightly. It was plain that although afraid of Skoliński, he was even more afraid of being alone.

'No! No! No! This too! This little pile too!'

Suddenly the door opened, and there in the doorway stood Cholawicki.

'What's going on in here?'

His tone was tough and unpleasant. The prince jumped up.

'Ah, Henryk! It's nothing, please don't shout. Tidying! We're tidying up! But there's no need to be upset. This gentleman was kind enough . . . but never mind, it's not so bad!'

He started to tremble. But without taking any notice of him, the secretary went up to the professor.

'Please leave!' he whispered furiously.

'Don't be angry, Henryk!' implored the prince. 'Please stay!' he said, turning in terror to Skoliński. 'Please don't go!'

Skoliński hesitated. But Cholawicki grabbed him by the arm and brutally pushed him out of the room, then went up to the prince.

'Do you see this?' he said quietly, showing the riding crop he was holding. 'I advise you . . . not to scowl! I'm sick of it! I've had enough!'

'Why . . . But, but . . . Henryk?! Mother of God!'

He threw himself onto the bed and pressed his face into the pillows. Never before had the secretary threatened to hit him. Shrill, childish sobbing began to shake his body.

Cholawicki was in no mood for compromise. He had just come back from Połyka, galloping all the way – his face had been slashed by branches. Even though it made no sense at all, he wanted to go back again, to have another chat with Maja. He'd made a quick dash to the castle to keep control of what was happening – and had instantly confirmed how very disastrous his absence had been.

The professor had managed to get to the prince!

He left him weeping on the bed, slammed the door shut and went to the professor.

'I asked you to stay hidden from the prince! I told you the prince is upset by strangers!'

'Did you say something to that effect?' said Skoliński apathetically. 'Oh yes, I think I remember . . .'

But Cholawicki no longer believed in his apathy. The haunted chamber seemed ridiculous now. How could he have been so naïve this morning?

'You listen to me! You're to leave the castle immediately! Your presence here is inconvenient for me – understood? And now you watch out. You can't actually do me any harm because I'm acting legally. But I want to avoid trouble. So if you keep this whole matter to yourself I'll reward you – you understand that for me in these circumstances a large sum is of no significance. But if you try to obstruct me, I'll find ways . . . radical ways . . . I haven't the time to play games with you!'

The professor glanced at him and realized that further resistance was pointless.

'I'll leave,' he said. 'But now you listen to me. You're taking the imaginary dangers into account, but you're ignoring the real ones. In your place I'd drop all this and get the hell out of here.'

'May I inquire why?'

'Because of that!'

He pointed towards the old kitchen.

'What nonsense!'

'It's not nonsense! I swear on my mother's soul! You do not realize quite how real and actual *that* is. You should watch out. I'd rather murder someone miles away from this place than commit any far less evil act here – in the vicinity. Evil has a special resonance here!'

His tone was solemn and admonitory. Despite all his fury, Cholawicki hesitated.

'What did you see in there?'

'That's my business!'

'Get out!' he shouted. 'You're to be gone in five minutes flat! Enough of this poppycock! And don't you forget – it's do or die!'

'And I would advise you not to resort to extreme measures. You have no idea! Don't forget that you have no idea what's going on in here – at the castle!'

But just then they heard the prince's voice: 'By your leave!'

Standing on the threshold of the gloomy room in his improbable dressing gown he looked like an apparition from another world. The secretary ran up to him.

'Why aren't you in your bedroom?!' he shouted, but instantly fell silent. The prince had changed out of all recognition! With one vague wave of his hand he moved him aside.

'Who is to get out? Did I hear that someone is to get out of the castle? Was that about you, perhaps?'

Despite all his agitation, Skoliński automatically nodded – the madman emanated such dignity and lordly pride.

'Unfortunately I shall have to leave,' he said with emotion, his heart full of pity for the wretched man.

'And why is that?'

'Because I say so!' shouted Cholawicki.

The prince was surprised.

'Since when are my functionaries in charge of my castle? I'm afraid that if you will insist on giving the orders, you shall be the first . . . to leave here.'

Cholawicki went as pale as the wall. He had never heard anything like this from the prince's lips before. The change in him was incredible! And he seemed to be entirely conscious!

'Excuse me,' he stuttered.

'You are my guest,' said Holszański, addressing the professor in the same majestic tone. 'I invite you to stay. Please ignore any tactlessness on the part of my functionaries. I shall put an end to it. You cannot leave. You are indispensable to me for tidying up! This castle is filled to the brim with rubbish and junk – this room, for instance. I am suffocating in all this rubbish. I'm drowning in it! It's doing harm to my health! You must rescue me! I might fall sick! Please save me – please save me – please save me – save me – save me . . .'

The lunatic's words came faster and faster, until at last they passed into a scream – and he slumped to the floor.

'Get off!' snapped Cholawicki, when the professor sprang forwards to help. He snatched up the prince's emaciated body and carried him off to the bedroom.

Only now did he fully appreciate the seriousness of the situation. The wall of solitude around the prince had been breached! His major asset had been torn away from him – he was no longer the one and only person without whom the prince was helpless. The prince wanted to keep Skoliński here! And what a tone of voice he'd used!

What was he to do? He laid the prince on the bed and ran back to the professor.

'You're to be gone in five minutes!'

But the professor shook his head. He was very serious.

'I'm not leaving.'

'What's that?! You're not leaving?'

'You heard me being invited by the prince.'

'But he's a madman!'

'If he's a madman, he should be declared legally unfit. For the time being I am here, and I have no intention of moving! I'm not going until the prince clearly demands it.'

'Are you planning to take charge of him?'

'Perhaps.'

The professor's decision was irrevocable.

And worse yet – so was the prince's. Cholawicki tried in vain to break through the madman's morbid insistence. After coming round from his faint, the prince sank into a feeble state – the heroic posture he had assumed towards his secretary was beyond his strength after all – with it his fear of Cholawicki had returned and he listened meekly to his stern, severe words. But even so he stuck to his guns, and Cholawicki realized that the prince would rather part with him than with Skoliński. That was that – the professor had wormed his way into the castle, and he'd simply have to come to terms with it.

Cholawicki had just as bad a night as the previous one, maybe a hundred times worse. The two crushing defeats he had suffered – one at Połyka, the other at the castle – had kept him wide awake, even though he hadn't had any rest at all for the past forty-eight hours. Maja! What on earth was wrong with Maja? Why had she run into the forest, why had Leszczuk chased after her, why had she locked herself in her room and refused to talk to him? He'd have to go there first thing in the morning. But if he went, he'd lose control of Skoliński and the prince again. So maybe he shouldn't go?

And on top of these torments came a dull fear of the professor's enigmatic words: 'I'd rather murder someone miles away from this place than commit any far less evil act here. Evil has a special resonance here'. And that towel – endlessly working away, down there in the depths of the castle, in the old kitchen – the thought of that towel inflating, shrinking, moving incessantly . . . while Skoliński, his enemy, was better clued up than he was, knew something that he did not . . .

It was dawn before he finally sank into deep sleep. But at ten Grzegorz woke him. A messenger from Połyka had brought a letter from Mrs Ochołowska.

Rubbing his eyes, only half awake, he tore the envelope open and instantly sobered up. Just a few words, hurriedly scrawled in pencil: *Please come at once. Maja is gone. I am very worried.*

X.

ON REACHING the station Maja told the stable boy to wait a couple of hours, and then return to Połyka at a walk. She was right on time for a train going to Lwów. That was even better than going straight to Warsaw.

In Lwów she had breakfast, and after a long wait she took an express train to Warsaw.

She was sure Leszczuk had gone to Warsaw. After stealing the money he couldn't go back to Lublin, to his club. He must have gone to Warsaw, as he intended – to make his tennis plans come true.

As for her, if anyone had asked why she had run away from home and why she was mindlessly going after Leszczuk, she couldn't have given a precise answer. All she knew was that she couldn't stay at Połyka anymore.

Everyone must have guessed by now that something had happened between her and Leszczuk.

Maja was ashamed – before her mother, Krysia, Żałowski, Cholawicki, the servants, everyone, everyone! The shame was killing her!

No, she couldn't remain at Połyka. Her Połyka days were over!

And besides, things between her and Leszczuk couldn't possibly stay like that, it couldn't end that way!

She had to see him again. See him in a different way. Make sure once again if he really was 'like this', and if she was 'like this'. But the main thing was to go after him. The force driving her on was stronger than she was.

Luckily the compartment was empty. She threw herself onto the seats and fell asleep, stunned by so many sensations.

But she soon woke up, and as if through fog saw a man sitting opposite, watching her.

Maja closed her eyes, doing her best to go back to sleep, but moments later she half-opened her eyes and peeped at him again. He was calmly and sternly looking at her. It was unbearable.

'Excuse me,' said the passenger, on seeing that Maja's eyes were open, 'if I'm disturbing you I'll move to another compartment. The porter brought my things in here before I'd had the chance to choose one.'

His voice was low and very pleasant, and his appearance was marked by great refinement. There was no hint of any improper intentions in his manner. Maja immediately felt like a lady, which delighted her beyond words.

'Thank you,' she replied. 'I shan't sleep anymore.'

Plainly the stranger wanted to say something, but he was holding back. She noticed this, and once again felt deep satisfaction, as well as something like gratitude. She had been through so many humiliations of late that she found the spiritual comfort emanating from her unknown travelling companion extremely nice. She sat and gazed at the countryside flying past.

'Do forgive me,' he said, a little embarrassed, 'but you've cut yourself. Blood . . .'

She quickly raised a hand to her mouth. A small cut sustained yesterday in the forest had opened – suddenly she realized she was sitting here before him covered in bruises and scratches.

Her mouth was bleeding. She started looking for a handkerchief.

'Oh yes, I fell off a horse.'

'Please help yourself to some eau de cologne. It's nothing serious, but while travelling one must be careful.'

He was doing his best to conceal the extent of his interest in this beautiful young girl.

Who could she be, with this astonishing mixture of innocent girlishness, womanly refinement, and something unusually brutal that was not just apparent in the wounds and bruises but also in her entire manner?

For some unknown reason he felt extremely sorry for her, and to save her embarrassment he hastily said: 'You must have taken a bad knock. I once fell off a horse onto some stones and smashed up my face.'

Maja went back to looking out of the window. How quickly the trees flew by! The day was sad, rainy, and the slippery chessboard of fields flashed past monotonously to the steady beat of the swaying coaches. What on earth lay ahead of her in Warsaw? And what would her mother say?

She took out a pencil and wrote on some pages torn from a notebook.

Mama!

Don't hold it against me. I've taken the money and I won't be back in a hurry. Please don't look for me. I've made up my mind.

But I haven't run away with anyone, just on my own, and on that I give you my word of honour.

I want to be independent. I have to start living a different life. I don't want anyone – especially you – to be watching over me and worrying about me. I must spend some time living entirely among strangers.

Tell Cholawicki that I'm breaking it off.

Tell the others any fairy tale you like about my sudden departure.

Dear Mama, I know what my leaving means for you, but I had to go. You don't know what happened to me. When I come back, I'll be happy to tell you, and we'll live together differently from before. It's not just my fault.

Maja

Once she had read through this rather vague message she decided to add some more:

I must be sure what I'm really like. I must find out what sort of a character I have.

And under that, she nebulously added:

I'm afraid I'm much worse than I thought. But in any case, a thousand kisses – please know that there was more love in me for you than you think. It's just that I didn't know how to show it.

She put the letter in an envelope.

And so she took the theft committed by Leszczuk on herself. But weren't they jointly guilty of stealing? Hadn't she incited him to do it?

They were coming into Warsaw. For some time the young man kept his calm, stern gaze fixed on Maja as she walked among the crowd down the station steps – until she disappeared from view. He whistled through his teeth. His heart ached with unbearable sorrow.

•

Maja had decided to reside for the time being with her friend Róża Włocka. She couldn't stay at a hotel because she only had about a hundred and fifty zlotys, including the hundred dropped by Leszczuk. She was also hoping Róża would find her a job to enable her to earn the money for her keep.

She and Róża had been quite close friends at boarding school, though Róża was almost three years older. It was about a year since Maja had been in direct contact with her, but they'd corresponded – though not often.

From these letters she knew that Róża was a student in Warsaw at the university, and that she occupied a little room on Krucza Street. At first Róża had complained of loneliness and boredom, and was determined to go home to her parents, who had a watermill and a sawmill near Tarnów, but then her letters had become more animated.

She wrote that she had moved to Czerniakowska Street and had formed some very pleasant relationships, about which there were lots of rather mysterious hints in her correspondence, supplied with equally foggy comments that 'one should know how to get by in life', that 'it's not worth getting upset', et cetera, et cetera.

Aware of Róża's modest means, Maja was sure the room on Czerniakowska Street would be nothing special in terms of size or luxury, and she was also afraid of causing her friend serious inconvenience.

But Róża received her with open arms. The room was wonderful. It was really a separate small flat with a tiny hall and a bathroom in one of the new houses in the district. Full of sunlight and air, it had a huge balcony with an extensive view.

'We'll fit splendidly!' exclaimed Róża. 'But without the formality! You could live at my place for a hundred years! So what brings you to Warsaw?'

'I've run away.'

'You've run away from home? What a story!'

'I've quarrelled with my mother and broken up with Henryk.'

'Have you gone mad? Why? Maja! Did he mess you up like that? You're all covered in bruises!'

'There was a jealous scene.'

'Aha! Well, then I'm not surprised you've broken up with him. Are you involved with someone else?'

'Yes, but he's married,' lied Maja, 'and he has to get divorced first. It'll take a while. Meanwhile I must pay my own way, you see? I can't accept money from home or from him.'

'Pooh! Easily done.'

The two young ladies inspected each other closely.

'You've changed,' said Róża.

'You've changed,' replied Maja like an echo.

Indeed, Włocka seemed completely different. Maja had known her as a shy, pretty but not very striking girl, but here before her stood a charming young woman, superbly dressed, fragrant with cosmetics, relaxed and self-confident.

She laughed, her eyes shone, she talked a lot and fast. But oddly enough, this gaiety was quite sad, as if at any moment she might break down into bitter weeping.

On examining Maja, Róża may have come to some conclusions too, because they both lost their high spirits and something unsaid was left hanging in the air. They both went on talking a lot and at length, but the conversation hovered on the margins of the things each of them was concealing. In fact they were sounding each other out, to see how far they could be frank with one another.

Next day at around noon Maja went out and spent a long time wandering the streets almost mindlessly. The bruises had faded during the night and now she looked passable.

Finally she headed towards the tennis club. She was welcomed enthusiastically. As a young champion, her position in the sporting world was very strong.

'Who's this?' cried the male champion Wróbel, running off the court to greet her. 'Dear God in Heaven! Our darling Maja's come! Here for the match, eh?'

'What match?'

'Don't you know? We're gearing up for the Dutch. The Davis Cup. I bet we'll smash them three-two, you'll see! But how come you don't know? What planet are you living on, lassie?!'

He had to go, because they were calling him from the court.

'Stop flirting, Wróbel! Let's play!'

Maja said hello to the manager, Mr Brzdąc, who was supervising the boys spraying the courts. From him she found out that Leszczuk had indeed reported to the club the night before, and wanted to talk to the owner, Mr Ratfiński. But as Mr Ratfiński was away, he'd been told to come back in two days' time. Had he left an address? No, he hadn't.

'Don't tell him I asked about him,' she said casually. 'He wants to join. He asked me for patronage, but I couldn't really recommend him! So is Klonowicz here?'

'He's just coming out of the locker room.'

Klonowicz was a candidate for the fourth racket in the match against the Dutch, but his participation hadn't yet been decided.

'Just imagine, I still don't know a thing! Between you and me, this place is a proper nest of intrigue. Plenty of backstabbing – what joy! Would you believe I was told that apparently Dymczyk has been trying to turn Wróbel against my playing. And it's a known fact that everyone counts on Wróbel's opinion.'

'That's nothing, it's the same everywhere, there's no need to get upset! In any case, there are new recruits on the way.'

'New recruits?' said Klonowicz sourly. 'I've not heard. There's Wróbel, Gawlik, Lipski and me, and apart from that nobody, because Wodziński is decidedly overrated.'

'On Thursday a new recruit is going to apply. He's called Leszczuk and he has major aspirations. Apparently he's a first-rate talent, but he lacks polish. That's what Brzdąc told me just now. Who knows if he won't come in handy for the Dutch.'

'What do you mean? That's impossible! What the hell?! On Thursday? At what time?'

'At six.'

Klonowicz said goodbye with a rather uneasy look on his face. Maja was sure he'd 'take care of' Leszczuk appropriately and do everything to prevent him from joining the club. And that was her aim!

If he were to get into the club and make a sporting career, he'd gain a different outward appearance – he might become one of those cultured, well-dressed young men with whom she socialized. And then she might not be able to resist the 'similarity' that was pushing her towards him.

'No, no, better not.'

At the flat she found a young blonde, lying on the couch with her feet on a table, whom Róża introduced as Miss Izabella Krzyska, a friend from the university. Maja noticed at once that Miss Krzyska was a striking beauty. She had huge blue eyes and a dazzling complexion – her teeth, ears, hands and feet completed the splendid whole.

'Do let's be on first-name terms,' suggested Miss Krzyska right away. 'I can't bear formality.'

Meanwhile Róża had fetched out a bottle of liqueur and offered it to her friends. Maja, who had met two of Róża's friends before now, was surprised they were all so pretty, but she didn't say a word.

For some time she'd been on her guard against Róża. She felt she was always circling around a topic that she didn't want to bring up directly. As a result they were treating each other with caution, because Maja had her own secrets too.

In the past they had hidden nothing from each other. They both knew they had changed a lot in the meantime, but neither of them was sure if the other had changed enough for them to be able to unburden themselves with total sincerity. They didn't know how to form a relationship on this new and altered footing.

Maja could see that Róża was somewhat embarrassed by the over casual behaviour of the little blonde, who was describing yesterday's outing to Wilanów in the company of some industrialists from Katowice. What's more, Miss Krzyska was examining Maja in every detail too, and was amazed by the bruises as well as the sudden changes in her voice – such as when she said 'nooo', or when her eyes betrayed something mysterious and evil, known only to herself.

And so these three Graces eyed each other, trying to tell if they could trust one another – each burdened with her own secrets, her own separate flaw.

'Come dancing with us,' said Róża to Maja. 'We're going with those acquaintances of Iza's, the managers of a factory in Katowice, they're here on a short visit and they want to have some fun. In any case the Chairwoman – Mrs Halimska – is coming with us,' she added, 'they're actually her acquaintances.'

'Who exactly is Mrs Halimska?' asked Maja.

'A very nice person and my great friend. You're sure to like her. Well? Agreed? It'll be good for you to meet her, she might be able to help with your plans. She's well-connected.'

At half past ten all three, accompanied by two older, very smartly dressed gentlemen and the extremely majestic Mrs Halimska, walked into the capital's most fashionable nightclub.

Maja had been expecting some nice, solid Silesians – meanwhile both representatives of heavy industry looked exquisite in their dinner jackets, and one of them was actually a Swede or a Dane and hardly spoke a word of Polish. Mrs Halimska turned out to be Russian by origin and combined eastern exuberance with west European gentility.

Wine appeared, and a light, refined conversation was soon underway. Maja was a little dazed by the play of lights and sounds, and the whirl of the dancing couples.

Soon two more gentlemen came to join them. One was a secretary at one of the embassies, and the other – a balding, rather sallow blond – was called Szulk and seemed to be a close friend of Mrs Halimska.

After midnight, two more ladies appeared in the company of a count, and once again Maja was surprised by their exceptional beauty and elegant, though modest gowns.

At the two little tables they occupied there was not – apart from Mrs Halimska – a single woman who failed to display outstanding charms, but this group of beautiful ladies from society made quite the opposite impression on Maja than it should have – of something suspect and tasteless – though their behaviour was beyond reproach.

Everyone's gaze was on them, and soon another gentleman came to join them – a stout, red-faced old boy who was received with great honours, and addressed as 'Minister'.

Maja had been taken up by the embassy secretary, enchanted by her perfect French. She danced a lot and drank a good deal, until Mrs Halimska leaned towards her and said: 'Let's not overdo it, my child.'

'Noooo,' said Maja, her head spinning.

Another foreigner appeared, a long, thin, serious Englishman. Meanwhile Mrs Halimska had embarked on a long conversation with Maja on general topics – she was kind and benevolent. But at one moment, when Krzyska began to laugh too loud under the influence of alcohol, Mrs Halimska said to her with mild emphasis: 'Tidy your curls, my child.'

Iza instantly sobered up.

And then came more dancing in a crowd that formed a single, large body, circulating heavily, arduously and fitfully. And there were lights, noises, fumes of alcohol, a nervous, agitated atmosphere in which Maja was getting lost – and was losing her memory of the things that had brought her here.

She came to. Standing beneath a pillar by the entrance to the bar was the stranger she had met on the train. His gaze sobered her up in an instant. She noticed that the diplomat was squeezing her a bit too tightly as they danced, so she moved away from him. He cast her an indignant look and immediately stopped dancing.

'I'll escort you to the table,' he said drily.

She was annoyed. What on earth did he imagine?

'Escort yourself as far from me as possible. I care about keeping my . . . distance,' replied the old Miss Ochołowska in her.

And to be rid of him she walked up to the stranger.

'Good evening, sir. We meet again.'

'Are you with that company – over there at those two tables?'

'Why do you ask?'

'Because I don't like that company.'

'Why not?'

'Too many foreigners. Too many dignitaries. And too many beautiful women, just like you.'

'Just like me, meaning like what?'

'Not so much depraved as being depraved.'

'How dare you?!'

He looked her in the eyes.

'Don't lose your way.'

'Nooo, I'm not losing my way, I'm just dancing.'

'And do you know what I'm doing at this moment?'

'You're standing here talking to me.'

'Oh no, not just that.'

'So what else?'

'I am showing you respect,' he said emphatically. 'Please know that I truly and sincerely respect you. You are worthy of it, and anyway it's my duty.'

The blood flowed to Maja's cheeks.

'I have no need of your respect!'

'That is not true, because you are greatly in need of respect. Anyway, it makes no difference. I respect you, and I shall always respect you, regardless of whether or not you want me to.'

She looked at him. Could he be trying to catch her out with respect? No. His entire figure, his strong, determined gaze and the shape of his head all inspired remarkable trust. He was exquisite – in the spiritual regard. Such a man might unexpectedly bestow his respect on someone, and this gift should be accepted, because it was a genuinely serious gift.

'Are you leaving already?' she said with regret when he bowed to her in silence.

'I have nothing to do here.'

'Please wait a moment,' she whispered, looking around anxiously. 'I'd like to have a chat with you. Come to the café here, upstairs, the day after tomorrow. At five.'

'All right.'

'Did you meet someone you know?' asked Mrs Halimska when Maja got back to the table.

'Yes,' she replied.

'Oh, you should have introduced him to me. Please don't be upset with me, my dear, but as I am the only older lady in our company, in a way you are all under my protection. I have nothing against fun, but one must observe form. And as for that foreign fellow,' she said, smiling, 'you dealt with him perfectly! I saw. These gentlemen must be kept on a tight rein. It's plain to see that you have breeding, tradition and a good upbringing behind you.'

At about four in the morning one of the industrialists settled the bill and the company left the club. Blissfully, Maja drew the invigorating early morning air into her lungs. The working people – janitors, labourers bowed over the tram lines and a few passers-by hurrying to their occupations at this early hour – paid no attention to the crumpled shirt-fronts and faces of the people getting into cars. They were used to this sight.

Before going to bed they sat a while on the large terrace, from where they could see the Vistula and the Saska Kępa district.

'Well, then?' asked Róża.

'Would you like me to be frank with you?'

'Of course!'

'The whole thing seems to me quite dubious.'

Róża laughed.

'You're right! It is dubious. Maja, give me your word of honour that you won't blab to anyone, and I'll tell you what it's about. Well? Word of honour?'

'Yes.'

'Catch!'

She tossed her an orange, peeled another one, and with her mouth full said: 'You see, it's the Mutual Aid Association, founded by the Chairwoman. Ha, ha, ha! Maja, God knows what you're imagining, but there's really nothing wrong with it, It's just Mrs Halimska's brilliant idea.'

Indeed, Madame Chairwoman's idea was innocent and brilliant all at once. The point of it, quite simply – as she herself put it – was an exchange of services, based on rational, civilized principles.

Rich industrialists, merchants and other globetrotters who came to Warsaw were eager to have some fun in the city, but most of them didn't have the necessary acquaintances.

At best they were condemned to consort with taxi dancers or other women of dubious morals, which after all – explained Róża – could be neither advantageous nor pleasant for them. Far nicer to go to a nightclub with a person from society – that meant an entirely different atmosphere.

'So you see: we give them our company, and they provide us with entertainment. It wouldn't be possible without Mrs Halimska. She has a superb reputation and she protects us from being compromised. She really is extremely tactful, and she knows just how to keep the right measure in everything. You saw for yourself that she can't be faulted in this respect. She has very wide-ranging connections, she has expert knowledge of people and she won't admit anyone who wouldn't know how to behave properly.

'Besides, she's already managed to bring together a team of very handsome young ladies and young divorcées from good homes. A crowd of pretty women has great magnetic force. You have the best proof in that even a government minister – in fact he's an ex-minister, but still – came to join us. That allows Mrs Halimska to keep making new acquaintances in reliable circles, and to act as a bridge between people who need each other – which brings her great advantages, strictly within the limits of decency, of course, for she is a very respectable woman in every regard. We are a sort of bait.

'I tell you, six or seven very good-looking and well-bred girls are a force that nothing can resist,' explained Róża excitedly. 'Old men and young want to join our company. The Chairwoman has organized this force and benefits greatly from it, and in exchange she helps us and provides for necessary expenses. Because frequenting nightclubs means we have to be well-dressed.'

'So you take money from her?'

'Well, actually, no. But sometimes. After all, if she gives us any, it's because it pays off for her. There's nothing wrong with that. It's a fair exchange. If I didn't take it from her I'd be completely dependent on my parents.'

'Do you want to know my advice? To hell with this association.'

'You're a fool! In the first place it's not an association – we just call it that as a private joke. And secondly there's nothing wrong with it. Anyway, I'm certainly not going to the coffee shop for a demitasse with the students! And finally . . . Maja, she liked you very much. She could come up with a job for you and help you in general. If you've broken with Połyka, there couldn't be a better opportunity for you.'

She looked at her keenly and with some anxiety.

'All right,' agreed Maja unexpectedly. Róża hid her astonishment. *This Maja is truly inscrutable. Seconds ago she turned up her nose, and now she's agreeing. What sort of a devil does she have inside her?* Maja's face was almost lifeless, without expression, but her lips were painfully twisted – and then all of a sudden she yawned.

'Let's go to bed.'

Next morning they went to see Mrs Halimska at her small but beautifully furnished flat on Kredytowa Street. The official purpose of the visit was to ask her to find a job for Maja, who had unexpectedly found herself in an awkward situation.

'Most willingly, my child, just come to the Europejska café tomorrow evening and I'll introduce you to a highly influential tycoon who's a good friend of mine. He will open many doors for you. But naturally, it goes without saying, people must help each other.'

They said goodbye very politely.

That evening Róża came home from the city in an excellent mood.

'You've made a conquest,' she said. 'She's very interested in you. Just imagine, the tycoon you're to meet tomorrow is Maliniak. You know – the one from America, a rich man who has come to Poland to invest capital and set up car production. I was at her place an hour ago to find out. She says you are the best of all of us, because you have exceptional charm and – how did she put it? You've got everything in you – child, lady, vamp, girl from a good home, even lass from the common folk – which makes you madly interesting. You know what, to hear that sort of compliment from such a connoisseur is quite something,' she concluded, embracing Maja in order to hide a hint of displeasure that she couldn't hold back. 'Aha! And there's something else as well! Dress as modestly as possible. She loved your frock too.'

'I'm very grateful to you,' said Maja. 'I can't think what I'd have done without you.'

They exchanged kisses. But they both knew that their former genuine intimacy had gone for good.

Self-interest had crept in between them, and on top of that they no longer trusted each other. In fact, Róża was surprised Maja had agreed to Mrs Halimska's help so easily, and for her part Maja suspected that Róża had gone further down this slippery slope than she would admit. Each was secretly amazed by the other, and even mildly despised her, but it suited both of them that the other was as she was.

Maja couldn't decide whether or not to go to the meeting with Mołowicz – as her mentor from the Café Club was called. What for? Just to tell him she'd become seriously involved with the society that he so disliked? She couldn't actually mention it, as she'd given Róża her word.

But on the other hand, the last thing she wanted to do was to mislead him by pretending to be different than she really was. His honesty compelled her to be honest too.

And on top of that she was afraid he would fall in love with her. She knew the force of her charm, and ever since she'd started rolling down an incline, it felt as if this force had grown even stronger. But for all the world she didn't want him to take a serious interest in her, because she couldn't possibly reciprocate or accept him as he deserved.

But as a result, she went. Oh, just to spend an hour with someone who wasn't suspect, dubious, compromising or compromised – who was neither Leszczuk, nor Cholawicki, nor the Chairwoman, nor Róża, nor finally herself, Maja.

'Hello, I thought you weren't coming.'

'I am a little late. I spent about half an hour over there, at the street corner.'

'Why did you do that?'

'I was wondering whether to come or not.'

'Better for you that you have come.'

'Maybe better for me, but worse for you.'

She felt sudden anger towards him. His tone seemed too self-confident – as if he were looking down on her, from the heights of his unswerving morality. What right did he have to speak to her

like that? Deep down she was willing to award him that right, and
that annoyed her even more.

'Why do you think it's worse for me?'

'Because I don't know if I'm going to improve in your company,
while you might lose a lot in mine.'

'Don't you think it might be the other way around?'

'Nooo . . .' She burst into reckless, hungry, insatiable laughter.
Leszczuk had once again taken control of her. Once again she was
'like' him. She sensed it with painful delight.

They sat on the veranda. It was drizzling and the day was foggy –
the trees, as if cringing, were dripping with water. Here and there in
the sky the wind was ripping up the monotony of clouds, and white
wisps stood out against the sad, leaden firmament.

Under this pitiful sky Maja's hungry laughter moved him deeply.

'Do you know what I think?' he said.

'What?'

'I think you're possessed.'

'What do you mean? By an evil spirit?'

'Not necessarily an evil spirit. One can be possessed by an evil
person too.'

'Ooo, don't you get stuck on me!'

He was taken aback. That was almost vulgar. That was how a girl
from the lower classes might respond – it wasn't in tune with Maja.
Whence this coarse, boorish accretion – where had she learned
that? But he noticed that she was looking sullen and irritated – so
he decided not to talk about her.

He skilfully steered the conversation onto general lines. He started
talking excitedly about art, poetry, politics and social issues, about
the thousand tasks that the modern era laid before the younger
generation.

He spoke with sincerity and gravity, and several times Maja let herself be carried away by his enthusiasm, putting in a couple of comments that showed intelligence and sensitivity.

He was pleased. His eyes shone; noticing that she understood him he carried on with even more ardour.

Maja was reacting not so much to the content of his argument as to his way of talking. To the friendly way he leaned over the table, to the low, refined sound of his voice, to the confidence with which he was treating her, and especially the indefinable inner decency of a true gentleman. She could breathe. Ever more sincerely, ever more freely she could breathe.

She was grateful to him for only bringing up general topics and not forcing her into lies she couldn't possibly utter.

He started telling her about himself. He was a recently qualified architect and was going to devote himself to urban planning. He talked with passion about the crazy expansion of Warsaw, and about this marvellous testimony to the vitality and resilience of the nation whose heart – Warsaw – was becoming mightier by the day.

He spoke about the problem of workers' housing, about communications, about how Warsaw had finally found itself an administrator who knew how to channel its blind strengths into an organized course – and the resulting benefits for the general good.

'You're not listening,' he suddenly said.

'What do you mean?!' she replied briskly. She didn't want him to think her impolite. What she liked best about him was that – with him – she had to watch out and keep an eye on herself.

'Why don't we go for a walk?' he suggested. 'The rain has stopped.'

They walked by the river, towards Poniatowski Bridge. Maja was deferring to him more and more. She felt obliged by his undeniably high standards, and wanted to keep him with her in that way.

He understood this, and imperceptible sparks of deep satisfaction flashed in his eyes.

Suddenly she became anxious and impatient.

'I must go now!'

'Where?'

'Oh, isn't it all the same to you? Anyway,' she said slowly, leaning on the bridge railing, 'you've only just met me . . . You don't know anything about me . . . How can you know what I'll be doing in a while?'

He fixed his keen, penetrating gaze on her. He took hold of her hand.

'Excuse me, but there's one thing I'm sure of – you won't do anything you'd have to be ashamed of,' he said.

'From what do you draw that conclusion, if I may ask?'

'From your appearance. A person has their character written in their face.'

Just then in his face Maja saw . . . stupefaction. She couldn't understand what was wrong with him. He was staring at her open-mouthed.

She hopped on board a tram that was just moving off and simply called from the platform: 'Day after tomorrow at five!'

She went to the tennis club. Once again she reminded the manager to be sure to get Leszczuk's address. She absolutely had to see him! To meet with him – to check up on herself – to make sure there was no connection between them, and that it was all an illusion totally devoid of foundation. Though Leszczuk wasn't due to report to the club until tomorrow, she waited in the street for quite a long time, in the hope that he might come along, and at first glance she'd be able to confirm they had nothing in common.

But Leszczuk didn't come.

That night Maja went to the Europejska café. She soon spotted Mrs Halimska, sitting with Maliniak underneath one of the enormous mirrors that made the room appear to stretch into infinity. Maliniak had grey hair – this detail surprised and embarrassed her – he was a man of over sixty, as white as milk, slim and straight as a reed.

Mrs Halimska greeted her as if they'd known each other for ages.

'My dear Maja,' she exclaimed with a Russian accent, 'allow me to introduce you, Mr Maliniak. What brings you here, my child?'

They had agreed that their meeting would appear accidental.

Maliniak stood up with difficulty and offered her his hand without saying a word. The waiters were buzzing around the millionaire with special servility.

Taking no notice of Maja at all he ordered two soft-boiled eggs and radishes, lengthily making sure in the process that the eggs were entirely fresh. He started eating, and did it with total ruthlessness, hardly responding to the Chairwoman at all, as with great mastery she tried her best to maintain the appearance of a genial conversation. Once he'd finished – a good ten minutes later – he addressed the ladies just as abruptly as unceremoniously.

'Right, I'm off,' he said and took a deep breath. He needed air.

'What on earth?!' cried the disconcerted Mrs Halimska, whose long story he had interrupted. 'You want to leave us already?'

'I'm off. My niece is sitting over there.'

He pointed. At a table by the opposite wall sat an elegant lady, closely observing Maja. Maliniak stood up. Without looking, he offered his hand to the ladies, and leaning on the arm of a page boy he crossed the room.

He didn't pay the bill for Mrs Halimska. Maja hadn't had a chance to order anything. The maître d'hotel came up to them, and with the most respectful familiarity consoled Mrs Halimska by saying: 'Mr Maliniak only ever pays for himself. And he has never tipped the staff a single penny. He thinks everyone has as much money as he has.'

The Chairwoman found it hard to conceal her irritation and disappointment. Outside she coldly addressed Maja: 'Well, it didn't work. You did not prompt any special interest in him, my child.'

Maja's hand began to itch. How dare this swindler talk to her like that? She remembered Mołowicz's tough, unsullied gaze. *So I'll give her a piece of my mind and leave. Enough of this filth!*

Suddenly she went pale and her face crumpled as if she'd been slapped.

In the crowd coming out of the nearby cinema a familiar back, a nape flashed past . . . She thought she recognized . . . The same gesture, the laugh . . . Maja lunged forwards. No! It was a workman walking along with a vulgar girl who was guzzling boiled sweets out of his jacket pocket.

Close up he was nothing like Leszczuk. But Maja was quivering like an aspen. Only now did she realize how violently she had raced forwards – how she had lunged frenziedly towards that gesture and that laugh, which reminded her . . .

'Do not fly off like that, I haven't your legs!' said Mrs Halimska, offended. 'And you are not listening to me. My child, if we are to live in harmony, I'd advise you to take more notice of what is being said to you.'

'Excuse me,' said Maja meekly.

XI.

LESZCZUK had fled from Połyka barely alive. The money he'd stolen was burning him like fire. And he was even more agonized by the thought of the squirrel – he couldn't forget the little creature's dying eyes and its final spasm of pain. Every time it came to mind his fists clenched as if ready to thump Maja again.

She had brought him to this! It was all because of her! She wanted to ruin him! She was mean and evil – there were no words for how depraved she was! He couldn't understand it, but at the memory of the scuffle in the forest he went cold, as if it were the work of Satan. The very idea that he could beat someone up like that! And then he'd taken the money . . .

But just as when he'd entered her room at night he'd been sure she wouldn't try to stop him, or betray him with a scream, now too he was sure she would do everything she could to avoid having to explain the theft.

And even if he were caught and sent for interrogation, he'd be in a position to compromise her. No, neither Mrs Ochołowska, nor Cholawicki nor Maja was going to prosecute him – they were too well aware that the young lady did not have a clean conscience.

And he needed the money like anything! Without it he couldn't go to Warsaw.

For Leszczuk, tennis was now a matter of life and death. There was nothing else to protect him from Maja's toxic spell. It was the only thing preventing him from going to rack and ruin and giving him the strength to run away from her.

Feeling extremely nervous, he went to the club to keep his appointment. There his fate would finally be decided.

He arrived at least an hour too early, so he took a seat in the stand for the main court and watched the players. It was an amateur match of no special standard. But these players soon went off, and then the top stars came onto the court.

Leszczuk had no trouble recognizing Wróbel and Gawlik, whose photographs he had seen in the magazines. He followed their playing in suspense. For him, each stroke was an opportunity for some high-speed self-examination – *can I play like that, can I possibly do it?*

Their game was much more powerful than Maja's – either of them could have beaten her. And yet their balls were not entirely unreturnable and they made lots of mistakes, obvious even to him. In any case, he now felt confident that his own game against one of these champions wouldn't cause a scandal – it would end six–three or six–four, he reckoned.

'Mr Brzdąc will see you now.'

The ball boy showed him to the buffet, where Mr Brzdąc introduced him to the administrator, Captain Ratfiński. Leszczuk timidly stammered his request, saying he'd come from the provinces and wanted to demonstrate his playing, knowing that the club was looking for new recruits.

The players gathered around them with glasses of lemonade in hand and towels slung over their shoulders. Leszczuk's offer stirred general interest, but wasn't taken very seriously.

'Please submit an application to join the club in the usual way, signed by two members,' said Ratfiński. 'It'll be reviewed in due course and we'll let you know.'

'I haven't got any money and I don't know any members. I'd like to be accepted straightaway.'

'And why exactly should we make an exception for you?'

'I'm a good player.'

'You don't say?' said Klonowicz ironically.

'I might even come in useful for the match against the Dutch.'

This was greeted by jovial laughter from those present.

'Will you look at him!'

'Where has this prodigy been hiding?'

'Wróbel! At last you've got a partner for the match against Holland.'

'Shh . . . gentlemen,' the captain silenced them, himself somewhat amused. 'Have you ever taken part in a tournament?'

'No.'

'So have you played against any of the reputable players?'

Leszczuk didn't want to mention Maja. He just replied stubbornly: 'No. But I'm a good player.'

Finally the captain grew impatient.

'Excuse me,' he said, 'but just think about it! How can you know you play well if you've never competed against a decent player before?'

'Try me out, gentlemen!' insisted Leszczuk.

At this point, with a smirk on his narrow lips, Klonowicz nudged him.

'Well, maybe we should give it a try?' he said. 'Let's do that for the fellow. But on one condition. Let's play three games on a trial basis, and if you lose all three you'll stop insisting. You see, it's not harassment, we just want to bring you down from the clouds and return you to plain old reality as soon as possible. Do you agree, Captain?'

'Yes!' replied the captain, who was afraid that Leszczuk would never stop pestering him at the club.

Leszczuk looked around in dismay.

'All right, but I'm not dressed and I haven't brought a racket.'

'That's no problem. They'll lend you some shoes in the changing room and you can use my spare racket.'

'Perhaps I'll come back tomorrow.'

'No, right away!'

In the changing room he rigged up a makeshift outfit, but he was extremely dissatisfied. The shoes were slightly too large, and Klonowicz's racket was too heavy. But worst of all, he was wearing an ordinary long-sleeved shirt and suit trousers. He was so accustomed to going about in light tennis clothes that this shirt and the Sunday suit he had put on for Warsaw even hampered him in the street. And at once he knew he'd look stupid in it on the court.

And there was still quite a number of people in the stands who had stayed put, attracted by the unexpected show.

'Let's play!' cried Klonowicz. 'Who's serving?'

'Wait a moment, a few balls first,' shouted Wróbel. 'That's not the way! Klonowicz has been playing all day, and he hasn't played at all! Let him warm up.'

Leszczuk's heart was thumping with all its might. He wiped his eyes because he couldn't see well – he was looking too feverishly, losing his sense of distance and proportion. Klonowicz casually sent across a few balls. They were so careless and feebly hit that not one of them was fit for a proper return.

Nonetheless, he sent them back as hard as he could. His concern was to get into the right ball length straightaway. But Klonowicz didn't hit any of the balls that Leszczuk returned, he just stood on the spot and sent him a few new ones as clumsily as before.

'That's not proper practice,' muttered Wróbel through clenched teeth. 'That Klonowicz is a first-rate swine.'

The Polish national champion had had very difficult beginnings. He knew how hard it was to get started. He suspected that Klonowicz despised his opponent from the very start, and just to amuse the audience was trying to destroy him once and for all by using the tricks and wiles of an experienced player.

They started the match. Klonowicz served first.

Leszczuk stood behind the line, expecting a fast, powerful serve. Klonowicz made the full, classic movement, in American style, Leszczuk leaped forwards and . . .

Klonowicz's ball fell just over the net, bounced aside in an unlikely direction and started rolling along the ground like crazy.

Leszczuk stopped in mid-court, disoriented, and the audience burst out laughing. At the last moment the older player had under-cut the ball using a system all his own, by twisting the racket in his hand. As a result, a swing that appeared to be forceful and normal produced a very weak ball of minimal bounce.

He served the next ball unexpectedly from below. It jumped straight at Leszczuk and hit him in the face, which prompted more gales of laughter.

'That's not how to play!' said Wróbel loudly.

'No, it's not!' said Klonowicz.

And served two more lightning-fast, powerful balls down the lines.

In fact this serve was not all that hard to return but Leszczuk, driven to nervous distraction, failed to reach the first ball at all, and hit the second with the racket frame.

The first game was a love game. The spectators applauded. Even the boy handing Leszczuk the balls was laughing.

Leszczuk's weakest point was his serve. His first balls rarely went right, and his second ones were too easy. This time he knew in advance that his first ball wouldn't go right because it simply couldn't.

He was so badly lost that for a while he forgot how to move, the physical process for hitting the ball. He slammed four balls into the net. The fifth was out. The sixth, soft and gentle, Klonowicz blocked, leaving him nothing to run for.

Only the seventh provided the opportunity for a couple of strokes – but thrown off balance, demoralized and jittery, Leszczuk couldn't muster more than an average performance and Klonowicz easily defeated him.

Damn, thought the boy feverishly.

And had no idea how he managed to serve the next ball. All he knew was that he shrank and then jumped – he hit it in the air with a different motion than usual. The result was a serve like lightning. Klonowicz didn't even move. He almost failed to catch sight of the ball, which landed like a bolt out of the blue.

A stroke of this kind was something quite exceptional – there were only a couple of players in the whole world who could match it.

'Pure chance!' proclaimed the spectators.

Only Wróbel appreciated the exquisite harmony, natural flow and perfection of Leszczuk's action. 'Well, well. That's great!' he muttered.

But it was this success that ruined the novice for good and all. He tried hard to reproduce the stroke. The result was grotesque. Klonowicz had won the second game. The third and fourth looked as if Leszczuk didn't know how to play at all – the balls flew off in every direction, until finally the bored spectators started to disperse; even Wróbel said quietly: 'Well, there it is.'

As for Klonowicz, he was sure Leszczuk had no idea about tennis. The captain went up to Leszczuk and declared simply and tersely: 'Waste of breath!'

Mechanically, Leszczuk went back to the changing room, got dressed, handed in the shoes and racket, and left the club . . . with his mind a blank. He walked slowly towards Chełmska Street where he was renting a tiny room from the family of a minor clerk.

On Puławska Street he stopped for a drink at Łopatka's, a third-rate 'retailer of spirits and alcohol'.

He drank a shot of vodka. It did him good. He had another. Then a large glass of lager, a herring sandwich and two more shots of vodka. Perfect. He drank it all standing up in a couple of minutes. Anything to stupefy himself and forget.

'How much?' he asked.

'Three vodkas, a lager and a sandwich – altogether that's one zloty twenty-five.'

'What do you mean, three vodkas, when I drank four? I'm certain!'

Mr Łopatko raised an eyebrow.

'I can assure you it was three – I should know what I've poured!'

'And I know I had four!'

Łopatko took offence.

'Are you trying to make a fool of me?'

Just then a tall fellow standing next to Lesczuk began to snigger to himself, heartily, yet with restraint. The boy glanced at him.

This was an individual who smelled of perfume, whose hair was pomaded, and who was dressed in formal striped trousers and a pale jacket; he had a charming little moustache on his upper lip, and an aquiline profile.

'What's wrong with you, sir?'

'Hee, hee, hee! Hee, hee, hee! It was my vodka you drank right under my nose! You drank my vodka.'

'Goodness! Then I'm paying for four!'

'Do forgive me, but it was mine, so I shall pay! You don't take money for vodka! Who do you think you're dealing with? You treated yourself to my vodka, so sit quietly and all's well – but don't insult a decent fellow.'

'All right, then I'm standing us two vodkas!'

'Ah, that's quite another matter! Top hole! Allow me to introduce myself. Ewaryst Pitulski, self-made man.'

Mr Pitulski cordially shook Leszczuk's hand and invited him to share yet another drink to return the favour, and then they sat down at a table and ordered two large beers.

Soon a great friendship had blossomed between them. Mr Pitulski hummed to himself, while Leszczuk smiled hazily.

'Let's go for a walk,' proposed Pitulski. 'Now's the most pleasant time. Lilac and willow-green tones, sir, at the onset of evening, plenty of dolly birds and the song of the city in general. Come on! For by temperament I'm a poet! I used to be a ladies' hairdresser, but it's a miserable trade, sir! There are better ones! What is your line of work, without wishing to be indiscreet?'

'Jobless,' he replied curtly. And at once it all came flooding back.

'But what do you live on?'

'Whatever comes along. What about you?'

Pitulski winked knowingly.

'Don't be too brazen, sir! One gets by, and that's all! Oh, but what do I see? A bench, and on the bench a maiden. A dear little cook, methinks, or a little chambermaid. The perfect thing for us! You'll see how I chat her up!'

And taking a seat on the bench, Mr Pitulski set all his skills in motion with such energy that a quarter of an hour later the fat little cook, bewitched and conquered by his flirtatious nose, had not only agreed to go to the cinema with him on Sunday, but had also confided in him all sorts of details to do with her living conditions: where her master and mistress lived, how many rooms they had and how they supported themselves – this was the information that Pitulski extracted from her as she bemoaned the lot of servants in general, and her own lot in particular.

The little cook finally went off, exchanging glances with him and inviting him to visit her in the kitchen – best to come between six and eight, when the master and mistress were in town and she had a bit of peace and quiet.

'That's my business!' said the former ladies' hairdresser proudly once she had vanished out of sight. 'But what do I see? A shop, and outside it a maiden. A dear little cook or a little chambermaid. You'll see how I chat her up!'

After a couple of hours filled with these romantic incidents, thickly interlaced with alcohol, Leszczuk and Pitulski were on first-name terms and had sworn undying friendship! It was all the same to Leszczuk. He didn't want to go home. He preferred Pitulski to his own thoughts. Now and then Maja stood before his eyes, as if real, and he could hear her voice – like the time on the stairs at Połyka, when she'd told him spitefully and pitilessly: 'Every coach imagines God knows what about his own playing.'

He shook himself.

'What do you need these acquaintances for?' he said to Pitulski, who was just bidding farewell to the tenth, perhaps the eleventh victim of his aquiline nose.

'Sucker!' cried Pitulski, reeling badly. 'Sucker!'

'Why so?'

'Marian, old boy, we're friends! Here's my hand on it! Each one of the little ladies means a zloty to me. Eleven little cooks means eleven zlotys! If you like, you can earn money too – indeed, why not? For a friend – anything! Naturally, not everyone has my gift, that's to say, not a single one ever resists me. They go for my nose, because it's prominent, or aquiline, conducive to romance.'

And Mr Pitulski briefly explained the essence of his romantic doings. He discovered all sorts of interesting details from cooks, shop girls, housemaids, milliners and other working women – for which a certain 'gentleman', whose name he refused to divulge to Leszczuk, paid him a zloty a piece.

Pitulski swore that he didn't know why this gentleman needed the information and what use he made of it – he was quite satisfied with fair payment for his work and his talent, and the innate virtues of his outward appearance, especially his nose, which was ideally fit for walks in the moonlight. No! He, Pitulski, never got involved in any shady business!

'But what do I see?' he cried, rambling a bit. 'A bench, and on the bench a maiden! A little chambermaid, or a dear little cook! Hm . . . what do I see? Beside the maiden on the bench is her ladies' handbag. You chat her up, and I'll sit on the other side and peep into her bag.'

By now it was past eleven. They were in Ujazdowskie Avenue, not far from the Belvedere Palace. At this hour the avenue was still quite busy, with plenty of late-night couples occupying the benches.

Leszczuk suddenly sobered up and realized what Pitulski was suggesting.

But at the same moment a wave of memories flooded back to him. Maja stood before his eyes as if real.

He didn't stop to think for long. He went up to the bench and sat down beside the stranger, who was a young blonde in a modest, navy-blue jacket.

Pitulski wandered off down the avenue.

'You're all alone, miss,' Leszczuk began and stopped short.

The girl was crying. A tear trickled slowly down her cheek.

'I'm sorry,' he said, 'I'll leave.'

'Don't go. It's nothing. It'll pass in a moment,' she whispered, as if to excuse herself.

'You'd rather I sat here?'

'Yes, because in someone else's presence I'll stop crying, and I can't stop on my own.'

She burst into a short fit of sobbing. He was amazed by her artlessness.

Is she quite so naïve, or is she trying it on? he thought.

'Why are you crying?' he asked, moving closer.

'I had a quarrel.'

'With whom?'

'With my fiancé.'

'Was it a very bad quarrel?'

'For . . . for good.'

'And where do you work?'

'I work as a waitress at a café. And he's a fitter.'

'What did you quarrel with him about?'

'He . . . started walking out with another girl . . . And he dropped me. Now I'm all alone in the world! Once again I have no one!'

Meanwhile, Pitulski had come into sight and was gradually approaching, his figure swaying gracefully. Once close to the bench he wiped his nose as if preparing for action, and sat down at a certain distance on the other side of the tearful waitress.

'But why are you talking to me?' said Leszczuk. 'How can you know who I am?'

He was very drunk.

At the same time Mr Pitulski subtly began to steer his arm into place and bent forwards. Leszczuk came to his senses.

'Leave off, sir!' he shouted.

The girl shuddered and grabbed her handbag. Pitulski was flabbergasted and, swiftly withdrawing, he stammered: 'Are you off your rocker?'

'Get out of here!'

'Oh, excuse me please!'

Mr Pitulski got up, offended.

'I see that a decent chap should be more careful with whom he has the pleasure. Just look at him! An arrogant puppy!'

His final words resounded from a certain distance, because he was hastily vanishing into the strolling crowd, though his figure was still swaying gracefully.

'You see, miss, he'd have taken your handbag.'

'But you defended me!'

'Well, yes,' he replied hesitantly.

He was confused. He couldn't understand the sudden about-turn that had taken place inside him. He was ready to defend the waitress against the entire world, even against himself.

He walked her home. She lived on Podchorążych Street. Her name was Julia Nowak, and she'd arrived recently from a village outside Płock, where her parents had a piece of land.

With total trust she told Leszczuk how very unhappy she had been in the first few months of her stay. She knew no one, she had no one to talk to, and after work she did nothing but cry and feel homesick.

'I was going to the dogs,' she said, 'until my aunt wrote to my mother telling her to take me home again.'

But just then she had met the fitter, somehow her mood had changed, he had even fallen in love with her and she with him, and they'd become engaged. It didn't matter that earlier on he'd been in love with a girl who'd dropped him and started walking out with another boy instead.

'But when that fellow dropped her, she came back to Władzio, so Władzio stopped walking out with me, and started walking out with her again. I fretted and fretted until I quarrelled and broke with him for good,' she said. 'Just my luck!'

'And where do you work?' she asked.

Disconcerted, for a while he didn't answer.

'Right now I haven't got a job,' he said.

'That's a bad show. What's your trade?'

'I'm a waiter.'

He didn't want to tell her about the tennis. He preferred to mention his other function, which he had performed at Mieczkowski's restaurant.

'I'll find you a job! I have a friend who works at a bar, and she told me they need help for the waiters. She's very fond of me. If there's still a place going, I'm sure they'll take you.'

She was so genuinely pleased that he didn't want to spoil her joy by refusing.

'That's perfect!'

'See what a good thing it is that we got talking! You'll have work!'

They agreed to meet tomorrow afternoon, because Julia worked one day from noon to evening, and the next from early morning to noon – and he bid her farewell before her gateway, as grateful as if she had done him the most incredible favour.

But as soon as they parted, he realized he couldn't meet up with her. What for? After all, she wasn't Maja! And he felt as if there were something wrong with him – increasingly so – and that contact with him was dangerous for this naïve girl.

A thought came back to him. He stopped before the mirror in a shop window and examined his lips. They were normal. Oh well – it could have been pure chance that his lips went blue that time, in the forest; perhaps he'd eaten something that was bad for him? Or maybe it was just that his lips were chapped? They probably weren't as horribly blue as he'd thought at the time. Yet he couldn't forget about it, and on top of all his external cares and anxieties he felt uncertainty about his physical state as well.

He still hadn't fully realized how deeply in love he was with Maja. As a result, he found the violence of his reaction to everything to do with her shocking and surprising. He couldn't understand her behaviour towards him – altogether everything that had happened between them was so remote from normal coexistence that he was hopelessly lost in it.

The similarity, his lips going blue, the weird and unpredictable nature of their relationship, the game of suppressed instincts and passions that had arisen between them – it all wove together into an inexplicable, ominous chain.

That night he had difficult dreams, and he must have tossed and turned in bed, because when he awoke the sheets were in disarray. But the next day – however – he went to meet with Julia. The thought prevailed that she'd be upset if she didn't find him at the appointed place. He didn't want to upset her for anything. There was something about her that made it impossible to hurt her.

And finally he'd had enough of it all! Yes! He'd break with tennis, drop his memories of Maja, and send back the money – he'd get the job at the bar and that would be the best cure for him. Quite simply, he was starting to be afraid of what was happening to him – and he wanted to stop it, change it, and start another life.

An hour later – now hired as a member of the bar staff – he was walking arm in arm with Julia across Krakowskie Przedmieście. As a reward he took her out for lunch, which they ate in the garden of one of the more memorable restaurants.

They had a delicious effect on one another. He was cheerful. He amused her as best he could, and she liked his easy, natural joy. Life seemed plain and simple, and as for him – how distant he was from the Leszczuk who'd fought in the forest . . .

His laughter was different. So was his speech. So were his gestures, and most important of all, his physical and mental state was different. With Julia he didn't feel like an inferior, he wasn't afraid she'd mock him, he understood her – and above all he was good to her, and knew that she was and would continue to be good to him too.

He was showing her increasing interest. Sometimes he felt scared that she was getting used to him and took everything in good faith. Sometimes he thought of warning her that she shouldn't get involved with him.

But he couldn't. He was so concerned about her not feeling lonely and unhappy. Whenever he saw her glowing at every sign of sympathy, he didn't know how to deny her more of them. She meanwhile was pleased that someone was walking out with her, taking care of her – and that she'd never go back to those terrible days of loneliness, the thing she feared most of all.

XII.

EVER SINCE Maja had run away Cholawicki had been torn between her and the treasure. Frantically, he sprang from one of these burning issues to the other, with a permanent sense of doing the wrong thing.

Whenever he sat at the castle, keeping an eye on the prince and Skoliński, he felt as if he were letting Maja go to ruin – he felt he should drop everything and go in search of her, snatch her away from Leszczuk. But whenever he left for a couple of days to look for her, he was assailed by a feeling of the utter hopelessness of these abrupt, improvised searches, and at the same time avarice and anxiety about the treasure bid him return immediately. So a couple of times, as soon as he reached Warsaw or Lwów, he went back on the next train to make sure nothing had happened at the castle in the meantime.

In fact, relations at the castle had settled and normalized – if one can talk of normalized relations between four men who are constantly on their guard against each other and against the grim, quivering thing that no one dared remove. Quivering . . . yes, quivering was probably the main feature of those days and nights at the castle. Each man quivered before each of the others, and on top of that the dusty towel, yellow with age, quivered on a peg in the old kitchen, incessantly and relentlessly.

And at the same time Cholawicki and Skoliński were fighting a silent, clandestine battle for the soul of the madman and for influence over his decisions.

Following his heroic, masterful 'taming' of the secretary, the prince had changed enormously. Skoliński's presence at the castle, and being able to rely on his support against Cholawicki were having a radical effect on his mental state. He had regained his pride and his imperiousness.

And the secretary knew that the prince would never forgive him for daring to threaten him with his riding crop. That had been a fatal error! That had had the most revolutionary effect on the prince's mentality. Thanks to the crop, Holszański had miraculously regained his lordliness! Now he treated the secretary with courtesy, but with majesty too. He gave orders. He expressed wishes – and had recovered his awareness of the fact that he, and no one else, was the master here.

He had also organized their communal existence at the castle. He had assigned Skoliński a spacious chamber not far from Cholawicki's room, given orders for it to be furnished and instructed Grzegorz to take care of the professor's comforts, and had done all this with such consideration and resolution that it looked as if he had returned to consciousness.

But Cholawicki was most shocked when Grzegorz appeared before him in a ceremonial, if faded tailcoat and a pair of ancient white gloves.

'What's this fancy dress?'

'Dinner is served in the Column Hall.'

'In the what?'

'In the Column Hall, at the prince's request.'

Cholawicki followed the butler to the room known as 'the Column Hall' because it was supported by four pillars that held up the Gothic ceiling, and there he saw a table laid for three that created a bizarre contrast with the pitiful state of the walls. Sunlight falling obliquely through the narrow windows bounced off the lavish crystal glasses and silverware diligently cleaned by Grzegorz, and there were flowers in a beautiful Nieborów jardinière.

'Is this party in your honour?' he ironically asked Skoliński, who was already waiting in the hall.

Just then the prince came in – amazingly – not in his dressing gown but in a dark suit, fully buttoned.

'Please sit down, gentlemen,' he said. 'From today we shall dine together. I have come to the conclusion that too much negligence with regard to food and attire is bad for one's health. One should observe a certain minimum of form. Do you see? Good old Grzegorz has even gone to the trouble of providing flowers. What an exquisite thing – flowers!'

And a refined conversation was held over the potato soup and roast meat, which Grzegorz solemnly carried round, quietly snivelling with emotion. After dessert, in the form of several fairly good apples, the prince nodded in farewell to the company and went back to his room.

Cholawicki decided to sit it out. From some of the prince's nervous reflexes he guessed how much latent fear and effort there was in all this. So he was hoping that sooner or later the old lunatic would snap, and then he would regain the advantage.

Skoliński on the contrary was pleased to see these signs of a better spiritual condition, and was trying his best to support them. The bond between him and the prince was the tidying, to which the kindly historian devoted himself with zeal, despite the fact that endless rummaging in a pile of rubbish and refuse was not among the most pleasant of occupations. But it did allow him to spend time on his own with the prince, and to gain ever greater trust.

He was careful not to ask too many pushy questions. Not once did he make the slightest allusion to that nocturnal encounter, when Holszański had demanded a 'sign' and had taken him for a creature from another world. He was waiting for the prince to go back to it first; for now he simply tried his best to win him over by being kind and gentle. And at the same time he looked through the rubbish carefully, in case he might find a document or object that cast light on the tragic story of Franio.

He also observed the prince's reaction to various gestures. As if by accident he would raise his hand, touch his throat, or sneeze – and watch how the prince reacted. But these gestures couldn't have resembled the sign, because none of them produced any effect. Perhaps the prince himself had forgotten what the sign was like? Anything was possible.

But the professor could tell that their relationship certainly wasn't as clear as it might seem on the surface. More than once he caught the prince casting him glances that proved he was watching the professor too, furtively examining him – that he was waiting in a constant state of tension for a revelation on his part.

Most likely, the prince had not entirely dropped the idea that Skoliński was in fact that mystical messenger from Franio, who for reasons unknown did not want to reveal his mission. And so their growing familiarity based on small improvements of a mundane, earthly kind, such as tidying the bedroom, was at the same time imbued with deep mistrust, strain, and anticipation of something 'from the other world'.

Oh, how hard the professor had to exert all his spiritual strength to keep going! This castle, so vast and empty, full of murmurs, endless labyrinths, dampness and depression, could shake the nerves of anyone unaccustomed or unacclimatized. And on top of that came communing with a tragic lunatic on a daily basis. And on top of that, eternal war with Cholawicki, the constant possibility of some underhand trick or attack. And on top of that the menacing towel, the ghastly horror of the chamber! Real dangers were interwoven with madness, insanity – and to cap it all with the bitterness of metaphysical reality – and this world was directly linked with the world beyond in the silence of the ancient interiors.

The professor didn't look into the old kitchen anymore. He didn't want to expose himself to the sensation of disgust and horror. More than once he asked himself why he didn't simply go in there and throw away that repulsive rag. But he was afraid . . . Although he didn't believe the thing was literally diabolical, he imagined some unfamiliar forces of nature must be involved here that required a cautious approach. He knew that at spiritualist séances breaking the chain could cause the illness or death of the medium. Anyway, that piece of cloth was on his side – he was using it to keep Cholawicki and Grzegorz in check. And anyway – and this was the main thing – something was preventing him from going near it . . .

Meanwhile, he had taken steps towards finding Mrs Ziółkowska. She alone could tell him about the 'sign'.

Luckily Cholawicki couldn't cut off Skoliński's communications with the outside world. He didn't want to go far from the castle for fear that Cholawicki would steel himself to do something radical in his absence. But he could take action by letter.

He informed Mrs Ochołowska of his presence at the castle, but without going into detail. He also wrote to one of his friends in

Warsaw, asking him to find and question Mrs Ziółkowska – did she remember what the gesture was like that had unhinged Prince Holszański?

The answer soon came. The housekeeper had easily been found. But she couldn't remember anything.

That was quite natural, after all these years. The professor's correspondent wrote that he had questioned her thoroughly, but she was going senile, and was not particularly intelligent anyway. Yes, indeed, she did remember that when she entered his room the prince had taken fright and started shouting 'the sign, the sign!'. But whether she had made a gesture, and what sort of a gesture it was, she couldn't remember.

'So what now, Grzegorz, my friend?' said the disappointed Skoliński when Grzegorz handed him the letter.

'Oh well, there's no helping it. We shan't find out.'

'We must find out! I'll have to have a chat with her myself.'

'If you go away, the secretary might make mischief!'

The professor braced himself to take a decisive step. If he couldn't go to Mrs Ziółkowska, she could come to him. He instructed his friend to dispatch the old girl to Mysłocz, regardless of the cost.

In strict secrecy from Cholawicki, Grzegorz put her up at the forester's lodge a couple of kilometres away from the castle. The forester was told the old housekeeper had come for a rest with the prince's permission.

Skoliński went to see her at once, that very evening. He found a plump, chubby-cheeked woman, extremely talkative, but senile.

'Why, to be sure, I remember as if it were today. There was flu, the prince was sick and so was Grzegorz, I go in with the coffee – yes, I was carrying a cup of coffee, maybe a tray – a tray sooner than a cup – or maybe a cup – and all at once the prince began to rave and shout, what a to-do! He took me for a ghost! But what sort of a sign had I made? Did I move my hand? Or maybe I nodded my head? Maybe I gnashed my teeth? I've been thinking and thinking but I can't remember, that I can't.'

The professor promised her a generous reward if she could, but the result of this was disastrous. Already agitated by the persistent questioning to which she had been subjected for several days, the housekeeper began to thrash about, trying out the wildest gestures and straining her memory, and consequently became utterly confused.

'Or maybe I raised a foot!'

'Why would you have raised a foot if you were carrying a cup of coffee?'

'Or maybe I grabbed my knee? I may have felt a rheumatic pain in my leg.'

He left her. He tried to slip into the castle without being seen, but Cholawicki must have spotted him through a window, because at supper he asked: 'Have you been out?'

'I went for a short walk.'

But the secretary doubted Skoliński would have left the castle without good reason, not even briefly. Thus they constantly monitored each other and spied on one another's movements.

It had come to a point where they all (because Grzegorz too was keeping an eye on the development of events) spent most of the day dozing, and at night they were on the alert. The night was the most dangerous time. The day was more suited to rest.

The only thing keeping the professor more or less sane was his work on cataloguing and evaluating the antiques. Each day he devoted several hours to this.

What marvels he discovered! From the pictures he moved to the wall hangings, the porcelain, the silverware, and the ancient armour from the sixteenth and seventeenth centuries, discovering more and more extraordinary rarities along the way. A couple of exquisite clocks from the reign of King Jan Kazimierz. Two famous Gobelins tapestries. A collection of priceless old Polish rugs.

And at the same time he made various architectural discoveries. The castle courtyard in particular still bore traces of beautiful but austere architecture. If only it could be restored to its original state, stripped of all the unsightly additions, what a fine residence Mysłocz would be!

Cholawicki assisted his research with bated breath. This was their only connection.

But for his part Cholawicki persisted in his efforts, doing what he could to organize a defence and a counter-offensive.

The whole story of the old kitchen had struck him like a bolt from the blue. Now that he was having to fight for influence over Holszański, he realized how little he knew about the prince's past, and that he had no key to his ailing psyche. He sensed that the professor, despite only having been at the castle for a few days, was much more in the know – he was in possession of some secrets that allowed him to act with a definite plan.

What on earth were those secrets?

Had his night in the old kitchen really given him insight into Holszański's past? Into the mystery of his madness? Was the one connected with the other?

Cholawicki hovered around the haunted chamber like a moth circling a candle flame; he stood in the doorway, closely observing the twitching of the towel – but he couldn't muster the heroism to stay the night in there, to find out something specific at last.

Something was preventing him.

He tormented Grzegorz with requests and threats. But the butler, who since the professor's arrival and the reactivation of the ghosts had been living in a sort of trance, making the sign of the cross a hundred times a day, refused to give him any further information.

'I know nothing! I don't know none of it!'

And so, deprived of any concrete evidence, Cholawicki writhed in powerless rage, feeling that he was losing the ground under his feet and would soon be disgracefully ousted from the prince's favours by his fortunate rival.

His last resort was to spy – relentlessly spy on Skoliński and the prince. Day and night he was on the lookout.

When he discovered that the professor had gone away from the castle, it immediately occurred to him that there must have been a reason. When it grew dark, Cholawicki discreetly set off in the professor's footsteps.

On the wet, boggy ground they were easily visible. Cholawicki had no trouble following them – until they led him all the way to the forester's lodge.

He approached cautiously, regardless of the dogs barking. There was light in a tiny window. At a loss as to what Skoliński could have been doing at the forester's lodge, Cholawicki peeped in at the window, and there he saw an extraordinary sight.

Alone in the room, a plump old woman was performing some sort of spells, or rituals; her face pensive and focused, she twisted her hands, raised a leg, and then grabbed her ear.

Now and then she stopped doing these things, only to start again moments later.

By now the secretary was so steeped in the atmosphere of ghosts that he cringed in terror. If anyone could summon up an evil spirit, it was this sorceress. Could this have anything to do with the haunted chamber?

What could the meaning of these gestures be? Were they spells? Their dreadful foolishness and absurdity only made them all the more uncanny.

From the barn, Matyjas the forester emerged, alerted by the dogs barking.

'How are you,' said Cholawicki. 'Listen here. Who's that woman inside the lodge?'

'If you please, Your Honour, that's the former castle housekeeper, Mrs Ziółkowska. She's come from the city for a rest, and the prince has given orders for her to stay at my place.'

'When did she arrive?'

'This morning.'

'Why is she twisting herself like that?'

The forester burst out laughing.

'Darned if I know! Ever since she got here she's been twirling like that non-stop.'

'Has anyone been to see her?'

'There was a gentleman from the castle. She did even worse contortions in his presence.'

'And who told you the prince had given orders for her to stay with you?'

'Grzegorz came to see me yesterday with these instructions, so I prepared accommodation for her right away, and told the kids they were to make an effort for her because I had to go to the forest.'

Cholawicki did some thinking. So Grzegorz was in league with the professor. They had both brought this woman here and hidden her at the forester's lodge. But what did they need her for? Now he

remembered that Grzegorz had once mentioned this Mrs Ziółkowska, the housekeeper at the castle many years ago.

'Tell her the prince's secretary has arrived and bring her out here.
I want to have a talk with her.'

'Yes, sir.'

Soon after, Mrs Ziółkowska appeared before him in a hat and
gloves, with a coat thrown over her shoulders. She was plainly surprised by this unexpected visit.

'At your service, Mr Secretary sir. Yessir, Mr Secretary sir. You
wish to talk to me, Mr Secretary sir?'

'Why have you come here, madam?'

'I? I? I came for a country holiday. I am in poor health, in a feeble
state . . . Fresh air . . .'

'Come come! You can save your tall stories for someone else!
What's the meaning of all this? What did the gentleman want from
you who came here today? You know who I am! So out with it! I
advise you to speak frankly, or I'll inform the police! Who brought
you here?'

'I've done nothing wrong!'

'I advise you to tell the truth or I'll summon the police.'

The poor, terrified woman didn't put up much resistance. She
confessed all, begging Cholawicki not to tell the professor. She
was innocent! She knew nothing! But the professor wanted her to
remember what sign she'd made twenty years ago when she'd gone
into the prince's bedroom with a cup of coffee. What he needed it
for she had no idea.

Once again she described in minute detail how she had entered
the room, made the gesture that she couldn't remember at all, upon
which the prince had started shouting 'the sign, the sign!', taking
her for a creature from another world.

Cholawicki strictly forbade her to mention their conversation to the professor. Even if she were to remember that gesture, she should pretend she couldn't. With threats and promises he made Mrs Ziółkowska swear to follow his instructions to the letter.

With a sense of relief he went back to the castle. At last he too had found a thread to follow in this labyrinth. His instincts hadn't been deceiving him. The professor and Grzegorz were leading a specific campaign – but what was this sign? And what did they need it for?

He watched the prince even more intently. He remembered something he had occasionally wondered about in the couple of years he had spent with him. He had noticed that during his nocturnal walkabouts the prince would sometimes disappear for thirty minutes or three-quarters of an hour. On many occasions when Cholawicki had looked in on him at night he hadn't found him, either in his bedroom or in the chambers where he usually wandered; only after quite a while had the prince suddenly emerged from God knows where, and every time his mood had undergone a distinct change.

He'd come back less conscious, and in more of a daze.

The secretary hadn't worried about it so far, but now he decided to investigate the goal of these expeditions.

But before that could happen, a trivial incident occurred that also gave him plenty to think about. Next day, when he arrived in the dining room for lunch, hanging on the walls he saw four family portraits of vast dimensions. Four of the grand Princes Holszański-Dobrowicki with the emblems of noblemen in high office, faded, but still exuding the regal purple of their splendid robes.

As if at the touch of a magician's wand, the room had changed its appearance. It had become well-dressed, and at the same time more inhabited.

'What's the meaning of this?' he asked Grzegorz.

'The professor found these old portraits stacked in a pile behind some cupboards, and told me to hang them up to give the prince a surprise.'

Cholawicki bit his lip. Skoliński's strategy was clear to him – to strengthen the prince's sense of family pride and authority, to free him from filth and neglect, and to reintroduce him to the social conventions to which the old aristocrat was so sensitive. The portraits had been hung up for this purpose.

But he dared not take them down. After entering the dining room, the prince behaved strangely. At first he seemed embarrassed, and passed over the portraits in silence. They drank their soup, talking as usual about general matters in an almost courtly tone. Finally Holszański smiled pitifully and sadly.

'Who put these up?' he said.

'I found these portraits while tidying the rooms and took the liberty of hanging them in here,' replied the professor. 'If you do not like them, they can be taken down at any time. There are lots of other portraits too. An entire gallery.'

'Ah, yes,' said the prince, scrutinizing the likenesses of his ancestors with a strange smile on his lips. And all at once he became animated, a blush rose to his cheeks, and his eyes shone.

'This is Józefat Holszański, the governor of Kiev province, my great-great-grandfather in a direct line. He was married to an Ostrogska. And this one's Jerzy, Castellan of Mścisław province, later Field Hetman. And this is the Starost of Pińsk. A famous colonel, a supporter of Zborowski . . . Alongside the Ostrogskis and the Zasławskis my family was the foremost in Ruthenia. You came up with a good idea, Professor. The portraits should be hung. This castle is too large to be populated by no one but the living – many generations are needed to fill it . . .'

He broke off.

'And I am the last of the line.'

Once again a feeble, hesitant smile darted across his lips.

Cholawicki guessed what he was trying to say: 'I am the last of the line . . . an idiot. How do these statesmen, commanders and dignitaries feel when they see the last scion of their clan . . . in this state?' Those were the unspoken words trembling on the prince's twisted lips.

And suddenly he shouted: 'No! Please take them down! I do not want them staring! Please put them back where they were! I do not wish it! But in fact I am not the last! For I have a son too! I have a son. My son lives! Where is my son?!'

He fixed his gaze on the professor, as if expecting a revelation.

He pushed away the table, making the plates rattle, then burst into sobs and raced out of the room, clutching his head in his hands.

'A week more of this treatment and the poor fellow will lose his wits entirely,' muttered Cholawicki ironically.

'I don't suppose so,' replied the professor coolly. 'A shock of this kind often produces the desired effect. I'm hoping the prince will recover his senses soon.'

'I didn't know the prince had a son,' said Cholawicki slowly, examining the professor. 'No one has ever mentioned it to me before.'

'Oh, what he says during these attacks is unreliable.'

'In any case the portraits must be taken down. Put them back where they were, Grzegorz.'

But Grzegorz was in no hurry to carry out the command, and Skoliński said: 'Better leave them here for now, Grzegorz. We'll see.'

The secretary stood up.

'It's true that you're the prince's guest,' he said, reining himself in, 'but that doesn't mean you have the right to give orders. Grzegorz, you heard what the prince said? Please take down the portraits immediately.'

'Young man,' said the professor, 'do as you wish! I am not responsible for your actions.'

'You'd better drop that high-flown tone! I am not a child and I can assure you that I refuse to be intimidated by ghosts.'

'And yet you are afraid.'

'Is that what you think?'

The professor lowered his voice.

'So why don't you remove that towel? If it's all the same to you? If it doesn't make you tremble and cringe inside? What could be simpler than to go in there and throw away the towel?'

The secretary couldn't find an answer.

Indeed, he couldn't steel himself to do it. In vain he had been trying to persuade himself that the presence of evil forces in the chamber was childish nonsense, just grist for the professor's mill, who by blackmailing him with 'ghosts' was gaining the psychological advantage. How many times had he gone up to the door of the old kitchen, stared at that relentless piece of cloth and been unable to pluck up the courage simply to grab it and throw it out of the window.

This impotence was casting a dreadful shadow over all his senses. It was keeping him in constant nervous tension and making him succumb – against his will – to Skoliński's ominous warnings.

What if he were to stay the night in there? To check what the professor could have seen? To know the same things he knew. But he found it even harder to muster the strength for this radical deed.

Did the prince really have a son? Could that be the source of his illness? Was this 'Franio', whose presence he so often imagined, actually his son? These questions tormented the secretary who, feeling that the prince was slipping from his influence, was urgently searching for the key to his soul.

That night he lay in wait in the next room, and when the prince began his nocturnal wandering about the castle, Cholawicki followed him, from chamber to chamber, through desolate galleries and cloisters. As usual, Holszański trailed slowly along the walls, stopping at the windows and whispering to himself, then he came back, lay down on the bed and dozed; half an hour later he went out again, as if driven by rising anxiety.

So it went on until about two in the morning. Doubting the value of his surveillance, the secretary was ready to go off and rest, when suddenly the prince went up to the door of Cholawicki's bedroom and listened. Then he slowly turned down a long, narrow corridor that led to the north wing.

The secretary moved after him. Why on earth was he venturing into this part of the castle? There were only small, cramped, empty box rooms here, clustered higgledy-piggledy on various levels.

But the prince went on, through narrow underground chambers with cloister vaults, and then he glided like a ghost through the enormous rooms in the north wing – the Rose Hall, the Arian Hall and the Knight's Hall.

Like this he went all the way around the castle, ending up near his own bedroom again. But then he turned towards the tower, where the castle chapel had once been.

Cholawicki finally understood why the prince had taken such a roundabout route. It was the only way he could get here without going past the old kitchen, which separated his room from the tower.

But Holszański didn't go into the tower; instead he turned once again and vanished down a narrow passage that led diagonally down to the rooms on the ground floor. This part of the castle, the least protected by nature, was the most solidly built. Stone walls of monstrous thickness rose up, forming cramped recesses, pointless and incomprehensible . . .

The old man went down to the very bottom, all the way to the dungeons, and here he stopped before one of the walls. A groan tore from his chest. He leaned his forehead against the wall and stayed in that position for quite some time. Then he sank to his knees, clutching his head in his hands in a surge of horrible pain.

It was very dark in here. Cholawicki couldn't tell exactly what the prince was doing by the wall. His actions seemed fantastical and meaningless, as if he were feeling the wall with his hands, or scratching on it. The secretary was reminded of Mrs Ziółkowska. This too was something like a made-up religious ritual.

'Franio! Franio! Franio!' the prince cried out in a hollow tone, his voice swollen with agony. And then he spent a long time doing something up against the wall again.

Suddenly he started to whine, softly and painfully, like a dog. Then again he cried: 'Franio? Franio?'

But this time it wasn't a groan, it was a question – the prince was clearly listening for an answer.

'Franio? Franio?'

And then silence. At last Holszański walked away. Crouching round a corner, Cholawicki saw the prince's face as he passed close by – it was in pain, drenched in tears. But what struck Cholawicki the most was that the prince's lips were so dark and bloody that they looked black.

As soon as he had disappeared from sight, Cholawicki ran up to the wall and shone his torch. What he saw was strange.

The prince's mysterious activity turned out to be writing. There on the stone floor lay an indelible pencil – this was what he'd been using to write sentences on the wall.

But they weren't sentences. More like individual letters, scattered in various places without connection, sometimes forming figures, sometimes drawn upside down. It looked like a riddle.

Apart from that, the wall was covered in dark purple marks in the shape of a small heart. Being a man of the world, Cholawicki was instantly reminded of a playful letter he had recently received from a certain lady. Instead of signing her name, this person had kissed the paper hard with painted lips – leaving exactly the same heart shape on the paper.

So the prince had been kissing the wall. After painting his lips with the indelible pencil. There must have been something hidden behind it. But it was made of stone, so huge and solid that no force could possibly disturb it. In any case, there was no evidence of that.

The wall formed an internal partition, dividing one cellar from another. It was extremely thick. Cholawicki peeked into the other cellar, but found nothing significant in there.

The letters on the wall fully engaged his attention. Without a doubt he had discovered the madman's secret shrine, his hidden 'temple of reverie', the place that for some strange reason the prince had chosen as a site for brooding, sighs and confidences. The recluse with an unhealed wound in his soul confided in a wall – for lack of a better friend.

Clearly he couldn't resist the need to express his secrets. But for fear of anyone discovering his confidences, he scattered the letters and mixed them up – at random, or according to a key?

Luckily, as he'd been terribly bored in the couple of years he had spent at the castle, Cholawicki had become an expert at solving puzzles and rebuses, knowledge that now came in handy.

It was highly probable that the word 'Franio' often recurred in this mystical journal, written on the wall. Indeed, the letter F appeared many times in various configurations.

By seeking out the other letters of this word Cholawicki had no trouble deciphering the prince's method. But he could only decode a few sentences and individual words. The rest remained obscure.

Perhaps the prince had changed the key. Or maybe because of his suffering and increasing madness he had drawn the letters haphazardly, forgetting the key he had adopted.

But what he did decipher was enough to understand the nature of the whole thing – and it was a first-rate source of information.

It wasn't a journal or confidences. Messages. Messages to this Franio! The sum of a vast jumble of individual letters was this:

Franio, my son, my one and only child, my boy.

You still cause great pain.

Your Father who loves you.

The prince had been carrying on this simple, unsophisticated correspondence on the wall for many years. The date made that plain – 1926. And further on it said:

Franio, my child, my son.

Still I wait and implore you.

Have mercy, your Father.

And then:

1931

When will you stop tormenting me?

Stop being angry! You are angry.

Are you still moving? I have seen. I looked in there, and I know you are moving.

Oh, when will salvation come?

Was that an allusion to the towel in the old kitchen?

Cholawicki skipped the oldest inscriptions, by now almost entirely faded. He moved on to the newest ones.

Franio, my son, my beloved one and only child.

Was it you who sent him?

Why hasn't he revealed himself with the sign?

Have pity on me.

If he has come from you, let him say.

Release me.

I am old.

Have mercy . . .

Let it end. Release me! Let me go! Forgive me!

Don't be angry.

You are angry!

Cholawicki wrote it all down in a notebook. He hadn't time to analyze the contents of these painful phrases. It was not impossible that the prince would drop in here again.

He examined a box in the corner containing trivial mementoes. A lock of hair, tied with a ribbon. A medallion. A couple of buttons. A few small coins – about two zlotys. A comb.

This was the secret shrine of Prince Holszański . . .

XIII.

Two days after the meeting with Maliniak that had ended so disastrously, Maja received a telephone call from Mrs Halimska, asking her to come and see her on an urgent matter.

The Chairwoman kissed her affectionately.

'Darling girl! Forgive me for being so upset the other day. That Maliniak would drive a saint to distraction! What a peculiar fellow! Can you imagine? It turns out I was wrong, and that both of us misunderstood . . . It's all going perfectly! Read this!'

She showed her Maliniak's visiting card, on which in a barely legible hand was written:

Dear Madam, If the young lady is looking for employment, she can be my secretary. Apply from 4 to 6 at the hotel, Wednesday, to my secretary, Mr Tocki.

'Dear child,' said Mrs Halimska. 'I am so happy. Congratulations! You have won the lottery! You'll be Maliniak's secretary! That's a triumph! The triumph of a lifetime! It will open up all sorts of opportunities for you! And I assumed he wasn't at all interested in you! Honey child, how can I apologize?'

Maja too was pleased by this unexpected success. Her feminine ambition was satisfied, especially with regard to Róża and her friends, who had received her initial failure with latent satisfaction.

But this job prompted her mistrust. Why on earth did he need a female secretary if he already had a male one?

However, Mrs Halimska met her reservations with laughter.

'You're off your head, honey! He's an old man, as you saw for yourself! Be sure that if this involved the least shadow of impropriety, I wouldn't suggest it to you. After all, I'm standing in for your mother!'

'Please leave my mother out of it.'

'How sweet you are to be so attached to your mother! Ah, you charming girl! But believe me, if you're going to be someone's secretary, best of all Maliniak's. An ailing old millionaire with one foot in the grave – you couldn't dream of anything more ideal for a young person. Trust my experience of life. No one could possibly object!'

'All right, but in that case he can hire an experienced secretary, and not me.'

'You don't understand! An ancient millionaire who's staring death in the face has his predilections too. He likes to have freshness and youth around him – for aesthetic reasons. He needs you the way he needs flowers. In fact it would be selfish to deny him possibly the final pleasure in his life. It may even be your duty! Just think how sad he is, how helpless, lonely and abandoned. He'll look at you, listen to your voice, and take care of you, and that may give him his last, pure and gentle joy in life!'

The first thing Maliniak's half Polish, half American personal secretary, Mr Tocki, had to say to Maja when she met him at the Hotel Bristol, was that he had no time for her. It was true, because at least fifteen people were waiting to see him and the telephone kept pestering him. Then he told her that for now she would be receiving five hundred zlotys a month, and that she was to appear at nine in the lobby, as she would be keeping Mr Maliniak company at supper . . .

When Maja asked what her duties were to be, at once he became very polite and looked her imploringly in the eyes.

'If you please,' he cried hastily, 'your first and only duty is not to take up my time. Please do not ever report to me on any account!'

And before she could catch her breath he pushed her out of the door, very cordially pressing her hand.

At nine on the dot Maja, in evening dress, caught sight of Maliniak emerging from the lift with the woman who had been waiting for him that time in the café and who was apparently his niece.

She introduced herself coldly to Maja, placing emphasis on her title: 'The Margravine di Mildi.'

'Come over here,' Maliniak said to Maja and, leaning heavily on the two women, entered the restaurant. He sat down at the far end of it, and from the six waiters who came running he requested two eggs, soft-boiled but fresh, and a small roll. The margravine ordered guinea fowl.

'What for?' muttered Maliniak. 'You'd be better off with an omelette and peas. And have them bring toast.'

The margravine bit her lip.

'And what can we do for you, madam?' the waiter asked, seeing that Maja had been totally overlooked.

'For me? I might also have an omelette . . .'

'Just a minute!' said Maliniak, coming to life. 'Hand me the menu!'

And he ordered a refined, lavish supper for her consisting of several dishes.

Maja did not dare protest. She had to eat everything that was brought to her, although under the hungry margravine's envious gaze her appetite was not great. Maliniak never took his eyes off her plate.

'This too,' he said, pointing at the tastier morsels. 'Good? Eh? And now a glass of wine.'

'I can't eat any more!' she groaned over a bizarre combination of pineapple and fruit-and-chocolate mush, coated in hot liquid.

'What do you mean, you can't? It's good! Eat it up! Zuza, pour the lady some more cream!'

'I really have had quite enough, thank you. I can't.'

Maja said this in such a firm, even slightly superior tone, that the millionaire withheld his efforts.

'What is it? Maybe you came here already full?' he said.

'Indeed, I had a fairly large tea.'

'That's no good. In future you must come to lunch and supper very hungry. I myself cannot eat, because I am sick. But I like to watch someone else eating.'

He became pensive, and for another half an hour or so he sat in silence. No one kept up the conversation. Clearly accustomed to these siestas, the margravine said nothing at all.

She was a fiery brunette of about thirty, with a passionate, secretive face. She made no effort at all to improve the girl's patently difficult situation.

'Well, that's enough,' said Maliniak all of a sudden. 'I'm off. Come tomorrow at . . . let's say four. But you have to be hungry! You'd better not have lunch.'

'And what will my functions be?' Maja dared to ask.

'Functions? Hmm . . . First of all, waiting. You must wait until I summon you. And your second function is eating. My niece the marquise and I like one to eat well. As for your other functions, we'll see. Well, goodbye. Move into the hotel today.'

Maja clenched her teeth.

'I'm not moving in.'

He was already walking away, leaning on a waiter's arm, but he stopped.

'What? Why not?'

'Because I have no intention of being hungry, or of waiting, or generally spending time with you. I resign.'

'Have Mr Tocki give you another two hundred zlotys.'

'I wouldn't stay for two hundred thousand, because you are ill-mannered!'

Maliniak opened his mouth. He hadn't expected this. His lifeless face beamed with deep satisfaction.

'Bravo! Excellent! I like you.'

She stood up.

'Excuse me,' she said, 'but it seems to me that further discussion is unnecessary. I said I'm not staying and I am not.'

'You're giving up your job – in my employment?'

She shrugged and cast him a glance that made Maliniak feel like a nothing, a nonentity, a former émigré. He went crimson, and it looked as if he was going to tear a strip off Maja, when suddenly he noticed the undisguised pleasure visible on his niece's face.

'Hey, Marquise!' he snapped. 'Don't rejoice too soon! She's not going anywhere!'

He took Maja by the hand.

'Let's not fall out! As you can see, I'm an old crank and a lout . . . but I haven't much life left ahead of me. Just a month or two . . . and I can see you need to be treated differently! Please forgive an old man. Come on! I'll have a hard time finding anyone like you.'

He asked her so sincerely that she felt pity.

'All right,' she said.

He started to cough violently. The staff carried, rather than escorted him out of the room. The margravine offered Maja her fingertips in farewell.

'Congratulations, little miss! You've found the best route to my uncle. Keep on like that and you'll earn superb interest on your lack of interest.'

'One does not address me as "little miss" but as "madam".'

'Oh, my God, what a creature you are. I didn't mean to offend you. My uncle loves young things like you that he can incite against me. Maybe you don't realize', she said emphatically, 'that you've been hired specially to annoy me. But it's not so easy to provoke me, and he'll be over it in a week.'

Before Maja had time to reply the margravine had turned her back.

So began Maja's employment as Maliniak's personal secretary. She moved into the Hotel Bristol.

A few days later she had learned her functions. Most of her time really was taken up by waiting. She never knew when Maliniak would summon her to his presence. As she didn't want to sit around in the lobby downstairs, she spent the hours in her hotel room – doing nothing. She had nothing to occupy her, and that tired her the most. She thought about Leszczuk. Eventually the bellboy would report that 'Mr Maliniak requests', and Maja would go to him, never sure how she would be received and what crazy idea would occur to the rich old screwball.

The very next day she'd been persuaded that the marquise was right. Maliniak really did seem to have engaged her to infuriate his niece.

As soon as Maja appeared before him, he subjected her to scrupulous inspection and declared that in his opinion she was not dressed smartly enough. He, Maliniak, liked refinement! He would take the liberty of supplementing her wardrobe – the final months of his life should at least pass in the company of exquisitely dressed persons!

He went to the shops with Maja, and ordered the marquise to accompany them. He started with the head. Soon Maja found herself in possession of several delightful little hats. Seeing Maja's beauty and knowing Maliniak's assets, the owner of the shop brought out all her finest wares.

'You should have a hat too,' he said to the marquise, who was present in the role of someone 'to add taste'. 'I shall choose one for you.'

And he chose her a monstrosity. A hideous, pretentious, overdone hat, in which the unfortunate Margravine di Mildi looked a fright and that aged her by ten years.

'I won't wear that,' she said, white as a corpse.

'What? You won't wear it? It's a gift from me!'

Poor di Mildi had to hide her rage and wear this horror. The same thing was repeated in other shops too. Maja came out of them twice as beautiful – and di Mildi ten times uglier. With subtle spite Maliniak stressed and highlighted her approaching old age.

These are things that one woman will never forgive another. Maja knew that in the person of the passionate marquise she had gained a deadly enemy.

Maliniak's behaviour towards this ageing international tigress really was pitiless. Was he taking revenge on her, suspecting her of looking forward to his death and the chance to bag an inheritance? Maybe he was in love with her and was taking vengeance for that? Or perhaps he just wanted to fill the final months of his life with passion, so he set these two women against each other, one starting out, the other coming to the end? Not only – under the guise of concern – did he condemn his niece to a diet, he pretty much starved her, allotting her scanty sums that barely covered her essential costs, and on top of that he never stopped thinking up countless subtle acts of malice.

Stifling her fury, the margravine surrendered to her uncle's caprices. This was a dreadful ordeal for the proud, demonic adventuress, queen of the sleeping car and the salon, accustomed to reigning supreme. She knew that, in Maja, Maliniak had found a wonderful plaything to set off against her, but she was expecting his fancy to pass. She just had to hold out!

She found it particularly unbearable that, for all his excesses, Maliniak actually treated Maja with a certain respect. Maja herself couldn't think why the millionaire was sometimes humble and servile towards her, like a peasant. These sudden changes were quite unfounded. But one day the mystery was explained.

'You must be from the landed gentry,' said Maliniak, 'from a manor house, eh?'

'You're right.'

'Parents gone bankrupt?'

'Exactly.'

'A pity,' he said. 'Were they rich?'

'We had about two thousand hectares.'

'Wow! What a fortune!'

She smiled on hearing the admiring tone of this man whose wealth was estimated at many millions. Maliniak picked up on her smile.

'You're laughing at me . . . But what I have is not a fortune. A fortune is a manor house with a park, teams of horses, a forest, fields . . . That's something else entirely. I know, because I spent my youth in the countryside, I'm the son of a peasant, and my father worked for one of the gentlefolk – for Count Ostecki of Plewo.'

'A relative of mine.'

From then on Maliniak treated her with even greater respect – and at the same time was even more tyrannical. Maja realized that her role here was dreadful and horribly humiliating.

She was a toy in Maliniak's hands. Serving to aggravate the marquise, allowing her youth and beauty to be exploited in this way.

Accepting gifts. Sometimes she thought of Molowicz and wanted to run away. But more often she thought of Leszczuk – and then she agreed to everything, accepting it all without protest.

And the marquise, though she had dined at more than one table, was amazed by the girl's cynicism. Meanwhile, all Maja's free time went on aimless walks about the city – on the lookout in case a familiar head flashed by, the back of a neck, a silhouette, in case that boy over there who was just turning around might happen to be . . .

By now she knew that Leszczuk had not been accepted at the club. But she didn't know his address. She had tried inquiring at the bureau of addresses. No luck. Anyway, she could have foreseen that he would hide.

Or maybe he wasn't in Warsaw anymore?

Her anxiety was increasing. She had disturbing dreams, in which she saw not just him but herself with him too.

The only thing keeping her calm and raising her spirits were her almost daily meetings with Molowicz.

But the young engineer was heading to these meetings with rising impatience. Maja had only given him very scanty information about herself. He knew she was Maliniak's secretary, but apart from that her personal life was a mystery to him.

He didn't want to inquire – he was sure the moment would come when she would tell him everything herself.

But he couldn't help noticing her dreadful anxiety. Her behaviour was very strange. She was looking for something . . . she was constantly on the lookout.

In the café she always chose to sit by the window, and during the most animated conversation her gaze would be fixed on the passers-by. While walking along, she often looked around behind her. Bah! She was quite capable of whispering out of the blue: 'Please wait a moment. I'll be right back.'

And she'd vanish in the crowd, only to return shortly after.

'Here I am,' she'd say.

Mołowicz guessed she was in love. It filled him with pain. One time he couldn't stop himself from asking her directly – was she looking for someone?

She didn't answer.

What puzzled him the most was that Maja was indifferent to elegant, well-dressed men. On the other hand, proletarian youths instantly caught her attention. And in a strange way this seemed to link up with the coarse accretions he had noticed in her, including her long-drawn-out 'noooo', a certain tone in her laughter, and the unexpected vulgarities in her behaviour, surprising in such a refined lady.

And those gloomy reveries of hers. The cruelty and malice in her eyes . . .

Finally he decided to take a risk. He couldn't go on waiting – and suffering.

'Maja, please don't cover up your past. Please tell me about it. You're too young – I'll help you to get out of it.'

'There's nothing wrong with me!'

'That's not true! There's something troubling you! If you really do trust me, please tell me.'

She went pale.

'No, I won't. And anyway, it's better for you like this. If you knew the whole story, you'd be disappointed in me.'

'You have lost your faith in yourself,' said Mołowicz with his characteristic energy. 'You must have suffered some dreadful humiliation. You're on the wrong track. I don't know what you do for that

Maliniak, but it's all unclear. Why do you refuse to rely on me? After all, you know that I . . .'

Maja dropped her gaze. It had happened. She knew he'd fallen in love with her, and was just about to tell her so. At the very least, she didn't want to expose him to a refusal.

'I'm involved with someone,' she said quickly, interrupting him in mid-word. Now he was the one to go grey.

'Aah,' he said, 'I thought so. I knew it from the start.'

They were walking along Nowy Świat Street. He was escorting her to the Bristol. The swarming crowds kept separating them.

Suddenly he grabbed her by the arm.

'Let's go this way,' he said, turning into Traugutt Street. 'We can't talk here.'

'Do we still have something to say?'

'Maja,' said Mołowicz, 'forgive me, please, but that won't do for me. Just stop and think. Even if you're in love with someone, it's definitely not a healthy or happy emotion. It looks to me as if you've got mixed up in feelings that you yourself would rather escape – but you haven't the strength to do it on your own. Maja! Please let me help you. If we join forces, maybe we can get you out of it.'

She knew he was right. She lowered her eyelids. Instantly she saw herself as his wife.

Could he really cure her of Leszczuk?

But how was she to confess to him? How was she to tell him the truth? It was impossible to relate. Should she confess that she was just like Leszczuk? It was laughable, it made no sense. And at the same time she was afraid of his standards. She refused at any price to become laughable and trivial in his eyes – she would rather tell a stranger than tell him. Her story might fill him with disgust.

'Let's go to a bar,' she said. 'Please get me some vodka.'

He frowned.

'Vodka?'

'You don't understand! It's an anaesthetic for a painful operation.'

'Aha!'

She was still hesitant. She stopped, as if about to run away.

But he took her by the hand.

'Let's go. You're going to tell me everything, mind!'

'Everything!'

They sat down at a small table. The room was still quite empty. Mołowicz fixed his strong, calm gaze on Maja.

'Tell me without vodka,' he said.

He was convinced he had already won. He could sense it. Joy flooded his heart. Maja was already under his influence. As soon as she betrayed her secret to him, she'd never break away from him again.

He leaned over the menu.

'I'm not going to eat anything,' she said. 'Let's have some beer.'

'All right.'

Mołowicz looked up at her from the menu and was stunned.

In that single second the girl's face had changed in a mysterious and terrible way. There opposite him sat Maja, but now she was a totally different, unreal Maja. This Maja was red, with downcast eyes, lips parted in a painful grimace, hands dropped awkwardly along her sides, and a dull, misty gaze. And she was leaning over the table lower and lower, as if about to lie down on it.

'Are you feeling faint?' he asked.

He beckoned the waiter over.

'Please bring some water. Quickly. Cold water.'

'Yes, sir.'

But Maja had already come round.

'Let's get out of here,' she whispered.

'Are you unwell?'

'I must go home.'

'When will we see each other?'

In horror, Molowicz realizes for sure that the girl is escaping him – escaping – that he's losing her and nothing will come of their conversation. That's why he desperately tries to set a date.

But instead of replying, Maja smiles. Her lips part – her teeth appear, sharp and even – this smile is ardent, determined, happy and angry all at once, and at the same time there's something conspiratorial about it. Molowicz is shocked because this smile is not aimed at him.

He doesn't want to look round. Anyway, he knows by now that Maja – with that smile and that look on her face – is lost.

'I'll walk you home.'

'All right.'

They leave. As Molowicz walks beside Maja in silence, he knows something is happening inside her. Some appalling changes. He's not looking at her, but he can guess. Once they've reached the Bristol he asks once more: 'Will we see each other again?'

She offers him her hand and says as if obliquely, to one side: 'It's not worth it.'

And walks away . . .

XIV.

Knowing that the waiters would change shifts soon, she went to the square where the bar was located, stood in the gateway of one of the houses and waited. From there she could see Leszczuk if he emerged.

She waited a long time. More than an hour. But she didn't feel tiredness. Just rising amazement.

'Oh, so I've raced here like a fool, and I'm waiting for him! Oh, so it's all over with Mołowicz! How did that happen?'

She hadn't yet come to terms with her own unpredictability where this boy was concerned. Whenever he came into her orbit, she immediately began to act against her own will, as if she were drunk – and she simply couldn't understand it: how come this Leszczuk had such power over her, Maja Ochołowska?

Hiding inside the gateway, she kept staring feverishly at the bar, but Leszczuk didn't appear. But someone else showed up outside the bar – a young girl, modestly dressed in a navy-blue jacket, had stopped at the street corner and was clearly waiting for someone too.

At first Maja took no notice of her, but after a while something struck her – could it be possible? She hadn't thought of that. What if she was waiting for Leszczuk?

Suddenly Leszczuk emerged and went up to the strange girl, they linked arms and walked off across the square towards Królewska Street.

So he – dared?! How could he?!

Suddenly, dreadful humiliation struck her like an electric shock. She hadn't foreseen this. He had another girl! That had never occurred to her. It seemed quite impossible for him to be involved with another woman. She started tailing them at a great distance. Several times Leszczuk looked round behind him, as if afraid someone was following him.

On Nowy Świat Street, where there were more people, she drew closer to them – and then she began to suffer a form of torture she'd never known existed.

In a light coat and a hat, Leszczuk looked like someone from her sphere – just as a cousin might look, or someone from the landed gentry – and as she watched him from behind Maja guessed . . . no, she knew for sure that yes, they were alike – that if he spoke, or laughed, or tilted his head, all these gestures were hers, Maja's, they were related to her, connected with her, actually meant for her!

But instead they were being received by that girl – accepted by that girl, who was walking with him, on his arm. And as she turned her head Maja got a sideways view of her eyes – large and happy, and her gentle profile. Miss Ochołowska peeped at those eyes with amazement and horror.

Could one really look at Leszczuk that way? With such a bright, cheerful gaze – so surely, sincerely and amicably? She, Maja, was incapable of looking at him like that; her gaze, when it rested on him, was always infected with shame, as it were – breathless, violent, restless, and full of stifled, dangerous passion, scornful.

Meanwhile Leszczuk and his companion had turned towards Poniatowski Bridge. Maja had to move away from them, because here it was emptier. But she noticed that she wasn't the only person adopting these strategies to follow the couple.

A dark-haired young man – judging by sight a craftsman, or something of the kind, with no hat and in worn-out clothes, as if on his way back from work – had turned after them into the avenue too, and had also slowed down. He seemed to have noticed Maja too, because a couple of times he watched her furtively.

The couple had now turned onto the steps leading from the bridge to the embankment. Maja speeded up, as did the unknown man. Suddenly Maja, who was not in a state of complete equilibrium, slipped on a fruit pit and fell. She flew down about a dozen steps.

The stranger caught up with her.

'Are you all right?'

He helped her to her feet.

'Thank you! I'm fine! Nothing broken.'

'You have to be careful on the steps'

Somehow he wasn't in a hurry to leave.

Finally Maja risked asking: 'It seems we both have something else on our minds.'

He hesitated, but then he admitted it.

'Yes, I think so too.'

'Are you interested in that girl?'

'And are you concerned about him?'

She nodded. He looked at her in surprise, but . . . Perhaps she was a dancer? Maybe she performed at that bar?

'So he's cheating on you with my fiancée?'

'That's your fiancée?!'

'You bet! Except I was interested in another girl for a while and we quarrelled. But I swear to God I'm not giving up – it's the second day I've been spying on them. If he won't back off, we'll come to blows! How dare she go to balls with him!'

'To balls?'

'And how! Today they're going to the ball at the Mermaid. Her aunt told me. There's an entertainment there to raise funds for some training courses, and lots of waiters are going. You tear his hair out to put him off seeing other fellows' fiancées – otherwise I'll give them a piece of my mind! But to think he's carrying on with my Julia, when he's got a girl who's so . . . Bah! My God, what's the world coming to? Wait here – I'll go and see where they've gone, and then we can talk some more. I'll be right back!'

Maja leaned against the bridge railing.

'Ma-ja! Ma-ja! Ma-ja!'

She turned round. There in the road stood a splendid, open-topped, seven-seater Buick the colour of café-au-lait, filled to bursting with a jolly company. Róża, Iza Krzyska, Mrs Halimska and two gentlemen, whom she had met before at a nightclub.

One of them was Krystyn Krzewuski, the other – the owner of the car – was Mr Szulk, a tall, sallow, fair-haired man who talked through his nose.

'What are you doing here?'

'Come with us! Just for an hour, to Konstancin! We've been out on the Lublin highway. We're on our way to Konstancin! Get in! Make room for her!'

'I'll never squeeze in!'

'Already done,' cried Krzewuski, lying in a bizarre position between the folding seats. Maja's presence raised the value of this outing for him by one hundred percent.

'I'm coming,' said Maja, approaching them, 'but I'm going to drive!'

'All right,' said Szulk, 'once we're out of the city I'll hand you the *ste-e-ring whe-el.*'

He had a habit of uttering certain words with special emphasis.

'Won't you be too cold?' fretted Mrs Halimska. 'That blouse is rather flimsy.'

'No! Let's go!'

They got into the car and set off. A violent rush of air swept over them. Róża coiled her hand into a trumpet shape and shouted into Maja's ear: 'Who was that fellow you were talking to?'

Beyond the city, Szulk let Maja take his place amid merry shouts. She leaned over the steering wheel and stepped on the accelerator.

'Just don't go too fast!' cried Mrs Halimska. But she was soon rendered speechless. The splendid vehicle moved off at full speed. The wind whirred in their ears. Trees and telephone poles raced past. Szulk leaned towards Maja.

'Do you know we're doing a hundred?'

'That's not much!'

And soon the speedometer was showing one hundred and thirty. Speed and terror had deprived Mrs Halimska of speech, but the young ladies began to scream. It was a mad ride – the cars they passed seemed to be standing on the spot.

'Take it off her!' Róża shouted to Szulk. 'You've gone crazy! We'll be killed! Stop!'

Out of fear she grabbed Maja by the arms from behind. But Krze wuski pulled her away.

'Hands to yourself, or it's death!'

Indeed, they were entirely at Maja's mercy, or rather her lack of it. At this speed, taking the steering wheel away from her could cause an accident. Only when she slowed down on a sharp bend did Szulk start to struggle with her, but she pushed him away; the car fishtailed, and again they raced at top speed. Mrs Halimska was praying and weeping drily as their tears were blown away by the wind. Suddenly sober, they were all gripping the car tightly, while watching out for obstacles in the road.

Just outside Konstancin she slowed down to twenty kilometres per hour and said: 'So now we've had a ride!'

Szulk took a deep breath and said in his nasal tone: 'I've never come so close to death before. How could you?!'

Everyone, except perhaps for Krzewuski, was annoyed with her. The Chairwoman didn't hide her resentment – she ostentatiously said nothing. Maja turned her head and laughed in their faces. Her laughter was so dangerous and provocative that only now did they understand to what extent she was toying with them, amusing herself by terrifying them. But Krzewuski exclaimed: 'To hell with your grievances! Can't you see she's magnificent?'

Truly, she had never been more magnificent. Her eyes shone, her teeth flashed between her parted lips, her slender, wind-lashed face was intense, and although she was smiling, her brows were knitted. They gazed at her in awe, as if seeing her for the first time. Szulk muttered nasally in French: 'She is more dangerous than her driving.' At once they all yielded to an indefinable excitement, and fell into an excellent mood. Their resentment vanished without trace. The men felt ashamed of having shown fear in front of her – something exuberant gushed from this girl. Even the jaded, whey-faced Szulk felt an abrupt need for some minor 'madness' that manifested itself in the following suggestion:

'Perhaps we should have a drink?'

'Let's go dancing!' cried Krzyska.

'Dancing again? Not worth it.'

'There's nothing else left.'

'Right! There's nothing else.'

The poverty of their entertainments was staring them in the face. Always the same. Maja slowly turned the car around, and only now was it apparent how poorly she controlled the vehicle – the engine stalled twice. Mrs Halimska threatened to get out immediately if Szulk didn't take the wheel.

'So what are we going to do?'

'We're going to the ball at the Mermaid!' said Maja.

'Where? The what?'

'Where is it taking place?'

'The Mermaid! An excellent idea!'

'We'll know lots of people!'

'Let's put on ball gowns!'

The car moved slowly down the highway, while they shouted like mad. Maja's idea was perfect! That was just what they needed! But Mrs Halimska was against it. In her view it smacked of eccentricity. But Szulk reassured her.

'I don't think there's any threat to us on the part of "local elements". We're quite capable of keeping ourselves separate! And why shouldn't we take a look at it?'

They went off to their various homes, because as Róża and Krzyska had proposed, the ladies were to dress up to the nines. That evening a jolly crowd started pouring out of cars outside the Mermaid.

In the cloakroom they could already hear the music.

And then the fashionable company made their entrance into the ballroom, where amid a hubbub pervaded with music, couples whirled to the rhythm of a waltz. In the vicinity the crowd thronged and the conversation buzzed. Balloons were floating overhead.

'Oho! Plenty of familiar faces,' exclaimed Krzyska, recognizing many of the employees from the local restaurants and cafés.

'Surely!' replied Szulk. 'This is a charitable do in aid of training courses for bellboys or something of the kind.'

'But it's a normal ball!' said Krzyska naïvely.

She found it odd that waiters could look so good. She was used to ignoring them in restaurants or cafés. And here suddenly she saw gentlemen whose everyday uniform tailcoat had changed into a festive, ballroom costume. Used to moving about in a large throng, they were nimbler and more at ease than the other men.

These people knew the discipline of daily work, which contrasted to their advantage with the overindulged and often pretentious manners of the gentlemen with whom she usually consorted. They were enjoying themselves gaily and naturally, being quite used to people having fun – something they rubbed shoulders with all the time at the clubs and bars – and they also had the self-control to rein in their impulses.

But Szulk suffered from a 'waiter complex'. He was one of those habitués who has a particular way of taking it out on waiters. He liked to exploit the privileged position of the restaurant guest who is always right and whose whims must be satisfied. He liked to be 'well served'. It gave him pleasure when a servile waiter appeared at the snap of his fingers. He didn't spare the tips, but he liked to feel he was the master of the establishment. Besides that he liked to teach the waiters manners, regarding it as his cultural mission, and from the heights of his infallibility he treated them sternly and ruthlessly.

'I am waiting!'

For this reason too the sight of the people dancing had a provocative effect on him. He was watching from on high.

'What awful dancing!' he muttered.

And up to a point he was right.

Only on closer inspection might one realize what a varied company filled the room. Waiters and waitresses only made up a tiny percentage of the guests. The ball was a charitable event, and anyone could come, as long as they were decently dressed.

Hairdressers and shopkeepers, shorthand typists and office girls, the proletariat and the petit bourgeoisie, common folk and gentlefolk – all of them thronged together, transported and united by the omnipotent tune of a waltz.

Wed-ding day! Everyone shouts hurray!
Everyone's merry and gay!
Onto the dance floor couples glide,
All that's missing is the bride!

With eyes agape, Maja was drinking in this extraordinary spectacle.

While her companions gave themselves over to feeble jokes and sought out things to ridicule, she was struck full on by this entertainment. She watched it as if bewitched – as if what was happening affected her personal fate.

The proud, haughty young lady watched the rather unskilful dancing, saw the disharmony of the costumes, and noticed all sorts of deficiencies and shortcomings that caused her pain. She did not find it amusing. To her it was tragic. She felt as if they were all dancing towards her and for her – that the whole party was jeering and laughing at her. 'Maja! Maja!' it seemed to be calling her. 'Come to us! Dance with us! Play with us! You're ours! Ours!'

Then she saw someone familiar. That fiancé of Julia's was standing in the crowd by the wall, looking around – and once again Maja felt a sharp pang of jealousy.

But, bored by his own boredom, Szulk suggested they sit down in the next room. Rustling their gowns, they ran after him. They occupied a table in the corner near the buffet and ordered some wine.

They were being stared at. It was plain to see that these were persons who had come here . . . well, to take a look, perhaps to gripe and criticize. Several ill-disposed glances were flashed at them, but on the whole nobody took much notice of them. The partying carried on as if they weren't there.

'It's extremely tactless of us to have come here,' said Krzewuski suddenly. 'I feel like a fool!'

'But why?' said Szulk, lolling in his chair. 'What's the problem? They're having fun, and we're allowed to have fun too!'

'I think it's more that they're having fun . . . at our expense!' replied Krzewuski.

Szulk's posturing and exaggerated refinement irritated him. But the rest of the company were also showing off involuntarily. The ladies were all too well aware of how different they were. Their every gesture, every word, every facial expression shouted at top volume – we're different, we're different! Even their discretion was indiscreet.

'Let's go and dance!' cried Róża with excessive lack of restraint.

'All right, but not with you,' exclaimed Krzyska, addressing the gentlemen. 'I want to dance with Andraszek. I've seen him! He's here!'

Andraszek was the nickname of a popular cabbie in Warsaw who drove the golden youth from club to club in his droshky at dawn.

'Mind you don't *fall in love with him*!' joked Szulk.

'That could only happen to you boys! For us women, men from the lower classes are quite out of the question. They simply don't exist! I'd never be able to love a farmhand or a workman.'

'Why not?' asked Krzewuski.

'What a strange question! Not because I'd look down on him. But what could I have in common with someone like that? What spiritual connection could there possibly be between us?'

'But in that case, how come men of our class sometimes marry and live happily ever after with their maids, for instance?'

Iza tossed her head.

'That's an entirely different matter! A man is stronger! He can pull a woman up to his level. If I were to marry a workman, I'd have to declass.'

'And I think all that is based on a gross misunderstanding.'

Szulk found this discussion annoying. He crossed his legs to reveal spotless socks while saying through his nose: 'Give it a rest!'

But Krzewuski did not yield.

'I'm certainly not advising you to marry an ignoramus,' he said heatedly. 'I am a hundred miles from such sentimental behaviour! That's not the point. But you are not entirely on a familiar footing with simple people. Men of different social classes come into contact in the army, or at work, and they gain each other's trust. Unless they work for a living, women from the intelligentsia lead an isolated existence. Hence your unjustified phobias! For you, as long as he's in a dinner jacket or has a manicure, a miserable weakling or an out-and-out rascal is worthier of attention than a decent, healthy labourer. The nation is still divided into classes and castes that don't know how to commune with each other!'

Though uttered with youthful zeal, this speech was received with indifference. No one cared to argue.

'Where is Maja?' asked Mrs Halimska, keeping a close eye on her flock as usual.

'She went to watch the dancing.'

Indeed, Maja was standing in the ballroom doorway, observing.

Stimulated by dancing and alcohol, the guests were starting to enjoy themselves. A great flurry of excitement ran through the room. The tremendous dynamism of joy and frenzy, the dynamism of people who don't often get the chance to party, pervaded and elated the crowd. For many a seamstress this was the night of their dreams.

She spotted Leszczuk, dancing with Julia, in a navy-blue suit and soft sky-blue shirt. He danced calmly and stiffly, with full respect for the ballroom ritual, holding his partner at a distance from himself. She meanwhile seemed modest and shy, but joyful.

At the sight of them, Maja hid behind the backs of the spectators. Ah, just a glimpse of him was enough for everything to become violent and passionate, terrible and unpredictable, wild and bad! If only she could be in his arms, like that girl! If only she could gently and innocently lean her head on his shoulder as that girl was doing!

How she longed for it! Once again the serpent of envy bit her in the heart. The whole ballroom was filled with envy. Her right was being violated. Her right, that she would avenge . . .

The dance ended. The breathless young men led away their flushed dancing partners and cigarettes were lit.

Władzio the fitter came up to Maja.

'They're over there!' he whispered.

As if through a fog Maja noticed that the boy was speaking to her humbly and with something like fear – as if to a higher authority, a divinity that was going to decide his fate.

Leszczuk and Julia were standing by the opposite wall, talking. Maja was separated from them by a constant procession of ladies and gentlemen. But between the heads of the crowd, she could see their heads, turned to face each other with a smile – and that was enough for her.

She started walking towards them, not straight across the room, but by a roundabout route, slipping along the walls to reach them without being seen. But the crowd parted before her. Heads turned.

Astonished glances were cast. Exclamations were made: 'Wow, will you look at that? My, my!'

Maja found to her fury that the crowd was giving her away, making it harder for her to reach Leszczuk. That was her only thought.

But they couldn't take their eyes off her! This exquisite, passionate girl, walking by in a ballgown, her lips clenched in a half-smile, was lovelier and more enchanting than anything they'd ever seen before, even at the cinema. Never had the world of beauty revealed itself to them with such overwhelming force.

The men goggled. And even the prettiest women were snuffed out like candles beside her; painfully aware of their own inadequacy they cast her jealous looks – why had she come here, putting their hands to shame with her own perfect hands, showing up their eyes with her eyes? Why did she have to come to their party?

But she envied these simple girls for being the way they were – and for the fact that any of them could go up to Leszczuk without being furtive, openly, as to one of their own kind. Oh, what wouldn't she'd give to be like the other girls!

She drew near to him and stopped just behind him; despite the hubbub she could hear his voice. How long was it since she had been so close to him?

Just then some strong, forceful, rhythmic chords rang out – and to the tune of a tango the violins began to sing:

Nobody knows like he knows
How to cause pain, to fool and pique
Nobody knows like he knows
How to vanish in the shadows
And come back after a week.

The music took control of the ballroom.

Leszczuk bowed to Julia, and they were just about to embrace when he felt somebody gently touch his arm. He looked round.

It was her!

She stood beside them, still and silent. She didn't speak. But that very instant Julia could tell that Leszczuk was lost to her. It was obvious. There was no doing anything about it. He'd been taken away from her!

Horrified, she took in the sight of them together.

Who on earth was this young woman, and why, oh why were they instantly as one? A twosome! Why was she suddenly an outsider, an outcast? Why in a single second had they become a couple, as if Leszczuk hadn't come to the ball with her, but with that girl instead?

'Julia!' he cried, holding out his hands to her.

But Julia was rapidly walking away from them, disappearing in the crowd, with her head drooping – rapidly. Władzio the fitter caught up with her.

'Julia!' he cried.

She burst into tears, while he took her by the arm and led her far away, into the furthest, empty rooms.

Maja and Leszczuk were left on their own.

Neither of them spoke. They just stood side by side. And once again there was hatred between them.

Meanwhile the tango was going wild. The violins were soaring to the heights, only to fall in a painful, stifled moan. The dull thud of the percussion marked the beat.

Maja parted her lips in a smile as if nothing had happened.

'Let's dance,' she said.

He wanted to refuse her, but it would have been impolite.

'All right,' he said, and suddenly they embraced as if it had been settled ages ago. They entered the circle of dancers.

He danced stiffly and cautiously with Maja – just as he had with Julia. He led her at a distance, and his dancing was maladroit, more like a ritual than a dance. Maja could sense his movements. They were . . . honest. They were the movements of a decent fellow from the provinces, full of respect for the dance, naïve but sincere.

But suddenly she felt herself rising to the same peaks as the music and then falling headlong into its darkest chasms. A superb dancer, she was lurking and hiding in herself! Gradually, imperceptibly, she began drawing him into the enchanted land of dance, where movement transforms into melody, and melody into movement. It was no longer he who was leading her. She was leading him.

And craftily, by degrees she ushered him into the song of the violins, into the thunder of the drum, into the sudden, unexpected voices of the flutes and into everything that was happening in the music.

Nobody knows like he knows
How to laugh when you're sad
Nobody knows like he knows
How to be bad.

sang the players.

Meanwhile Maja, serious, with knitted brows, could feel him awakening to the dance – and with mute joy was discovering subtlety in him, sensitivity, poetry, the merging with the music of a born dancer. How did he know all this? *How has he understood it? Here's hoping he'll understand more! The change of key too!* And with all her being she silently sent him furtive signs of the singing that was taking possession of them.

And the musicians noticed this couple; maybe they were struck by the 'similarity' they shared, or maybe it was their dancing . . . suffice it to say that at once the orchestra started to play in a different way, becoming eloquent. It struck the dancers with an intense wave, it led them and joined company with them. The flutes sounded different. The voice of the saxophone was different, and as if drunk on their own beauty, the violins and cellos raced each other in delight.

> *But when he's dancing with me*
> *My bloodless lips go pale*
> *It's dark, my eyes can't see*
> *Only one thing do I feel . . .*

The ballroom swayed and flowed. Was it they who infected the other couples, did their passion spread to everybody else? Something was making their hearts beat faster, intoxicating them, forcing them to surrender totally to the dance.

She was no longer leading him. Now he was guiding her as the music commanded, while she merely prompted or hinted . . . The ballroom danced. The couples whirled, pretty and absurd, young and old – even Mr Pitulski, who was there too, pale and impassioned, had raised his flirtatious nose and extracted miracles from his partner, bending her fantastically in all directions.

However, worried by Maja's prolonged absence, Chairwoman Halimska appeared in the doorway with Róża, Krzewuski and Szulk.

'Where on earth could she be?' she said.

Just then she spotted Maja with Leszczuk. At the same moment they all realized that something strange was going on. Was it the music? The dancing? The attentive faces of the people watching, full of emotion? It was hard to identify the source of this impression.

'With whom is she dancing?' said Mrs Halimska.

And Róża whispered, as if to herself, in a strangled voice: 'As I live and breathe, I've never seen anything like it!'

Szulk scowled.

'That fellow dances *a-pall-ing-ly*!'

'Oh no, that's not the point!'

'So what is?'

'Why don't you just shut up? You don't understand a thing!' she said softly, her eyes fixed on the dancing couple.

Instinctively she could sense Maja's wild happiness.

But Szulk understood better than anyone else. Although he wasn't emotionally involved with Maja, envy was choking him. With a nervous gesture he scratched his ankle with the tip of his patent leather shoe.

'She is compromising herself!' said Mrs Halimska at last, though she would have been quite incapable of explaining what was compromising about the dance. 'Do something! We must bring her back!'

The tango had broken up and ended before she'd finished saying these words. The couples drifted apart, the hubbub returned, everyone went off to right and left, and in the chaos Maja vanished from their sight.

Meanwhile she and Leszczuk were still on the spot where the end of the music had surprised them. Suddenly they both felt completely at a loss. The spell was broken.

'Let's go,' she murmured.

They began to forge their way through the crowd. Both he and she could feel the intrusive staring, and a strange sense of shame came over them.

Mr Pitulski and his flirtatious nose flashed past them – with no fewer than six gleeful ladies in tow, whom he was treating to vodka and sandwiches – and aimed his flirtatious nose in their direction.

'Wowee, wowee!' he cried arrogantly.

'Wowee, wowee!' repeated the ladies.

As soon as the dance ended, resentment towards this couple had stirred within the crowd. Those who had yielded to their irresistible charm now became malevolent and mocking. Some coarse jokes were made, and someone even tried to trip Leszczuk. Other people's happiness annoyed them and Maja's beauty provoked them.

But Maja and Leszczuk moved through the crowd with the one and only thought of getting out of their sight and escaping. They quickened their pace.

Someone whistled right beside them.

'If you're ashamed to be seen with me, I can leave,' said Leszczuk.

'Why should I be ashamed?'

'I'm not meant for you, Miss Ochołowska.'

She stopped, leaned against the wall and sank her deep, serious gaze into him, taking in his entire figure, sternly and searchingly.

'And I think,' she said, 'we really are meant for each other, Mr Leszczuk.'

Taken aback, he didn't answer.

'Who was that Julia with you? Why don't you go to her? She's waiting!' she sneered. But he doggedly replied: 'I'm not leaving.'

And added with a touch of fatalism in his voice: 'You've often appeared in my dreams, and it's always the same.'

'What's it like?'

'In this white room. And on a peg in the corner – there's something, I'm not sure what. It's moving.'

He shuddered. While she instantly remembered the dream that troubled her so often.

They both felt anxiety and didn't question each other further.

'How's the tennis?'

He went red.

'No good.'

'Didn't they take you at the club?'

'No. How do you know?'

'It was I who saw to that.'

'What?'

'I went there and talked to Klonowicz.'

'Aha . . .'

And suddenly he seized her by the hand and crushed it so hard that she almost screamed. He leaned over her, just like that time in the forest at Połyka. His face went dark, and his teeth, those teeth that were perhaps their most 'similar' feature of all, sharp and even, flashed between his twisted lips.

'Why are you doing all this to me? Why are you so eager for my life to go wrong? You want to spoil everything for me. You've stuck your claws into me.'

She pushed him away.

'Don't take too many liberties!' she shouted. But he took no notice.

'Why have you got it in for me?'

His tone of voice was frank. She gazed at him – he had an honest look. She remembered the dance, and the knowledge she had gained about him in the course of it. He had to be subtle, sensitive, intelligent.

And yet . . .

She raised her head. They were standing at the top of the stairs leading to the exit. A short while ago this space had been deserted, but now there were several dozen people walking to and fro, right in front of them – ladies with balloons, gentlemen in tails and suits, in soft and stiff collars. All strolling by – and all spying.

Suddenly someone bowed low to her.

It was Szulk, with Róża and Krzyska standing behind him, arm in arm, with naughty looks on their faces.

'Do forgive me for disturbing you,' said Szulk formally to Maja, while bowing to Leszczuk, 'but the Chairwoman is asking for you.'

'I'm just coming.'

'Allow me to introduce myself: Szulk.'

At the same time the two young ladies approached.

'What's all this flirting in corners? We've been missing you!' they cried, laughing. Szulk instantly introduced Leszczuk to them.

'Very nice to meet you!' they said.

'I'm just coming,' said Maja nervously. But they had surrounded Leszczuk.

'Please come along too, sir.'

'Let's all go!'

'Please come to our table!'

The orchestra struck up a foxtrot. A flood of jaunty, light, erratic sounds assailed the crowd, who started forming couples again.

Maja hesitated. She didn't want Leszczuk to go with them. But there was nothing to be done – they led them off to the Chairwoman. Once again, in his formal, nasal tone Szulk set about introducing Leszczuk to each person in turn: 'Mr Leszczuk!'

Maja blushed. Leszczuk bowed awkwardly and shook the hands offered, while Mrs Halimska muttered: 'How very nice! Please take a seat.'

They were inspecting him with barely disguised curiosity. It was Szulk's idea – to bring them here and 'see what sort of a thing it is'. They were all madly intrigued.

Who was this? Where had the crazy Maja got this boy from? What could it mean? What was going on between them? There had to be something, that was for sure!

Szulk in particular was deeply offended and furious that Maja had betrayed their company. He had decided to punish and ridicule her, and was deliberately striving to play up every explicit aspect of the situation. He and the others could barely control themselves!

Szulk addressed Leszczuk with excessive courtesy. He poured him some wine, but Leszczuk's hand shook, spilling the liquid, partly on Róża's dress.

'I'm sorry.'

'Have you known each other for long?' Szulk asked Maja, the politeness of his tone making up for the inappropriate nature of the question. Maja raised an eyebrow.

'Oh, Marian is a much older friend of mine than you are!'

Szulk choked on his wine. What a tone she had used! He didn't address waiters that way! Who did she think she was, the little upstart? So they were on first-name terms?!

It was a surprise for Leszczuk too. He didn't know they were on first-name terms either.

But dangerous sparks had appeared in Maja's eyes. By now she knew they wanted to make fun of her. What a fine crowd! What a collection of big-city riff-raff!

'I've had the pleasure of seeing you *some-where be-fore*, sir!' said Szulk. 'Do you share my impression?'

'At the Europejski bar, perhaps,' said Maja. 'He's an assistant waiter there.'

This was a new blow for Szulk! A waiter! Not even a waiter, but a bus-boy! He reached for his cigarette case and lit a cigarette to hide his rising irritation. Maja's girlfriends' eyes were out on stalks. Wow, that Maja! Mrs Halimska sipped her coffee in silence. Young Krzewuski squirmed on his chair, embarrassed.

Szulk offered Leszczuk a bowl of orange salad.

'Would you like some of these *pas-tries*?'

'No, thank you.'

'What can one *offer* you, *dear sir*? A little *dish* of *some-thing* perhaps?

'No, really, thank you very much.'

He kept ostentatiously waiting on Leszczuk, dishing out salad for him and offering the plate in a parody of a professional waiter.

This could just about pass as readiness to embolden an outsider who was bound to be feeling alien and exotic in their company. And Leszczuk really did feel dreadful, because he knew they were watching and judging him, looking out for opportunities to laugh at him. Not wanting to be impolite, he took the salad, but – without knowing what had taken hold of him – started to eat coarsely and noisily.

He wised up instantly. What had come over him? He'd never eaten like that at Połyka! Was it because no one at Połyka had expected him to eat that way? Nonetheless Szulk said spitefully: 'I see you like it!'

Leszczuk felt clumsy and unhappy. He started to sweat! Though on court he never sweated, not in the worst heat. Beads of perspiration appeared on his forehead. He was suffering.

And Maja was suffering too. That sweat, the slurping, those clumsy gestures! Once again she was convinced he was from another world entirely! He horrified her. Once again he seemed savage! Uncouth! Unpredictable! The eyes of the assembled company flitted from her to him and from him to her – curiously, intrusively.

In the background people were dancing.

Szulk continue to clown around, offering Leszczuk more and more dishes, until finally he summoned the waiter.

'Menu!'

And at that moment his anger broke loose.

'How badly you stand!' he roared at the waiter. 'Please stand properly! I'm *can-cell-ing* my order! I am not *ac-cus-tomed* to such conduct! Please approach once again and stand correctly!'

'All right, that will do,' said Mrs Halimska, trying to calm him down.

But by now he had lost his cool entirely. The waiter, old and tired, made an attempt to explain himself, but wasn't allowed to speak.

'I refuse to argue! Please approach the table once again and take my order in a *de-cent man ner*! Got that?'

Everyone felt uncomfortable. This was going too far, at least with regard to Maja. But the rage in him, suppressed for a long time, was being vented. If he couldn't tear a strip off Leszczuk, he'd do it to this waiter in his presence!

'Please stop throwing your weight around,' snapped Maja suddenly.

'I'm not throwing my weight around,' replied Szulk coldly. 'I'm just demanding decent service!'

'Then why don't you demand it in a decent manner, Mr Szulk!'

He was dumbstruck! Her tone! And that 'Mr Szulk'! She was way out of line!

'Please be so good as to take note of the fact that I am not a child and I do not accept remarks from anyone!'

'Why not? If you make remarks to others, you should accept them too!'

It was impossible to tell if she was being serious or just mocking. Either way, the note of contempt was undeniable and painful.

'I am not in love with any waiter!' he replied scathingly.

Miss Ochołowska looked at him as if at an object.

'You've guessed! Indeed – and I have even got engaged to one – this very day!' she said nonchalantly.

The effect was electrifying. Mrs Halimska quietly squealed. Róża and Krzyska opened their mouths, unsure if Maja was being serious . . . But when the silence dragged on, they all understood that this time she wasn't joking. Finally, staring down at Leszczuk, Szulk said: 'Well, er . . . congratulations on your taste.'

With downcast eyes, Leszczuk didn't move. He couldn't gather his thoughts. But Maja placed a hand on his hands and said calmly, with a deep sigh of joy: 'This is my fiancé!'

Just then a procession of dancers burst into the room and interminably threaded its way between the tables, before finally disappearing through another set of doors. Male and female dancing partners flew past, swaying to the beat, holding balloons, with their hands raised, pulling off tablecloths as they went by, and stirring a jolly commotion.

They had to give way to this playful invasion. They stood up.

'Enough!' said Szulk. 'I'm paying!'

He reached into his pocket as the waiter handed him the bill. But his hand came back empty, while his face showed astonishment.

'I haven't got my wallet,' he declared. 'But I had it five minutes ago.'

The gentlemen hastened to assist, taking out their wallets. They started looking around in all directions, as if Szulk's wallet were hanging in the air somewhere.

'Perhaps it fell out of your pocket,' said Mrs Halimska.

'I had it here, in the back pocket of my trousers,' said Szulk, drawing aside his coat tails.

'Maybe you left it in the cloakroom – nobody could have taken it off you here.'

'No, I definitely had it!' he said, and turned to Leszczuk, who was sitting next to him. 'Perhaps you would stand up,' he said. 'We'll see if it didn't get mislaid from this side.'

Leszczuk moved, but didn't stand up. Silence reigned. Everyone was struck by the fact that he alone was sitting, while the rest of the company had long since risen from their seats.

Maja went pale. She had spotted the corner of the wallet behind Leszczuk, in between his back and the back of the chair. As the boy moved, the wallet fell deeper. He had felt that and stopped moving.

'*We-e-ell?*' said Szulk slowly.

But just then Maja leaned forwards and hit him in the face with all her might. His pince-nez fell from his nose. There was instant mayhem. The gentlemen threw themselves between them, and the Chairwoman shrieked piercingly: 'She's gone mad!'

Meanwhile Maja grabbed the wallet and slipped it into her handbag. At the same time she tugged at Leszczuk. He stood up. And as soon as they were standing side by side, once again for the umpteenth time everyone got the impression that this was a couple, and that the two of them were identical.

'Ha!' said Szulk. 'You have prevented me from summoning the police!'

Hastily they all headed for the cloakroom. Maja and Leszczuk stayed behind.

'Wowee!' cried Mr Pitulski, walking past them, from the heights of his flirtatious nose.

'Let's go,' said Maja.

XV.

THE SCANDAL OF Miss Ochołowska spread far and wide within Warsaw's social circles. Szulk put it about to left and right, and Maja's girlfriends confided the story to others in the strictest confidentiality. At last everyone knew the secret of beautiful Maja Ochołowska, who in the course of her short time in Warsaw had already managed to intrigue everyone with her disturbing manner. In love with a bus-boy! Engaged to a bus-boy, who was, *nota bene*, suspected of pilfering Szulk's wallet!

Crowds raced to the Europejski bar, but Leszczuk was no longer there. The day after the ball he'd been dismissed, no doubt as a result of Szulk's intervention.

And Maja suddenly found herself completely isolated. The Chairwoman's entire flock had moved away from her smoothly and instantly. Even Róża had loosened her ties with her. She was no longer invited to any nightclubs or parties. All she had left was Maliniak and the marquise whom he was driving to distraction.

Anyway, she wasn't angry about it. She didn't need people. She was living in a sort of trance.

'No! He didn't steal!' she kept persuading herself. 'He didn't steal! No! It's impossible!' How could he? Just at the moment when she'd finally owned up to him!

But the obvious facts contradicted that. Who else could have stolen the wallet, if not he?

But when she remembered the way he'd danced, and when she closed her eyes and saw his honest, pleasant face, it seemed impossible.

And yet at Połyka he had committed theft!

And when she remembered how rudely, how coarsely he'd eaten that salad – and sweated – she realized he was alien to her, from another environment with which she could never be familiar and where any kind of boorish behaviour was acceptable.

But one more vision of Leszczuk persecuted Maja too – with blue lips, his face hideously altered by those lips. And then she thought he must be sick, a degenerate – which in its turn was disputed by his unquestionable physical fitness, evident at first glance.

She was getting lost in these contradictions.

Straight after leaving the ball, when she had rounded on him to admit it, he'd sworn he hadn't stolen the wallet. She couldn't get anything out of him, except that he didn't know who had planted it on him. But he said it oddly. Maja sensed that he was treating her with disbelief.

And could there be any wonder? After all, from the very start of her acquaintance with him she had behaved eccentrically to say the least.

And to tell the truth, she was seeing herself with rising disbelief too. The scandal at the ball – slapping Szulk in the face – hiding the wallet – this entire series of rough, crude, even dishonest acts would unbalance someone a hundred times better grounded than Maja. At the same time all these acts were rather naïve and humiliating, as well as childish, if not foolish.

And once again Maja was in the dark! Was she childish and naïve? Or spoiled and cynical? Or crude and common? What was she like, and what was she capable of? It was all so muddled and unclear, so random.

In the gloomy lobby at the Hotel Bristol someone took her gently by the arm. She looked round. Her mother.

Mrs Ochołowska had aged ten years. Dark furrows had appeared around her mouth and under her eyes – that was Maja's first impression.

'You've found me, Mama?'

She wasn't unduly surprised. It was obvious that her protracted presence in Warsaw couldn't be hidden for long. For some time she'd been preparing for this encounter.

'Aunt Wiktorowa wrote to tell me that she'd seen you in the city. I also inquired at the club. To begin with I thought you'd gone to Lwów,' babbled Mrs Ochołowska as she followed Maja down the corridor to her room. 'Apparently you're Maliniak's secretary?'

'Yes.'

'Maja, is it true that . . .'

'What?'

Mrs Ochołowska sat down heavily and stiffly.

'My dear child, tell me! Are you really engaged to him? Is he here with you? Is it true what people are saying?'

'Mama, you're over the top.'

'Over the top? So you think everything's all right?'

Maja laughed.

'Well, there's nothing unusual going on!'

She stood before her mother and started talking, casually and calmly, as if there really was nothing unusual going on. She controlled her own emotion, because the last thing she wanted was for her mother to share her agonies. No, her mother had to be kept well out of it!

And in her slightly childish tone Maja explained that she was actually very pleased she'd run away from home and come to Warsaw. Yes, in fact it had turned out perfectly! Admittedly, she had caused her mother some anxiety, but from time to time a radical break was necessary and had a healthy upshot. She had taken the job with Maliniak and was earning her keep. It was very salubrious. As well as that she had met lots of people, and was rubbing shoulders with society . . .

'You know what, Mama, I think I've gained enormously,' she said naïvely. 'I've deepened. I'm starting to embrace life seriously. And as for Leszczuk, I do see him occasionally, and I made a fuss about him at the ball because he was being accused of things he hadn't done. I try to look after him a bit, I'd like to help with his tennis plans, but you simply can't imagine what the intrigue and envy are like in the sporting world. The story about the engagement is nonsense! Fairy tales and gossip. But it can't do me any harm because I've broken up with Cholawicki for good.'

Mrs Ochołowska couldn't believe her own ears. She would never have supposed Maja was so good at putting up a façade. She had travelled here with an aching heart, full of trepidation – but here was Maja, quite content and on an even keel. Listening to her gave one the impression that everything was straightforward, self-explanatory and natural.

She simply couldn't understand the girl!

'I might be returning to Połyka soon,' Maja continued as naturally as could be. 'But there's one thing . . .' – at this point she blushed – 'about that money . . . You know what, I'm extremely sorry. I do realize what such a large amount of cash means in your situation. I'm saving it up from my salary and I'll pay you back, you can be sure of that!'

'But my dear child, can't you see that you're compromising yourself? That people are talking about you?'

And with a lump in her throat as she read the signs of suffering on her mother's face, Maja kept telling herself: 'I must reassure her! I must reassure her!'

And so blithely did she present her entire existence in Warsaw that Mrs Ochołowska began to feel ashamed of the tears she had shed for no reason. In any case, she knew Maja well enough to be aware that it would be fruitless to apply pressure. The promise to return to Połyka soon had the effect of calming her. In parting she said: 'There's someone else here who'd like to have a word with you.'

And moments later Cholawicki appeared in Maja's room.

Mrs Ochołowska discreetly withdrew – of the two evils she now preferred Cholawicki to Leszczuk. Meanwhile, the couple shook hands and stood facing each other.

'You've changed,' said Cholawicki.

'You've changed,' replied Maja like an echo.

In fact, as soon as her mother had left the mask had fallen off. Cholawicki was amazed to see her beauty, but it was no longer Miss Ochołowska's respectable, ladylike loveliness. Now there was something ambiguous, uncertain and debased about it.

But Maja was no less surprised by his appearance. Cholawicki looked like a ghost. He was thin and sallow, his eyes were flickering and his hands were shaking – he seemed to be having a nervous breakdown. She could tell that he was only keeping upright by a constant effort of will, and two vertical lines had appeared on his brow that hadn't been there before. And a few grey hairs on his temples too . . .

She was so sorry. She felt nothing for this man, but he was suffering because of her.

'We haven't seen each other for three weeks,' he said.

And suddenly she realized just how recently she'd still been at Połyka and how much had changed since then.

He looked at her intently and said: 'It's a waste of breath! You're not coming back to me. It's over.'

'How do you know?'

'I can see. It's no use talking.'

She sighed.

'You're right.'

He tried to restrain himself, but failed.

'Three weeks I've lived on the thought of finding you and having a talk with you. But it's no use!' He smiled spitefully. 'Good luck in the lap of nature with that shepherd boy!'

'Are you sure I'm with him?'

'It's obvious, isn't it?! I didn't believe what I was told – today, only an hour ago –but now I do! You're not just similar anymore! You're identical! You've been infected by him! You've become coarse and common, like him. Congratulations – now there's nothing to keep you apart!'

'I have a request for you. Please don't share those observations with my mother. She doesn't need to know.'

After a long silence he looked around nervously and said: 'In an hour I'm going back to Mysłocz. This is just a brief call. I must go. Here everything is lost. But I have a request for you too. You are privy to my affairs – I hope you won't tell anyone and you'll keep my plans to yourself.'

'You needn't worry. How's it going there?'

'Not bad.'

He looked around him again, and Maja thought something had unsettled him.

'How did you deal with Skoliński?'

How far she had wandered from his affairs! She spoke of them like something antediluvian.

'Skoliński? Skoliński is still at the castle. He's making a catalogue. I came to an agreement with him.'

He rose from his chair, took a couple of steps into the corner of the room where the washbasin stood and went back to his seat.

'Would you like some water?' she asked in amazement.

'No.'

'And how's the prince?'

'So-so. Still hanging in there.'

He stood up again and approached the washbasin, where Maja's scarf was hanging on a metal rail. Cholawicki inspected it closely.

'Why is it moving like that?' he muttered. 'The window is shut.'

'What's moving?'

'Can't you see? It's quivering from top to bottom.'

Only when she went nearer was she able to see the almost imperceptible motion.

'What's so odd about it? The vent is open, and there's a hot water pipe running through the wall here. That instantly creates an air current. I don't understand what you mean.'

He sprang at the window and closed the vent. The scarf stopped quivering, and Cholawicki ran a hand over his brow.

'I'm losing my mind!' he whispered.

'What's wrong with you?'

'Nothing, nothing.'

But suddenly she remembered her dream about the moving piece of cloth that frightened her so much, and that Leszczuk had dreamed about too.

'I once had a dream about a piece of cloth that was moving like that, on a sort of hook,' she said automatically.

Her words had an unexpected effect. Cholawicki went pale.

'What's that? What piece of cloth? Describe it to me in detail.'

Briefly, Maja told him about her dream. A basement, or a room, a narrow window, white walls, a metal hook, and on it something that kept inflating, a piece of cloth or a duster, or maybe an animal. She couldn't really tell. Something so repulsive and evil that it was hard to talk about it. She'd had this dream several times, and always woke up feeling exhausted and bathed in sweat.

'Was there a stove in the room? A kitchen stove?'

'No. Or maybe yes. I can't exactly remember. But do you have that dream too? What does it mean?'

However, she couldn't get any information out of him. Answering in monosyllables, he immediately started to take his leave. Maja thought he was going mad. He seized her by the hand.

'I have a request for you. If you ever dream of that piece of cloth again, be sure to write to me about it. Please. It's important! Well then, goodbye.'

And once again Maja was beset by a pressing thought. What was the meaning of those dreams?

Luckily she had no time to sit and wonder about it. Maliniak summoned her and declared that in two days' time they were moving to Konstancin. He was bored with living at the hotel, and was longing for sunshine and greenery. And he thought that in the fresh air he'd do even better at tormenting the unfortunate 'tigress' for whom he had already bought some outlandish countryside *toilettes*.

The marquise's hatred of Maja had reached morbid intensity. She was restraining herself to no purpose, knowing that it was grist for her dear uncle's mill, that this was exactly what Maliniak wanted. She, a European adventuress in the grand style, a demonic, raven-haired, pale vampire with crimson lips, couldn't bear having to yield to this provincial goat, this chit of a girl, this little goose who had wormed her way into Maliniak's favours.

She too had been hearing strange stories about Maja and she did not fail to report them to Maliniak. The fine young lady from the manor house was in fact a dubious creature mixed up in shady business! She ostentatiously hid from Maja the remains of her personal fortune that Maliniak had not yet taken away from her. She treated Maja pretty much like someone from the demi-monde. But Maja herself was no longer sure who she really was or how she should be treated.

And then these endless doubts were interrupted by a telephone call from Mrs Halimska.

'My dear child, how are you? I am so annoyed with Szulk! My dear, could you possibly meet me this evening? I've a small matter to discuss with you.'

For Maja this proposal, and the Chairwoman's honeyed tone, were a surprise. Mrs Halimska hadn't given a sign of life since the ball. They arranged to meet at one of the minor cafés – it was plain that Halimska would rather not appear with her in public.

But when Maja arrived, she received her effusively, though slightly differently than usual.

'Well, well! I never imagined you were so determined! You'll get by in life with that sort of personality, my dear! I never suspected you of so much cunning! If you hadn't hit him and given the affair a totally different character by doing so, he'd have summoned the police, and that boy would have been in trouble. À propos, do you really want to marry him, my darling?'

'Why do you ask?'

'Well, perhaps I have a right to ask. I've been taking care of you for quite some time. You owe me Maliniak, and I believe I can also be helpful to you in the future, because perhaps with your family now . . . you won't be going back to it, will you? In your situation you won't be able to manage without me.'

Then she spent a long time demonstrating to Maja that she alone could save her social and financial situation. Then she got down to business.

'My golden girl, I placed you with Maliniak, and in exchange you must take care of a small matter for me.'

'What is it?'

'It's a trifle. Also to do with a wallet, not Szulk's, but Maliniak's.'

'What?'

'I'm relying on you to extract a document from it. A design to do with the expansion of those new industrial premises of his. You'll bring me the sketch for a couple of hours, and then you'll put it back in the wallet. Not a living soul will know.'

Well – thought Maja – *a week ago she wouldn't have dared to put such a proposal to me. Well, yes, but now she regards me as his fiancée and she knows I'm like him . . .*

And at the same time if I were to refuse, Halimska could take revenge on me – which in her position would be a catastrophe. Maja decided to postpone the decision.

'But what if Maliniak notices?'

'How could he? He puts that wallet under his pillow at night, and he's a heavy sleeper. We'll have the whole night ahead of us.'

'I'll think about it.'

'All right. I'm willing to wait. I know you won't be ungrateful . . .'

A hint of threat had appeared in the Chairwoman's honeyed tone. Maja took a close look at her. *Aha, so she's like that! And I am like that! And so is Leszczuk . . .*

No! No! It's not possible! Neither Leszczuk, nor she . . . I must see him again! I must make sure again!

They often met up now, and spent long hours together. But the conversation wouldn't take off. Above all, they were too embarrassed to bring up the most salient issue. Neither of them said a word about their surprise 'engagement' at the ball. Nothing on the topic of their future together, or even some temporary solution. They had so much to discuss – but they wasted time on trivial remarks such as: 'The streets are most crowded at this time of day'.

They were on neither formal nor first-name terms – which also made it harder for them to communicate.

Maja decided to let him in on the Chairwoman's proposal.

She was nursing the mad hope that Leszczuk would respond negatively, or at least unwillingly. The slightest reluctance on his part would fuel her will to resist. If she knew that he was eager for her not to get involved in such enterprises . . . But if not, if it were all the same to him, then it was all the same to her too, and what would happen, would happen!

She repeated her conversation with the Chairwoman to him. Perhaps he could give her a hand? It could be far easier to pull it off together.

He did not show the least surprise. At once he set about discussing the details of the matter. The only reservation he expressed was of a purely practical nature: 'But won't they catch us?'

If Maja still nurtured any illusions, they evaporated once and for all.

She didn't know that at the very same moment Leszczuk's final illusions were evaporating too. For Leszczuk was just about certain she was the one who had taken Szulk's wallet! To be fair, he had some suspicions about Mr Pitulski too, but Maja's present performance dispelled his remaining doubts. Yes – she must be either a madcap, a kleptomaniac perhaps, or smarter than he was, with no scruples at all. That had to be the case, because a normal young lady of her class simply wouldn't associate with a boy like him.

But he hadn't the strength to defy her. She was too close to him. He had too strong a sense of sharing the same feeling, a desire to get the best out of life. And even her display of initiative made it easier for him to express something that had been weighing on his mind for a long time.

'I'd like to have another try at the club.'

'What's that?'

'I could thrash Wróbel!'

She shrugged, sick and tired of the whole business. Wróbel was one of the best players in Europe, and for several years his name had been a permanent feature on the Myers list – the idea that Leszczuk could beat him was unthinkable.

'I've invented a new stroke. I can beat anyone if I want to.'

'What nonsense!'

'Let's go to a court and I'll demonstrate.'

Soon they came upon a sign that said 'Tennis Courts' and went in. Maja felt indifferent, apathetic. They hired some shoes and rackets, in the process of which Leszczuk spent a long time inspecting the racket strings before choosing one that was already badly clapped-out, with a beautiful frame.

And there they stood facing each other on the court, as at Połyka. But they had no desire to play. They weren't suitably dressed, and besides . . . Tennis was no longer enough for them, and there wasn't the same lack of restraint between them – just stiffness, difficulty, awkwardness.

'Please serve,' he said.

Maja served, and he returned it – a fairly sharp drive that sank just across the net, as if suddenly undercut by an invisible hand, and fell almost vertically to the ground. No player could have reached it in time – it simply wasn't worth running.

The same thing happened with the next few balls. She changed her way of serving. After that, she sent him some powerful drives to the back line. Every ball he returned landed just across the net, as if cut short. In these conditions there wasn't really much of a game. At the same time, from the formal point of view there was nothing to fault. It seemed Leszczuk had mastered the art of cutting the ball short to a hitherto unknown and unachievable degree.

'How's it done?' she asked in amazement, coming up to the net. He smiled.

'It's a sort of invention. One has to hold the racket like this,' he explained, 'and tug it like this just as one hits the ball. That gives it a special turn, so it's bound to drop just across the net. It's not a trick, like "undercutting" the ball, it's just that one holds the racket a different way, and that makes the ball move differently.'

'But fancy no one coming up with it before!' she cried.

Indeed, it was incomprehensible! One would think there were no strokes or grips that hadn't been tried and tested by millions of players on thousands of courts the world over!

'Plenty of people must have played this stroke by accident, when the racket twisted in their hand. But the whole point is that the first time one hits the ball this way it seems silly, as if nothing can come of it. A miss, and that's all! It looks like such a silly way to hold the racket that it doesn't enter the picture. Only when one practises a bit does one see that there's something in it. And the second point is that one needs a special racket to do it – an old one, with soft strings, and these two strings at the side have to be looser. One can't play like this with a good racket.'

She wanted to ask him how he'd come up with it, but the question was difficult to pose in an impersonal form. However, he guessed what she was thinking.

'I discovered it ages ago in Lublin,' he said, 'but I've only brought it to perfection lately. The world's best player couldn't take a set off me now!'

'It makes tennis completely impossible! They'd have to introduce some new rules. That return can't be allowed into play!'

'I could beat anyone!' repeated Leszczuk doggedly.

He leaned towards her. 'Nobody can be told I've invented this method,' he said, without looking at her. 'I'm quite a good player, but if someone doesn't know what's up, he won't think there's any cheating going on, he'll just think I'm good at shortening the shots, and that's all! I don't have to do it all the time, just now and then. In each set I can make up for a couple of games that way, and no one will realize. If they arranged a trial for me at the club now, I'd con the lot of them! They'd just have to be persuaded to play with me. I'd tear them to shreds!'

Maja gave him a sideways look. Aha, so he was like that! There was familiarity in his tone, as if he knew she would understand him, and was counting on her support.

He smiled hesitantly and asked in an undertone: 'Well? If I were to win . . . it'd make life easier for us too. At least I'd have some status.'

Aha – so he was approaching it that way . . . matrimonially? She wanted to move away in disgust, but – that was her smile, her way of talking, she could have said it in exactly the same way. And besides, was she any better? Just a silly, vulgar boy and a young lady who's *déclassée*.

'We'll see,' she said unsurely and as if involuntarily. 'There's going to be a demonstration match at Skolimów soon. Perhaps something could be arranged. I'll give it some thought. If one were to beat Wróbel in public, they'd have to organize an official match.'

His eyes sparkled.

'For sure!'

And at once they felt close to each other, in perfect understanding. Oh, why were they only united in evil? Why was it enough for them to start scheming and at once they felt in perfect harmony, as all the obstacles to communication vanished?

She bid him a speedy farewell. She went home and got into bed, but before going to sleep she jumped out of it again, took everything that might remind her of a hanging piece of cloth – the towels, her scarf, her blouses on hangers – and put it all away, or laid it on a chair so that it wasn't hanging. Nevertheless, the dream haunted her again. And once again in the dream, against the background of a white wall with a narrow window was a piece of cloth, or an animal – something moving, some horrible thing in such dreadful, stifled motion that both of them – she and Leszczuk – were paralyzed by terror, they were at its mercy, just waiting for the thing to come closer. And then she saw something else. She saw the piece of cloth pushing itself into Leszczuk's mouth, and he was choking. She screamed . . .

XVI.

THE DEMONSTRATION match at Skolimów, which took place two days after Maliniak, Maja and the marquise had moved to Konstancin, attracted crowds of spectators. It was not in fact a major sports event, but the holiday and the splendid weather had drawn many people from Warsaw, not counting the local inhabitants and visitors to the town.

The stands were packed full. This sort of contest, regarded as a bit of fun, purely for entertainment and free of the ballast of responsibility, often gives the players and the audience greater satisfaction than the serious national tournaments.

And frequently at these secondary events, where risk is not recklessness, the best shots are played.

Added to that were the pleasant coolness under the trees, the greenery, patches of sunlight, and a band playing in the distance. Everyone was in an excellent mood, sipping lemonade carried around by some grimy boys.

Naturally, the cherry on the cake was Wróbel, the Polish national champion, who first of all played singles against Lipski, whom he thoroughly thrashed, to the delight of his fans. After the break there was going to be a doubles match: Wróbel and Antonówna against Maja and Klonowicz.

Antonówna, a far weaker player than Maja, equalized the chances to some extent, but even so no one was in doubt that, at the peak of his form, Wróbel would smash the opposition. Though thanks to his tricks and experience, Klonowicz played far better in doubles than singles.

'Well, that's enough of a good thing, let's get on with it!' said Ratfiński, bucking up the players, while the spectators clapped and whistled out of impatience as well as delight.

'I'm frightfully off form today,' declared Klonowicz just in case. 'I've had a headache all morning.'

'I can see you're as pale as a corpse!' said Antonówna in a sympathetic tone, which prompted laughter, because Klonowicz was tanned the colour of coffee.

Everyone was familiar with his hysterical quirks before every public appearance.

Whereas Wróbel really did have stage fright, even though the match was a piece of cake for him, and even though he'd shown excellent form a quarter of an hour ago. He was nervously tossing up his racket and looking around impatiently.

'Let's go!' he said.

They were greeted with applause. The first balls were played without any great thrills – the spectators' heads turned right and left – when suddenly Maja slipped and fell. Klonowicz ran over to her, but she sprang up without his help. However, when she took a few steps, it turned out she was limping.

'Oh dear, I won't be able to play,' she said.

'What's wrong?'

'My ankle hurts. It's out of the question!'

Consternation set in.

'So now what? There's no extra woman!' cried Ratfiński. 'The match has gone to hell! At least you're not badly injured, Miss Ochołowska?'

'No, it's nothing. I've pulled a tendon.'

'Klonowicz will have to play singles against Wróbel.'

'What? Me? No way! I'm not in the mood!'

'We can't call off the match. The spectators have paid!'

Ratfiński came out to the umpire's chair and announced: 'Ladies and gentlemen! Miss Ochołowska has hurt her foot and won't be able to play. Instead, there'll be a singles match between Wróbel and Klonowicz.'

But this decision was received with whistling and protests. Klonowicz was too weak to play Wróbel. And besides, he was unpopular. The rabble rousers started screaming: 'We object! Klonowicz out!'

'What an ill-mannered rabble!' hissed Klonowicz.

Limping, Maja went up to him.

'Take Leszczuk in my place,' she said. 'He plays just as well as I do. He's sitting over there, in the stand.'

'What Leszczuk?'

'The one you played three trial games against.'

'Oh, that one!' cut in Ratfiński. 'But he's clueless.'

'I've played him lots of times! He's a better player than I am! You can go ahead and take the risk. He was completely demoralized by Klonowicz that time! I can vouch for him,' said Maja feverishly, and, horrified by the prospect of singles against Wróbel, Klonowicz proved extremely conciliatory. Besides, after those three love games Leszczuk didn't seem a threat to him.

'That would be an idea. It could work for doubles. And by the way, I really did put him off his stride a bit that day. If he turns out to be completely useless, Wróbel and I can play, we'll muddle through somehow. But will he agree?'

He and Maja went over to Leszczuk and beckoned him out of the stand. But then Klonowicz and Ratfiński both realized why Maja had twisted her ankle. They only had to look. Both had heard a thing or two about Miss Ochołowska's curious adventures, and now they were in no doubt. If she was embroiled in a love affair, it could only be with him!

'I see!' said Ratfiński in distaste. But it was too late to back off. The crowd was growing impatient.

'Ladies and gentlemen!' announced the captain. 'Miss Ochołowska will be replaced by Mr Leszczuk.'

'Who?'

'We object!'

'Start the game!'

'Get out! Get out! Be – gone, be – gone, be – gone, be – gone' – and all the stands began to chant, revelling in their own screaming on a hot summer's day.

To this accompaniment the players came onto the court – Leszczuk and Klonowicz against Wróbel and Antonówna. Under his breath, Klonowicz gave Leszczuk a lesson: 'Just don't get in my way! Do your best to play as little as possible!'

Wróbel's powerful serve interrupted these instructions. The game had started.

Klonowicz didn't return the ball.

Nor did Leszczuk return the next one.

'Thirty-love,' announced the umpire.

Again Klonowicz failed to return the ball.

'Forty-love.'

'There's no playing!' pronounced the spectators.

But the fourth serve turned out weirdly. Wróbel, who didn't like to stand on ceremony in any, not even the weakest match, had a very difficult, powerful serve. Despite which, the accidental amateur not only hit the ball back, but managed to drop his shot so short that it was impossible to return.

'Forty-fifteen.'

In his turn Klonowicz was lucky. He played the ball back to Antonówna. It wasn't a very powerful shot. Antonówna returned it to Leszczuk because she thought he was weaker.

'To her!' whispered Klonowicz. 'Avoid Wróbel!'

But with all his might Leszczuk sent the ball back to Wróbel, and raced to the net. The stroke was superb, the ball shot off like an arrow. Miraculously, Wróbel returned it. Klonowicz had no difficulty returning that ball, but failed to drive it home.

And suddenly, to the spectators' amazement, a duel took place at the net between Wróbel and Leszczuk. A few high-speed volleys, a lob by Wróbel, a smash by Leszczuk and that was it.

Thunderous applause rang out.

But before the clapping had stopped, Wróbel was serving to Leszczuk. And again there was an abrupt, confident drop shot. What was going on?

Soon the first game ended in victory for Klonowicz and Leszczuk.

'Don't get in the way!' fussed Klonowicz, who thought it was he who had won the game.

But the spectators were no longer in doubt. The result, as well as Leszczuk's superb actions, the indefinite yet palpable refinement of his strokes seemed to imply that he was indeed a thoroughbred player. All of a sudden, the plain Sunday entertainment had become a sensation. However, many people thought it was a temporary run of luck, something that could happen to anyone.

But in the second game, those who knew Wróbel – and almost everyone did – were amazed by the change that came over him. The Polish champion grew serious, tenacious and sullen. Concentrating hard, he got down to action with close attention. He looked the same as during the toughest international tournaments. He started playing solely to Leszczuk.

And in his turn, Leszczuk only returned the balls to Wróbel's side. Klonowicz and Antonówna were entirely eliminated. Unparalleled, strong, violent drives crossed the net on the diagonal. It looked as if the two players could only see each other on the court. At one point Klonowicz tried to run up and send the ball home, but Wróbel shouted: 'Stand aside!'

Another storm of applause erupted. Everyone understood there could be no question of carrying on with the doubles match. These two players were too curious about each other, too keen to fight it out. By now they were already playing singles.

Many people stood up from their seats. Shouts rang out: 'Singles! Singles! Singles!'

Ratfiński announced that 'at public request' the doubles game had been suspended, and instead there would be a match between Wróbel and Leszczuk. This announcement was met with more screaming and shouting; as soon as Klonowicz and Antonówna had withdrawn, leaving the two rivals on court, at once a deathly hush fell. Then there was a sudden burst of applause in honour of Wróbel. Wróbel spun his racket in his hand, cast the audience a strange look, and smiled rather sadly.

No one could fail to notice his emotional state. Wróbel's strange behaviour made the spectators even more agitated – only now did it occur to them all that their favourite might be at risk of defeat.

The idea seemed unlikely, and yet Wróbel's unusual gravity gave the match a dramatic quality. Once again a hush fell. But he stood in position and called to the umpire: 'Let's start!'

And at once the first shots showed that the Polish champion hadn't the slightest chance!

After five minutes there wasn't a shadow of doubt.

If Wróbel was undoubtedly one of the best players in Europe, then on the other side of the court an incredible, elemental talent had appeared, compared with whom all his opponent's technique and abilities seemed nothing but plain hackwork.

In truth, this was a youthful and inexperienced talent, making up for calm and equilibrium with fury. Nonetheless, no tactical errors could offset this natural advantage.

No one was clapping anymore. The audience was witnessing the defeat of their favourite.

Wróbel seemed helpless, and there was something tragic about it. Leszczuk's best shots were met with profound silence, as dictated by respect for Wróbel's tragedy.

He meanwhile was bringing out everything he could. He knew he was fighting for his public, who any moment now would turn away from him – he was no longer striving for victory, but for making sure the defeat was not too awful.

But all his best shots proved ineffective, as if he'd been deprived of his sting.

Whenever he gained the advantage in a game, the other fellow undercut the balls. And those drop shots, hit with incredible technique, unerring, were impossible to return!

There was nothing to be done about them!

To a point where his helplessness was becoming comical.

But no one was laughing. The set ended in deathly silence. But when the umpire announced the score, six–love, a loud roar and cries of bravo set the air shaking. The audience went mad.

Leaning on his racket, Wróbel listened. Once upon a time he had been cheered like that too.

During the second set, now and then clapping interrupted the game.

The crowd had gained a new favourite! And what a fine one! Leszczuk had become their wonder, hope, glory, delight – their dream come true! They only had eyes for him! They were thrilled by Wróbel's defeat.

He did his best to defend himself, to the very last. He lost with honour in three sets, six–love, six–love, six–love, and when the match was over he approached Leszczuk, holding out his hand.

But the crowd snatched Leszczuk away from Wróbel and lifted him up.

Wróbel left the court and walked off, stopped by no one.

Meanwhile the players had gathered around Leszczuk.

'What the hell, what the hell!' Ratfiński kept saying. 'What the devil, gentlemen, what the devil! I'll be damned!'

'The Davis Cup is ours!'

'And he lost against Klonowicz!'

'It's the greatest day in Polish sport!'

'You deceived us,' said Ratfiński to Maja, who had totally forgotten about her ankle, 'but never mind! It serves us right!'

Leszczuk broke free of the crowd and went up to her.

'Let's go,' he said, without a shadow of joy.

An hour later they were walking down a shady avenue in Konstancin.

They were coming up to the villa Maliniak had rented. It was a sizeable, two-storey building, wooden, very attractive, like a miniature manor house with a small garden.

'Here we say goodbye,' she said, stopping a certain distance from the villa.

The whole time they had hardly spoken to one another.

'How are we going to do it?' he asked, pointing at the villa.

'We still have time,' she said nervously. She was so exhausted by the dreadful, deceitful match – but he replied: 'It's no use putting it off. I'd rather get the whole thing over and done with.'

'This is his window,' she said. 'My room is next door, but the catch is that there's no way out of it except through Maliniak's room. I could extract the wallet myself and give it to the relevant person, but either I'd have to spend the rest of the night outside, or return to my room through his, and that might wake him up.'

'So then what?'

'During the night I'll drop into his room and check to see if he's sound asleep. If he is, I'll light a match in my window. Then it'll be possible to enter his room through the window, take the wallet – it's under his pillow – and give it to the person who'll be waiting in a car outside the park entrance. All together it shouldn't take more than two hours. The wallet will be handed back to me through my window. If anything goes wrong, if he wakes up for example and notices the wallet is gone, I'll light a lamp in my room, and lower the blinds halfway.'

'All right! Let's do it tonight.'

'Tonight?'

'Tonight! At once. But I have to know the layout of his room.'

He gave her a pencil. She scribbled a map on a piece of paper and handed it to him.

At the last moment, as they were taking their leave, she wanted to back out of it, to say she disagreed, that it wasn't necessary – but she lacked the energy.

During the match Leszczuk had revealed every feature of his character to her. She was resigned to her fate. Was it worth risking the Chairwoman's revenge if in a month or two of communing with this boy she might do things that were far worse?

Leszczuk didn't go back to Warsaw for the night, but rented a room in a nearby boarding house and threw himself onto the bed.

He was tired, but he didn't fall asleep. He gave no thought to his triumph over Wróbel. Tennis had ceased to interest him. Tough. It had happened, and it couldn't be undone.

But he could have beaten him honestly!

Now he knew that he would have had the advantage over him without resorting to dishonest means. The result would have been less spectacular, but real.

Tough. It had happened . . .

From now on he would always have to fake his playing – because the public would always demand crushing victories.

And as for Maja, that was tough too. Tough. It was plainly their destiny, plainly only this sort of tie could unite him and Miss Ochołowska.

All right then. Now he wouldn't walk away from her for anything. What would be, would be; as soon as he'd started cheating at tennis it had become all the same to him. The sooner the better . . .

He was feeling nervous, though he was ashamed to show it in Maja's presence.

The sky was cloudy, and the avenue outside Maliniak's villa was almost black. The trees grew densely here.

He stopped among the trees and waited for Maja's signal.

Passing through the half-open garden gate, it wasn't hard to get underneath Maliniak's window, all the more since there were trees here too, and plenty of shade.

As Leszczuk looked out for Maja's signal – the lighted match in the window – he grew more and more anxious.

If it were only a matter of theft, he'd be scared, but not as much, or at least in a different way.

But apart from the specific danger, this also involved another one that he couldn't fully identify.

No – she was not normal.

It was not natural for a young lady of her class to do such things – she was associating with him – and she had run away from home . . .

He thought about how their acquaintance had been rather unnatural from the start.

And those mutual dreams . . .

And those lips . . .

And the similarity . . .

He would be a hundred times less afraid of this act if it didn't have to be performed with Maja. Perhaps she had gone mad? Maybe she was sick?

Finally the faint glow of a lighted match flared in Maja's window and instantly went out. The sign that Maliniak was asleep.

He waited another ten minutes or so, looked around to make sure no one was coming, and quietly entered through the open gate. It was about one o'clock.

He put his head through the window of Maliniak's room and listened. A deathly silence prevailed.

Without further reflection, he entered through the window. He froze, ready to flee on the instant if something moved.

But there was nothing moving. It struck him that Maliniak's breathing was completely inaudible. Something wasn't right. What if he wasn't asleep?

Leszczuk took a step forward and stopped again. Should it be this quiet?

But he was too close to back out now. He was two paces away from the bed, and could just about distinguish Maliniak's head. It looked as if it were stuck to the wall.

And he was not asleep. He was gazing at Leszczuk with his eyes not just wide open but bursting out of their sockets. Or so it looked. But the most shocking thing was that the head wasn't moving at all, not even twitching.

Leszczuk stepped back abruptly and bumped into a lamp that fell with a crash. Maliniak's head didn't move – he just went on staring, his eyes goggling and bulging, and . . . his lips were dark blue, almost black.

Leszczuk sprang at Maliniak and pulled him by the arms. The head flopped to one side.

Maliniak was dying.

In total silence, without breathing, with his eyes bulging. Only his fingers clenched and unclenched . . .

Around his neck there was a tightened noose of solid cord. The end of the cord was hanging from the bed.

Someone had strangled Maliniak with this noose at the very moment when he was entering the room. But who? There was nobody in there. Definitely! Could there be someone hiding under the bed?

He peeped. Nothing. Nothing. No one in the room . . . Who had pulled the cord?! Who had throttled him?

Leszczuk's hair stood on end. He raced to the window, jumped across the sill and fled blindly down the avenue.

So Maja had strangled Maliniak!

It could be no one else but her! No one else could have got into his room, only Maja. Nobody could have got in through the window, or he'd have seen them.

Only Maja! Maja had crept in, put the noose around his neck, pulled the cord – and on hearing him come in, she had withdrawn. Anything else was an illusion! This was a fact in all its nakedness.

Why do it? For what purpose? Why at this exact moment? Who could possibly know? Maybe she'd been trying to extract the wallet herself, but Maliniak had woken up and she'd strangled him.

Leszczuk didn't try to probe the motive or the process of the murder. For him it was enough that she had done it.

Was she mad? Deranged? Or was she a monster, thoroughly depraved?

And this was the girl to whom he was so irresistibly attracted! He found her so alluring! He was similar to her! Was he really joined by some bond to this crazy, horrible girl?!

He couldn't understand it, but he could feel his connection with her so deeply that whatever she did it was . . . as if he had done it – it belonged to him – it was his . . .

So in spite of the thoughts that were flying through his head like a flock of startled birds, he immediately asked himself the question – could I have done something like that? Could I have throttled Maliniak?

Everything turned on this question.

Because if he could have done it, it meant that she could have too . . . And if she could have done it, she had.

Everything implied that she had, and the only evidence against was that such an insane, monstrous act was impossible for her – but indeed, she could put a noose around a sleeping man's neck, and pull it tight . . . No, she must have acted in a state of insanity.

And suddenly Leszczuk stopped in mid-run.

At a standstill, he wondered if he could have done it . . . He studied himself. He looked deep inside himself. Was it at all possible? For him to go in there like that, put it in place, and pull – cruelly, savagely . . .

He wondered . . .

All at once, as if caught by an unexpected thought, he whipped a mirror out of his pocket.

His lips were dark blue – almost black!

And at the same time he recognized in himself a sort of relaxed feeling – as if he were eluding his own attention.

He started running. But it didn't help – he felt he was evading himself, losing himself somehow, as if he couldn't catch hold of himself. Something had taken control of him. He wanted to shout but he couldn't anymore. With clenched lips, mute, he tore headlong across the fields, knowing only that he bore with him those blue-black, evil, dreadful lips!

XVII.

FEELING TENSE, Maja approached the door to check Maliniak was asleep and to give Leszczuk the sign with a lighted match.

But just at that moment she heard the window creak in his room, and immediately after the floor creaked too.

Could Leszczuk already have entered – before she lit the match? Perhaps he didn't want to wait any longer – or maybe he had peeped through the window and determined that Maliniak was asleep? Either way, it wasn't a good thing. She listened.

Suddenly she heard the clatter of a falling lamp that resonated throughout the house, and straight after that something that sounded like violent activity.

She raced to the window and was just in time to spot Leszczuk fleeing in panic through the garden gate. Then everything went quiet.

In Maliniak's room silence reigned.

For about five minutes Maja stood by the door before making up her mind to open it.

And again, silence. Truly deathly stillness.

What had happened?

Maliniak was lying on the bed, throttled by a cord around his neck. His lips were parted, livid blue and black.

Leszczuk . . .

She felt faint and sat down by the bed. Her thoughts were racing. What was she to do?! Leszczuk! Hide the fact?! But there was no hiding it!

Someone came down the stairs and gently knocked at the door. Maja didn't open it. They knocked again. Finally they started to thump on the door and yank at the handle.

She opened it.

There in the doorway stood the Marquise di Mildi with a lighted candle.

'What are you doing here?' she asked.

Then she went up to the bed and screamed, and five minutes later the whole house was on its feet – the valet, the cook and the night watchman. Lights were switched on, the telephone was put to work, a hullabaloo was raised.

Maja was stunned, she tried to leave the villa, to get some air, but the marquise grabbed her by the hand.

'Please don't leave until the police arrive.'

'I'll be here, outside the house.'

'Oh, no! Please stay with us.'

Maja went pale.

'Why?'

'I don't know what's going on! I found you beside my uncle. I categorically insist that you're not to go anywhere until the authorities arrive. Please don't move anything!' she said, addressing the servants.

A car drove up to the house and a police officer entered, accompanied by several constables. He moved everyone into the next room, and having secured the evidence, began his initial questioning.

'Which of you discovered the murder?' he asked.

'I did,' said Maja.

'It wasn't you, it was me,' the marquise interrupted her. 'Me, me, me!'

The 'tigress' surged forwards, pale with red blotches, looking dishevelled in a monstrous Persian dressing gown gifted her by the deceased. On top of all the misfortunes she had suffered lately she had a stye in her left eye, which was dreadfully swollen.

'I alerted the house! I wish to make a statement!'

'Please have your say, madam,' said the police officer, seeing that he couldn't easily shake off this hysterical woman.

'Officer!' she began. 'This is the most mysterious crime I have ever read about!'

The police officer couldn't hold back a smile.

'I can tell you've read a good deal about crime,' he said.

'No, no, that's not what I meant to say! I'm in such a jitter! Officer, it's a mystery! Last night I had a headache, I couldn't sleep, so I went downstairs to get a pill from my uncle. The door into his room was locked shut. I knocked – no one answered. I started banging, and then this lady opened the door to me, and at once I saw that my uncle was dead. He was still warm.'

'So the door was locked from the inside?'

'Yes.'

'And the window? Was the window open?'

'No, it was shut.'

Maja wanted to interject that in fact the window was open, but she lacked the strength.

'So the only access into Mr Maliniak's room was from the adjacent room?'

'Yes.'

'And who occupied that room?'

'Miss Ocho . . .'

The marquise opened her mouth, goggled, and spread her hands.

'It's not possible!' she shouted. 'I must be mistaken! Maybe someone came through the window . . . Please check if there are any footprints under the window.'

She was staring at Maja in horror.

'Can you confirm that the door leading into the hall was locked from the inside?' the police officer asked Maja.

'Yes, it was. But I . . .'

'Please speak calmly.'

'I was in my room. When I went into Mr Maliniak's room, I found him already dead.'

'And why did you go in there?'

'Because I thought someone had come in through the window.'

'So the window was open?'

'Yes.'

'She's lying,' said the marquise scornfully. 'She's lying! The window was shut. But do check for footprints below it. If someone had come in through the window they'd have left prints, because the ground is soft. Search the whole garden!'

She threw herself on Maliniak's body.

'She killed you! She killed you!' she cried. 'Oh God! Oh God! Oh God! I knew it, I always knew it would end this way!'

'Now we must wait for the investigating magistrate to arrive,' said the police officer, glancing at his watch.

The marquise slumped onto the sofa.

'I feel faint,' she gasped.

But the policeman on guard under the window called: 'There are distinct footprints here! Someone ran off this way!'

The officer went outside, but soon returned. His face betrayed surprise.

'There are footprints from the gate to the window and back again. There can be no doubt! They're freshly made.'

Instantly the marquise regained consciousness.

'What's that? There are footprints?' she asked.

'They're very clear. From the gate to the window.'

'Impossible! The window was shut! That's nonsense!'

She ran outside before anyone had time to stop her. But not even seeing the footprints for herself was enough to convince her.

'Impossible!' she screamed hysterically. 'Out of the question! When I tell you the window was shut! My uncle always closed the window at night. It's a coincidence! Someone must have walked about here yesterday! Please check!'

The investigative magistrate drove up and repeated the investigation.

'There's no two ways about it. Someone went in through the window,' he decided. 'Look, there are footprints on the floor too.'

From this point on the margravine held her tongue. For her, Maliniak's death was a dreadful catastrophe, because she knew he hadn't left her anything. On top of that, Maja, who had seemed to be sunk with no hope of salvation, was floating to the surface again!

She fell into a sort of stupor, and just smiled derisively now and then, with her swollen eye and in her patterned yellow-and-green dressing gown.

Meanwhile the magistrate was closely examining the pillow, on which Maliniak's head was lying. 'Look, sir!' he said quietly. 'This is strange! You see how the head is pressed between the pillow and the wall. It looks as if the murderer was hiding under the bed and pulled on the cord from there.'

'That's absurd!' replied the officer and immediately added: 'This murder is altogether strange. Whoever heard of something of the kind – strangling the victim with a noose? Maybe it was suicide?'

'No! He was plainly throttled.'

'From under the bed?'

The corpse's lips were going blacker by the minute. Both men averted their gaze. The officer looked under the bed, and brought out a handkerchief that had fallen from it onto the floor.

'Maybe this handkerchief strangled him?' he said ironically. 'There was nothing else under the bed!'

After a detailed interrogation Maja was allowed to go. But as soon as she left the villa, her legs gave way beneath her. She was absolutely wiped out.

What about Leszczuk? What on earth had happened to him? How could he have done it? – that was the one and only thought rattling around in her head.

What the hell for? Why? And how? Ah, so he was a monster! And what about her, seeing she had helped him? Enabled him? They'd done it together, together . . .

She had to see him! It simply wasn't possible! And yet he'd done it! He really had!

But she couldn't find Leszczuk at the boarding house. She was told he hadn't come back for the night.

She went to Warsaw, but she couldn't find him. For two days she searched in vain, and even made discreet inquiries at the club.

In sporting circles consternation reigned. A big official match with Leszczuk had been organized, but meanwhile the newly discovered champion had vanished, without leaving an address.

Luckily it hadn't occurred to anyone that the disappearance of the superb tennis player could be connected with the murder in Konstancin. Who would have suspected a young man on the threshold of a brilliant career of something like that?

'What has become of him?'

For Maja, seeking out Leszczuk, understanding how he could have done it, and confronting him was a matter of life and death.

She felt close to insanity. If only she could see him, if only she could understand, or at least find out . . .

She was riding on the number nine tram in a state of total prostration when suddenly the man sitting opposite spoke to her.

'I do apologize most sincerely, miss, but are you aware of what you're doing?'

Amazed, she looked up and saw a serious gentleman of over fifty, with hair that was turning grey and an extremely intelligent face.

'What I'm doing?'

'If it goes any further, you'll rip up your entire sleeve.'

Maja noticed that her sleeve was in shreds. She had been unconsciously tearing it in her agitation. The gentleman smiled and tipped his hat.

'My name is Hińcz,' he said.

She shuddered. That was the name of the famous Warsaw clairvoyant whose extraordinary attributes often prompted amazement. He could read out letters that were in sealed envelopes. He could find missing people and objects.

Many a time he had managed to predict future events accurately, though in fact plenty of his predictions did not come true. Yet there was no charlatanry in it – Hińcz really was distinguished by some mysterious sense inaccessible to all other mortals.

As well as that he was a man of immense knowledge, a scholar whose works in the field of telepathy had gained major recognition abroad.

'Yes, I am indeed the Hińcz you're thinking of,' he replied jokingly to Maja's inquiring look. Her immediate thought had been that he could help her to find Leszczuk. But she didn't know how to begin.

'Boldly,' said Hińcz, continuing to smile genially.

'I see that you really can guess people's thoughts.'

'Oh, no, it's just long experience that allows me to sense who needs my help. If I'm to be honest, I confess that I began the conversation because you seem to be in need.'

'You're not wrong,' she whispered. 'I'm looking for someone.'

'I'm getting off here,' he said. 'If you wish, we could talk about it now. I have half an hour to spare. I'll see what can be done.'

She accepted his offer with gratitude. They got off the tram and went into a small café on Nowy Świat Street.

But just as she was about to speak, she bit her tongue. In her situation, confiding in the clairvoyant wasn't safe. Then again, no one else could possibly help her!

She made up her mind.

'I'm looking for someone,' she repeated hesitantly.

'Whom?'

'It doesn't matter.'

'All right,' he said. 'Don't tell me. All I need is an object belonging to the person, an object with which they've been in close contact. Do have anything like that?'

Maja remembered that she had Leszczuk's pencil in her handbag. Should she give it to him or not? If she did, he'd be able to see through all their secrets!

But suddenly becoming serious and as if nervous, Hińcz took hold of her hand.

'You can be frank with me,' he said, 'and I advise you to speak out.'

'Why?'

'Because I can be of use to you. I don't accept any fees, and if I've taken an interest in you, it's for other reasons. You are a first-rate subject for me. I spotted that on the tram.'

His scholar's passion shone in his eyes.

She handed him the pencil that Leszczuk had lent her a couple of days ago to draw a map of the villa. He examined it carefully.

'There are toothmarks here,' he said.

'Yes, its owner often chewed it. It's a habit of his.'

'All the better.'

He closed his hand around the pencil and closed his eyes. Suddenly the hand began to tremble and he started breathing heavily.

'Let's get out of here,' he said abruptly. 'I can't concentrate. Come to my house! Let's be off at once!'

He hailed a taxi.

'Did you . . . sense something?'

'This is the strangest pencil I've ever come across!' replied Hińcz in an undertone, looking at her closely.

Maja felt uneasy. For a long time now so many strange and terrible things had been happening around her. Maybe this Hińcz was a charlatan, or perhaps he knew she was mixed up in the Maliniak case and was trying to find something out this way.

Meanwhile he sat down at his desk, and with the pencil in his hand, he said: 'I can see him. A young lad, about twenty years old, dark blond, light hat. He's walking . . .'

'Where?'

'Just a moment. Please don't interrupt: he's walking along a highway, I can't see the direction. Aha, a kilometre post. One hundred and fifty-seven. He's at kilometre one hundred and fifty-seven. He's tired, but . . .'

'What?'

Hińcz concentrated.

'No, no! He's not walking, he's writing . . . He's writing something with this pencil on a wall. A thick, white wall. Just a moment, he's walking down the highway! What on earth does it mean? He's in danger.'

'Danger?'

'This man is in danger . . . great danger. He must be saved at once! There's something he wants to do . . . And on the whole he's mad, or . . . There's something around him, or inside him. Ah! He's writing something on the wall again. I can't understand it. Now I can't see anything.'

Hińcz let go of the pencil and looked at Maja.

'We must save him,' he whispered. 'I can't understand all of it. I'm seeing two people at the same time – the one walking along and the one who's writing – that has never happened to me before. But they're both in dreadful danger. You see, I don't really know. But I've never come across an object as evil as this pencil before. It's the worst thing I've ever held in my hand. And it belonged to that man. Anyway, when I saw him walking along the highway I could sense it – that fury is starting to build up inside him. Maybe it's insanity? But what's strangest is that to look at he seems absolutely normal.'

'Do you believe there are objects that are good and evil?' asked Maja, examining the pencil. Her head was full of confusion.

'There are many mysteries in this world that are beyond the understanding of the human mind,' he replied. 'You see, with my attributes, or talents perhaps, I'm always coming upon these enigmas. But the more mysteries there are, the more one thing becomes obvious and clear, namely the simplest dictates of conscience, moral law. There are lots of things we don't know, but we know what's good and what's evil at once and for certain. You might be surprised to hear me say it, but I'm a man of deep faith.'

He changed his tone.

'That boy can't be left like this! Something bad will happen to him. We must find him right away. But how?'

'The one hundred and fifty-seventh kilometre?' asked Maja.

'Yes. I saw the signpost clearly.'

Where might Leszczuk be going? Why was he on foot instead of travelling by train? What sort of a highway was it?

Or maybe Hińcz was wrong, and was talking nonsense?

Maja remembered that the road from Połyka joined the Lublin highway at kilometre one hundred and sixty-two.

'Can you describe roughly what the countryside was like?'

It made sense – a flat, wooded area, cut across by stretches of water.

'I can guess where that might be. I know those parts.'

She briefly explained the geographical situation. Hińcz looked at a timetable.

'The fast train leaves in two hours. We have no time to lose. Pack up your essential items. We'll meet at the station.'

'Are you coming with me?'

'Naturally.'

On the train Maja told Hińcz the whole story of her acquaintance with Leszczuk in the finest detail.

She was entirely frank. She didn't even hide the fact that he had killed Maliniak. She was too tired by now to conceal anything at all.

In any case, Hińcz inspired total confidence in her. She told him about the dreams, about the horrible blue lips, and the dreadful effect they had on each other.

'If he killed, then I could kill too,' she said feverishly, 'we have identical natures! I know it! If he's like that, then I'm like that too . . . and I am like that!'

Hińcz concentrated. His wise, searching gaze seemed to penetrate Maja to the core.

'This is one of the most bizarre stories I have ever heard,' he whispered. 'But don't lose hope. Anyway, this story should be exceedingly simple and psychologically understandable. If he really is so similar to you, then it's obvious why you have such a bad influence on each other. You are exceedingly lively, intense, aggressive. So if a nature like yours comes across a kindred nature, then this impetuous, stormy energy is multiplied, he arouses you, and you arouse him, and so it accumulates without end. This energy is in itself a priceless treasure. But if it's not directed towards good, it changes into a destructive element. And that's what must have happened in the given instance,' he went on, 'since from the first moment you lost mutual trust and respect. Yes, it would all be plain and simple if only . . .'

'If only what?'

'If only there weren't some . . . other factors tangled up in it. The lips. The dreams. The pencil. All these are phenomena of a different order. Shall I tell you frankly? I think he's possessed.'

'Do you believe in that?'

'I believe that a person can create conditions within himself that can give evil easier access to him. That sort of person attracts evil like a magnet. And there are many people and many places in the world that are imbued with evil. Watch out for yourself, but above all don't lose hope.'

She felt as if she were dreaming. None of this could be true. It smacked of the Middle Ages, of witches. And yet an ultra-modern person was saying it.

So Leszczuk was possessed? He'd killed in a fit of madness?

That filled her with hope. But also horror.

The thought that Leszczuk was wandering the roads somewhere in this state, unaware of anything and incapable of defending himself was dreadful.

'Please save him,' she whispered.

By now they were approaching the station at Koprzywie. Dusk was engulfing the little town – it was seven o'clock in the evening.

Maja easily gained the information they needed. Someone very like Leszczuk had arrived on the morning train and taken the road to Połyka.

Hińcz's presentiments and Maja's guesses proved accurate.

They took a droshky and set off as fast as possible.

The castle came into sight in the distance among the trees, its foundations wreathed in mist.

But Hińcz told the driver to stop.

'We're being foolish! I saw him on the highway. Let's go there – that's the starting point for our search.'

So they went down the highway, to kilometre one hundred and fifty-seven. Hińcz looked around.

'Yes, this is what I saw. He was going in that direction.'

For quite a time they drove in silence. Suddenly Hińcz told the driver to stop again, got out and walked up to a small fruit tree planted by the road. He examined it carefully.

At first glance it was no different from the other small trees. But on closer inspection it had plainly been slashed with a knife. Here and there, the bark had been torn off. Some of the branches had been slit at the base and were only holding on by a hair.

Hińcz scrutinized these wounds with great attention.

'Let's go!' called Maja impatiently. 'That's just the usual sort of mischief done by village louts!'

'Can't you see that this tree has been damaged in a particular way? A lout would chop off some of the branches if he felt in the mood. But these branches have only been cut halfway through. That's not the work of vandals but of anger. This was done with refined anger.'

'So you think Leszczuk . . .'

'Highly possible.'

A shiver ran down Maja's spine. Why on earth had he tormented this tree? Had he gone mad? She herself was close to madness.

'Let's go, let's go!'

Soon they came upon some labourers on their way back from roadworks.

'Yes, indeed! We saw a young fellow like that, about three hours ago, walking towards Koprzywie . . .'

'So it appears he was wandering about the district. He probably went back to Koprzywie for the night. It's possible we'll find him at the inn.'

They turned around, but one of the labourers stopped them.

'That fellow must be mad,' he said.

'Why?'

'He came up to me and asked the time. I gave him the right answer, but he trod on my foot – he almost broke my toes.'

'Maybe by accident?' asked Hińcz.

'Get away! Perhaps if he'd trodden with his sole, I wouldn't be telling you. But he stomped on my toes with his heel. He deliberately twisted his leg to crush me with his heel.'

'He's lost his mind!' whispered Maja.

'Worse,' said the clairvoyant. 'Can't you see that all this is *exceedingly* evil? I'd rather he'd hit that man than trodden on his foot with his heel. That heel proves the fact that his behaviour exceeds normal limits.'

'Why on earth are we looking for him?!' she exclaimed. 'If we find him we'll have to hand him over to the police!'

'Calm down, calm down. Maybe he didn't murder Maliniak? Anyway, the fact that he's not sound of mind is plain to see.'

He said this to comfort her, but Maja was still in extreme despair.

In spite of all, she couldn't believe Hińcz when he said that Leszczuk was possessed. It sounded too fantastical.

She was sure he had gone mad. And if not, he was a murderer.

They got back to Koprzywie at about midnight and headed straight for the local Hotel Polski, which was the only passable inn in the whole town.

The hotel was a small, wooden house with several guest rooms on the upper floor. On the ground floor there was a restaurant, managed by the portly Mr Kotlak, who bowed low on catching sight of Miss Ochołowska.

'Indeed, indeed. A gentleman of that description arrived not long ago. He rented a room and he's probably asleep by now, because his light is out.'

Maja and Hińcz conferred briefly. It was hard to predict how Leszczuk would behave at the sight of them. Anything could happen.

Hińcz decided that it would be wiser to wait until morning than to wake him at night, so he rented rooms for himself and Maja, and ordered supper.

They were eating their meat course, when all of a sudden Leszczuk came in and sat at a table by the window.

Luckily a jolly company consisting of several tipsy farmers shielded them from him.

With bated breath Maja looked at his haggard face.

Was he insane? He was behaving normally. He ordered a steak in a low, timid voice; he seemed abashed and infinitely sad – it was enough to bring tears to her eyes.

Her heart ached, and she wanted to approach him, but with a commanding gesture Hińcz restrained her.

He wished to do more observing. They heard Leszczuk asking about the road to Połyka.

'I tried to go there today, but I got lost in the forest and came out on the highway,' he said.

'So this is the boy?' whispered Hińcz, keeping a close eye on him.

'Visiting Mrs Ochołowska, my dear sir?' asked the inquisitive restaurateur.

'No, in fact I'm going to the forest.'

'To the forest? To look at a tree?'

'Nooo, it's a different matter.'

He started eating, but minutes later he pushed the plate away. His gaze was fixed on an object lying on the window ledge beside him.

It was a fly trap – a glue-coated strip of paper on which dozens of flies were close to death, using the last of their strength to extract one foot, only to bury the rest even deeper. The strip was covered in the ghastly struggle of small creatures dying of exhaustion.

'Please take this away from here,' said Leszczuk hastily.

'The flypaper? Where am I to take it?' asked Mr Kotlak in surprise.

'Anywhere! Just so it's not near me! Quickly!'

The restaurateur looked at him in amazement, but he took the flypaper and moved it to the next window.

At this point a strange thing happened. Leszczuk stood up – then abruptly made for the flypaper and started finishing off the flies with a finger, one by one.

The farmers got up from their bench and stared at him in astonishment, while the landlord asked: 'My dear sir, are you killing those flies?'

'They shouldn't suffer,' said Leszczuk in a voice that sounded stifled and alien.

And as he spoke, he went on killing them, faster and faster . . . and it was so very strange that finally one of the farmers said: 'That's enough now!'

Instantly Leszczuk threw himself at the man. He was foaming at the mouth . . .

With both hands he seized the farmer by the head and tossed him over his back with incredible force. Then he started grappling with the horrified man, dragging him around the room.

The other fellows raced to the rescue.

Maja and Hińcz were pushed into a corner. A maelstrom broke out on the floor, and the buffet came clattering down in a crash of breaking glass.

And at once a terrified, horrible roar tore free of this stack of humanity: 'God Almighty! God Almighty!'

Leszczuk threw his entire body at the window, smashing it to pieces as he hurtled outside.

But before fleeing he stopped for a moment, looked around and . . . killed one more fly on the sticky paper.

He was gone.

The farmers spilled out after him in a horde.

'Catch him! Stop him!'

The little town awoke. Windows and doors opened, and frightened people stood in them. The chase flew through the little streets like an ominous apparition.

Hińcz couldn't keep pace with Maja, but tearing ahead, she grabbed him by the hand and did not let go. They ran along at the rear.

'They'll kill him!' whispered Maja feverishly.

They heard the sound of a new roar in the distance. The country folk had surrounded a cottage on the edge of town. Armed with sticks, scythes and pitchforks, they were climbing the fence and forcing their way into the outbuildings.

'He's hidden in here!' they cried. 'He's in the loft!'

'He grabbed me by the ear!' howled the owner of the cottage.

'He was killing the flies on the flypaper! Punch him! Hit him!'

'Set the house on fire!'

If Leszczuk had battered them twice as badly they wouldn't have been so enraged. What had driven them mad were those small but wild actions, like grabbing the man's ear, or killing the flies. That was real villainy! Beat him up!

Maja approached them.

'People, have you gone crazy? He ran off through the barn in that direction.'

'Which way?'

Many of them recognized Miss Ochołowska from Połyka. Some of them doffed their caps, but at once voices spoke up: 'He hasn't escaped! He's here! He raced in this way and climbed the ladder to the loft.'

'But I'm telling you, he ran off in that direction!'

Imperceptibly, Hińcz turned into the yard and, taking advantage of the confusion, led a horse out of the stable, tied a large bunch of straw to its tail and lit it. The horse reared and galloped off into the fields.

'He's getting away!' they shouted, hearing the hoofbeats, 'he's taken a horse!'

They all raced to the back of the house.

Meanwhile Leszczuk had ripped open the roofing and slid to the ground in a flash.

Briefly, Maja caught sight of him standing there, dazed, wild and trembling, utterly lost. She wanted to cry out. But in a couple of bounds he had run to the well, located on the other side of the street near the outbuildings. It was deep, round and narrow, with an enormous wellsweep.

Without a second thought, Leszczuk jumped feet first into the bucket and went down the well with it.

The peasants came back screaming: 'Wait! He hasn't escaped! He set the horse alight! Guard him! He's here! He's up in the loft!'

They surrounded the house again. Maja and Hińcz were fearfully expecting the peasants to notice that the well-sweep was submerged, though moments earlier the bucket had been swinging high in the air.

Several of them leaned against the well casing, and they'd only have to look down to find Leszczuk – that is, if he hadn't plunged to the bottom with the bucket. Or perhaps the bucket had taken in water as it fell – in which case Leszczuk's fate was already sealed.

In spite of all, the peasants were afraid to go into the loft. They were jostling each other.

'Hey, you!' shouted Mr Kotlak to a boy. 'Go and fetch my shotgun! It's behind the wardrobe! With all speed!'

Maja ran as fast as she could towards the hotel, raced into the deserted restaurant, and fetched out the shotgun from behind the wardrobe. It was loaded. Without thinking, she fired both barrels into the air.

She tossed the shotgun to the ground and fled.

Alarmed by the sound of the shots, the peasants came running.

Hińcz caught up with Maja.

'Did you fire the gun?'

'Yes, yes. But let's run to the well.'

From afar she could already see that the sweep was in its normal position. Leszczuk had managed to escape. But what would happen now? Where should they look for him? What further atrocities was he ready to commit? They looked around in vain. All trace of him had vanished.

'He's gone mad!' said Maja, feeling crushed. 'He's a raving lunatic! Death would be the best thing for him!'

And the terrible thought that he had gone mad because of her, that she had driven him to it . . .

But Hińcz took a different view.

'No!' he insisted. 'This is something else! There's a surfeit of evil in his actions! A lunatic would have beaten the people up, but not killed the flies! Especially that last fly. After extracting himself from a scuffle like that, it must have taken more than just madness for him to stop and squash a fly. And how strangely it began. At first he was crushing those flies out of pity, because he couldn't bear their suffering, and it was only while killing them that a fit of madness came over him. Killing the last fly was a demonic act. But he doesn't look the type! I beg you, don't give in to doubt! Have faith! We shall save him!'

After a couple of hours' fruitless searching, they went back to the hotel. At about seven in the morning Mr Kotlak knocked at Maja's door to say that one of the farmers wanted to have a chat with Miss Ochołowska on an urgent matter. Maja, who hadn't slept a wink all night, immediately went out to meet him. A man of about forty, robust, strong and lean, bowed to her.

'I've something to tell you in private,' he said.

'What's the matter?' she asked once they had gone outside.

'I wanted to say that the fellow who got into a fight with people yesterday is at my place.'

'At your place? Meaning where?' she asked, hiding her emotion.

'At my cottage. I have a piece of land about five kilometres from here, at the edge of the forest, in Zaniwcze. The fellow's asleep now, and I told my wife to keep an eye on him.'

'Who sent you to me?'

The peasant smiled knowingly.

'I don't live far from Połyka, miss, so one time I saw you with the same gent and I know he's from the manor.'

'I'll repay you.'

At once she summoned Hińcz and they drove off with the peasant. Before leaving, the clairvoyant forced her to drink a glass of warm milk.

The splendid morning gilded the stubble. A vast silence reigned in the fields. Hińcz questioned the peasant about the details.

'God forbid! If not for me, he'd be a goner!' said the peasant.

'How so?'

'This morning I went into the Połyka forest for firewood. I'm walking along, when I see something black in a copse, in between Zaniwcze and Dębinki.'

Maja shuddered.

'I think to myself, is it a boar or not? Until I get close, and I see this fellow removing his trouser belt and looping it around a branch. At once I could tell what was brewing, but when I coughed, he stopped right away and just stood waiting a couple of minutes. So he waits, and I wait – I wait, and he waits – until I see him coming up and pressing against me.'

But even though he seemed quite well-educated and looked intelligent, he couldn't find a more precise term.

'So he pressed against me,' he said. 'After that he followed me all the way home, pressing against me the whole time. He didn't press against anyone else, just me. Oh, there's my cottage,' he added, pointing at a small farmhouse, entirely secluded at the edge of the forest.

'You can help us,' said Hińcz. 'If he refuses to go with us, he'll have to be tied up and carried to Połyka. But just a minute. Wait a bit. First we'll go up to the fence quietly, and then you can bring him into the yard – I'd like to see how he "presses" against you.'

'What for?' said Maja fretfully. 'He'll run away from us again.'

But Hińcz did not share her fears. From the peasant's words he concluded that Leszczuk was utterly exhausted by now. On the other hand, he felt it extremely important to know the precise nature of his madness.

'It's very interesting that the peasant couldn't define this "pressing against". Once again we're probably dealing with something that deviates from the norm. Don't forget that the tricky part has only just begun. Until we have the key to his illness, we won't be able to overcome it.'

Indeed, Leszczuk's behaviour fully confirmed his expectations.

The peasant brought him out of the house as agreed, and walked right across the yard with him several times. Leszczuk could have stirred pity in the hardest of hearts.

He was staggering, crestfallen and helpless – and simultaneously the same sad docility, the hopelessness of someone who was ruined showed in his entire figure, in his every movement.

And indeed, as the peasant had said, he 'pressed against' him in a way that couldn't be denied.

It looked as if he wanted to tell the peasant something but couldn't – as if he were trying to make contact with him in some way.

He moved up close to him, huddled up to him, and followed him, as if a mysterious magnet were attracting him with special force.

This behaviour didn't look very conscious, but it was only apparent in relation to the peasant. Though his wife was reluctantly watching these manoeuvres, Leszczuk paid no attention to her at all.

The peasant was amused – he kept casting glances at the fence behind which Hińcz and Maja were standing, and making funny faces.

'There's no need to tie him up,' he said on his return to them. 'He's seen something in me and he'll follow me like a dog.'

It was decided that Maja would go to Połyka first and get everything ready to receive Leszczuk. The main thing was to hide the whole matter from the boarding-house guests.

In any case, Hińcz was afraid that seeing the girl might prompt an undue shock in Leszczuk. He hoped that with the peasant's help he'd be able to deliver him to Połyka without much trouble.

So Maja rode bareback along the road across the forest. And shortly after, a horse and cart drew up at the side entrance of Połyka manor, then Leszczuk was carried out of it and transported to one of the rooms upstairs.

He could no longer walk. He was dropping with fatigue. He hardly knew what was happening to him. He didn't even recognize Połyka. A reaction occurred, and on finding himself in bed, he instantly passed out.

XVIII.

MAJA's arrival at Połyka caused quite a stir among the boarding-house guests. In particular Miss Wyciskówna and the doctor's wife were inflamed by the news.

'Do you know who arrived this morning? Ochołowska!'

'What do you mean? She only left yesterday, and she's already back today?'

On learning from the press of Maliniak's murder Mrs Ochołowska had immediately set off for Warsaw.

'Not the old one, but Maja! I saw her with my own eyes through the window!'

The newspapers had been writing extensively about Maliniak's mysterious death, and Maja's name had often been repeated in these reports. The doctor's wife was excited.

'And do you know that she's not the only one to have arrived? Someone was brought here! Carried upstairs! I heard through the door.'

'Marysia told me there was a fracas in Koprzywie yesterday.'

But both ladies' exhilaration reached its climax when the maid Marysia told them in the deepest confidence that it was Leszczuk who had been carried in and lodged upstairs.

Ever since, they had been on constant watch in the dining room or on the veranda.

But there was nothing going on. Maja did not appear. The house was filled with blissful afternoon silence.

Meanwhile in the room upstairs the blinds were down. Leszczuk was asleep.

Towards evening the doctor appeared. Hińcz had a long and exhaustive conversation with him.

'There's nothing wrong physically. The wounds are superficial. The fears you're speaking of could be related to a nervous condition. It would be advisable to send for a psychiatrist.'

But Hińcz took a different view. He suspected that the illness was not nervous but spiritual.

He asked the doctor for a sedative for Maja, and took a soothing potion himself as well. Their main need was to recover their strength.

And so silence reigned at Połyka – that is, until the following afternoon, when Leszczuk regained consciousness.

'Where am I?' he whispered, rubbing his eyes.

'Please don't move,' said Hińcz, who still wasn't letting Maja in to see him. 'You've been unwell.'

'But where am I?'

'At Połyka.'

Suddenly he remembered everything, and sat up abruptly in bed.

'What on earth have I been up to? Who are you? Aha, the peasants wanted to beat me up? And I . . . ? Aah.'

He grew weak again and closed his eyes. But shortly after he said: 'Are you a doctor?'

'No.'

'Please tell me the truth. Have I gone mad?'

'Of course not!' replied Hińcz. 'You were behaving rather fitfully yesterday, but you must have been agitated.'

He made every effort to reassure the boy.

But as soon as he remembered the events of the night before, Leszczuk sank into gloomy apathy. He closed his eyes and said nothing.

Hińcz slowly explained how they had found him, merely concealing the fact that he was a clairvoyant. He said he had been taking Maja back to Połyka, and by chance on dropping in at the hotel they had found him in the restaurant.

'So she is here?' asked Leszczuk.

'Would you like to see her?'

'No,' he replied in terror.

And added: 'I'm getting out of here.'

Hińcz took the pencil from his pocket.

'Tell me, please,' he said, 'where did you get this pencil?'

Leszczuk didn't answer. Only when Hińcz had repeated the question several times did he grudgingly reply: 'That one? It's not mine.'

'Not yours? Take a good look at it. Those are your toothmarks.'

'This pencil? Ah, right. I found it.'

'Where did you find it?'

'At the castle. I was there one time and . . . I picked it up off the floor in this white roo . . .'

He didn't finish. He had remembered the white room from his dreams.

'It must be the same room that I dreamed about,' he muttered reluctantly and turned over onto his other side. 'I'm going to sleep.'

'Just a moment. Was this pencil already chewed when you found it?'

'Yes.'

'And did you chew it too?'

'I don't know. Yes. It's a habit of mine.'

He fell silent and lay with his eyes wide open, staring at the ceiling. Hińcz realized he wouldn't learn any more from him.

But Maja was stirred by his account. So the pencil was from the castle? Leszczuk must have found it that night when he lost his penknife! He must have been carrying it in his pocket ever since.

Ah – and soon after his lips had gone blue – that time on the walk in the forest. And what's more, he'd found it in the white room – she too had instantly thought of the white room from her dream. She had already suspected more than once that there might be a room like it inside Mysłocz Castle.

Could there really be something uncanny about all this?

She told Hińcz about the castle and about the dreadful sensation produced by every encounter she'd had with this mysterious, desolate place that lived a life apart.

Yes, the room from the dreams had to be a room in the castle. These discoveries made a huge impression on her.

The thought of Skoliński sprang to Maja's mind. She didn't want to involve Cholawicki in this business at any price – she knew he hated Leszczuk. But if Skoliński was still at the castle, perhaps he'd be able to provide some information.

Hińcz fully agreed with her. In his view, the weird and loathsome pencil could prove the key to the enigma. This above all had to be explained.

'You know what? Let's pay a visit to the professor. I'm curious about the castle. We'll leave Leszczuk in Marysia's care. She's an energetic girl, and he's still too weak to defy her.'

They walked along the causeway between the swamps. They went through the underground passage, and Maja led the clairvoyant through the dark and empty chambers.

She was hoping she'd manage to reach the professor without running into Cholawicki, from whom she wanted to hide her arrival at Połyka for as long as possible.

On the first floor she stopped.

'Wait here.'

But from the depths of the suite of rooms they heard voices and saw a light coming through a half-open door. She wanted to withdraw, but Hińcz stopped her.

'Let's go closer,' he said. 'Even if someone sees us, it's no big deal, and I'm curious to know what's going on in there.'

Maja too was curious about the noises, so contrary to the silence she was used to finding here. They went closer and saw a scene like no other.

At the table the prince, Cholawicki and the professor, being waited on by Grzegorz, were holding an informal conversation, as if nothing had ever divided them – and exchanging polite platitudes in the shabby wreck of a dining hall. On the surface, there was nothing remarkable about it – on the contrary, the conventional correctness of the conversation seemed downright excessive and exaggerated.

And yet the talkers' exhausted, weary faces turned their smooth sentences and their suave manners into a sort of weird and dangerous sport. It looked as if they were making the greatest effort to talk away things that were infinitely more serious.

But the most astonishing fact was that – for all the correctness of the conversation – their gestures were somehow . . . uncoordinated, fantastical. Now and then, Skoliński or Cholawicki made a strange movement – for example, one of them would bend a finger downwards, while the other would reach for a serving dish with a move that was too wide, too rounded – and even Grzegorz kept pouring water into the glasses in a special way.

'What does it all mean?' whispered Hińcz.

With a finger to her lips, Maja let Skoliński catch a brief glimpse of her. He understood, and soon after he appeared beside them.

'Please come to Połyka with us, Professor,' whispered Maja. 'We must have a talk with you. I don't want Henryk to know about it.'

'All right. I want to talk to you too.'

As they made their way to Połyka, on hearing Hińcz's name the professor asked: 'Are you the famous clairvoyant? Who sent you here?'

'All in good time, Professor! In the first place, tell me please, is there something abnormal going on at the castle?'

'How did you know?'

'I have reasons to suppose so.'

'Finally, God in heaven, I'll be able to talk it through with someone!' cried the overjoyed professor. 'You've come just in time. I wouldn't have been able to stand it for much longer!'

And he told them everything he had endured so far in that dreadful place. The kitchen. The towel. The prince. Cholawicki. Mrs Ziółkowska. The sign. The whole story unwound before Hińcz and Maja, like a tale from the thousand and one nights.

'So I wasn't mistaken,' whispered Hińcz, moved to the core. 'There are some alien forces at work here.'

'What do you mean?'

'Professor,' said Hińcz, 'you must take care of yourself. We saw you at supper. Why were your movements so . . . bizarre?'

The scholar was embarrassed.

'I keep attempting to find the sign. I try to take every opportunity to draw out the prince in this regard. I've got into the habit of "finishing off" every gesture in a slightly different way from normal.'

'That's very dangerous.'

The professor was under no illusions – he knew that he too was gradually succumbing to some weak-mindedness in these terrible circumstances. In his view, the situation was extremely menacing.

They had reached the manor, and Maja led them through the side entrance to her room upstairs.

'I was hoping I'd discover the sign and succeed in rescuing the prince from the state that is killing him morally and physically. Unfortunately, so far I haven't advanced an inch in my quest. I am dreadfully weary of it all, I can hardly keep going . . . My resistance is waning by the day. I'm afraid it's even worse for Cholawicki. That man is betraying visible symptoms of insanity.'

'Could he really be in such an awful state?'

'How should I know? I know nothing anymore! Or perhaps it's not that our resistance is waning, but the pressure of those mysterious forces is increasing . . . It's no wonder a person finally ceases to understand and loses confidence in his own mental powers. These are phenomena that surpass my intellect. I'm inordinately pleased that you've come to help. You know this sphere of phenomena better than I do. Can all this be explained in a natural way?'

Hińcz in his turn told Skoliński the story of Leszczuk.

'That would mean that this force is infectious – that it attacks people,' whispered the professor.

'I may be wrong,' said Hińcz, 'but in my opinion the moral and spiritual meaning of these remarkable symptoms is beyond doubt. I believe that the least enigmatic fact is the motion of the towel. Anyone who has taken part in a spiritualist séance knows that some unfathomable forces raise objects, hurl furniture, or even hit the assembled company. These phenomena do not necessarily have to be supernatural. There must be as yet unexplored forces of our psychophysical constitution at work here.

'Let us imagine that, in a fit of intense concentration of his vital forces, the ill-fated Franio must have transmitted a particle of his energy to that towel. Have you not observed that its motion is similar to that of a medium?

'So this part of the puzzle could be . . . if not explained, then at least related to familiar examples, to experiments conducted at séances.

'I believe,' he continued, 'that here we are confronted with an incident of exceptional intensity. Franio must have reached a maximum degree of stress that a normal person simply cannot imagine, and unleashed forces that are now acting within a range that is hard to establish. Some of this aura must have permeated the pencil and spread to Leszczuk. There's one detail here that's exceedingly interesting – to wit, that all these symptoms are in some way connected with the lips.

'Leszczuk's lips went dark blue a couple of times. We know he was in the habit of chewing the pencil. But it turns out the pencil had already been chewed before then. And I'd bet my last penny it was Franio who chewed it – on that pencil Leszczuk's toothmarks are mixed up with Franio's.'

'The lips,' said the professor. 'Several times I too have had something wrong with my lips. At least twice I've noticed that they were throbbing, or rippling – but then it stopped.'

'Evidently this force attacks the lips most easily,' said Hińcz pensively.

'And lips were mentioned on those scraps of paper left behind by Rudziański too.'

'But you say this doesn't fully explain the mystery,' said Maja to Hińcz.

'That's the point, it doesn't. This force that's assailing us is by no means neutral in the spiritual regard. It has a distinctly negative

stamp. It is an evil force. I repeat what I have already told you –
I feel it to be remarkably evil and I'm putting my trust in this
feeling. It may well be that it spreads automatically by means
of "infected" objects – but I am convinced that it can only take
root in a person who is spiritually susceptible to it. Why hasn't it
caused greater harm to the professor, although he has spent such
a long time close to the chamber? Because the professor has been
resisting its spirit. And why was Leszczuk "infected"? Because a
series of disastrous circumstances made him lose faith in himself
and weakened him.'

'Yes,' said Maja in distress.

'Do not give in! We shall fight.'

'So what remains to be done?'

Hińcz concentrated.

'A great deal. We must strive towards an explanation of these matters. Above all we must sound out Leszczuk – I am in favour of not
hiding his state from him. Once we make him aware of his position,
he might regain his capacity to resist. We must find out from him
what happened with Maliniak. And talk him out of the idea of suicide.
And generally have him tell us something about his state of mind!'

'It won't be easy,' said the professor.

'We'll see. But that's not all,' said Hińcz, knitting his brow. 'That
peasant puzzles me. Why was Leszczuk especially drawn to him?
And why did I see two people when I was holding the pencil?
Leszczuk walking along the highway, and some other fellow, who
was writing on the wall. Could that have been this Franio?'

The professor took a faded old photograph out of his pocket.

'Was he by chance anything like this photograph?'

'Is this Franio?'

'Yes.'

They examined it with curiosity.

'Yes, he was the one writing on the wall,' said Hińcz. 'That's him.'

'Don't you think he looks like Leszczuk?' asked the professor.

'What's that?!' replied Hińcz in astonishment. 'Does he, indeed? But no, he doesn't! There's no likeness. Take a look – their features are different. The same sort of thing is going on here as with you,' he said, pointing at Maja. 'They don't look alike, but they give that impression because they share similar natures. The likeness is only in the expression of the eyes, in the line of the lips, in the character. You three are joined by the same fervour, vitality, the same passion for life – take a look, Professor.'

Hińcz covered Franio's eyes with a slip of paper. Instantly the likeness vanished.

But Maja shuddered on realizing that he had spoken of 'you three' – as if they formed a single family.

Meanwhile Hińcz was lost in thought, with a vertical crease on his forehead.

'My friends!' he said. 'There's no fooling ourselves. The situation we happen to be in is unusually difficult and will demand our best effort. We must get a firm grip on ourselves. No mysticism, no fatalism. And meanwhile – let's go down to supper.'

'To supper?' said Maja in amazement.

'Absolutely. We have to eat! And in any case we can't hide from the boarding house any longer. Believe me, the more naturally we behave, the better.'

They entered the dining room. The doctor's wife, Miss Wyciskówna and Councillor Szymczyk, as persons *au courant* with Maja's tempestuous past and her even more tempestuous 'criminal' present, drank in the traces of exhaustion on her face, while, in blissful ignorance, a newly arrived young married couple with a child unreservedly devoted themselves to their food.

Maja did her best to utter Hińcz's name as faintly as possible, and at once declared as naturally as could be: 'Mr Leszczuk has come with us, but the peasants beat him up in Koprzywie and he'll have to spend some time recovering.'

'Aaah,' said Miss Wyciskówna.

Maja was moved by the sight of the familiar old dining room, lit by two oil lamps. It felt as if she hadn't been in here for centuries.

'And the dear professor stays at the castle and never looks in on us!' chirped the fat doctor's wife cordially.

'Oh yes, I have befriended the prince,' said Skoliński, 'and I'm studying the archive there.'

But these explanations weren't enough for Wyciskówna. The fact that Maja looked dreadful was understandable. But the professor? And this new gentleman reminded her of someone – could it be . . .

'I think that's Hińcz,' the doctor's wife whispered to her. 'You know, the psychic! I've seen pictures of him in the weeklies!'

Hińcz! Miss Wyciskówna felt as if she'd seen the king of England! Despite which she replied sourly: 'Maybe it is that soothsayer. I'm not interested.'

Silence reigned at the table, one of those awkward silences that, the longer they last, grow heavier and harder to break. Somehow nobody could find a topic of conversation. And strangely, this silence started to be unsettling. Perhaps the presence of a personality such as Hińcz, a 'medium' and a 'spiritualist', made both ladies feet uneasy. And . . . they started talking about ghosts. Hińcz tried in vain to stop them. The doctor's wife told a ghastly story, and Wyciskówna returned the favour. It was impossible to close their mouths! They were simply revelling in it!

After supper Hińcz went into the garden, and as he walked down the narrow paths of the old park, he tried hard to see these dark and complicated matters as clearly as he could.

Never before had he felt such impotence. So what if nature had granted him the power of partial and quite accidental 'second sight' when this clairvoyance did not explain anything – but on the contrary, thrust one into an even worse state of uncertainty, bidding one commune with mysterious, inscrutable powers.

Hińcz was constantly brushing up against this metaphysical world, the nature of which he could not penetrate.

As a result he was more and more inclined towards faith. Amid the world's dreadful ambiguities, he was ever more clearly aware of the simple, certain truth that the one and only mainstay for man, his one and only weapon and law were the values of character, and his one and only signpost was morality. He was sure that if Maja and Leszczuk regained a good moral frame of mind, they'd emerge from all their difficulties victorious.

So he was pleased to have found in the professor an ally gifted with the values of the soul. On the other hand, the stupidity and shallowness of those smug boarding-house guests – the lady clerk and the doctor's wife – filled him with the worst misgivings. If they discovered the whole story, those women would do nothing but sow panic and alarm. Terror would strip them of their last vestiges of dignity and common sense.

Hińcz took hold of the dismal pencil and inspected the tooth-marks in the moonlight. Who else had chewed it? Whose teeth – and in what state of frenzy? He exerted himself, focused hard, stood up

straight, and with his hand extended, tried to perceive something –
to draw aside the hem of the curtain again.

In vain! Could the reach of these forces, here, close to the castle,
be too great? Or else he too was lacking in disinterested calm and
spiritual equilibrium – he was labouring to no avail, he was failing to see anything. Although the crushing impression of evil – of
something evil in the pencil – pervaded him again.

He slowly walked back to the house. But in the dining room
he found the doctor's wife, the lady clerk, and the newly arrived
young couple gathered at a small table in the corner. Hińcz was
now so sensitive to any anomaly that instantly it struck him that
these persons were sitting too close to the table, in too confined
a space.

At the sight of him the lady clerk let out the squeal of a small
child caught red-handed, and the rest of the company too seemed
simultaneously embarrassed and agitated.

What on earth were they up to? He wanted to walk past them,
but on the table he noticed a large sheet of paper with letters written
on it, and on the paper a small plate turned upside down.

'Are you holding a séance?' he asked.

The company sniggered.

'We're going to!' squeaked the young husband.

'Apparently this lady is a medium,' cried the young wife, pointing
at Miss Wyciskówna.

'We are all extremely interested in spiritualist matters,' said the
doctor's wife effusively, casting a winsome glance at Hińcz.

'Would you like to take part in the séance?'

Aha. It was an ambush. These people had discovered his identity –
and in this clumsy way they meant to draw him into a frivolous
game, in the hope of some first-rate thrills. Hińcz was seized with

the desire to flog this imbecilic confederacy of dunces, unwittingly playing with fire.

At the same time, it crossed his mind that a séance could be held – but with Leszczuk.

Yes! That was an idea! By this route, not a very bright one, it would be possible to gain new light. This experiment might work. Except – might it not be too risky?

Hińcz became so pensive that he stopped hearing the peevish voices of the amateur spiritualists. Suddenly hoofbeats rang out – and a tall man in riding clothes came in.

Cholawicki!

'I'm told Miss Maja has arrived,' he said by way of greeting in an unpleasant tone devoid of expression, without looking at anyone.

'Yes, she has,' the nosy ladies hastened to inform him, delighted by the new sensation.

'Is she upstairs?'

'Yes, that's right!'

'Mr Leszczuk is back too,' added Wyciskówna, as if it were of no consequence.

Cholawicki headed for the stairs, but Hińcz stopped him.

'I'm just on my way up and I shall inform Miss Maja that she has a visitor.'

He wanted to warn her, and also to stop Cholawicki from going up. But entirely ignoring his words, Cholawicki stomped up the stairs.

And when he turned into the passage he saw Maja, standing at the door of one of the rooms with Skoliński beside her. The secretary stopped, as if bewitched.

From the moment he had said goodbye to her in Warsaw his sufferings had intensified. The awareness that she was lost, that Leszczuk had taken full possession of her wouldn't let him live.

As soon as he was informed of Miss Ochołowska's arrival, he had set off for Połyka as if scalded by red-hot iron. He didn't know that Leszczuk had come with Maja until the lady clerk told him about it.

By now Cholawicki was on the brink of total collapse. Maja was a reminder of the days when – at any rate – he still belonged to the normal world. This further increased his acute jealousy.

'Maja,' he said soundlessly.

Quickly she moved away from the door.

'Look who's here!' she said with a forced smile, trying to get a grip on herself.

But he was intrigued to see that she was guarding the door against him.

'Who's in that room?' he asked.

'Let's go downstairs!'

He flashed her a look, and instead of replying he pressed the handle. He was carried away by envy.

Maja tried to obstruct him, but he burst into the room. Hińcz raced after him, enraged by this unexpected sabotage that could do the utmost harm to the patient. He was dumbstruck. Leszczuk's bed was empty! He wasn't there!

He had vanished. And the open window showed all too clearly which way he had left the room. A large maple tree near the window had provided the perfect ladder.

Cholawicki was forgotten! Hastily throwing on their coats, everyone ran outside and scattered about the forest.

'Where could he have gone?'

'Let's drive over to the peasant!' cried Hińcz. 'He's sure to have gone there again!'

Maja hurriedly gave orders and they boarded the britzka.

In silence, Cholawicki mounted his horse. He had no idea what Leszczuk's flight meant, nor this urgent pursuit at which he was present; what decided him was Maja's emotional reaction – at the sight of the empty room she became totally oblivious to him.

He galloped after them, almost pleased that they'd forgotten about him – he could digest his misery in peace.

They were driving up to the cottage when Handrycz, as the peasant was called, ran out to meet them, laughing and rejoicing.

'He's flown back to me again!' he called from afar.

Sure enough, Leszczuk emerged from the house and walked up to them. He looked as if he were drunk. He wobbled up to Handrycz with the obstinacy and blindness of a drunkard. And at this point Maja ran out of strength. She rushed towards him.

'What are you doing? Have mercy!' she cried.

Hińcz tried to hide her from him. It was too late. Leszczuk had spotted her.

'You're after me again!' he shouted in complete madness, his eyes wild, and flew at her. They caught him. But he tore free in an insane frenzy.

'She's a killer! A killer! A killer!' he roared.

They rolled on the ground. Mrs Handrycz ran up with some halter ropes. Meanwhile Cholawicki was watching the scene from up on his horse, taking no part in it.

They overpowered Leszczuk and carried him into the cottage. At this point Cholawicki dismounted and slowly approached the window. From here he could hear every word.

'Go away!' Hińcz shouted at Maja. 'You drive him out of his mind!'

Leszczuk burst into tears. Hińcz went straight up to him and put a hand on his shoulder.

'Listen to me!' he said firmly. 'You're haunted by an evil spirit! Can you hear me? You're possessed by the devil!'

Keeping the boy's low intellectual level in mind, he wasn't going to play at any academic circumlocution. He put it in the simplest terms.

He was met with silence.

But at this point, still holding Leszczuk by the shoulder, Hińcz clearly and precisely told him everything he had learned from the professor and from Maja. He spoke slowly, trying to make sure the words got through to Leszczuk's conscious mind.

He told him about the haunted chamber and the pencil – and about what they had been through in recent days. As he presented the whole situation, gradually his hand left the wretched boy's shoulder, and began to stroke his hair.

Could he hear? Could he understand?

Hińcz hadn't the least guarantee, yet he went on talking non-stop for half an hour.

Leszczuk turned his horror-stricken gaze on him.

'Are you really saying this? So that means I'm . . .'

'Yes. But don't give in. We're fighting for you. Please help us.'

'So that's why I ran after the peasant?'

By now he had regained consciousness.

'Save me . . .' he whispered.

'Do take advantage of this moment of better awareness. Right now you are fully conscious,' Hińcz assured him. 'Please answer my questions as precisely as you can.'

'Ask away.'

'What draws you to this peasant?'

'I don't know.'

'Have you ever met him before?'

'Never.'

'So you don't know. But do you realize what you're doing in these moments of madness? Can you remember?'

'Yes,' he whispered. 'But I can't stop myself. It's as if I were drunk, or . . .'

'And when did it first come over you?'

He struggled with himself a while before answering: 'It was then . . . after the murder of Maliniak.'

'And why did you kill Maliniak?'

'What?!'

He sat up in bed.

'She killed him!' he cried and his face went dark. 'She did it! She did it!'

Hińcz shook him violently.

'Calm down!' he shouted, seeing that the boy was sinking into darkness again. 'What are you saying? Stop and think! Damn it all, pull yourself together!'

'She put the noose around his neck and pulled it tight through a hole in the wall I saw it!' gasped Leszczuk and fainted.

Hińcz brought him round with a wet rag.

'Do you know what you said just now? Go on talking! Tell us exactly what happened.'

'What for?' he replied apathetically.

'Because she wasn't the killer! You were seeing things! Perhaps you'd already gone mad by then?'

No! He wasn't mad! He remembered perfectly. She was strangling him when he entered the room. She'd put the noose around his neck while he was asleep, threaded the end of the cord through a gap in the wall into her bedroom and pulled. At first he couldn't understand – only later had he guessed what had happened.

The cord must have been pulled downwards, through a gap between the wall and the floor. The house was shoddily built, it can't have been hard to loosen the floorboards. She'd crept into Maliniak's room in advance, put the noose on him while he slept, and threaded it through the gap – then she'd lit the match to give him the signal to come in through the window, and as soon as he entered, she'd started to throttle Maliniak. She'd planned it all cunningly to put the blame on him. Who would suspect her of it if he had climbed through the window?

Hińcz wiped his brow.

Could it be possible? Perhaps it was. For in these conditions anything was possible. What if Maja had been drawn into the orbit of these powers too, and had strangled Maliniak in a fit of madness?

But he swore to himself that under no circumstances would he let himself be carried away by gruesome flights of fancy. He focused his attention on the facts.

What did it mean? After all, Maja had told him she hadn't lit the match. So why was Leszczuk so sure she had given him the signal by lighting a match?

He asked Leszczuk about it again, then ran to Maja, who was sitting on the front step in agonies of anticipation.

He repeated it all to her.

'He's out of his mind,' she said. 'In the first place, Maliniak's bed stood against the opposite wall to the one between his room and mine. And second, I didn't light the match. Who could have killed Maliniak, if it wasn't him? You know what? The longer I think about all this, the more I come to the conclusion that the most relevant person here would be a psychiatrist.'

Maja was starting to succumb to resignation, but Hińcz refused to admit doubts. He decided to rely on trust. If they couldn't trust each other, he would trust both of them.

If Maja claimed she hadn't lit the match, and Leszczuk claimed to have seen the light of a burning match through the window, then they were both right.

If each suspected the other of murder, then neither of them could have done it.

So what on earth had happened? An evil spirit? But that name shouldn't be abused either – unless there were no other explanation.

Just in case, he asked Maja to draw him a map of the villa and to describe the course of those dramatic events once again in detail.

Reluctantly she satisfied his request. She had no illusions. And he had to overcome the same reluctance in Leszczuk before he'd agree to tell him the whole story again with the map in his hand.

And that was when it appeared that Leszczuk had been wrong about the layout of the rooms! Maliniak's room adjoined Maja's room on one side, and a little hallway on the other, where the stairs to the first floor were located.

'Did you see the light in this room, or this one?' asked Hińcz for the umpteenth time, pointing in turn at the window of Maja's room and the window of the hallway. Each time, Leszczuk pointed at the hallway.

'In this one. In her room.'

'And was Maliniak's bed against this wall?'

'Yes.'

'Then you're mistaken. That's not Miss Maja's room at all.'

'It makes no difference to me,' he replied lifelessly and almost inaudibly. 'If there's something like that inside me . . . If I am . . .'

He turned to face the wall, and Hińcz could get nothing more out of him.

But Maja didn't believe him either when he explained that he was solidly convinced that Leszczuk was telling the truth – and that he had not killed Maliniak.

'Who else could have killed him? Either he doesn't remember, or he's afraid of the responsibility. That stuff about the wall is puerile.'

'Let's go home,' said Hińcz at last. The worst thing was that he couldn't bring them face to face. He was afraid that neither he nor she could withstand a confrontation. And Maja had to go home separately again, because the britzka was needed to take Leszczuk.

'I'm going to the castle,' said the professor. 'You can manage without me, but I can't leave my old gentleman unattended for such a long time.'

'All right, but we must organize regular contact. If nothing happens, please call in at Połyka tomorrow afternoon. Aha, one more thing. Where's Handrycz? We'll have to sound him out too.'

He summoned the peasant.

'Come to Połyka tomorrow morning. I must have a chat with you.'

But at this point Mrs Handrycz put her oar in.

'My old man's not going nowhere,' she said firmly.

'And why not?'

'He's got other work to do.'

'Don't argue!' said the peasant, sensing an opportunity to earn some money. 'What time am I to come?'

'And I say you're not going nowhere!' she screamed. 'It's nothing more than stuff and nonsense! You're to see to the cottage!'

Hińcz took a close look at her. This unexpected resistance made him wonder.

'All right,' he said, 'no means no.'

But he promised himself he'd come here the next day to investigate this mysterious couple.

They set off. They'd reached the forest when suddenly they heard the sound of a galloping horse, and at the point where the tracks crossed, the dark figure of a rider flashed past them.

Cholawicki . . . The drumming of hooves and the dull thud of a riding crop broke the silence of the forest.

What fury there was in that galloping! Hińcz stared anxiously into the forest, but the horse and its rider had long since disappeared.

•

Cholawicki handed his half-dead horse to the stable boy and entered the castle. Shortly before, he'd raced at a gallop, but now he walked very slowly through the empty chambers, his head and hands feverishly trembling. He had overheard Hińcz's entire conversation with Leszczuk. He'd found out the whole story!

Aha, so the force in the old kitchen really was evil!

Could it spread to people? Why hadn't it infected him so far? And why had it singled out Leszczuk in particular? That was curious – why?

The secretary was flabbergasted. How could it be? So he, Skoliński, and the prince, who spent all their time at the castle, had not been attacked, but Leszczuk had . . . even though he had been far away, in Warsaw . . .

He opened the heavy, studded door and stood on the threshold of the old kitchen. He lit a match. The towel was moving tirelessly but almost imperceptibly. It was quivering, shrinking and working away – working away non-stop . . .

As so many times before, Cholawicki gazed at it in silence. How horrible! How extremely revolting! He felt panic and a choking feeling . . . And a sense of idiocy.

So this piece of cloth was persecuting Leszczuk and Maja. It had singled them out. Cholawicki couldn't help sniggering, and his own snigger made him shudder.

He had to admit that even if it was nothing more than a blind, automatic force of nature, some sort of spiritualist-protoplasmic energy, it knew whom to target, he thought.

Why was that? Was this restless, spasmodic sign of life attracted by the mysterious tensions that had arisen between Maja and Leszczuk?

Cholawicki preferred not to investigate. All he knew was that the towel (to give it a name) was in league with him against them.

He remembered how he had tried to shut the professor in here for the night; the man had slipped out of here.

But now the aura of the cloth had latched onto Leszczuk. If only he could get more familiar with it – if only he could exploit this mystery infection – get hold of it – stay for the night, and see . . . If the pencil had had such a disastrous effect on Leszczuk, then what on earth could this . . .

Oh yes, it was horrible. But wasn't he himself horrible? Ruined, desperate, deprived of Maja and the treasure – he had lost on both fronts.

He had known it for some time, ever since the professor had come to live at the castle – ever since Maja had run away with Leszczuk. But only now did the opportunity for revenge present itself.

And Cholawicki burst out laughing again.

'I'll really get you moving,' he muttered.

He stood up and slowly walked towards the towel. As he came closer, he was surprised to find that something he hadn't dared to do for all this time was proving so incredibly easy. He no longer felt the nastiness of the weird phenomenon – all he could feel was his own nastiness, and although his face was twisted with fear, it wasn't fear of the towel, but of himself . . .

XIX.

MEANWHILE Hińcz was in a whirl of feverish activity. Among these enfeebled, disoriented people, he alone represented a reserve of mental energy and the will to resist. He knew what a great responsibility rested with him.

He must strive to clarify the situation! To examine everything that wasn't sufficiently clear, to follow every clue – that was the method he adopted.

He wrote a letter to the investigative authorities in Warsaw:

By reason of extremely urgent business, I regret to say that I cannot come to speak with you in person, he wrote to the judge, yet I regard it as my duty to share a certain intuition that has struck me in connection with the murder of Maliniak.

As we know, the theory so far in this inquiry is that the murderer came in through the window. However, it remains to be explained why he used a noose, and in addition the position of the body, in particular the head of the murder victim, has brought the authorities many difficulties.

And so, gentlemen, I would strongly advise you to subject the wall between Maliniak's room and the hallway to close examination. Please for the moment adopt the hypothesis (without being put off by its apparent absurdity) that the murderer placed the noose around the neck of the sleeping Maliniak, threaded it through a gap in the wall, then went into the hallway and pulled

*on the cord from there. Then he cut off the cord right by the wall
and pushed it back into Maliniak's bedroom.*

*I am fully aware that this assumption, quite fantastical in
itself, totally precludes the fact that the door of Maliniak's room
was locked from the inside, in view of which the murderer could
not have entered and placed the noose. Whereas if he entered
through the window he could not have got into the hallway.
Nonetheless, I would consider it highly advisable to investigate
this idea as if it were possible, for I am entirely convinced that
this is what must have happened. Would you please inform me
at once of the results of your research, as that would facilitate my
ongoing work. I remain yours etc.*

Hińcz was placing his entire authority on the line.

At about five in the afternoon, Skoliński arrived.

'At last!' said Hińcz. 'I've been expecting you! Please take care
of our patient, while I go and see Handrycz. It's not the least of the
riddles we must solve.'

'I don't know if I'm doing the right thing by staying away from
the castle,' said the professor. 'Cholawicki didn't appear at lunch
today. He sent word that he's sick. I'm afraid he's up to something.'

'Soon we'll deal with that fellow face to face,' replied the clairvoyant. 'And the ghosts in the chamber too.'

'You want to declare war on the towel?'

'Of course! That is the source of the evil and we must get to it.
If Cholawicki tries to obstruct us, we'll neutralize him by force.
There can be no pussyfooting around! But first I must gain as much
information as possible and – most crucially – fortify Leszczuk and
Maja psychologically. Then we'll make our way to the castle and
simply destroy the towel.'

'That might carry unpredictable consequences,' cried Skoliński.

'Tough. Anyway, we'll see. This evening I'm going to conduct an experiment of great significance.'

Skoliński stayed with Leszczuk, who had once again sunk into a state of torpor and was lying in bed without moving.

Maja wasn't coming out of her room. The professor went to and fro between them, but he too was full of forebodings, anxiously thinking about the prince and about Cholawicki's sudden illness.

Towards evening, Hińcz returned.

'There's something suspicious about that peasant,' he reported the result of his visit to Skoliński. 'His old woman wouldn't let me see him. I don't know why she's digging her heels in. But I discovered some facts in the next village. It turns out Handrycz came here from Lublin about fifteen years ago with his wife. The wife is the daughter of a local farmer, but she was in service in Lublin, where she met Handrycz and married him. When her father died, they came here to take on the farm. Handrycz has no family here and no one can tell me any more details about him.'

'Oh dear, if only we could discover that sign at last!' groaned the historian, worried about the prince's fate.

'Professor,' said Hińcz, 'this evening we're going to carry out a decisive test. Please stay for supper. It may be that before the day ends the mystery will start to unfold.'

He had serious concerns about this experiment, which could end in disaster. Hold a spiritualist séance with Leszczuk as the medium? Hypnotize him, and by taking this doubtful path strive to form a clearer idea of the forces that had taken possession of him?

It was an extremely dangerous game indeed, for which the boy might pay with his health and his life. No one could foresee the outcome of such a séance.

And yet Hińcz was determined to go ahead, in order to break through the wall of darkness that surrounded them.

May the experiment succeed! The mystical nature of the goings-on in the haunted chamber made this method appear very promising. Except that – to Hińcz's despair – he would have to resort to the help of the boardinghouse harpies for lack of anyone else to take part in the séance.

It made Hińcz's flesh creep to think that those idiotic females would be taking part in such a risky experiment.

After supper he suggested: 'Well, then? Let's hold a little séance. That will occupy our evening.'

'Ah!' cried Wyciskówna and the doctor's wife. And Wyciskówna added: 'I am happy to serve as a medium.'

'No, I have a better medium. If I am suggesting a séance, it is because I believe Leszczuk is an excellent medium. We'll ask him to take part.'

Wyciskówna and the doctor's wife were beside themselves with joy. A séance, and with Leszczuk too!

A round table was made ready in a snug, corner study. The blinds were lowered, and a dimmed lamp was placed to one side – such were the modest, yet thrilling preparations.

Hińcz explained to Leszczuk what he intended to do with him. The boy did not protest.

Hińcz couldn't possibly guess quite how terrified Leszczuk had been on hearing that he was in the power of some mysterious influences.

This news, which could have shaken someone more sophisticated than he was, acted like a thunderbolt on this simple boy.

So he was in the power of the devil?

Leszczuk wouldn't go into the subtle details. For him this force could only be demonic.

He didn't believe it. He couldn't believe it. But everything spoke in its favour.

Either way, there was something horrible inside him – he could sense that.

So revulsion and fear of his own being had made him sink into a complete stupor.

Maja was not to take part in the séance – her presence was impossible in view of Leszczuk's participation.

'Please have a supply of smelling salts and dressings to hand and wait in the next room,' Hińcz advised her.

'Dressings?'

'Yes. We don't know what might happen.'

They took their seats around the table. On Leszczuk's right sat Hińcz, on his left the professor, then the two ladies and the married couple. Paper and a small plate were made ready. Hińcz got down to business very cautiously. To start with, he decided to hold an ordinary séance with a small plate.

'Oho, it's moving,' whispered the horrified doctor's wife, when after about fifteen minutes of nervous anticipation the plate began to shudder and then roamed about the paper.

While the doctor's wife responded with reverent terror, Miss Wyciskówna by contrast was deeply convinced that all this was 'poppycock', 'cant' and 'fooling the guests', a belief that she demonstrated by making suitable faces and pouting.

However, the saucer began to spin about the paper faster and faster, with ever more determination.

Suddenly it stopped, with the line that Hińcz had marked on its edge pointing at the letter J. Then rapidly, with increasing speed, the letters A, M, and A followed.

'Ja-ma,' read the doctor's wife in a whisper.

'No prompting, madam,' the clairvoyant reproached her.

But the plate repeated the word over and over again. It went crazy, flying across the paper, slipping from under the fingers of the assembled company and repeating: 'Ja-ma-ja-ma-ja-ma-ja . . .'

'What is your name?' asked Hińcz.

The plate moved violently.

'Fra-ja.'

'Fraudster,' said Miss Wyciskówna, adding an ironical twist.

'Ja-fra-ma,' tapped out the plate.

'Repeat!' ordered Hińcz, endeavouring with the utmost attention to understand the meaning of this gibberish.

'Fra-ja-ma,' replied the plate this time, and then instantly spelled out the word 'No'.

'You don't want to say?'

'No.'

'Why not?'

'Lead,' tapped out the plate and stopped.

'He's insistent,' whispered the doctor's wife.

'Even if he started to move, he won't tell us anything,' said the professor in a slightly hoarse voice, 'because the line is blurred.'

'What's that?'

It was true. The line marked by Hińcz in pencil on the plate had faded.

'Lead,' repeated Hińcz and stood up. 'It means lead the element. Wait here, please, I'll fetch a lead pencil.'

'I have a pencil,' said Wyciskówna.

But as if not hearing her, Hińcz left the room and returned soon after with a small black pencil. He used it to draw a new line on the edge of the plate, and they all leaned over it again.

Just then the doctor's wife became dreadfully scared.

'I'm leaving!'

'Do not break the chain,' shouted the clairvoyant menacingly. And at that moment the plate moved again, like crazy. It started hurling itself about the table, racing to the edge, as if trying to fall off and smash to pieces. It was in a frenzy – such unconscious but obvious fury that they felt as if an animal were thrashing beneath their fingers.

Just then Skoliński said: 'He's sleeping.'

They glanced at Leszczuk. Indeed, he was asleep, his face deathly pale, with beads of sweat on his brow – he was in a deep sleep. His lips had gone blue, almost black, and he was panting.

'Do not break the chain,' Hińcz quietly ordered.

This order was superfluous. No one was moving. They were all riveted to the spot, in anticipation. Then came crackling noises and static discharges in the room. The plate rose half a metre up and plummeted, shattering into tiny pieces.

'Who are you?' asked the clairvoyant.

This strange question was justified. Leszczuk's features had undergone radical change. His nose had sharpened, his face had grown thinner and somehow alien, imbued with an aura of terrible hatred. His teeth showed behind his black lips and at the same time his body began to 'pulsate'. Not to tremble, but to 'pulsate' – or so at least it seemed to those watching in the semi-darkness.

'You'd like that?' said Leszczuk in a voice that wasn't his. 'All right. All right. Now I shall forgive you. You will see. Now you will see. First myself, then you.'

He tore a hand free, raised it, and passed a finger across his throat.

'That's how I'll forgive you! That's how I'll forgive myself and you!'

He tore the other hand free and stood up, swaying. With both hands he began to make strange gestures, as if stuffing something into his mouth. Straight after that his face went purple and he crashed to the ground, wheezing.

The doctor's wife had an attack of nerves and fell off her chair to the floor. The young couple simply fled. Hińcz and the professor sprang to the rescue.

But how were they to save him? From what? Leszczuk was suffocating on invisible matter – so it seemed – with no chance of rescue.

Hińcz worked feverishly to wake Leszczuk up. And finally, when it looked as if all was lost, his efforts proved effective – the boy awoke and instantly stopped choking. He was gasping for breath.

'Where am I?' he whispered.

They carried him upstairs. The whole house was as if deserted. The terrified guests had taken refuge in the furthest rooms.

'Where is Maja?' the professor suddenly wondered.

They tried calling, but she didn't answer. She should have been waiting in the little parlour. At once Hińcz noticed her lying on the floor, unconscious.

They easily revived her.

'What happened to you?'

'I fainted.'

She knew nothing, only that she'd been sitting here, as instructed. Apart from that she couldn't remember a thing. Hińcz muttered and sighed with relief as he closely inspected the minor injuries she'd sustained in falling.

'Well, it could have ended worse – for both of you.'

'Was the experiment a success? Did you find something out?'

'Quietly, now. Have a bit of a rest, and we'll give some thought to the material we've gained.'

Hińcz looked in on Leszczuk again, who was lying on the bed, exhausted. He didn't ask any questions, but his eyes, wide open and immobile, were shot through with deathly, almost bestial grief and alarm. When Hińcz tried saying a few words to reassure him he replied nervously: 'Don't tell me. I don't want to know. I don't want anything!'

That's not good, thought the clairvoyant, *he won't be able to cope with this for long.*

Without going far from Leszczuk's room, Hińcz and the professor discussed the séance at length.

'My dear Professor,' said Hińcz, 'it seems we were present at a scene that took place in the old kitchen. As for me, I am virtually in no doubt that Leszczuk's body was occupied by Franio.'

'Is that possible?' whispered the professor.

'Of course, that sort of thing happens at a séance. But one needn't automatically ascribe supernatural meaning to it. We don't know how it happens, because we aren't fully aware of our psychological characteristics, but it is at séances that other personalities appear through mediums. In this case, it was Franio.'

'Yes. That was to be expected.'

The professor took out the photograph. Yes – Leszczuk had become like Franio.

'In my view, now we know what happened in the old kitchen on that critical day,' said Hińcz, 'and I think you will agree with me. We were witnesses to Franio's final conversation with the prince, in the course of which he committed suicide. He performed this terrible act with the use of the towel – by stuffing it into his mouth and twisting his face, just as we saw. He choked himself on the towel in the presence of the wretched prince. In this regard Leszczuk's movements at the séance were clear and vivid. Why didn't the prince prevent him? Maybe he was paralyzed by fear? Maybe he couldn't stop him for practical reasons? And passing his finger across his throat like that,' he suddenly wondered, 'what do you think, isn't that the sign we're looking for?'

But the scholarly historian shrugged.

'I've tried a similar gesture a thousand times on the prince and on Mrs Ziółkowska without effect. In any case, it wasn't forgiveness. It was more like menace.'

And the professor repeated Franio's gesture, but at once stopped. 'That's not quite it,' he said.

'He did it another way!' confirmed Hińcz in turn, copying Franio-Leszczuk's movement.

'No, not like that.'

'So like what?'

They were both stumped. Suddenly Skoliński cried: 'He did it with his left hand!'

Yes, that was the difference. Could Franio have been left-handed? In any case, Skoliński hadn't tried that gesture yet.

'I'm going to see Mrs Ziółkowska!' he cried. 'It has to be tested.'

'I'm going with you,' said Hińcz, not entirely convinced of the professor's perceptive powers.

'Wouldn't it be better if you stayed here? Can we leave the two of them alone like this, after such a shock?'

But the clairvoyant had no such fears.

'We'll go in the britzka. We'll be back in an hour. If they've survived the séance successfully, they're not in any danger for the time being.'

Just in case, he left Maja with special instructions, telling her to keep an eye on Leszczuk, but under no pretext was she to go into his room.

He put Marysia in overall charge. Then he and Skoliński set off for the forester's lodge where the housekeeper was staying on holiday. Along the way they continued to comment on the unexplained details of the séance.

Ja-ma? Had Leszczuk been saying Ja-ma? What did Ja-ma mean? Why had the medium gone on to supplement it with the syllable 'Fra'? Fra – meaning Franio?

They were soon lost in conjecture. 'Ja-ma', 'Fra-ja-ma', 'ja-ma-ja' – what sense lay hidden in this gibberish?

'Ja Ma-ja – "*ja*" means "I", so that could be "I, Maja"', said Hińcz. 'But why "Fra"? Or perhaps . . . Fra-ja-ma . . . Fra – Franio. Ja – that's a reference to himself, I, Leszczuk. Ma is short for Maja. Just a second . . . Could the medium have been trying to stress the connection between these three persons? Fra-ja-ma – and thus a creature formed of the three of them, a combination of Maja, Leszczuk and Franio? One could explain it like that, or one could also do it another way. How little we know about the world and about ourselves!'

Mrs Ziółkowska was not at home. They had to wait a long time for the housekeeper to return from Koprzywie, wearing a black shawl and a huge hat. At the sight of the professor, she spat in disgust.

'What? Not about those signs again! I can't recall a thing!' she shouted. 'Please leave me in peace!'

'Just a moment! Do you remember this?'

The professor made the gesture.

'No!' she shrieked. 'I do not! What an idea! I've brought nothing but trouble on myself by coming here!'

'Please try hard to remember. Maybe it was something like that?'

'Something like a smack in the face!'

They had no alternative but to get in the britzka and leave. The professor was disappointed, but Hińcz took a less trustful view of Mrs Ziółkowska.

'That old bird is fibbing. Did you notice how flustered she was in the first instance? And actually, if she was bringing the prince food on a tray that day, she probably had it in her right hand. So she only had the left one free, and if she did make a gesture, it was with her left hand.'

'I'm getting out here,' said the professor as they passed the road leading to the castle. 'It's high time I went back to my post. But who's this in a hurry? Grzegorz?'

Grzegorz was running towards them in the moonlight, waving his arms. They jumped out of the britzka.

'Has something happened?'

'I've been looking for you everywhere, Your Honour. I've been to Połyka.'

'What's wrong? You can talk freely before this gentleman.'

'Things are bad! God forbid! I hurried to warn you that things are bad.'

'What is it?'

'The secretary spent the whole night in the old kitchen!'

This news struck Skoliński and Hińcz like a thunderbolt. Cholawicki in the old kitchen?

In a few broken sentences the old servant gave his report: 'Yesterday I noticed that the secretary was in a worse state – he just walked about the castle smiling, and didn't look in on the prince at all. Last night I dropped by his room, but he wasn't there. I thought he'd gone out, or something . . . At dawn I called on him again – the bed was untouched, he wasn't there. But a short time ago something prompted me to look in at the old kitchen. So I do, and I see the bed's rumpled, as if someone's been lying on it.'

'Well?'

'I raced off to the secretary, and he just burst out laughing, but somehow so . . . I think he's gone completely mad! "Don't obstruct me," he says, "for I have scores to settle." Then he called for his horse and rode off. I think to myself, I must fly to Połyka to find the professor, for things are bad! But on the way a peasant told me you gentlemen had gone this way, so I've been waiting. We must do something at once, or there might be a misfortune! The prince is alone at the castle!'

Hińcz and the professor exchanged glances.

'Let's go back.'

'Can he have lost his wits entirely?'

'Anything is possible!' said Hińcz. The worst thing is that anything is possible! You return to the castle with Grzegorz immediately. Keep an eye on the prince. I'm going to Połyka. We shouldn't have left them on their own.'

'What's your plan?'

'If Cholawicki gets in the way, we'll have to tie him up. We must take control of the castle and gain free access to the chamber. If there's no alternative, we'll throw out the towel, set fire to it, and destroy it regardless of the consequences! This state of affairs is intolerable in the long run. I refuse to be blackmailed by that cloth any longer, even if the devil himself is sitting in it.'

Hińcz whipped up the horse and drove off sharply to Połyka. He was now set on anything. By the time he arrived, it must have been eleven at night. It struck him that the dogs hadn't been unchained.

'Where is Miss Maja?' he asked the maid.

'Miss Maja left with Mr Cholawicki and told me to give you this letter.'

Hińcz opened the envelope.

'Dear Mr Hińcz,' he read, 'please do not look for me. I'll be back in the morning. Maja.'

'Was Mr Cholawicki here for long?'

'No. He talked to the young lady in the garden, and then she went with him, taking the buckboard. Madam is back from Warsaw too.'

Indeed, Mrs Ochołowska appeared in the doorway looking despondent, with dark circles around her eyes.

'Could you please explain to me what is going on here, sir?' she said.

Only now did Hińcz notice the hullaballoo in the house. The servants were bringing out suitcases in every direction. Miss Wycis-kówna, the doctor's wife and Szymczyk flashed past inside, all dressed for travel. Mrs Ochołowska was entirely at a loss.

'I arrived a quarter of an hour ago from Warsaw,' she said, 'where I went in connection with the dreadful story about Maliniak. I couldn't find Maja there, so I came home. Apparently you brought her back. But what's going on? Everyone wants to leave, right away, on the night train! And where has Maja gone? Would you please wait,' she addressed the lady clerk, the doctor's wife and the coun-cillor, who had just walked up, 'at least until tomorrow?'

'Impossible!' said Wyciskówna. 'I have received an urgent mes-sage. I must go!'

'And I shall keep you company!' cried the doctor's wife.

'And I shall take care of the ladies,' said the councillor.

The young couple were on their way too. No one wanted to stay at Połyka for the night.

Panic, thought Hińcz, while also seeking some explanation for Mrs Ochołowska.

'I'm afraid I am to blame,' he said at last. 'Unfortunately certain qualities of mine, of which you are sure to have heard, can frighten people away. And I was careless enough to have organized a little séance after supper. It seems to have induced this mass exodus.'

'Where is Maja?' asked Mrs Ochołowska, as if not hearing him at all.

The same question was hammering away in Hińcz's mind.

XX.

IF UNTIL NOW Maja had regarded Hińcz's suppositions with mistrust, feeling them to be improbable, if not absurd, now, following the séance, she believed them.

Deep down she had been convinced that Leszczuk had either simply gone mad, or was feigning madness out of fear of responsibility.

But now she really was starting to believe he was possessed, haunted by an alien power. All his actions had to be connected with that chamber. He'd been infected by some inscrutable aura.

In which instance, anything was possible!

So he wasn't as she had imagined by nature – so the murder and those other, earlier acts were all the result of that outer force?

And perhaps he hadn't killed Maliniak at all? Maybe it was this force that had killed him?

But in that case he wasn't lying in suspecting her of the murder?

And if he suspected her . . . maybe the idea really had led him to flee Warsaw, to go mad, and become susceptible to the influence of the chamber? And that would mean that he loved her. Yet . . .

Maja walked about the room, from corner to corner, struggling with herself.

Should she go to him or not?

What she found most agonizing was that he couldn't bear her presence, and that they were apart.

Go to him or not? What if it did him harm and he had another attack?

But she felt it was necessary.

She was sure that she alone could cure him.

If he loved her . . .

If only he loved her – if only it were true that he'd got into all this trouble because of her and nothing else. Ah, his salvation was in her hands, she was the remedy for him!

She pressed the handle.

He was lying in bed and didn't even shudder when she entered. They looked at each other without speaking. Maja felt odd.

Imagine being in the grip of an alien force! Being the object of an attack, having an intruder inside you, capable of taking over your soul at any moment? Not being fully responsible for anything? What a dreadful, ridiculous idea!

'Do you really think it was I who killed Maliniak?' she asked.

He said nothing, but his gaze remained vacant and terrified. How could she convince him? What should she say to him?

It was as if Leszczuk had entirely ceased to react to her.

'Maybe it wasn't you,' he said at last, 'but it's all the same to me.'

Oh, those terror-struck, stupefied eyes!

'What do you mean?' she whispered.

'Just that. I'm doomed already, lost for ever and amen.'

'I'm not to blame . . .'

He sat up in bed.

'You are not to blame? Then who is? Didn't you tempt me in every possible way? I've reproached you for it several times before! I didn't pick up this evil spirit from the pencil, but from you. It was there inside you from the start! When you stole Szulk's wallet. Whenever you talked me round. Because of you I played a dirty trick at that tennis match, and no wonder God has punished me.'

She didn't know how to reply. He was right. The look in his eyes was dreadful! If only she could have a clean conscience. But instead of raising him to her level with love, she had spurned him, mistrusted him – and pushed him lower and lower.

How naïvely he put it. The devil, he'd said. Quite simply. And maybe that was fully justified.

But she was amazed by what he'd said about Szulk's wallet.

'I robbed Szulk?'

Maja was close to believing she had done it. She was totally confused. So he suspected her of that too?

But she found his indifference unbearable! The apathy! The bestial terror!

'Don't talk like that!' she shouted. 'It's not true! Anyway, I love you. I love you! You love me too, I know it!'

She wanted to tear him free of this state at any cost. Could she have lost her influence over him?

'Please leave me alone,' he said slowly, 'this is no time for romance. It's here inside me – and it might be inside you too. If it's in me, it's in you. How can I know if it's you that's talking to me now, or . . . I don't know . . . if it's definitely . . . you . . . You know what? There's just one thing left – go and fetch a priest, I want to make my confession.'

She left the room.

For a while she couldn't get her head around what had happened.

He suspected her, no more nor less, but of having this 'evil' inside her too. An evil spirit. That was how he imagined it. He didn't trust her. He was afraid of her. And she was afraid of him. She couldn't help feeling terror at the sight of him. They were afraid of each other.

Maja felt he was expressing it too naïvely and literally. And yet so many weird things and anomalies had occurred around her lately that she couldn't be sure of anything.

They feared each other, and this terror, black, superstitious, was killing any chance of salvation!

He wanted to make his confession . . . Maybe that was the wisest and only thing to do in their situation? Summon a priest. Maja couldn't believe she was really having this thought.

She fell to her knees in the corridor, and for the first time in many years she sank into ardent prayer.

She couldn't have said to whom or for what she was praying. She was desperately calling for someone's help, begging for someone's mercy on her and Leszczuk.

Maja's energy was completely drained. Her helpless mind could only latch onto one desire, for all this to be well and truly over. Never mind how – she'd had enough of this torment!

She kneeled in a dark corner, with her face in her hands. She couldn't feel the warm tears trickling through her fingers. Imperceptibly, exhaustion came over her, and such profound apathy that it almost felt like peace.

The house seemed to be asleep in silence. The lamp in the corridor dimmed.

Was it a dream, or a hallucination? All of a sudden Maja felt as if someone was hauling her to her feet and leading her away through the darkness and silence.

In the void ahead of her a door opened noiselessly, and then closed behind her. Her only clue to this was the deepening darkness. Behind nearby walls she could hear a rising hum. It wasn't the cry of branches in a gale, nor waves of torrential rain beating against the windowpanes.

All this was dreamlike, yet real. If she'd stretched out her hands, she'd have touched wet stone walls. She knew this with a sort of irrefutable certainty. And she continued to walk into the depths of this mysterious cloister without hesitation, trusting the one leading her, whoever it was.

Somewhere in the distance a small light shone. It was growing larger and more distinct. She realized that it was a multicoloured stained-glass window of the kind sometimes seen in the corridors of old monasteries. A random mosaic of small panes of coloured glass, patched together any old how.

She was meant to see something through the colourful bits of glass. But the contours of the window were moving, the lines were writhing and tangling like snakes. She strained her vision, but in vain.

At this point she felt sure she wasn't asleep.

She wanted to smash the stained-glass window, but she sensed that she couldn't raise her hands.

She was holding them to her face and eyes just as she had a while ago, when she'd been kneeling to pray. Her fingers were throbbing with warm blood, and sticking to her tear-stained cheeks. She could clearly see light between her fingers, but it was multicoloured, not monotone, as before.

She definitely wasn't asleep! She could even hear her own breathing, quickened, sometimes interrupted by spasmodic sighing.

But she was incapable of any movement. As if paralyzed.

The someone who was at her side – no one else – finally took pity, now that she was wrestling with her own impotence. He must have pushed the little window, because the coloured, tangled bits of glass vanished.

She peeped through a narrow gap in a thick wall. She knew she would see something evil there, something awful. She gathered all her strength to conquer her fear. Because she must, at any cost, she must finally see what was hiding there.

It was like seeing through a thick curtain. The image seemed strange, as if she were looking from below or above, not normally.

Yes, from below. There were shadows of people trailing about a white chamber, looking strangely foreshortened. Huge feet walking on long legs. The torsos appeared tiny, the heads non-existent.

One of the ghosts came close to Maja. It leaned towards her. Through the curtain she could see the outline of a face, somehow familiar, and yet so altered that a shiver ran through her. (No, she wouldn't have felt that shiver in her sleep.)

Who was it? Leszczuk, for sure. Whom else did she expect to see here? The eyes were out of their sockets, the eyeballs huge and white, like a drowned man's. The face was blue and puffy, the lips swollen and black as iron.

A nightmare.

Two enormous hands reached out to Maja. The fingers, as crooked as talons, were curling and unfolding rapaciously. But they couldn't grab hold. They came up against the white curtain. Their claws became entangled in it. They tugged and yanked at it – but they couldn't tear free.

Suddenly there was a flash of insane fear in the dislocated eyes. The talons withdrew. One hand, the left, seized the throat and choked it, forcing the black lips to part in a dreadful spasm, revealing the teeth. The other hand fluttered in the air, like the wing of a wounded bird.

The phantom began to shake. For a while it staggered torpidly, then suddenly tumbled face first towards Maja.

She heard a weak, stifled scream. Her own voice. But there was more surprise in it than alarm – because in that instant she had recognized that the ghastly phantom was not Leszczuk.

Someone familiar. Who? . . . . For God's sake, who was it?

But it was Handrycz! Definitely Handrycz.

The hallucination vanished. And yet the phantom's face lingered in Maja's memory. She couldn't be mistaken, even though the features were so dreadfully altered.

Suddenly the whole strange image was gone. The curtain, the white room, the human shadows . . . Just the memory of Handrycz's face refused to go away.

Where on earth had Handrycz come from?

She was still in the same somnolent state, but was consciously unwilling to tear free of it. She was agonized by unsatisfied curiosity. She waited – would the vision start up again and continue, providing some sort of explanation, or additional information?

Who had led her, Maja, down those passages? Why had he shown her that chamber, familiar from somewhere, just as Handrycz's face was familiar?

But nothing else would appear beneath her closed eyelids. Instead, complete awareness of time and place returned. The torpidity was leaving her body. Instead, pain had awoken in her tired knees and tightly clenched fingers. Now aroused, her mind began to work away again, ever more anxiously.

If it wasn't a dream, what did the vision mean? Where had it come from? She couldn't make coherent sense of her scraps of memories. In fact, what memories? An underground passage leading to the castle, a room she'd seen before in a dream, and Handrycz's face? Why Handrycz, and not Leszczuk? Why was the phantom choking itself with its own hand? Yes, its left hand?

How much she'd have given to have someone here who could help her to understand it all. Her efforts to solve the riddle alone were in vain.

Tiredness, nervous exhaustion? That could have justified the dream and the hallucinations. But she hadn't been asleep . . . Could it have been a premonition, shaped into visions prompted by her fevered imagination? If so, what did it portend?

But Leszczuk wasn't there! she told herself in amazement. *Is that good or bad?* Was he no longer there, or had he remained entirely beyond the range of these nightmares?'

Before she could calm herself down by dissuading herself from attaching weight to delusions, she heard soft footsteps at the far end of the corridor.

Someone was walking towards her.

'Mr Cholawicki is here,' she heard Marysia's hesitant voice behind her.

She sprang to her feet. What on earth did he want? Should she receive him or not? But then it crossed her mind that something might have happened at the castle.

He apologized for appearing at such a late hour, but he wanted to talk to her on an important matter.

His eyes were shining feverishly.

'Let's go into the garden,' she suggested, and soon they were among tall trees, immersed in the dark-blue celestial expanse.

'Above all I want to tell you that I'm no longer your enemy,' said the secretary very quietly, 'neither yours nor Leszczuk's. I give up. I've changed greatly since yesterday, as you're about to find out. But please keep this entirely to yourself. There's very important news.'

'All right.'

'Do you know what the old kitchen at the castle is, and what's been going on in there?'

'Yes.'

'Then listen. No one has ever dared to stay all night in there. Not so long ago I couldn't summon up the courage either. But the night before last – I did it . . .'

He took a deep breath.

'Now I know what's going on in there with that towel,' he said. 'And I came specially to tell you this because . . . there's something happening in there that's to do with . . . you.'

She shuddered. With her? Was he telling the truth? But how could he know she was mixed up in this business? Even if he'd heard about Leszczuk's illness, he didn't know its foundation.

Perhaps Skoliński had given the game away? No, that was impossible.

Besides, she only had to look at him. If before then Cholawicki had looked like a ghost, now he resembled death itself.

She felt her throat tighten.

'What?' she dared to ask. But he shook his head.

'I can't reveal it to you,' he whispered. 'It's impossible and . . . anyway, I can't. Don't even ask. All I'll tell you is that it's to do with you and Leszczuk . . . You must go there alone and see for yourself!'

'I must go there alone?'

'Yes, you must. No one but you will understand it. It's about you and him. Listen, what does it mean? Can it be that you . . . that he . . .'

'What?'

'Nothing! Nothing! Go there alone. You'll see. And you must go right away. Tonight. Everything depends on it! His life, and more than that!'

'But what's it all about?'

'Don't ask! But if you don't go at once, you'll never save him!'

Maja jumped from mistrust to terror, then fury, then helplessness . . .

She didn't believe Cholawicki. She could sense a trick.

How could he have suddenly become her and Leszczuk's guardian angel? She knew his jealousy.

But then how could he know all this? Perhaps he was deliberately trying to lure her into that room? But what if he was telling the truth?

His enigmatic, elusive words were driving her insane! They were increasing her uncertainty!

And she realized she had to go and see what was happening in there. Until she knew, she'd never have a moment's self-confidence and peace.

She and Leszczuk were slaves to this mystery, slaves to anyone who wanted to blackmail them with it, finally slaves to their own frenzied fantasy.

They'd be afraid of each other. They'd never be sure of anything.

If lack of trust had killed the love in them earlier, what would happen now that they really had no idea who they were anymore?

So she had to go and see, and finally know what it was – yes, only then would she be able to save herself and him!

But what if Cholawicki were drawing her in on purpose? Maybe she'd see things in there that she couldn't withstand?

Or maybe there was nothing there, just a spurned fiancé taking his revenge? She only had to look at him, at his vacant eyes and face . . .

'Do you want to go there with me right away?'

'Yes, right away. It's high time. Tomorrow it could be too late.'

She smiled.

'So that's a yes? All right. Let's go.'

She went to fetch a coat.

But once alone in her bedroom she had another flash of dreadful panic.

She leaned her brow against the wall – she felt as if she were fainting.

But she got a grip on herself. The awareness that she must save Leszczuk, and that she was sacrificing herself for him, gave her strength.

'I'm ready,' she said as she descended the stairs, addressing Cholawicki, who was waiting for her with his gaze fixed on the ground.

They didn't speak a word to each other the entire way.

And with every beat of the horses' hooves Maja became more certain that he wished her ill and was taking his revenge.

But she'd had enough of it all!

She could no longer fear that chamber, be dependent on it, know nothing, or live in a fog, in a cloud of mist.

She had to see! Find out for herself! Make sure! Know something at last!

And her personal fate didn't matter to her now. She'd suffered too much.

Maja understood that there are times in life when one must summon up all one's courage and be prepared to risk absolutely everything if one wants to save one's dignity and humanity.

'This way,' said Cholawicki, leading her through the chambers.

He opened a heavy door with metal fittings and shone a torch. 'Here.'

She raised her head.

She saw a white room – the same one she'd seen in her dreams. On a peg hung a dusty towel, yellow with age. Aha, so that was it. Yes, it was quivering ever so slightly . . . almost imperceptibly . . .

'All right,' she said.

The sound of her own voice surprised her.

Then Cholawicki grabbed her by the arms.

'Stay here,' he said. 'Sit down on the bed – and wait. So – farewell.'

He lowered his voice.

'You won't survive it,' he whispered. 'You won't!'

And his face contorted into a horrible, malevolent mask.

She tried to push him away. But he gave her a mighty shove onto the bed, leaped out of the chamber, slammed the heavy door shut and locked it.

She didn't even try to open it.

Total darkness filled the room. And through the door Cholawicki said to her: 'I'm still here. But I'm about to walk away. I'll have gone and you'll be left alone. And then you'll see – you'll see something you can't endure! If you've never gone mad with terror before . . . Well, I'm off now. I'm leaving you . . .'

His footsteps died away.

XXI.

HIŃCZ ran upstairs to Leszczuk.

'Do you know what has happened to Miss Maja?'

'Why do you ask?'

'Cholawicki was here. Apparently she rode off with him.'

He was so worried by her departure that he wasn't in the least concerned about the effect this could have on Leszczuk. He suspected Cholawicki of the worst things imaginable.

'I have no idea,' muttered Leszczuk apathetically.

It seemed nothing was capable of jolting him out of his fearful anticipation.

Hińcz wasn't listening anymore. He called Marysia.

'Is there a gun here?'

'There's the late master's revolver and a double-barrelled shotgun.'

'Please bring them to me, but don't let anyone see you. And some cartridges.'

The horses drove up to the porch and the boardinghouse guests were about to take their seats when suddenly the clairvoyant jumped into the carriage with the shotgun and the revolver, and before Wyciskówna and the doctor's wife knew what was happening, he'd thrown out their suitcases.

'Let's go!' he shouted to the driver. 'To the castle! Twenty zlotys for beer if we're there in half an hour!'

They set off. But just then Handrycz caught up with the carriage and jumped onto the footstep.

'I've been waiting here for you, sir. I have something to say! I've been waiting for two hours!'

'Get in!' said Hińcz. 'You can tell me on the way. I'm in a hurry.'

'Where are you going?'

'To the castle!'

'And a good thing too, because there's something to do with the castle going round in my head.'

Gradually he explained to Hińcz exactly why he had come.

Ever since that fellow had started pressing against him, he'd been in a sort of non-stop daydream . . . As if he were trying to remember something, but couldn't. Had he lost his marbles, or what?

And it had something to do with the castle. But he couldn't remember a thing.

He'd told his wife, she'd sworn at him and chivvied him off to work, but he'd decided to go to Połyka and ask for advice, because something about all this was . . .

'Listen here, are you by any chance a lefty?'

'What?'

'Do you find it easier to use your left hand?'

'Yes, my left hand works better than my right.'

Handrycz was somewhat surprised by this question. But Hińcz did not reply.

Now they were driving up to the castle, but before the carriage had pulled up in front of the castle gate, two figures emerged from the shadows of the night – Skoliński and Grzegorz.

'There's no doubt,' said the professor. 'She has gone into the castle with him. The peasants saw them, but he has locked the gate! It's impossible to get inside.'

'Let's go through the underground passage.'

'It's too far. Besides, he's sure to have blocked entry from that direction.'

They stood there helplessly. Suddenly from a window of the corner tower the secretary's voice rang out.

'Have you gentlemen come to call?'

He laughed. He was caustic!

'Is Miss Maja inside the castle?'

'How did you guess?!'

'I wish to talk to her – without delay.'

'That's not possible! Right now Miss Maja is spending some time in the old kitchen! At her own request! She decided to investigate what's going on in there and asked not to be disturbed! I'm sorry, but I cannot let you in.'

'I want to talk to the prince.'

'The prince is asleep.'

'Open up or we'll break down the gate.'

'Ah, so it has come to this! Unfortunately! Miss Maja came here voluntarily, and as I've said she does not wish to be disturbed. And I can't let you into the castle because the prince has forbidden it.'

'I want to talk to the prince.'

'Very good! The prince will talk to you gentlemen himself.'

Indeed, soon after the prince appeared in the window.

'Please go away!' shouted the old man, waving his arms. 'I'm not letting anyone in! I forbid it! This is my castle! Begone! Begone!'

The professor stepped forwards.

'Prince!' he cried. 'But it is I! Your guest! I'm a permanent resident of the castle! Please let me in.'

But as if entirely transformed, the old man went on waving his arms around.

'Begone! Begone! I won't allow it! Franio has forbidden it!' he screamed, as if in a state of ecstasy. 'Franio!! No one is allowed in!'

His snow-white, bird-like head disappeared. It looked as if he had slumped to the floor. Cholawicki took his place.

'As you can see, gentlemen, the prince's will is categorical,' he said in an official tone.

'Sir,' said Hińcz, 'let's not talk to each other like children. You are just as well aware of the prince's state of mind as I am. We have reasons to suppose that you have abused Miss Maja's trust. Do you want us to apply force?'

'Ah, so it's like that, eh? Well, in that case I'd be inclined to talk to you, but privately and without witnesses. Come up to the gate, please, and we'll talk through the Judas hole.'

Hińcz went up to the gate, and in the mist Cholawicki's lips appeared in the tiny window.

'My dear sir,' said those lips mockingly, 'as you can see, the law is on my side, as I have the prince's formal injunction, and Maja too appeared here voluntarily. The poor thing wants to see for herself what haunts the old kitchen, as she's got it into her head that those ghosts have taken possession of her and her young man. You seem to have made a major contribution to this notion of hers. But that's not the point. I too am eager for her to spend the night in that kitchen. You see, I have already abandoned the treasure and her love. But I do have scores to settle with her, and I believe the chamber will settle them for me. So I imagine, or rather I am sure, as I have spent the night in the old kitchen and now I know what's in there. The professor managed to escape – but she will not.

'So what do you want, gentlemen? If you drive me to extremities, I'll get my revolver and kill her, the prince and myself – I assure you, life is of no great value to me anymore. It's up to you. If you want me to kill her, force the gate. But to be frank, I'd rather not resort to such radical means. I'm hoping the chamber will take revenge for me, and I won't need to have a hand in it.

'So what do you want? A little common sense, gentlemen. If you'll wait quietly, you still have a chance, for if she comes out of the chamber alive I shall let her go, but otherwise – her fate and the prince's are sealed.'

'If you think you'll succeed in freeing yourself of responsibility like this, you are mistaken,' said Hińcz.

'Oh, no one will be able to prove anything against me,' replied the lips nonchalantly. 'She wrote down in black and white that she was coming here of her own accord. I didn't abduct her. And the fact that the prince won't let you in is not my fault. In truth I must admit that I've finally discovered the sign . . . The prince is in my power. Well then, goodbye.'

Hińcz heard malicious, fitful laughter and the sound of footsteps walking away.

The desperate clairvoyant returned to the professor. Total impotence was killing him.

Should they wait? Wait until Maja paid with her life or health for her unwise step? Wait until Cholawicki wreaked his vengeance on the prince, meek and submissive to all his whims? Wait passively until he led them both to the edge of the abyss, whence there was no return?

'How could she!' whispered the professor in despair. 'How could she!'

'If only we could get inside and overpower him, or shoot him before he manages to carry out his threats,' muttered Hińcz. 'This is dreadful. She's in there alone! Alone!'

'I've been in that chamber. I know what it is. She won't survive it. Especially now, when she's exhausted, mentally weakened by everything she's been through. May God protect her!'

The castle was crushingly huge in the moonlight. The vast edifice was lost against the black-and-purple sky. Two madmen – and Maja . . .

'If Cholawicki appears at the window, shoot,' ordered Hińcz, loading the shotgun.

He closed his eyes.

The thought that this madman had control of Maja and the prince, that the hideous power of the chamber had become a tool in the hands of that scoundrel, who in a fit of insane jealousy had lost the remains of his humanity, was appalling. What was to be done?!

Just then he spotted Leszczuk, who was standing among the trees, leaning on a bicycle. What, he was here too?

This unexpected arrival didn't suit Hińcz at all.

Despite the darkness he could see that the boy was pale as death.

'What are you doing here? Go back to Połyka! There's nothing for you here!'

'Is she in the old kitchen?' he asked with trembling lips, and the bicycle fell to the ground.

'Well, what of it? She is! But you can only get in the way! Go back!'

Leszczuk looked at him.

'Why did she go there?'

'Go back!'

'No. She's in there. She went there on purpose to see. But she can't be left there. The same thing will happen to her as to me, or worse.'

'We'll get her out,' replied Hińcz, contradicting himself.

'No,' said Leszczuk in a hollow tone, 'because he'll take revenge. It's out of jealousy. There's only one remedy. Let him lock me in there instead of her. He has scores to settle with me too. He'd rather get me than her!'

He moved forwards.

'Excuse me, sir!' he called out.

No response.

'Excuse me, sir!' he repeated.

'What is it?!' replied the secretary, cautiously keeping out of sight. 'Who's talking?'

'Set Miss Maja free, and I'll go into the chamber.'

'What's that?'

'Give us your word that you'll set her free, and I'll remain in her place. I'm curious to see what's going on in there too. Agreed?'

Total silence reigned.

Leszczuk rightly supposed that the secretary hated him even more than he hated Maja. The offer was enticing.

'No!' said Cholawicki at last. 'You want to get in here to attack me. I don't believe you!'

'What if these gentlemen tie me up? Have them tie me up. You can supervise – they'll tie me up right here in front of the gate, where you can watch. Then they'll step away from me and you'll be able to pull me into the castle and do what you like with me.'

'You fool!' whispered Hińcz, pulling him away. 'That's madness! He'll catch you but he won't let her go. You won't survive it!'

'Yes, I will,' he stammered. 'If she can withstand it, so can I!'

Hińcz, Skoliński and Grzegorz surrounded him. They were sure he was suffering another attack. But Leszczuk was fully aware of the consequences of the offer he was making.

'I'm sure he won't let her go, but it's all the same. If he locks me up in that chamber, at least she won't be alone! Two's always better than one. Even if I can't help her at all, she'll be less frightened!'

He was talking quickly and passionately, trying to convince them as fast as possible.

'It's impossible to say what she might see in there. I want to be with her! And if he does me in immediately – you only die once! There's nothing better to be done. If you have any other idea, then speak up!'

Hińcz had to admit that there was no alternative. Their helplessness was total and utter.

'If you gentlemen tie him up securely, here, in front of the gate, within my sight,' said Cholawicki, 'and if you then step back two hundred paces . . . Yes. Agreed. I have nothing against it. If he's curious, let him see.'

'Tie me up with halter ropes,' said Leszczuk, lying on the ground.

Grzegorz leaped towards him.

'But sir! You saw! Tie him up and hand him over, like a lamb to the slaughter?! That's like killing him with my own hand! Someone else can tie him up – I won't do it!'

'It's out of the question!' whispered Skoliński, pulling Hińcz away. 'Let's not forget that he's already infected by it. Even if Cholawicki does put him in the chamber with Maja it could have unpredictable consequences!'

'Tie me up!' said Leszczuk impatiently. 'Tie me up! I'm not afraid! If she found the courage, then so can I! I'm not afraid of him or of ghosts! I tell you, I'm not afraid! I can withstand it! I tell you, I'll survive! Even if the devil himself . . . I'm not afraid and he won't do anything to me! Nothing!'

Hińcz passed a hand across his brow.

The idea seemed as crazy as it was hopeless. Hand the boy over, bound and defenceless, to the mercy of his infuriated rival?

Who could know what Cholawicki would do to him?

Even if he did put him in the chamber with Maja, wouldn't Leszczuk have another attack? And didn't the secretary know the secrets of the chamber better than they did – what if his calculations were more accurate?

No, such an idea could only be born of extreme despair!

And yet . . . he was starting to believe that Leszczuk could buoy up and save Maja.

What had brought about the change in him?

This was no longer the Leszczuk who was terrified of spirits and devils, like the typical peasant, fatalistically waiting for insanity to strike him again. Whence the change?

Hińcz took a close look at him as he lay on the ground, waiting for them to tie him up.

Yes! Leszczuk had stopped being afraid! It was plain to see that he wasn't afraid and wasn't going to be, whatever happened. He wasn't afraid. He had reached the limit past which a person is ready to expose himself to anything, feels brave enough to take the ultimate risk, and can even withstand things beyond his strength.

What had transformed him?

'Gentlemen!' said Hińcz. 'Fetch the halter ropes from the horses and tie him up!'

And they started to bind him. And when they stepped back two hundred paces, the gate opened and the secretary hauled Leszczuk inside, like a spider dragging a fly into its web.

There was total silence . . .

The professor glanced at his watch.

'It's coming up to two,' he said.

What had happened to Leszczuk? Had Cholawicki put him in the chamber? What was happening to Maja, locked up, in anticipation? And what about the prince?

The torment of helplessness! All they had left was the waiting. The quarter hours ticked by. When would dawn break?

'It's all in vain!' fretted Skoliński. 'We're condemning them to certain doom! Even if they come out of the chamber alive, Cholawicki will finish them off another way. He won't let them out in one piece. That's a pipedream!'

But there was a chance, albeit minimal, that Cholawicki would not resort to extreme measures. If he locked Leszczuk in the chamber, Maja would untie him and then they'd be able to put up some resistance.

Or perhaps the secretary would come to his senses, be scared of the consequences – and then maybe something would happen, something would occur?

However, if they tried to force their way into the castle there was no chance. Cholawicki would carry out his threat.

So in darkness and trepidation they waited, praying for dawn to bring salvation. The professor, who hadn't forgotten his own dreadful experiences in the old kitchen, fell to his knees, shielded his face with his hands and trembled all over.

'Where's Handrycz?' asked the clairvoyant.

Only now had he noticed that the peasant had vanished some time ago. He wanted to send him to the village to summon people to help.

Suddenly a horrible scream split the silence.

They froze. It was Maja's scream.

They couldn't see the window of the old kitchen – it was hidden behind the outer castle wall – but that was where the scream had come from, signifying ultimate horror. And the silence that followed was deathly.

'That's enough!' shouted Hińcz.

They lunged at the gate and started battering against it.

It gave way.

Hińcz, Grzegorz and the professor burst into the castle.

They raced headlong up the black stairs.

On the first floor they heard revolver shots. It was the old prince firing, again and again, while at the same time shouting: 'I won't allow it! I won't allow it! Begone! Don't interfere! Franio!'

Hińcz caught him and knocked him over.

They raced on, to the haunted chamber.

However, the door leading into the atrium that divided the kitchen from the rest of the castle slammed in their faces, and it was just as massive and heavy as all the castle doors.

Hińcz started thumping his fists against it.

They heard Cholawicki's cold, measured voice.

'Just a minute! First I'll take care of them – then you – and then myself. All right . . .'

And the secretary's footsteps began to move away towards the old kitchen. He didn't even hurry, certain that the door would hold out until he'd dealt with Leszczuk and Maja.

Hińcz started firing his revolver at the door, while the professor blasted it with the shotgun. It was an act of despair. The revolver bullets stuck in the wood, and the professor's buckshot hardly made any impact at all.

The prince came running up.

'I forbid it! I forbid it! Franio! Franio is in there!' he shouted. 'Franio has come! You want to kill him! Begone, he's coming out right away.'

All at once, Hińcz and the professor stopped shooting. They listened . . .

They listened – what would they hear? Would it be Cholawicki's revolver shots, or something else . . . What was going on in there?

The continuing silence seemed interminable.

'I tell you, Franio has come and he'll forgive me! I have seen the sign!' cried the prince.

Suddenly footsteps resounded – Cholawicki's slow footsteps – and the door opened.

They flew at him. But instead of defending himself, he quietly drawled: 'Go and see, gentlemen – go and see – please go and see.'

Incapable of further speech, he pointed towards the old kitchen.

The tone of his voice was so strange that they all stopped, as if on command.

The door of the old kitchen was ajar; Hińcz, the professor, the prince and Grzegorz approached it – and were dumbstruck.

Maja and Leszczuk had vanished without trace.

Instead of them, in the middle of the room, stood Handrycz, looking foggily around him, like someone who has woken from a deep sleep.

The towel was nowhere to be seen.

'Where are they?!' cried Hińcz. 'What have you done with them, you murderer?'

He grabbed the secretary by the arms. But Cholawicki was stunned, his eyes goggling as he pointed at Handrycz and whispered: 'I haven't done anything!'

Suddenly a body sank to the floor. It was the prince, falling to his knees before Handrycz with his hands outstretched and his face flooded with tears.

'Franio,' he said. 'Franio!'

'How on earth did you get here? Is it you? Is it you – Handrycz?' asked Skoliński, barely conscious of the absurdity of his questions.

But the peasant didn't answer, he just cast a hesitant gaze around the walls and said, as if to himself, in deep confusion: 'So I . . . have been here before . . . I was here . . . in the past . . .'

And he fainted too.

But before the clatter of his falling body had died away, Cholawicki emitted a frantic scream and dashed out of the room.

There stood Hińcz, the professor and Grzegorz, like three speechless question marks.

XXII.

MAJA didn't even try banging on the door that Cholawicki had slammed shut. She didn't try pleading or shouting for help. She knew it was pointless. She sat down on the bed and stayed there without moving, in anticipation . . .

Of what?

It was dark in here. In the darkness she couldn't see that horrible object moving on the peg, but she knew it was there – and that it was moving.

At first none of it seemed nearly as terrifying as Skoliński had said or as she had imagined.

She was even pleased to be finding out for once and for all exactly what it was like in here. And she was prepared for anything.

Time passed. And in the darkness she could sense the movement intensifying, and a strange fury growing, thrashing about on the peg.

And at the same time her mind was working away relentlessly, coming up with all sorts of fanciful ideas about what was going to materialize in here.

To no avail she tried as hard as she could to divert her attention away from it, doing her best to think about sober, matter-of-fact things. But under it all the question continued to rattle about – what was it going to be? What on earth would emerge?

Would this thing attack her? Or would it just appear to her – perhaps the mere sight of it would be enough to shatter her forever?

Or maybe the thing would get inside her – infect her, get control of her as it had Leszczuk, and she . . .

And then there was the conviction that if Cholawicki weren't absolutely sure she couldn't withstand it, he wouldn't have locked her in here – he wouldn't have brought her here . . .

It was dark.

She could hear voices through the window – she thought she could make out Hińcz's voice, but she wasn't sure . . . and she couldn't go up to the window anymore – it was too near the corner where the piece of cloth was moving.

She could feel herself weakening. In vain she kept reminding herself that she'd come here of her own free will, that she could conquer her animal fear, and that her own and Leszczuk's fate depended on her succeeding.

But in the darkness, instead of gaining strength, she was growing weaker – and now she could feel her facial muscles twitching, cold sweat on her brow and rising, deathly panic.

She kept herself going with the remains of her self-respect.

No, she would not surrender. She would not give in! She couldn't let that thing moving in the corner . . .

But then her teeth began to chatter. And the convulsive motion was definitely increasing.

'Oh God, oh God!'

Suddenly she heard Cholawicki approaching – but his tread was heavy, and he was talking. To himself?

The door opened. She lunged towards it.

She was ready to beg Cholawicki to let her go.

But something struck her hard and fell to the floor, and when she stepped back in shock, the secretary slammed the door shut.

'You have a guest! Have fun together!' That was all he said, and then his footsteps died away again.

She dared not speak. Until finally she heard a stifled voice, as if choking . . . it was Leszczuk's.

'It's me.'

With the greatest effort of will she whispered in amazement: 'How did you get here?!'

'Please untie me,' she heard instead of an answer.

She leaned over him, and as she worked at loosening his bonds, he explained in a whisper what had happened and why he had let Cholawicki tie him up.

Maja felt as if it were wrong to speak in here – as if the human voice would disturb something in the chamber – and provoke it.

On the one hand, Leszczuk's presence had torn her free of her panic-stricken torpor, because it was something human and comforting in this inhuman place. But on the other, standing there beside him in the darkness, she hadn't the least guarantee that he wouldn't go mad with terror and attack her, do something awful, or have a fit – and that made the ghastliness twice as great.

If she was afraid, how on earth must he be feeling?!

She couldn't see him. She couldn't monitor what state he was in at this moment.

They were both silent.

'Is it over there?' he suddenly asked. 'Which direction is it in? Over there?'

He took her by the hand and pointed.

'Yes.'

'Is it moving?'

'Yes.'

They stopped talking. And once again there was extreme repulsion, horror, frenzy increasing in the silence, convulsive motion. Maja thought that now, now it would begin, now that he was here, something was bound to happen between them, there was no helping it! And instead of reassuring her, his presence in the darkness terrified her even more.

Wasn't he going to be seized by madness any moment now? Wasn't he going to do something atrocious? It was plainly fated to happen!

Curled in a corner, she dared not move. She waited.

And she didn't dare ask any questions, because she was sure she'd hear a note of terror in his reply – then she'd be unable to hold out and would tumble headlong in fear!

She was sure he couldn't move, couldn't speak out of fear.

Suddenly she heard: 'Well, then? So there's nothing? And I thought there really was something going on in here.'

She grabbed him tightly by the hand.

'Can't you feel . . . that it's moving? Moving?'

He burst out laughing.

'I can't feel a thing! You're imagining it. Why should it be moving? If you like, I'll throw that rag out of the window and be done with it!'

Had he gone mad? Had he forgotten where he was? Maja found his tone impossible, improbable.

'Be quiet!'

But he took a few paces into the depths of the chamber.

Maja's heart stopped beating!

Now! If he touches it! Something's bound to happen! Don't let him touch it!

She felt as if something would go bang – or wail – something would suddenly make its appearance . . .

But meanwhile he was moving about in that corner.

And whistling!

Whistling through his teeth.

'I can't find it by feeling. Aha, I've got it! Is it hanging on a peg? It's just an ordinary towel! What a fuss about nothing. Away with it!'

She glimpsed his silhouette against the window – and the wave of his hand as he threw out the towel. She thought his hair looked strange.

'That's the end of the ghosts! And if that Cholawicki comes after us I'll smash his face in. We must sit here until morning, and then . . .'

He didn't finish his sentence.

The top of the kitchen stove set against the wall lifted up, came right off, and crashed to the stone floor with a clatter. Something had blown the stove apart.

She screamed.

And there in the stove something was digging, moving and gasping – a bulky shape.

Until finally the faint light of a match flooded the room.

In this light she saw the tall, distinctive figure of Handrycz, slowly scrambling out of the ruins of the stove.

He was trying to say something, but just then shots rang out from far inside the castle.

'Escape this way!' shouted the peasant. 'There's a tunnel here! Quickly!'

And as Maja and Leszczuk disappeared into the bowels of the stove, he stood there, looking around him, his face focused and mournful.

'I have been here before,' he whispered.

EPILOGUE

'AND SO,' said Hińcz, as he and Professor Skoliński entered the old kitchen, 'we can more or less reconstruct the tragedy that took place in here long ago.'

It was bright. Outside the birds were chirping. Free of the towel, the room looked nice and pleasant.

'Let's imagine the events of that final night,' the clairvoyant continued, 'when Franio reached the zenith of his rage. As ever, the prince came up to the door and begged him for mercy. Franio responded with scorn. "I'll forgive you!", he cried, drawing a finger across his throat, which meant he'd do himself and his father in. You see this chink in the door? It was through this gap that the prince saw Franio make that gesture. Then, in a fit of fury, the wretched young man seized the towel and suffocated himself by stuffing it into his mouth and winding it around his neck. The prince fainted. And when he came to, he found Franio in a lifeless condition.'

The two men leaned over the stove.

'Yes,' said the professor, 'there's a hole knocked through at the bottom, a sort of chimney that goes all the way down to the cellars. Probably some unfinished alteration from many years ago.'

'I can see it now!' said Hińcz, squinting. 'On waking from his faint, the prince loses the rest of his wits. He bursts into the chamber, he doesn't know what to do with the body, he wants to hide the dreadful fact from himself and others, so finally, in haste, in a frenzy, he puts the body into the stove – and it falls to the very bottom!'

The professor pulled his head out of the stove.

'Aha, now I understand why he set up that chapel in the dungeons. That was the place where, according to his reckonings, the beloved corpse remained.'

'He didn't know that the chimney joins an underground passage that emerges beyond the castle grounds. He didn't know that Franio hadn't choked himself, he'd just lost consciousness. It didn't occur to him that no one could strangle himself that way. And finally he didn't know that once he had got outside the castle, Franio would entirely lose his memory as a result of nervous shock.'

'I'm surprised none of the locals recognized Franio in Handrycz,' said the professor.

'I asked Handrycz about that,' replied Hińcz. 'He told me that he woke up in Lublin a couple of weeks later, suffering from typhus. Some people took care of him. He ascribed his amnesia to the illness. There he met his present wife. They only came back here years later. Anyway, she alone guessed that her husband had something to do with the legend of Franio and the castle, but she kept it secret from him for understandable reasons. And what about the prince? Blindly latching onto his last hope, as madmen do, the prince had persuaded himself that Franio's cruel gesture was a sign of forgiveness! He never stopped expecting Franio to forgive him, as he had said he would.'

'So Cholawicki sat in here all night and didn't see a thing. In that case, how did he find out about the sign?'

'From Mrs Ziółkowska. That old crone was in league with him, and she told him about our discovery during the séance. He saw nothing in the chamber, though he spent the whole night here. The towel moved more and more fiercely – then more and more feebly. Nothing appeared.'

'So in fact there was nothing haunting this room?' asked Skoliń-ski with disappointment.

'Nothing. Except that the towel kept moving.'

They left the chamber and found themselves in the castle court-yard. The sun was blazing.

The glaring light of noon exposed the sombre desolation of the old castle. There were clumps of grass protruding from crevices amid the loosened foundation stones, cracked plaster, russet patches of mouldering brick, grey damp stains and green blotches of lichen.

'In a few years there'll be nothing left but a heap of rubble,' mut-tered Hińcz reluctantly.

'Maybe, maybe not.'

'Do you want to restore this old wreck?'

'My arrangement with the prince does not foresee that option for now. Well, Handrycz will be the heir, I'm just the custodian, if that isn't too grand a word. I am to take care of the movable property, conduct expert research, and deliver the valuable items to museums . . .'

'It'll remain a ruin,' put in Hińcz.

'Time will tell. Of course, if no one takes care of the castle, it'll fall into decay. But the prince still has time to think about it all.'

'You believe so?'

'I see him on a daily basis and I'm sure he's making a complete recovery. That old man was like his castle. There were layers of something like cobwebs and dust building up in his psyche. That thug, Cholawicki, made a major contribution to it. He tormented and harassed the old man, now feeding his hopes, now mocking him, now terrorizing and frightening him. He knew how to exploit the prince's mania, though he didn't understand the reasons for his state of mind. A scoundrel, a cold, sophisticated scoundrel.'

'But he fell foul of his own villainy.'

Lost in thought, the professor waved his cane, hacking down the large burdock leaves and stiff thistles proliferating against the wall.

'That is the result of every villainy.'

'And what now? Will he shake it off?'

'What? The gunshot? For sure. The doctors immediately affirmed that it's a light wound. Dr Darasz claims this is the way two kinds of suicide shoot themselves – the clowns and the cowards. A bullet in the chest? Well, then, two broken ribs, a few torn muscles . . . Mind you, a bullet from a decrepit old piece of junk like that one is huge. But he'll pull through.'

'And the prince doesn't know anything about it?'

'No. He hadn't regained consciousness when we carried Cholawicki out. Grzegorz will keep quiet, if only out of affection for the old man. So will Handrycz.'

'You mean Franio. And what does Franio say about the prince's plans?'

'He doesn't seem to have any objections.'

'So in the end you've won your game, Professor. The castle will remain with the prince and Franio, and the furniture will retire to museums? Just as you dreamed?'

'I hope so. But I'd rather the castle didn't go to waste either. These old walls can hold out for many years to come. It may be a ruin from the outside, but the inside core of the walls is still healthy. Solid stone. One would only have to replace the ceilings and floors, reinforce the foundations and apply new plaster, and the corpse would be resurrected.'

'Yes, just as we've resurrected the prince.'

'One single shock won't be enough in this case. It'll take years of effort and expense. But I'm hoping the money will be found.

And will make a good profit, because God knows what could be housed in these old rooms. An orphanage, a school, a museum . . . The treasures that are hidden here could be left as they are, but given proper care.'

They walked around the gloomy walls along the moat, tripping over broken cobblestones and sinking into weed-choked holes.

'A real-life illustration for the fairy tale about the sleeping princess,' said the professor, pointing his cane at the tower that rose high above the leprous walls, the mighty buttresses and crumbling battlements.

'But new life is already awakening here. Look, Professor. Grzegorz is opening a window, Mrs Handrycz is here already and is rustling something up in the kitchen. Franio is managing the new farmhands. Everything's about to change.'

'The evil spell has lost its power. The role of the poisoned apple was played by . . '

'The towel,' said Hińcz in solemn earnest. 'It should be lying here somewhere unless someone has found it by now.'

'This is the spot,' said the professor, leading Hińcz along the walls. 'There's the old kitchen window.'

'Where on earth is it? Ah, here we have our joker!' said Hińcz, pointing at the towel, which stood out against the grass.

Thrown out by Leszczuk, there it lay, not looking in the least bit threatening. And yet both gentlemen scrutinized it mistrustfully from a certain distance.

The professor gulped. In spite of all, he felt terrible abhorrence prompted by this piece of material that still seemed to be quivering and contracting, though almost imperceptibly.

'It has to be burned,' he said in disgust.

'Oh no!' replied the clairvoyant. 'That towel and the pencil are the one feature of this whole episode that hasn't yet been investigated.

I'll take it to Warsaw and have it subjected to scientific examination. We'll see what it is! What sort of energy stirs it?'

'But be careful! Don't forget that one can't come into contact with it without paying the price!'

'Oh!' said Hińcz. 'The longer I think about this business, the more inclined I am to assume that we only owe a small part of Leszczuk's madness to the towel's vibrations, undeniable as they may be. These are mysteries, without doubt. But the real reason for his madness was Maja. You see, when an unresearched, mysterious element plainly appears in human life, we tend to be quick to attribute all sorts of things to its effect. That is a major error. There are definitely many forces and phenomena in existence that transcend our knowledge of the world, but we should not exaggerate their influence. A man forges his own destiny. The deciding factors are character, consciousness, and faith – not blind, obscure auras. Every human life, every adventure we have is a little unclear and mysterious. We move around in a world that hasn't yet been fully explained. But the clarity we do have is sufficient for a person of good faith.'

He lowered his voice.

'In this particular case I am not afraid of the automatic effects of this cloth. We shall always be able to cope with it, even if our lips go black as coal. À propos,' he added casually, 'I don't know if you noticed that Leszczuk's pencil was an indelible one . . .'

The professor glanced at him.

'But never mind,' said Hińcz, 'even so it doesn't explain anything. I tell you, our efforts to understand it all were a waste of time. Our life progresses in semi-darkness. There are probably plenty of mysteries that we could solve in a natural way, but there will always be a small number that are insoluble. That has always been true. But at any rate there's one thing we know for sure – there was nothing going on in the old kitchen. It's just that the towel moved more at night, that's all. People went mad in there under the pressure of fear and imagination – as they have since the world began.'

'Whatever the case, I'd rather not touch it with my hands,' said the professor, cautiously raising the towel with a stick.

Hińcz smiled indulgently.

'For an academic, you're not much of a sceptic, Professor.'

'Ha, if I hadn't been a witness to the uproar caused by this rag . . . Brr! I get shivers every time I remember the night I spent alone with it!'

'So it turns out that even in the brain of a scholar the imagination can outweigh the capacity for rational thought.'

'Most definitely. But you must admit, as someone who is closer to supersensory phenomena than I, an ordinary homo sapiens, you are too much of a sceptic.'

'For instance?'

'Since you ascribe the blackening of Leszczuk's lips to the fact that the pencil was an indelible one, maybe you'd try explaining why the towel was moving? Because it's a fact that it was moving – it wasn't an illusion or a trick of the imagination.'

'A sceptic would say there must have been a draught moving the rag. And he'd look for chinks in the wall where the towel was hanging.'

The professor burst into forced, insincere laughter.

'And that clarifies it all? There are no more mysteries . . . ? In that case, dear sir, since common sense has triumphed over delusion, perhaps you'd deign to give me one more piece of evidence of critical scepticism by placing that filthy object into a suitcase with your own fair hand?'

Hińcz bit his lip. He frowned.

'Don't be angry,' continued the professor solemnly. 'My proposal is a serious one. Do you understand my point?'

'Yes,' muttered Hińcz.

And he slowly leaned towards the towel. But just then, quick as a flash, the professor seized him by the outstretched hand and pulled him back a pace.

'Stop!' he exclaimed. 'That's quite enough for me . . .'

'What do you mean?'

'First of all, I saw that you hesitated and held back, even though you're not afraid of the "automatic effects of this cloth". Isn't that how you put it? But secondly, you were still determined to do it. A very interesting experiment for a student of the human psyche.'

'And the conclusion?'

'That you are not a sceptic after all. Just like me.'

'My dear Professor,' said Hińcz, patting him on the arm, 'is it worth being a pure sceptic, without admixture? That would strip life of all the illusions that give it so much colour. It's nice to fathom a mystery, but for cognitive experience, not for the triumph of disbelief. Would some sort of negation please you?'

'Long live romanticism,' quipped the professor. 'Let's leave it at that. And so . . . let's use a stick and not our hands to confine the towel safely.'

They put it into a small suitcase and drove back to Połyka.

'Have you seen Maja?' Skoliński asked, as they alighted in front of the house.

'No. I haven't had a chance to talk to her yet. But I have news for her. I received a telephone call from the investigative magistrate in the Maliniak case. Do you know who killed him? It was the marquise. They found the gap in the wall through which she had threaded the noose. And everything came to light when the romantic crime novel, *In the Vampire's Snare*, fell into the magistrate's hands. It turns out the marquise literally copied a major scene from that book. The murderer rigs up a noose behind the bed in such a way that it only takes one tug for it to fall over the sleeper's head.

'Naturally she had the whole thing prepared before Maliniak went to bed, and that explains how she was able to strangle him, despite the fact that his bedroom door was locked from the inside. What perfidy! If Leszczuk hadn't been an accidental witness to the murder, and if Maja hadn't opened the window to let him in, no force could have saved her from false suspicion. Shh . . . here she is. Professor, don't let her know we have the towel in this suitcase – let's not expose her resistance to a new test. Take it into the house quickly.'

Unfortunately the professor was in too much haste, and a calamity occurred! The little case caught on the handrail and snapped open. The towel fell out two paces ahead of Maja, who was just approaching the britzka.

She stood rooted to the spot.

'It's nothing! Nothing!' shouted Hińcz, trying to conceal the towel with his own person.

She burst out laughing.

'Don't worry,' she said, 'it doesn't frighten me anymore.'

And she gave the dangerous rag a light kick.

'Aren't you afraid?' asked the professor in amazement.

'Not in the least. Leszczuk threw it out of the window and nothing happened to him.'

'Bravo!' cried Hińcz with emotion. 'Does this mean you've both overcome your fear? The towel no longer has any effect on you?'

'None at all. And do you know why, gentlemen?'

She pointed at Leszczuk, who was walking down the path towards them.

'That's why,' she said.

They gave a cry of astonishment. Leszczuk's hair had gone white!

As they were on their way home from the castle together after their night in the kitchen, they hadn't noticed. But now in the daylight his head was as white as snow, as if he'd been bewitched.

'You need good understanding of a woman's soul,' explained Maja as if joking, though actually with emotion, once the three of them were sitting on a bench by the tennis court. 'Alone in the chamber I was hellishly afraid, but I felt much more frightened when Leszczuk ended up in there with me. I couldn't see him in the darkness. I imagined he was even more scared than I was, so I was even more afraid – so to speak – for him. Then, when he threw away the towel, whistling as he did it, suddenly I knew for sure he wasn't at all afraid. But that was even worse. I thought he was too vacuous, not intelligent enough to be afraid. His appearance in the room lost all value for me. Before, I'd thought he was sacrificing himself for me, but now I realized it cost him nothing. You see, I didn't know him. To me, he was more obscure than that chamber. I thought he was different from me. And only this morning when I realized that it was while he was throwing out the towel and whistling that his hair had gone white – only then did I understand . . .'

Maja stammered and blushed.

'He found the strength in himself because you had been brave enough to go into the chamber. He was infected by your courage and determination,' said Hińcz, without concealing his joy. 'But I have news for you. We know who killed Maliniak.'

'I'm not interested.'

'Why on earth not? Aren't you curious?'

'No. I know for sure it wasn't him. And it wasn't me. You see,' she went on slowly, casting her gaze around the old manor house, the garden and the outbuildings beyond it, 'for a long time we doubted each other, but once we began to trust one another, then nothing, not the wildest story could infect us with doubt anymore. And no aura could latch onto us. We are . . . impregnable.'

'Thank God!' cried the clairvoyant. 'At last you've understood that! In this world, full of obscurity and mystery, darkness and confusion, wonders and errors, there is just one infallible truth – the truth of character!'